FORGED

IN THE

FALLOUT

BEN GREEN

Loamseed
PRESS

Forged in the Fallout (Rimduum Book 1)

eBook ISBN: 978-1-7348218-2-6

Paperback ISBN: 978-1-7348218-1-9

For my family: past, present, and future.

ROYAL CRAFTS

GOLDCRAFT

PHYSICAL AUGMENTATION
METAL: GOLD
BODY & FORM

SILVERCRAFT

MENTAL AUGMENTATION
METAL: SILVER & NICKEL
MIND & SPIRIT

SHIELDCRAFT

PROTECTIVE AUGMENTATION
METAL: TUNGSTEN & LEAD
PROTECTION & HEALING

INDUSTRIAL CRAFTS

COPPERCRAFT

ANIMAL DOMINION
METAL: COPPER
ANIMAL CONTROL & COMMUNICATION

TINCRAFT

PLANT DOMINION
METAL: TIN
PLANT CONTROL & COMMUNICATION

IRONCRAFT

ELEMENTAL MANIPULATION
METAL: IRON
FIRE, WATER, AIR, EARTH, SHADOW, LIGHT

BUDGECRAFT

SPATIAL MANIPULATION
METAL: ALUMINIUM
TELEPORTATION

MODERN CRAFTS
(REQUIRES GESTURING)

MECHCRAFT

MECHANICAL MANIPULATION
METAL: TITANIUM & PLATINUM
MACHINE CONTROL & MANIPULATION

BLUECRAFT

ELECTROMAGNETIC MANIPULATION
METAL: COBALT
COMMUNICATION & ENERGY

TIMECRAFT

TEMPORAL MANIPULATION
METAL: MERCURY & CHROMIUM
SLOW TIME & SPEED TIME

UNCOVER THE TRUTH

CONFLICT IS a stone wedged between my shoulders.

I'm at eighty feet, leaning from a sandstone cliff on the western edge of our family property, my hands braced in a gap. It's mid-October in the Blue Ridge Mountains. Red-orange trees glitter on display. The sun is a neon half circle on the horizon, throwing the forest into shadows and dappled patches of light. But I only have a few minutes to soak up the sunset, feel the cool wind on my face, the grit of the rock against my fingertips.

I wanna freeze this moment, catch it in a bottle like a firefly.

This is everything simple about the world.

Then there's Dad. Once I'm down the mountain again, I need to check his oxygen, make dinner, and get him settled for the night. Before I came out, I told him to take it easy. I hope he listened. His night terrors, his breathing, his dependence on me, they all get worse when he works himself into a state of exhaustion, which for him is as easy as taking a walk out to the orchard.

A hundred yards away, familiar chalk-gray smoke rises from the chimney of our cabin.

"Clayson?" A cautious voice drifts over the top of the cliff.

It's Ara. Dad's actual nurse. Very young, very tall nurse. Why is she here a week early? I'm suddenly self-conscious of the layers of grime caking my arms and face. I bet I smell from cleaning up after our goats.

I clear my throat. "Ara? Almost up."

After a few more grabs, I pull myself over the rim of the cliff. When Ara sees me, she backs up a few paces. The scrubs she usually wears have been replaced with a simple long sleeve blouse and jeans. Something's off. I've never seen her *not* in scrubs. And though she's gotta be the most hands-off nurse assistant to ever make house calls, this is different. Even when she takes Dad on hospital trips out west, she shows up in the same pink scrubs.

I close the distance between us and groan inside. Ara must be near six feet tall. I'm five-four on a good day, though Dad says I'm a man now. I've grown as much as he had at my age. Okay, Dad.

"Hey, uh, Ara. You guys have a trip planned?"

It wouldn't be the worst thing. I would get to climb whenever I wanted. And there's a bunch of long projects I could finally get done if this *is* a hospital trip. I could even sneak down to the local gas station. There are always a few old-timers reading the newspaper and drinking coffee. They love to talk, and without a computer or a cellphone, these are my only non-Dad conversations.

Ara looks past me, but I catch the raw umber of her eyes and the way the sunset casts her tan features into darker shades, cutting gaunt shadows into her cheeks. Simply looking at her makes me nervous.

She squints at the forest below us. "Something is wrong."

A spell of vertigo ripples up my spine, settling in a blotch at the crown of my head. My mouth goes dry. "With Dad?"

"What?" She never makes eye contact with me. It's like she tries but gives up. "I—no, I mean I don't think... I didn't see him in the house."

My insides twist into a knot. "He wasn't in the house?"

"Well, I couldn't find him."

The knot in my stomach becomes a solid rock. "You're his nurse! I told him—forget it."

At a dead sprint, I take the trail winding away from the clifftop. Dad didn't listen to me—again. I pass the dried-up waterfall and head into the clearing. My breath is unwavering and clear, but it makes me think about him. Did he leave the house? Did he take his portable oxygen?

I glance back at Ara. She's vanished. What is going on?

I push through the pines, ignoring the well-worn path I usually take. When I reach the gravel driveway, I scramble around Dad's flatbed, march up the side porch steps, and burst through the kitchen door. The smell of rosemary potatoes and chicken hits me from the crockpot I set up this morning.

"Dad!"

No answer. I rush to the den, but the room is empty. The TV's doling out what Dad calls "news for taffies." If he were in the house, he would've changed it to an eighties action movie.

I'm frantic.

His bedroom's empty. The living room and his office plastered with old sci-fi posters—empty. I check the basement. Nothing.

I grab his portable oxygen and race from the cabin. The screen door clatters shut behind me. The sunset etches the shapes of black trees into the sky. I'm trapped in strange slow motion. The crisp fall air brushes my face, leaves tumble through the air, unsure if they wanna reach the ground. It's like someone doubled the gravity on my body.

Around the cabin, the ax lays against a pile of freshly split wood.

He's been trying to do chores again. He thinks he can work and keep it a secret from me. It means he's in the shop. I slide open the hanging door, but I don't see him.

The distillery equipment is working, the burner creating heat, the condenser beading up our homemade biodiesel, dripping it into the tank. He should be standing there. I rush around the table.

His back rests against the cabinet door, his face pale as his breath rattles in his chest. He's hyperventilating. At last, looking at me, he grimaces. I shake my head, slipping the oxygen mask over his face, opening the valve. I've found him in time. I never want to learn what it would feel like if I don't find him on time.

"Dad..."

After a few deep breaths, he pulls the mask away. His face tightens in concentration to form each word. "I'll be fine, Clayson. Thought you were climbing. You didn't have to run all the way out here."

He offers me the mask. I push it back.

"Second time this week. I'll have to record this one."

He's told me what this feels like for him: a throbbing pain in his chest and a sensation like his blood is bubbling. He calls it shaken soda syndrome. He's not funny.

"You and that log," he says. "It's not that bad."

"Scale of one to—"

"Zero."

"Come on, it's the one thing I can do to help. By the way, Ara's here. Medical trip?"

He shakes his head. "She must not be here for that."

"It'd be a bit early," I say, "but you always seem better when you come back."

"Don't want to leave you"—he draws air deeply through his nose and lets it out— "by yourself."

"I'm pretty sure I turned fourteen... recently."

His face scrunches up in thought. "Maybe."

And he means this. Spanglers don't celebrate birthdays. I don't even know the exact day. Though, when I was a kid, I got Dad to admit it was in October. I set the date right in the middle, the fifteenth.

"Dad, just go. What am I gonna do, throw a party with the goats?"

"You have friends."

"Had. I left school three years ago. And I'm not sure any of my old friends would be up for a birthday party. If I had a phone—"

"No." Another difficult breath shudders from his mouth. "It can't have been that long."

Of course, he ignores the phone conversation yet again. He calls them inefficient. What's inefficient about instant communication?

"It *has* been that long," I say. "It doesn't matter. I read college-level textbooks. I follow the news. I can name any rock or metal you put in front of me. What else? I can fix a transmission. My beard would grow in if I didn't shave every day. Come on, we make our own biofuel. I don't need school. I'm grown up. And you've said it yourself: Spanglers mature faster than other people. Look at you. You look fifty. You're thirty-two. You had a kid when you were, what, seventeen?" I stand and turn off the equipment.

"You need friends," he says, getting that I'm-sorry-I'm-sick look on his face.

As always, I dismiss the idea. "I've got you."

"I don't count."

When the rasp in his breathing is nearly gone, we head for the house. I haunt his steps until he makes it to his chair in the den. It's warmer inside, which is good for him. There's always something relaxing about the inside of the cabin. I think it's the heat from the embers in the fireplace, but it could simply be all the soft tones, pinewood, and woven rugs.

Above his head on the pine boards is a small coat of arms. The symbol is a blazing white sun tagged with our last name: *SPANGLER*.

I turn my attention to the news still blaring on the TV. The anchor reviews the details of a health crisis somewhere in eastern Africa. It's a breaking story, which always interests me, but as I search the couch for the remote to turn up the volume, the channel changes to a movie with an alien robot attacking someplace in the Rocky Mountains.

5

"Taffy news," Dad mutters, setting the remote on the coffee table.

I can get my news fix later. "Dad, what about Ara? Her car's not even out there. Starting to think I was hallucinating."

"Guess she'll come back when she wants."

I shake my head, and her words from the clifftop come back to me. "She said something was wrong. Did she mean with you?"

He pulls the oxygen mask away, his mouth hanging open. His eyes dart to the window and then to me. "I'll keep an eye out for her."

"You don't find it weird she might be wandering around our property? Should I go find her?"

He shakes his head. The steady hiss of oxygen covers the low sound of him clearing his throat. When finally, I try to retreat to the kitchen to check on dinner, Dad puts a hand on my arm. "Clayson, wait."

His sky-colored eyes fixate on the framed picture of my mother on the mantle. I glance in frustration. Small bands of her strawberry blonde hair are woven in tiny braids, but the rest of it ripples over her shoulders. They're both five foot three unless you ask Dad—says he's a fingertip taller than her. Terry and Lena. She's like a movie star, beautiful and out of reach. Pale against her shimmering black gown. I *wanna* like her, but it's complicated.

I'm never allowed to be around her when she comes to visit. House rules. Dad protecting me, I guess. But it's not the same for him. Whenever he's overwhelmed or stressed out, he seeks the strange vitality—a visceral power—that only comes from a long gaze into his past with her.

He sees me looking at the picture. "I'd like to think we'll be a family again soon." His eyes unfocus, staring out the window. "Maybe very soon."

He can't mean she's coming back here. "This is our life Dad, like it or not."

He squeezes my arm tighter. "No, it isn't. This can't go on forever."

"Maybe I should adjust your oxygen down."

He coughs a laugh. "Okay, okay. But maybe tomorrow…"

He drifts off, settling into his chair to watch his movie. I retreat to the kitchen, test the chicken and potatoes, and fill a pot with mixed vegetables. When everything is done, I set the table and return to the den.

Dad's out cold.

I adjust the blanket on his lap. "So much for keeping an eye out for Ara."

I fall into our nightly routine, wrapping his dinner and putting it in the fridge. Then I return to the den and change the channel back to the news and eat off the TV tray. I do the dishes and clean the stove as night settles over the cabin.

Not bothering to turn on the lights, I watch something on a travel channel about Azerbaijan nightlife.

The world is a connection of a thousand cities. I've been to exactly zero. No vacations. No plane rides. Not even a long car trip. Someday, I'd like to travel, but once more, I push the thought from my mind. When the show's over, I turn down the sound and head to the porch swing to wait for the stars to appear in the sky, all part of the ritual of our solitary life here in the mountains.

But clouds hide the stars tonight, and Ara is still somewhere on the property. Both these things are foreboding signs which leave me wary of the night.

I wait on the porch for a long time. Long enough to glimpse the lamplight eyes of a raccoon in the grove and to feel the temperature drop with the last of the sun's purple glimmer. Moonlight shapes the pale pieces of gravel into something like gems.

Down the gravel road sits the camper my parents once drove everywhere, padlocked. I'm not allowed inside. Which doesn't matter. It's not like we could mow around it and drive off somewhere. It's missing the two front tires and sitting on cinder blocks. Been there, stuck in the weeds, since the transmission went out, the day my mother left us.

I start to drift into sleep, but a muffled cry startles me awake. It's darker now. I sit upright, stilling the porch bench beneath me, listening for the sound again.

A growling scream shatters the placid evening. I run back to the den, where my father fights a night terror. I work to unclench his hands from the blanket, to wake him, but the moment he stirs to consciousness, the door flies inward—Ara steps in.

"Therias, they know you're—" A flicker of embarrassment brushes her face. "Night terror?"

I nod, but my mind bounces to a strange word—Therias. Did she call Dad the wrong name?

Regaining himself, Dad takes a drink of the glass of water next to him. "What? Know what? Who—"

"The council knows you're alive. They've sent Bazalrak."

Something tingles over my scalp, some forbidden knowledge. It hangs suspended in the air. If only I could grab it, make sense of Ara's words.

Dad bolts to his feet. The oxygen mask snags on the tank and rips free of his face. "What? When?"

"Now," she says. "As soon as they find a budge leading to the Blue Ridge Mountains."

"Do they know about Clayson?" Dad asks.

The oxygen mask hisses. "What's going on?" I ask.

Ara scans my face. "Therias, it's time he knew."

"Why are you calling him that?"

Dad raises his voice. "Do they know about Clayson?"

She shakes her head. "Not that I can tell."

A visual weight lifts from him. "Okay," he says, then growls in frustration. "You and I will have to return to the conjurers, but Clayson... he can't go there. Tell Azbena to meet me... you know where."

Ara's mouth firms into a straight line. "Okay."

8

Frustrated, I wave my hands in the air. "Hold it. Who is Azbena?"

"Well..." Ara stares at her feet. "Therias..."

I shake my head, tension building across my shoulders.

Dad hangs his head. "I figured there would be time."

Heavier clouds cover the moon outside—at least it seems that way—but there is something unnatural in the deepening shadows in the den.

"Do it," Dad says, bowing his head to Ara.

Her hand drops to his shoulder. A few seconds pass as a strange light gathers along Ara's arms and face. I step back, unable to process what I'm seeing. Dad's shoulders relax, and he stands, breaking contact with her. A fierce glow snaps into focus in his eyes, a look I hadn't seen since before he was sick.

Ara's breath becomes a thick fog. For the briefest second, tiny human-shaped shadows stumble around inside her breath as it hangs in place. The shape of an ax darkens the center of the cloud. Ara cuts it away with a wave of her arm.

She and Dad trade a look filled with understanding.

"Bazalrak," they say.

"What? What's Bazalrak?"

A bright glare from the motion flood lights shoots through the window, but when I move to check, Ara yanks me backward.

"Time to budge," she says.

Pieces of reality break away from my mind. "Budge what? Guys, slow down."

Dad clamps his hands around both of my biceps, showing more strength than he has in years. "The camper."

He drags me toward the kitchen, Ara behind me. The range light is still on over the stove, but we race through the side door into the gloomy evening. I follow in Dad's wake. We get about fifteen feet from the cabin, but my mind is stuck on the stove light. Turning it off is the only thing that makes sense.

"The stove light... if we're leaving," I say, whirling around.

A scream breaks over the night. But it's me. I'm screaming.

Ara is on fire. Thick fog swirls around her while glowing molten rock inches up her jeans, slowly devouring her.

I try to shout for Dad, but it comes out as air instead of words. I can't breathe. I press my fingertips hard against my temples. What's happening?

Somehow Ara still moves. She rounds the side of the cabin, her burning, clouded figure still visible as she stops behind Dad's flatbed. I feel a wave of nausea roll me back. No, not nausea. The earth is moving—a wall of earth sprouts in front of the car, bathed in the same thick fog.

"Dad? What's—"

Ara's fists become balls of flame and rock. "Run! I'll give you a few seconds."

Dad's arms around my chest, attempting to haul me from the scene. "Deliver my message to Azbena," he tells her. "Don't worry about us."

Another massive shudder shakes the ground. Liquid fire erupts over the earthen palisade, sizzling against the dirt.

That's when I turn and run, faster than I have ever run in my life. We flee up the road to where the shape of the old camper rises in the dark. A dull orange glow from the fire behind us flickers against the flecked red and yellow stripes on the aluminum body. Weeds and bushes hold the camper in place.

Dad stops at the door, somehow breathing steadily. He was ahead of me. He ran faster. How is he not out of breath? On a good day, he can't do five jumping jacks without folding over and wheezing for five minutes straight. How is this possible? Ara had put a hand on him. What had she done? Inject him with something?

He shakes the old padlock on the door.

"Dad, your breathing..."

He smiles, takes a breath in through his nose, and says, "We need the key." He picks up a rock from the ground.

Nothing is registering in my mind. "What's happening?"

He reaches inside the rock and pulls out a slim leather case.

After glancing at me, he parts the drawstring and frees a pair of tinted glasses. They're bigger than should fit in the case. And the case was bigger than could have fit inside the rock. The darkness is playing tricks on my mind.

"Here. Put these on." He presses them into my hand. "Open the camper."

I stare at the lock. "It's locked. I need—"

"Just put them on. I can't use them. I-I won't."

I unfold the glasses and slip them over my eyes. It's like looking through two yellow glass ashtrays. "Now what?"

A cool male voice, edged with malice and the threat of danger, calls from down the road. "Brightstorm!"

A strange shadow crawls along the ground toward us. The earthen wall lies in a heap of dull, molten goo, glowing like the seams of hell itself. Ara is gone. The unnatural shadow grows closer.

"Dad, come on. What are we doing?" I'm pushing him away from the camper, but he won't move.

"The lock, quickly."

I growl in frustration, but when I reach for the lock, strange thoughts push their way into my awareness—satisfaction, like having solved a riddle. Or no, more like a revelation. Eureka. The lock vanishes.

"Where did it go?" I say.

"It's still there. The glasses let you bypass it. Now in!"

The front of the camper still rests on cinder blocks. Though I half expect the thing to have magically grown new tires. Nope. We're not going anywhere in this thing.

"This is crazy," I mutter. "What is this?"

"Good forgework. Your mother's, I think. Now get in the camper before Bazalrak spots us."

I shake my head confused.

The smooth voice rises over the night. "Therias."

I yank the camper open. Dad scrambles around me in the tight space, heading for the cab. I blink. This is my first time inside.

It's tidy but covered in dust, a monument to my parent's former life. Which apparently, I know absolutely nothing about.

"Clayson, get up here," Dad says.

I find Dad removing a plush cover from the aluminum steering wheel. Then he sits in the passenger seat.

"Sit down, and you don't need the glasses anymore," he says, pointing to the driver's seat. "The keys are in the ignition."

I set the glasses on the dashboard. "But the front wheels."

"Turn the key, put your hands on the steering wheel, and push the accelerator."

"This is nuts," I say. "I'm barely fourteen." Fear is working its way through my bloodstream, but I trust Dad to protect me. I turn the key.

The engine sputters to life. The camper shakes, and the headlights flicker on.

In front of the camper, four figures pause on the gravel road for a brief second and then turn toward us, squinting against the light. None of them are taller than me and Dad, and that's saying something. Their gray uniforms look homemade, spun from some type of heavy cloth—canvas maybe—embedded with shimmering pieces of metal.

The one closest is a burly man with a dozen glimmering face piercings. He stares through the camper window, grimacing at the bright headlights. A giant ax rests on his shoulder. Can he see us? I hope he can't see us.

"Who are these people?" I say.

Dad reaches across me and grabs my seat belt, buckling me in. "Now or never, Clayson or our situation is about to get a hundred times worse." His voice is grave. "Answers when we get there."

The metal steering wheel is cold in my hands. I step on the gas.

Reality shatters. There's pressure against my calves, and my stomach lurches as the camper rockets upward. Or it seems that way. The force of movement pushes my body into the seat.

Beyond the windshield, a black void rushes by. Maybe. We're racing upward like some space readiness test.

We snap abruptly into place, and the weight lifts from my body. My stomach settles.

I catch a glimpse of the bright evening sky before the front of the camper drops into the dirt. Pushed against the dashboard, Dad and I exchange glances.

Dad grins. "Oops. The cinder blocks weren't part of the original coding. Forgot. No front tires."

"Where are we?" The horizon is skewed.

We've landed in some kind of RV park. A few kids in an RV next to us stare in disbelief. Dad waves at them, and they drop away from the window. I glance at the crooked skyline between a few power lines. Nickel-colored mountains lean inward, carpeted with yellow and orange.

"The Rockies," my father says with a strange reverence.

I laugh. Hysteria is the only emotion I have left. Maybe I'm still asleep on the bench in front of the cabin. "As in the Rocky Mountains? No, that doesn't make any sense. How can we be halfway across the country?"

"We budged here. It's how our people get around. We don't use trains or cars or anything so limited."

"Our people? You're gonna have to explain better than this, Dad."

He taps his fingers on the dashboard. "When we're safe."

My vision floats to the window. "We're still not safe? Those other people, did they... kill Ara?"

He looks at me confused, then puts a hand to his forehead. "The fire? No, that's craft. Uh, how do I explain—like magic, but not. It's technology. Forgework. Coding. She was using ironcraft —control of the elements—to give us some time."

"Magic?" I say, looking out the window at the Rocky Mountains.

He fumbles with the latch on the glove compartment. "You're not going crazy, Clayson."

Rifling through handfuls of old ketchup packets and napkins, he finds a map, but instead of opening it up, he tears the cover off, finds a pen, and scribbles something in the corner. I lean over to look. The word *GAMGIM* is scrawled along the side.

He stands, and with the camper still tilted forward, climbs uphill out of the cab. I follow, frustrated.

Before he slips out of the door, I grab his sleeve. "Okay, I'm not crazy, and..."

His head dips, and he takes a deep, clear breath. "There's a lot to say." His clear blue eyes find mine. "When you were a baby, I decided you would have a better life if you and I moved to the surface."

"Surface?"

"We have a proud heritage, Clayson. A line of noble mountain dwellers extending back thousands of years. Loamin."

The look on my face must communicate my confusion. Strange words tumble around in my brain: craft, budge, the Rockies, magic, mountain dwellers. Now Loamin.

He places a hand on my shoulder. "Think of us like—and I hate to say it—but, like dwarfs. Though we don't use that word."

I'm suddenly aware of the amount of space between the top of my head and the ceiling of the small camper. "Dwarfs?" I say. "I'm short, but come on."

"Tall for Loamin," he says.

He opens the door wider and steps out. I follow him. A cool, dry wind swollen with pine scent brushes my face. It's sunset again, at my back. We really did change time zones.

A handful of vehicles are scattered through the park, but only a few people wander among the trees. Closest to us, light pours from the windows of a modern camper. The door opens, and two kids come tumbling out. They give us confused looks and then join their parents in camp chairs around a small grill. Their mother watches us closely, her gaze moving between us and the missing wheels on our camper.

"We're so close to home," Dad says. "The Rockies."

He marches over to a small metal mailbox nailed to a pine tree encrusted with sap. He drops the note he made from the map cover inside the box. "Nearly every Loamin left on earth has gathered underneath these mountains. And now, Ide keep us, we have to go back."

A figure blocks out the sunset, casting a shadow over me. "Would you really come home, Therias?"

It's my mother's voice. I look over my shoulder, but first, I lock away two competing feelings: contempt and hope. Will I even talk to her this time? A reaction forms on Dad's face, wild with a joy I could never feel at her appearance.

Moving past me without a single word, she pushes wisps of her strawberry blonde hair away from her face. Her skin is the color of ivory, except around her eyes, where they're red from crying. What had she been crying about?

Dad clears his throat, water in his eyes. "Ara reached you then?"

She nods. "Would you really come home?"

A figure pops into existence behind my mother. The tall, sallow-skinned man inclines his head to me, then to Dad. His suit jacket hangs limply from his shoulders, an off-white color as if it had once been bright.

When he straightens, he finds something other than us to look at. It makes me think of Ara's lack of eye contact. They're both extremely tall. How are they connected to this world? Are they Loamin or something else?

The man carries a small golden ring box sandwiched between two hands, like something sacred.

Dad takes a quick interest in him. "Hello, Vor. It's been a long time. You haven't changed."

"No," he says with a deep bow. The word is strangely stretched out, melodious. "And good evening King Therias."

Dad inclines his head but returns his attention to my mother.

Her spotless white dress is soaked with light from the sunset. It's almost blinding. I try to meet her eyes, but she's already walked around me. She must feel nothing for me, and I can't understand that because even though I haven't been allowed to interact with her there is a familiarity between us I'll never be rid of.

He reaches for her hand, and slowly, painfully so, she lets him take it. My father whispers, "Azbena." It echoes inside my mind as if I'm remembering it, not learning it.

When she finally smiles at him, it's so forlorn I almost can't look at her. "It's over," she says. "The council found you, despite my efforts. This oath you made not to use craft... come back to me."

This man and woman are suddenly foreign to me. Not Terry and Lena, but Therias and Azbena. They're a dim reflection of that framed picture on the mantle. My understanding of the world shatters and reassembles itself into an insurmountable object. Everything I've believed about my family, about myself, is a lie.

AWAY ON VACATION

DAD BRUSHES a wisp of my mother's hair behind her ear. "You came."

She steps back, as cold toward him as a January blizzard.

"Ask me," Dad says to her.

"Therias, I—"

"Ask me, please."

Her eyes return to his, and she lets a ghost of a smile bleed through her sharp features. "Do I love you?"

Dad touches her face. "More than anything."

In the back of my mind, I sense the weight of history in this strange exchange. A shared story I know nothing about.

She nods sadly. "I do, Therias. More than anything. Please come home. We can face this together. Rebuild our lives."

The nearby family starts cleaning up their meal, casting us wary glances.

Dad looks in my direction. "Now more than ever, I can't. Clayson he—"

Her chin drifts upward. "Stay in your isolation then, Therias. You keep doing this to me," she continues. "Pretending there is a chance for us. I can't. I can't do this. You need to give up conjur-

17

ing. Use craft again. Help us. Help us rebuild the city. Be with me, with your daughter."

Her last word strikes a hot iron through my brain. "Daughter? Do I—do I have a—"

"Sister?" Dad acknowledges this with a dip of his head. "Clayson, come here."

Vor's head moves inch-by-inch as he follows my footsteps.

Dad shakes his head. "I have kept so much from you."

My mother squints at him, confused. "Like what? I mean, what else?"

When I try to meet her eyes, she makes no effort to connect with me.

"Do you see it?" Dad looks right into my eyes. "She can't... I can see you, but your mother can't. Doesn't even understand someone else is standing here with me. I've kept this truth hidden for your safety."

I try again to meet her eyes, but she still scrutinizes her husband's words, confused, searching for meaning she can't discover. "What can't I see? What are you talking about, Therias? Who are you looking at?"

I stumble for the right words. This woman is my mother. "Dad, sh-she can't see me? How is that possible?"

"Craft," Dad says.

"Craft?"

"Uh, like magic but made through metalwork."

"Magic... so the fire around Ara? And teleporting—"

"Budging," Dad says, encouraging me to use the right word. This is turning into something like our lessons on mechanics. I ask questions, he answers vaguely.

"Okay, budging," I say. "It's like magic, uh, craft."

Dad tousles my hair like I'm five. "Fast learner," he says. "And yes. That's craft. But the kind used on you and your mother... it's nothing I've seen before. And I've tried everything—for her and for you."

18

My mother almost yells at him. "Therias, you're doing it again. Would—please look at me."

My head is spinning. "For me?"

With both of her hands, my mother directs Dad's face back to her. "What are you talking about, Therias? What's happening?"

He faces her. "Clayson, I'm going to talk to her, but I'll be talking to you at the same time. There are usually parts of my words she simply blocks out. Things related to you. It's been that way since before you were born. Well, even during your birth, she kept forgetting you were a part of her, thought she was sick or cursed by craft. It was difficult. Do you remember, Azbena?"

Her eyes widen like she's remembering the trauma of my birth, or for her—I suppose— something painful, but that she doesn't remember as childbirth. "When I was sick before you left? Of course, I remember."

I don't understand, but I try to listen, force my mind to slow down. I pretend they're only something on TV because. at this point, my life might as well be one of the post-apocalyptic movies Dad watches.

"Before she even started showing, she hid away. No one knew. Not even your sister. And when you came, Clayson" —he takes her hands again, on the verge of letting tears slip out— "you wouldn't sleep, for days and days, and she couldn't feed you. You were dying. One night, desperate, I took you to the surface, thinking the change in pressure might shock your system. And it worked. You stopped crying. Slept. Even ate something. I knew then that whatever craft made you invisible to her made it impossible for you to truly sleep unless you were on the surface."

My mother interrupts. "You left me. We both knew what taking the mithrium would mean, but you didn't have to leave. My father lost his life trying to use the mithrium. It's time to face the council together."

He nods. "She thinks I left because we took something from the council, something dangerous. But I left because of you, and I stayed on the surface because of you, Clayson. I tried to bring you back down many times, but you wouldn't sleep."

I catch something in their words. "Mithrium. What's that?"

Vor dips his head even lower like the very word is frightening.

"I don't need to go over that all again. Get to the point, Therias," my mother says. Her eyes redden. I've always pushed her to the side, but I'd been working without all the right information. What does she mean to me now if she's never understood she had a child?

Dad has no such conflict for her. He's trying to balance both my questions and my mother's demands. I see him through fresh eyes. He gave up everything to raise me. I've always known that, but this scrubs away all my confusion about their relationship. He loves her. She loves him. But they couldn't be together.

"For the moment," he says, "my obligations haven't changed."

"It was Theridal Silverkeeper," my mother says, all emotion drained from her voice. "Your friend. He and the rest of the council cast a decision beyond my ability to rule against it. They suspect I know your whereabouts. I've denied it, but Silverkeeper found you somehow. He sent Bazalrak with a team and a troll mech to retrieve you."

I freeze. "You mean that guy at the cabin? The guy with the ax and all the piercings? Is he dangerous?"

"Definitely," Dad says, and then to my mother, "And Silverkeeper and I aren't friends. Not since his accident."

I rub my face. "Okay, first there's Bazalrak and now Silverkeeper. Some strange council. Dad, am I supposed to be keeping track of all this? And—"

"Relax, Clayson," Dad says.

"Relax? Fifteen minutes ago, I was in the Blue Ridge Mountains. The biggest thing I had going was a travel documentary about Azerbaijan. And now—"

"Deep breaths, Clayson. Give me a few more minutes to sort things out with your mother."

I throw my hands in the air, frustrated, taking a step back. I nearly topple over Vor, who's so quiet he could be a Navy Seal. A very timid, weak Navy Seal.

My mother lets go of Dad's hands. "Vor, the necklace, please."

Vor slinks over to her and hands her a necklace made from a bike chain studded with dull blue glass. "You're confusing me. Here. Ara said you might need this. It gave me hope you were going to use craft again. But I was wrong, wasn't I?"

She tries to hand the chain to Dad, but he shakes his head almost imperceptibly. "I can't," he says.

She drops her hands to her side and clenches her jaw, retreating even further from him. "There's no time for your principles, Therias. Let me protect you?"

"I made an oath," he says.

"Bazalrak will be just as happy to kill you as to bring you in a prisoner."

I step between them. I need answers. "Who are these people? Dad, what did you do?"

"The Knights of Shale," he says. "The military body that serves the Keeper's Council and the royal family."

"I've lost my influence in the council," my mother says.

"Dad, I thought you said she worked in the government, in D.C."

"Technically," Dad says, "she runs the government. We all do. Our family, I mean. She's the steward of the Kingdom of Rimduum, and I'm—I was the King."

"Are the king," my mother says softly.

"So, we're some kind of dwarf—I mean, uh, Loamin—royalty?" I shake my head. "Okay, I'm done."

Reluctantly, he takes the necklace from my mother and passes it to me as quickly as he can.

"What's this? A birthday present?" I say. It's probably some magical necklace that can call a hoard of black bears to fight off the enemies of the royal family—which apparently includes a dude with a huge ax named Bazalrak, and an old friend of my father's named Silverkeeper, who helps run a shady political council.

My mother's eyes shift toward the pine trees at the edge of the RV park. The sun is escaping for the second time today, and shadows elongate the shapes of my parents against the asphalt.

"Ara said you would need my concealer also," my mother says. "Who are you trying to conceal? They know you're alive."

"Do you trust me?" Dad asks her.

She sighs but nods.

"Let me guide your hands. You weave the craft."

She calls Vor forward again, and he opens the golden ring box, revealing its contents. A small golden candy rests against a shimmer of green velvet. She pops it in her mouth, and Vor steps away. A second later, she draws a pin from her hair. She pierces her index finger. I expect blood to well up, but instead, gold liquid becomes a pinprick at the tip of her finger. She holds it over her palm and lets a few drops start to accumulate.

Dad drags me in front of her as she dips her finger in the golden blood and brings her hands forward. He takes her wrists and gently leads her hands to my face. "Hold still," he says. Whether this is a command to me or my mother, I can't tell, but I don't move as he helps her trace her fingers along my cheekbones and above my eyebrows. I shudder.

What will this do to me? First, Ara becomes a ball of liquid fire, then I use a pair of weird glasses to open a lock, then we teleport magically to the Rocky Mountains. I have to get Dad to slow down and talk to me. Answer my questions.

When they finish, my mother pulls away, blinking. The skin on my face tightens. There's a weird feeling at my joints like I've hit my funny bone, but all over. I reach upward out of instinct, but Dad catches my hand and says, "Let the concealer set."

He guides her hand to rest on my shoulder, and for a moment, I think she might be able to cut through whatever power has her blind to me. Her face crinkles, eyes darkening. She steps behind me, her hand still on my shoulder.

22

Vor stiffens and bows to Dad.

"It was good to see you, Vor," he says.

"And you, King." Vor's voice has a strange quality to it, as if he's far away.

Who is he? He seems so much like Ara, but maybe it's the height or his mannerism.

I glance at Dad, but as I do, the tiny weight of my mother's hand disappears from my shoulder. I turn to where she had been standing, a single pink orchid rises from the pine needles. She's gone. So is Vor.

My father's eyes dart to the trees, and then farther to the horizon, to the pinnacle of the mountain. He bends and plucks the flower from the ground. "I wish the mithrium had never been found," he says.

When he catches me staring, he points to the mountaintop behind us. "See that peak? How many mountains in the world are about the same elevation? Fourteen thousand feet, give or take."

"I-I don't know. Hundreds?"

"Hundreds. There used to be hundreds of cities, each with millions of Loamin living in peace and comfort." He laughs, and it's bitter, angry. "This mountain—Helgrimral—and one other—Whurrimduum—are all that remain of our once-great civilization. Two cities left. Hundreds of millions dead."

I glance toward the sign hanging over the entrance of the RV park: *PIKE'S PEAK*. "Dead? How?" Can there be a whole city beneath us? I suppose if we can instantly teleport from the Appalachians to the Rockies, anything's possible.

"I'll explain as much as I can, but we've got to get moving," Dad says.

He flies like a storm to the camper door—reminding me the effects of his disease are gone—wrenches it open, and calls to me. "We have to get you out of here."

I barely make it to the entry before the door hinges back on me, but I follow him, leaning to one side to stay balanced on the angled floor of the RV. He steps into the bedroom, sets down the flower, and rummages through a small closet. Stacks of old clothes fly through the air as he frantically tears through his belongings. I stand with the necklace in my outstretched hand, waiting for who-knows-what-else to happen.

I blink when he pulls an unopened energy drink from the bottom of the closet. He wipes off the dust and motions for me to sit at the table. I duck to avoid the kitchen cabinet as I sit.

He takes the opposite seat as I lay the necklace between us. The sun, already below the horizon, sends the last of the day's light filtering through a lace curtain onto the table, striking the necklace. Suddenly, blue and white shimmering refractions speckle the inside of the camper.

Dad's forearms drop on either side of the necklace, muting the brilliant droplets of light as he sets the brown-labeled can on the table.

"This will get you to safety. We've been above granite for too long." He turns the energy drink so I can read the label: *GAMGIM.* "Using two types of craft at once split their power, but I think your mother's concealer will hold, and here... drink it," he says, popping the tab.

I turn the can to him. "Sorry, no. What do you mean by two types of craft? Craft is magic, right? That's what you said. Like when we teleported here, or the lock on the camper."

He glances out the window but sighs and scratches his head. He lines up the necklace with the can. Pointing to the can, he says. "Budgecraft. Aluminum. It can move things from place to place. Got it?"

Trying to shake as much disbelief from my brain as possible, I aim my thumb toward the cab of the RV. "Like the RV?"

"Correct. The RV works by budgecraft, aluminum. Now, this" —he points to the necklace my mother gave him— "is a little more complicated, but we won't need it. The moment you drink this energy drink, you'll budge to Gamgim, and Rugnus will be there waiting for you."

"Rugnus? Who's—wait, you're not coming with me."

"I need to go back to the conjurers with Ara. Bazalrak's after me, not you. No one even knows you exist. You can disappear. I'm sorry I didn't tell you anything until now, but Rugnus will take care of you until I make contact. He'll take you to Helgrimral... uh, they call it Tungsten City now. You can hide there, blend in. Start your own life. Please drink it, Clayson."

"Wait. I can't do this. I don't understand. There were cities under the mountains? And now they're gone? But not the one you're sending me to? And... I'm not following. So, who's Rugnus? How do you know him?"

Dad pushes the can closer to me. "I'm sort of his mentor. He's about your age. Your soon-to-be friend. Drink."

"I'm not going somewhere without you. What if you get worse?"

"Clayson, I... being sick it's... I'm only sick because of living on the surface. It happens to all Loamin. Well, all of us except you. That's why we're here. And I stopped using craft a few years ago. It used to protect me from the effects mostly."

"The year you got sick?"

"Yeah."

"So, we're on the surface because of me? You're sick because of me?" The bottom drops out from under me. The walls of the camper appear impossibly far away.

"No. Don't think about it that way. There were other reasons I had to leave too."

"Why are they—Bazalrak, the council—why are they chasing you? What's mithrium? You took it? Stole it?"

"That's a longer story. But mithrium is the most dangerous substance on earth. It can level whole cities. It did level them, nearly all of them." He takes a deep breath. "I-I won't leave you with Rugnus. Not forever, but I need you to listen to me before we run out of time. I-I love you, Clayson. I know I've kept this world from you. But I need you to trust me. Drink this. Find Rugnus. He'll keep you safe."

For the first time in a long time, Dad seems healthy. His

25

breathing is strong, his eyes clear, urging me to drink from the can. For three years, I've been tethered to his side. He smiles at me, rubs my shoulder. It's his way of setting me free from him.

I shake his hands off of me. "No. I'm not going to leave you."

"You have to! I-I can't let... It's not like I won't see you again. I'll find you. Okay? I'll come for you when the time is right."

"I haven't been away from you. How will I contact you? I don't even have a phone."

"I've told you: you don't need a phone. There are much better forms of communication in the Loamin world. And I promise: I will find you as soon as it's safe."

With this promise, I pivot away from him. A city under the mountain filled with magic. If there is, I've never seen it on a travel show. Excitement lights a fire somewhere deep in my bones, in my DNA.

I take the can. It's cool to the touch. I drink about half of it in two big gulps. I gag, almost spit it from my mouth. It tastes like someone left a steel wool pad at the bottom. I catch my reflection in the mirror on the fridge, and for a brief second, my lips shimmer with tan light.

But that's not the only oddity. I have a new face. My nose is thinner and pointy. My forehead, glistening with sweat, is more stretched out—my chin, softer. No stubble. My hair's changed from brown to black—my eyes, from green to brown. Even my dimples are gone. "What did that drink do?"

"No, that's the goldcraft, the concealer, your mother put on your face. It's temporary. Goldcraft can change your physical body. But... using two types of craft splits their power."

He looks at me expectantly. Did he assume I would disappear? I drank from the can. Was I supposed to—what was it called —budge?

"What about this?" I hold up the necklace.

"I said we won't need—"

The table trembles.

"What was that?" I say.

Dad counts under his breath. "One one-thousand…two one-thousand…three one-thousand—" The windows rumble, and he snatches the necklace from the table, bolting for the door.

"Outside!" he yells.

I stand so quickly, I hit my head on the kitchen cabinet. Groaning, I barely make it to the door before the ground quakes again. The RV across from us tips sideways and crashes on the pavement, revealing a hulking metal figure making its way toward us. The giant monster is a hybrid of gears, and riveted sheets of metal—like some crazed artist created Quasimodo from clock parts and a seven forty-seven jumbo jet. Its mechanized biceps flex as it shoves the RV out of the way.

"Dad, what was in that energy drink?" I say. "Am I hallucinating?"

He grabs my arm and leans over to me, whispering, "Stop calling me Dad. They'll guess who you are."

Towering above me, the massive troll-shaped machine spits lightning at the nearest power line. A high-pitched, electric current buzzes and the light bulbs pop in the few surrounding streetlamps. RVs, feeding off the park's power, go dark all around us. Even the power in the little park office down the road flickers and dies, leaving the late-evening glow highlighting the monster's metallic skin. The campers run in a panic. Those still in their RVs peel out at breakneck speeds.

In two giant steps, the Robo-troll could close the distance between us but remains motionless. Through gaps in its metal cranium, tiny gears rotate like clockwork, and a blue flame pulses in each eye.

"Azbena coded these," Dad says. "The budge should have worked by now. The mech has to be blocking it. No wonder she thought we needed the necklace. You'll have to disable the foilgrip."

I stare at him.

He groans. "Foilgrip uses budgecraft to block people from

27

budging. The mech has anti-budgecraft capabilities, preventing the energy drink from working within a certain area."

The Robo-troll hasn't shifted, but its blue-flickering sockets stop pulsing, and the flames inside deepen and focus, shaping into beady, dangerous eyes.

Gears in its neck click and spin as it cranes its head toward us. Iron bumps run the course of its long nose down to a fixed, bemused grin. The troll is more a statue now than a monster, waiting in the darkness for us to move.

A few more RVs zoom past the troll, their headlights twisting the shadows around its face, and for a moment, I imagine it's all a nightmare. What else could this be?

I step carefully over to Dad as the Robo-troll's eyes track me. "Should we run? Try to get outside its range?"

He shakes his head. "No. A Behemoth unit like this one can run about fifty miles an hour, easy. You have to use the necklace to take control of it, disable the foilgrip. Though three crafts at once..." He shakes his head. "It can work. Let's just hope none of this craft is a weakness for you."

I'm making every effort not to think about what will happen if it attacks us. Its titanium hands pinch together like vice-grips.

"It would catch us," he says. "Azbena's coding is always good. The necklace. Put it on."

I shove it toward him. "But she said you had to—"

"No! I can't." He never snaps at me this way, but his expression softens. "I can't use it. I made an oath to the conjurors. Please, put it on."

I undo the clasp but fumble to secure it at the back of my neck. Dad reaches over and tucks it into my shirt.

"It has to be touching your skin."

He waits. When nothing happens, his shoulders slump. "This is my fault. I shouldn't have kept you in the dark. This is going to be harder than I thought. Okay, you have to focus on what you expect it to do."

"What do I expect it to do?" I say.

"I might be too late," Dad says, pointing down the road at a group of campers. "Bazalrak is here. Whatever you do, don't let his shadowcraft touch you."

"Shadowcraft?" I strain my eyes. Not campers, Loamin. The same group who chased us from the cabin. No beards. No armor. Only four short figures this time, one with a giant ax swinging freely from his hands. They weave between two abandoned RVs, and I lose sight of them.

Dad shakes his head and says, "Okay, we better run."

"You said—"

"We're out of options. The line of trees over there. Don't look back. I'm right behind you."

I take a deep breath, steal a quick glance at the Robo-troll blocking the road, and then, like a maniac, sprint for the tree line. Not far behind, Dad urges me to go faster. The machine hesitates for a moment, but then a rhythm fills the air—grind, buzz, crunch, grind, buzz, crunch—faster and faster.

Catching up with ease, Dad nudges me to the right, into a thicket of elms. Passing the clump of trees, we run through a wide picnic area. Light shimmers against a small creek ahead of us. I can't help picturing my mother's glamorous white dress, the sun setting—like a halo around her wispy, braided hair. Only minutes have passed, but for the first time ever, I miss her.

I never miss her. I've always thought of her as out of reach, uncaring. But what she had to go through to bring me into this world... the person I've placed so much blame on is innocent. No. More than that. She's a victim of some magic that cut her off from her child. From me.

A sensation, like cringing from nails on a chalkboard, crawls up my spine. The next second, static electricity pops along my skin. All at once, display lights pop up before my eyes, overlaying reality with a sharp, bluish hue—like I'm suddenly wearing night-vision goggles. Red outlines, people-sized, ahead of us twenty feet, growing closer.

I lose my balance, tumble next to the stream. My hands move to my eyes on instinct. I try to scrape away the extra color.

"I think the necklace is working," I say between breaths.

My pulse beats fierce drumming bursts in my ears as the Robo-troll stomps into the mud along the bank of the stream and stops. The display outlines it in green, yellow ripples rhythmically emanating from its exterior.

A virtual text box now hovers beside the troll. Words like video game statistics hang in the air:

MEDIUM GEAR TROLL - BEHEMOTH
TOTAL OBJECT RATING - 9
FOILGRIP - ENGAGED
KEY PHRASE - FIREBANE

"What's happening?" Dad asks. He bounces on his feet, eager to run again, warily eying the troll. Its beady blue orbs follow his movement as he comes to my side.

"Everything's blue. There are words floating in the air."

"Find the foilgrip. Disengage it with the key phrase before the knights reach us."

The knights.

In the display, three of the four red outlines skulk around in the trees. They form a wedge as they slowly creep toward us. The troll looms over the trees. The fourth outlined man—or dwarf, or Loamin, or whatever I'm supposed to call people now—stalks up behind us, clicking his tongue, which must be hard to do with so many piercings. He leans casually against the troll's leg. His body covered in strange red light, his face is peppered with metal studs and rings, a few through his eyebrows, a half dozen rings in his lower lip.

"What a wonderful day for the Kingdom of Rimduum and for the Council of Keepers," Bazalrak says. "To find you after...what has it been...fifteen years. Let's bring you home, Therias. We'll have a grand feast to celebrate the return of the King-which-had-been-lost...or rather, lost himself."

"Bazalrak," Dad says, his shoulders square and his face unreadable. "I hope you have a good cause for disturbing my evening."

Bazalrak lets his ax blade drift to the earth and grins, his silver lip rings twitching upward. He taps what I can only assume is some mark of rank on his collar. "General Stonedoom now."

Dad smiles. "They truly call you by your family name, torturer? They must be down to the last Loamin under granite to have made you a general."

"Your friend Silverkeeper appointed me."

"He should have come himself."

"The head of the council? No. Besides, these days he refuses to budge anywhere. But I was happy to come in his place. So, are you going to resist? I would love it if you did. As a general, I'm so busy. I don't get enough opportunities to torture people anymore."

The other Loamin emerge from the brush but stay on the opposite side of the stream. Three of them: a man with a carpet of spiders like a cap on his back; a woman with almost cartoon-shaped arms, out of proportion with the rest of her body; and a teenage boy my age, holding a massive railgun with a grin about the same size.

"Once a torturer..." Dad says.

Bazalrak shrugs a laugh. "The great king returns to his judgments." He clears his throat, switching his tone to something more formal. "It has come to the attention of the Council of Ten Keepers and the Knights of Shale that after having abdicated your crown—thus forfeiting your privileges in the Kingdom—you were recently discovered gallivanting around the human world. Fizzblooded as you are"—Bazalrak smiles—"you are granted an audience in the high courts of Rimduum, before the Council, in the castlestack of your forbearer, the noble and illustrious Erikzin

Brightstorm." Bazalrak's eyes fall on me. "And who might you be? Don't think your little mask will keep your identity safe for long."

Dad steps between me and Bazalrak. "Your business is with me."

My attention snaps to the job Dad gave me: disengage the foil-grip. Whatever that means. I scan the surface of the troll and, to my surprise, find what I think I'm supposed to be looking for. Something, I'm sure, I couldn't see without the necklace, similar to the way the glasses let me unlock the camper. Two red words pop up in another over-sized text box next to the Robo-troll's elbow:

DISENGAGE FOILGRIP

Budge. That's the word Dad used for teleporting. Anti-budge must be keeping me here. I fix my eyes on the floating words, and they morph into different words:

SPEAK KEY PHRASE

An icon of two hands hovers underneath, repeating a visual tutorial of the gesture I should make to disengage the foilgrip. Can anyone else see this? They must not.

Bazalrak glares at me, slowly sharpening his ax against the troll's metal leg. Behind me, splashes of water, as the other three Loamin draw closer.

The key phrase? What was it?

The moment the phrase pops into my mind, Bazalrak's ax returns firmly in his grip. The strange combination of a cringe and static electricity runs the length of my spine.

"Firebane!" I shout, gesturing like I'm snapping the troll's elbow. The yellow ripples emanating from the troll vanish.

Bazalrak swings, and I raise my arms to protect my face. The moment I do, one of the troll's arms springs outward, absorbing the attack. Bazalrak's ax hits an invisible energy field around the troll. With a crack and a burst of gray light, Bazalrak is hurled backward. My mouth drops open in shock. Did I just control this thing?

Dad comes to my side, but Bazalrak scrambles to his feet, yelling, "Azbena must've already been here. They're trying to budge out! Grab the boy!"

One of the other Loamin, the man with the cloak of spiders, pushes my father away and seizes me from behind, brown light seeping from his forearms. A few spiders scuttle over my shoulders.

Dad's staring straight at me. "It will be okay," he says.

My skin crawls, and suddenly I taste the aluminum from the energy drink again. Bazalrak brings his ax up, eyeing Dad. Nausea rolls my insides into a knot, and I gag. My stomach is a sea of violence. Gravity increases over my whole body until I sink into the darkness of the earth.

HIDE IN GAMGIM

I'M SCATTERED into a billion grainy pieces. No sound. No light. Then all at once, it's like a hundred million ants are gluing together all the little bits of me. When it's over, I sense I'm wading in a void, and each attempt to move is met with resistance. Maybe the void is filled with sand. I hope it's not the particles of all the people who've never made it out of this nothingness alive.

Is this budgecraft? It feels similar to when Dad and I teleported using the camper—extra gravity and a wave of crippling nausea through my gut, if I have one of those still. This is a thousand times worse this time. If it is budgecraft, I never wanna use it again.

My vision clears. I reappear. Or maybe just appear? I shake a spider from my arm and smash it under my foot with a crunch. It must be from the Loamin who grabbed me. Brown light bleeds down my body like water. The ground absorbs it. Is brown always the color associated with a budge, with teleportation?

I pat my body to make sure I'm not missing any parts, then I turn to my surroundings. A dense forest rises around me, dark trunks and limbs nearby and ghostly shadows beyond. The air is thin, forcing me to take deeper, more steady breaths. I must be high in the mountains. A heavy quiet dampens the night.

The blue light and floating video game words from the bike chain necklace are gone. I try to adjust it, use my mind to turn it on, but it's only a weight around my neck again.

There's a crisp snap to my right. I turn my head and catch a handful of leaves shifting, an icy wind rousing them from their sleep on the forest floor. My imagination shifts with the wind into places unknown and frightening, to axes and spiders, magic and fire.

"Hello?" I say. "Who's there?"

No one answers.

I'm alone. I left Dad behind with those people—Loamin. He wouldn't use the glasses to open the camper. He wouldn't use the necklace. He was defenseless. Would Bazalrak kill him? The image of the general's ax swinging downward fills my mind. If they capture him, what will he face? Regret becomes something even heavier than my typical responsibilities. I wanna go back and help him, but I don't know how.

Long minutes pass, maybe a full half-hour. I can't tell. I pace out a small area around me, but I don't venture out farther into the forest. I can't be sure where I am or what to do. Elms and oaks, vaulted ponderosa, and other evergreens grow in the turf between slabs of quartz, so mixed and matched it's unnatural, as out of place here as they would be in the Blue Ridge Mountains.

A twig snaps somewhere in the forest. Dread washes over me when I glimpse a figure lurking within the trees, far enough away to be only the shadow of a tree, and yet it moves more freely, dark against the moonlit grove. I try speaking, but my throat tightens, and all I can manage is a dry squeak as the shadow melts into the darkness of the forest.

I jump at a low whistle, whirling around.

It's not a shadow this time.

A lean, short figure in crisp black jeans, a white t-shirt, and a light jacket patterned with gold flowers approaches me without caution. He's about my age, with heavy black eyebrows and dark eyes, which highlight his beige, rectangular face. Ethnically, he might be from some middle eastern country or southern Europe. He's an image out of that travel documentary about Azerbaijan. My mind has snapped, and I'm hallucinating.

But the clothing's not right. Not middle eastern. A bright yellow beanie sits on his head. He holds a billy club, the size of a preschooler's tee-ball bat, waving it around in the air, one hand on his side, breathing heavily. "Clayson?"

My feet shuffle back a few steps. "Are you—"

"Rugnus," he says. "Uh, but could we just actually dispense with the intros"—another large breath— "until we're sitting someplace a bit less hazardous."

I swallow, thinking of the shadow in the forest. "Hazardous?"

He waves an arm around. "Gamgim. Filled with wraiths, especially after dark." He casts a glance to the fading evening light. "Which gives us maybe three minutes or so to get out from under the trees... so."

"Wraiths?"

"Oh." Rugnus leans in and looks at my face. "Oh, wow. Uh, so you don't know anything. Okay. Wraiths can steal your craft permanently. Like your favorite ones—strengths. Ironcraft for me. Wouldn't so much as be able to lift a stone from the ground. Trollbrick. It'd be awful."

He takes off the yellow beanie and rubs his head. Two shining, ink-brown eyes catch what light can filter down through the trees. His hair's cut so close to his scalp I'm surprised the woolen beanie didn't cling to it like Velcro. Side by side, we're physical opposites. Brown-eyed verse green-eyed. Thin verse stocky. The list would be lengthy.

"I'm not exactly following," I say.

"Yeah, no, sorry. Too many words. Just follow me below ground to the summation hall; that's where the king—uh, your dad—wanted me to take you first. And... wow. Your concealer is wearing off."

I reach up to my face. It's broader, returned to its old shape. My hair is thick and wavy again.

Rugnus blinks, pulls at his beanie, and shakes his head. "Man, it's like you stole the king's face or something."

"Wait, what?"

"Your father. Look just like him. He didn't tell me that. Which makes sneaking you into Tungsten City...difficult. Okay, have to go."

He grabs my arm, and we sprint through the forest.

"My dad," I say, keeping an easy stride behind Rugnus, "we've gotta help him. Bazalrak—"

"—is a brittleboned, washed-out ironhead. Your father can deal with old Nugget Face. You and me... first stop in the tour of the Kingdom of Rimduum—your summation. Not that we can't do it elsewhere." He breathes heavily, more exasperated than out of breath this time. "This is where your dad did his summation. He's nostalgic like that."

I almost stop running. Dad is always nostalgic and ceremonial. Funny Rugnus knows this about him. "True," I say.

Another twig snaps to my left, and we both jerk our heads in that direction. Nothing's there.

"Can have a nice long conversation... the second we pass the tree line," he says, smiling.

I rush after him in the fading light, hopping over rocks and weaving around tree trunks. After a few minutes, the canopy thins, and we reach the edge of the strange tree-mixed forest. Moonlight floods over the ground. Loose rock—scant brush growing over it—stretches out in each direction, forming a clear distinction between the forest and the clearing. Beneath my feet, gravel replaces the soft grass, the pine needles.

A twenty-foot wall of concave granite skirts the edge of the other side of the clearing. Rugnus comes to a stop before a tomb-shaped outline, a rectangular doorway cut into the granite wall. He's about to usher me inside when he stops dead, staring past me into the forest. My skin crawls when I crane my neck around.

37

Something moves in the trees. It's the same shadow I saw when I first arrived.

"Is it a wraith?" I ask.

Rugnus shakes his head. "We're past the tree line. Would've passed out and wet ourselves. Woke up unable to use one of the ten crafts."

"Note to self: there are ten crafts," I mutter.

Rugnus gives me a strange expression, but his attention stays on the movement in the trees.

A girl emerges from the forest. The cut of her green evening gown and the shape of her body make her a glimmering diamond. As she grows closer, the moonlight reflects off lengths of shimmering metal dancing in her long hair. The emerald fabric stands out against the linen-brown color of the tree trunks. When her features become clear, my breath catches in my throat. Her eyes are green like mine.

It's my mother, but it isn't. She's much younger. This girls' face is rounder, her smile more generous, unreserved.

"It's not possible," she says, a disbelieving smile lingering over her features.

I scrutinize every detail: every effortless footstep is as if she glides over the grass; the dozens of thin braids throughout her flowing strawberry blonde hair; the rushing of her voice, like water moving over rocks—two tin bracelets lined with thick green fabric shimmer on her wrists.

"Are you...you would have to be..." I can't say it.

"Unless you're Therias in disguise...or this is a trick? No. I think...I think... how could she not tell me. I have a brother." She smiles again, dimples forming within her gold, glowing blush. The same dimples Dad and I share, but not my mother. This is my sister.

Before I can even process this revelation, she sweeps towards me and wraps me in her arms. Everything about her is a mirror of our parents. I feel only one thing: this is my sister. Everything inside of me says it's true.

Rugnus whistles. "Princess Andalynn." The words out of Rugnus' mouth carry a hint of mockery.

Andalynn. Yes, that's her name. It's beautiful. I squeeze her in return, and a feeling passes between us, an admission almost. Ghostly strands of the thin wire in her hair graze my face, and by some magic—or craft, I suppose—her thoughts lay open to me, accompanied by the feeling I get when I solve a puzzle. A realization. A moment of revelation.

She didn't know I existed. All those years raised apart from each other. Telepathically, my unspoken wish passes between us —that we had shared lazy summers together in our cabin in the Blue Ridge Mountains. Then—only in my mind—there's a garden bursting with neon purple and green flowers, shrouded in moonlight, a memory from her childhood. She wishes we could have played there together.

"I didn't know," I mutter into her hair.

She peels me away, and we marvel at each other. "When Mom and I heard the news, Father was still alive... she wouldn't tell me anything, so I tapped into the old family communication network on a hunch, and that's when the message popped up. Gamgim."

"Are you saying you didn't even know Dad was alive? How could you not know? Our mother knew. She even came to visit a few years ago. If you could call it a visit." It makes me guilty, but I can't stop myself from resentful words about her. "Why didn't she tell you about Dad?"

Andalynn blinks, confused. "I knew she was hiding something. When we learned Father had been found, she started acting strange. I...she doesn't know." She pauses. "What's your name?"

"Clayson," I say, so quietly I wonder if I even say it. I pull the necklace out from under my shirt. "You should know, she gave us this right before Bazalrak showed up. She helped me escape."

"Escape? But she and the council sent the knights to get father. Did they see you?"

"No, she used something, a gold liquid—blood, maybe—to change my face. Dad wants me to stay hidden. I—"

"Clayson, there are things our father didn't tell you," she says. "I can only guess where he wants you to go." Her eyes plead with me. Her words become more deliberate. "I-I... come back with me to the castlestack at Whurrimduum. We can figure everything out together."

Hope whispers to me through her eyes, a hope I will follow her—enticing because I have no idea what else I should do.

But something still nags me.

Dad had been the king, but he'd left the kingdom behind—left my mother and Andalynn—to raise me alone. If he had wanted us to return there, we would have returned years ago. My mother never told Andalynn about me because she doesn't know I exist. All of this weighs on me, but something else, too. If I go with her, will I become something like a prince? Dad had said these underground places had some sort of war. Is that what I would be walking into?

Rugnus speaks up behind me. "Okay, Princess. Not sure where your royal guards are, and I know you finally climbed out of your tower...or whatever, but let's just stop you guys right there. Therias sent *me* to bring Clayson to Tungsten City. So yeah, we'll go ahead and go now."

Andalynn shakes her head. "Who are you?"

Rugnus eyes my sister warily. "Kind of my personal business, ain't it? Not recording, are you?"

"Whoever you are, Clayson is coming with me. If indeed my father sent you, I'm afraid you will be disappointed."

"Uh, no. Maybe in Whurrimduum you can just bat those long eyelashes everywhere you go, and people fall in line, but we don't have to obey your orders. Right, Clayson?" He leans toward me and whispers loudly, "She doesn't have you under silvercraft or anything, does she? That mother of yours can do some wicked things with silver. I'm sure she passed it on."

"What?" I say. "No, I don't think so." I'm more confused now.

Andalynn sighs. "Clayson, the people of Whurrimduum need you. You could be the true heir to the kingdom. Mom and I... well, the Keeper's Council is trying to seize power from us. This could change everything."

"Andalynn, Dad kept all this from me. I'm still having a hard time understanding what you're talking about. Craft, and-and the council, and nuclear magic, and genocide, and underground cities. I—"

"I could help you understand." She opens her hands to me. "Look, I'm not trying to force you to come with me."

Rugnus considers her words. "Well, that's new for a monarch. Thought that was your favorite pastime: forcing people to do things. Hiding the truth from them."

Andalynn crosses her arms, and the moonlight catches new reflections off her tin bracelets. She shifts, and the trees behind her move, some of them straining forward, others sending out limbs as if to grab us. Is she controlling them? Could this be another type of craft, manipulating plants and trees? Tin. Her bracelets are made of tin.

"I would never force him," she says. "Though I could. And I could certainly silence you if I wanted to. I could do that as easily as bending a few trees." Some of the outstretched limbs start to recede. "But there is too much burned blood already between our two cities. Why bother with someone as foolish?"

Rugnus gawks. "Foolish?"

"You accuse Whurrimduum—the monarchy and the council—of keeping secrets from the people, but Tungsten City's democracy is a mask for mob justice and hateful individualism."

Their words expose something of the difference between the two remaining cities: one is run by our family and some sort of a council, and the other is run by its people.

Something groans from the forest, like a hundred murmuring people trapped behind a closed door. A mass of debris, or dust, or fog leaches from the edge of the forest, bright lights sparkling inside a swelling cloud.

Andalynn and Rugnus speak at once. "Wraiths." Then Andalynn looks at the dark doorway cut into the granite. "Are you taking him for summation?"

Rugnus nods.

"Fine. I don't like being even this close. Let's get below."

We rush through the doorway, pounding down flight after flight of gray, stone-carved stairs. At the end of the stairs, we come to a cavernous opening lit with fire from torches lining the walls. In both directions, a hallway curves away into the dim light. High above me, millions of thin tendrils like the metal strands adorning my sister's hair fall to the floor opposite me braided together into sturdy metal walls. If I didn't know better, I would say the strands are roots from the forest above us.

Tiny shimmering droplets trickle down millions of wires to the center of the metal walls, where large basins—woven from the same strands of metal—gather the droplets into shining pools of mercury.

"What are these?"

"Called summators," Rugnus says, "Each basin is made from all the metal types. This place is where each initiate used to come to begin summation, long before the invention of the mobile summator."

This vague definition is meant to satisfy me, but it only raises more questions. The dark room, filled with stone and metal and magic and strangers. What am I supposed to do here? What's an initiate? Or summation? And if Dad refused to use this stuff, this craft, why does he want me to go through some ceremony in this place? Andalynn places a hand on my back. "I had my summation completed here. It's where all the royal family would come to begin their own."

Rugnus scoffs, then turns to search the wall closer to the door. It's formed from tiny stone cubes, like children's blocks. Some of the cubes jut outward towards us, giving the whole wall a deep texture.

He motions me over. "Harvest two of the slate cubes, then we

42

can complete the survey using the formal summator." Under his breath, he says, "Don't know why we couldn't just use a mobile summator."

Andalynn grudgingly gestures toward the wall. Apparently, she agrees. Summation, whatever that is, is my first stop in this strange world. I select two cubes, breaking them off carefully from their place on the wall.

"What now?" I ask.

Rugnus opens his mouth to speak, but one of the buttons on his pants pockets starts to glow bright white.

"Great," he says. "I *am* a fool." He turns toward me. "The Knights of Shale are here. Must have followed her."

"Excuse you? They didn't follow me," Andalynn says. "How?"

"Could Dad's message to Rugnus—the one you intercepted— could it have been found by someone else?" I say, a creeping worry eating at me.

Andalynn folds her arms across her chest. "Those old networks are open, but that's about as possible as reaching the heart of a dungeon."

I don't understand, but Rugnus must. His face changes.

He squints at her in the soft torchlight. "Apparently not."

Her hand goes to her mouth. "What if they found out she helped father? Bazalrak may know about you as well. I need to get back to her." Caught in the torchlight, the color on her face deepens. "Come with me. Our family has to answer to the Council of Keepers. What's your choice?"

It was the same thing my mother had said to Dad: face the council together. I can't meet her eyes. "If Dad...it seems like he wants..."

This unfinished statement hovers between us.

She fiddles with a bright gray-blue ring on her index finger, separating it into two smaller rings. She hands me the second half. "We can use this to communicate. You need to be facing a reflection for it to work. The stronger the reflection, the better. I may not be able to answer, but if I'm alone, I will. Go."

She hugs me and vanishes.

Rugnus clicks his tongue. "I guess she was telling the truth. For an ironhead, she's pretty...uh, nice. Pretty nice. I mean, once you get past the monarchy thing."

"Okay, how do we get out of here?" I ask.

"No worries. That's why I brought this." He reaches behind his back to the holstered billy club. It's made from Aluminum, which must be the theme for the day.

"Is that a budge? Or budgecraft?"

"Not a budge, *the* budge. This is Icho."

I start to ask him why his billy club has a name, but his shirt button is bright enough to burn a hole in his leg, which can only mean whoever's here is getting closer.

On cue, Bazalrak's smooth, sing-song voice reverberates from somewhere down the hall. "Who's down there?"

I can feel the shadows deepening around us. It's an effect I saw at the cabin, and at the RV park, anytime this Bazalrak showed his face. What did my father call it? Shadowcraft. His voice concentrates in my mind: *don't let his shadowcraft touch you.*

Rugnus tightens his grip on Icho. "Your summation will have to be a little less formal. Let's not tell your dad. He was set on you completing it here. Old traditions are tougher than granite."

The strange room, with the basins and flowing stands of metal, echoes now with nearby voices. With one hand on my wrist, Rugnus levels his club, Icho, between us. In its sharp, reflective surface, he checks the state of his beanie, adjusting it slightly.

At the last second, a tangible shadow leaps from the wall, covering half of Rugnus' chest and face. His eyes widen, his mouth opens in a scream, but the budgecraft works.

It's nothing like the camper or the energy drink. It's both smoother—no added gravity, no sickness—and more disorienting. I'm shocked to find myself in a totally different place, but the moment I begin to look around the basement-like room, Rugnus grabs my shirt.

His face twitches involuntarily, his mouth still open in a scream, but only a hiss escapes. A whip-shaped piece of the unnatural shadow that attacked him is still latched to his torso. It squirms, trying to bury itself deeper inside his chest. He collapses to the ground.

"Rugnus!" I yell.

More lights illuminate the room. The shadow over his face absorbs into his eyes, discoloring his pupils. This is shadowcraft. Dad's warning smashes into this critical moment. Bazalrak's background in torture now makes total sense.

Rugnus' voice strains to break free from his mouth. "Nnnnn....lluuu....leh....lead."

Lead.

Each craft has a metal; maybe lead can fight this. "Lead? You want me to find—"

He pushes me away, gesturing vaguely to one side of the room.

I search the room, frantic—three walls made of stone. The fourth wall is an aquarium, with giant, pale crabs scrambling over dark orange coral. There's no end to the back of the tank, only a void and the shapes of strange things floating in the deep. A giant bean bag. Pedestals with strange objects spotlighted in neon colors. A rusted gear suspended above us by a black braided rope.

Metal, metal, metal. I need lead!

There are two doorways, one next to the aquarium, one next to a series of shelves.

Shelves.

The walls are shelves. The whole place is a storage room. Thousands of metal and glass objects are arranged like some hyper-organized, sanitary antique store.

Rugnus' groaning transitions into sobs.

Panic. My hands comb through my hair roughly. I have to find a lead needle in a haystack of precious metals.

FLEE THE FALLOUT

ALL THE USELESS stuff about metal and stone Dad taught me comes into sharp focus. He told me once that knowing the difference between cobalt and nickel could save a life. I had laughed, but he wasn't kidding.

Rugnus grits his teeth and groans.

The first column of shelves is filled with gold—the second, silver. There are neat piles of coins, goblets, chains, and tendrils of wire like the silver ones in my sister's hair. There's even a bottle of shimmering gold paint that reminds me of the liquid, or blood, or whatever it was, my mother smeared on my face. For humans, it would be an unimaginable treasure. I don't know about Loamin.

In the third column, I find scores of objects made from lead and another dark-gray metal—tungsten. The first thing that sticks out to me is a clam-shaped wooden container with a lead figurine of a cat. I grab the figurine, and stark, white light erupts. Should I feel something, like the extra gravity when I used the budge, or revelation when I shared thoughts with my sister?

I'm out of time.

Rugnus is barely coherent when I press the figurine into his hands. I try to force whatever magic—craft—I can into him. "Come on, don't die."

And like the flip of a switch, the shadows disappear from his body.

His eyes snap open and white light blinds me—like looking into two flashlights. As they return to their normal ink-brown, he gasps.

"Whoa!" He jolts to his feet as if I gave him a shot of pure adrenaline. "What did you do?" He crosses the room, dancing to the beanbag, before finally glancing at the figurine in his hand. The excitement drains from his face. "Not napcraft."

"Napcraft?"

"That'll work," he slurs. His eyes roll back into his head, and he drops onto the beanbag. In less than a second, he's snoring so loudly I think he might strip a layer of skin off the back of his throat. He curls up with the figurine like it's a plushie. I sit next to him for a few minutes, trying to shake him awake, but whatever napcraft is, it will have to take its course.

Great. Now I don't have a guide.

I explore the rest of the room. The two doorways lead to smaller rooms made for different purposes. The one next to the shelves is some type of testing area—if I had to guess—filled with broken crates, boulders of various sizes, and burned-out walls. Two fluorescent lights brighten the entryway, but the room is lit mostly by torches spread out evenly along the walls. In some places, the floor has been overrun by lava, now cooled into black ripples. Closer to the door sits a diorite table, the floor beneath it heavy with sand.

The other doorway leads to an even smaller room with a primitive cooking pit in the center, surrounded by a few small cushions. The aquarium forms one side of this room as well. A single cabinet stands against the far wall. A dining room?

None of the rooms has an exit from this place. Then again, why would there have to be when you can budge anywhere you want?

I sigh. It will take time to adjust to this new reality.

I return to Rugnus' side, staring into the aquarium as something desperate takes my heart and submerges it deeper into the pool of shock my life has become. My head shakes, trying to rid itself of the strangeness of everything. How can any of this be real? At the same time, this secret world explains so much of my life, so many of Dad's secrets.

Rugnus has to wake up. He's my guide. Or at least Dad wants him to be.

A whistle made from copper hangs from a hook next to the aquarium. I take it from its spot and blow on it, hoping to wake Rugnus from the napcraft. A tingling sensation prickles my skin —meaning craft, maybe—but Rugnus is unphased by the bright notes of the whistle.

There is a tap against the aquarium glass. The pale crabs have stopped moving. One of them pulls his claw back from the glass wall. Curious, I blow on the whistle again, weaving a simple pattern of notes. The hair rises on the back of my neck, and goosebumps bubble their way along my arm. The crabs form into a line and tap the pattern against the glass.

"Whoa." I return the whistle to its place, and the crabs return to the coral.

Another form of craft. Another strange physical sensation. Did I sense anything with the lead figurine? No. But why?

Ten. Rugnus had said there are ten types of craft.

The best I can, I review every type I've come in contact with.

Aluminum is for budgecraft. Every time I use budgecraft, my stomach drops, and gravity doubles. It was that way with the camper and the energy drink, but not for Rugnus' club. Why was that different? Something to ask him when he wakes.

The silver strands of my sister's hair. What type was that? Mind control? I was able to see her thoughts and even memories, if only briefly. There was a feeling of having solved a puzzle or having figured out a riddle. Like when the lock on the camper vanished. Was that silver? It didn't feel like metal. The lenses were made from yellow glass. Maybe glass can work similarly to metal? Or the metal gets added to glass?

I'm grasping at straws, but the object-laden shelves seem to confirm this theory about glass. I find yellow glass objects in the silver column. Red glass objects in the gold column. Gold. My mother's blood. That was by far the strangest type of craft so far. It tightened my skin like a sunburn. It changed my physical appearance. A pair of red glasses glint in the candlelight. Would they change my face again, make me look like another person?

I don't dare try anything.

The ninth column holds a more unrecognizable metal—cobalt maybe—but it also has more glass than all other shelves combined, blue glass. I'm not sure what type of craft it would be, but it reminds me of my mother's necklace. I take it out from under my shirt and compare it. It's titanium, not cobalt, but the beads are the same blue glass. The bike chain itself looks like it fits better in the eighth column. Is that the type of craft that lets me control the troll mech? I try to recall the sensation I felt when the mech turned on. Static? But something else. A nails-on-chalk-board cringe. Two columns. Two crafts. Two metals.

"Light." Rugnus' voice calls me to his side.

"What?"

"Light," Rugnus says again, this time gesturing behind him or over his head. There's a flashlight on a pedestal.

"Light. Okay," I say.

The flashlight sits under a spotlight of soft brown. I pick it up. It's not heavy. Aluminum again. I thought aluminum was budge-craft, but maybe it's just a flashlight. How would I know the difference? I pace in front of the shelf, then sigh and move back to Rugnus.

He squeezes his eyelids even tighter as I come around the beanbag and point the flashlight at him. I flip the switch, but no light comes on. Rugnus looks confused as he opens his eyes. He pales again when he sees the flashlight. "Oh, no."

I've made a huge mistake. It *is* a budge.

There's a heartbeat where I only stare at Rugnus, and then I'm sick to my stomach. The gravity doubles.

I'm suddenly freezing cold. I'm in a long room, maybe the foyer of some fancy hotel, like something I've seen on TV. An edge of cold tips my fingers, my nose. My breath exits in a fog.

What did I do?

The whole place glitters like diamonds. Iced-over palm trees line the polished marble floors. Pillars rise to a vaulted ceiling where a frozen waterfall drops down the wall. A sheet of icy glass runs the length of one side of the foyer.

If I weren't so cold, I'd be stunned by its beauty. I want to run my hand over the marble pillar next to me, but it's covered in veins of ice. The air temperature is below freezing, and all the surfaces look as if they wouldn't give my hand back.

I flip the switch on the flashlight, hoping it will budge me to Rugnus' vault. Nothing.

Then I see the body.

A man's body, cold and rigid, still upright. A horrified expression is frozen on his face. It's almost as if he's still alive, trapped in the ice. The flashlight clatters to the floor. I pause, but the cold gnaws at me. Carefully, I move past the body.

"I'm so stupid." Even my whisper echoes in the cavernous room.

I tuck my cold hands closer to my torso as I move toward the long windows.

Another body.

As solid as a glacier, except more freezer burned. This one is a woman sitting on the edge of a short wall, her face calm. A frozen, purple lizard, the size of a football, sits in her lap. Her frozen eyes appear to follow me.

I come to the tall windows. The world outside is almost unimaginable.

Hundreds of skyscrapers made of stone and glass and metal all encrusted with shards of ice. Half of the city lays under crested waves of snow, the result of an avalanche on a nuclear scale.

Beyond the skyline, a stone wall—no, not a wall, the viscera of a mountain itself.

Until this moment, I hadn't understood the size of these cities beneath the mountains. What was it Dad had said to me? There had been war. Millions of Loamin had been annihilated—hundreds of millions. His words raise bile in my throat.

What happened here?

Next, I look up. And up. And up. I'm inside a cavity that could only have been made by a drill bit as wide as a city. Miles above, at the height where clouds should be, the wall disappears behind an angry white sun. Flares of molten light ring it in uneven pulses. Of course, it has to be smaller than the sun, but it gives off so much light, and it hangs so far away I can't tell the difference.

Then I look down. And down. And down. Though there seems to be a level where many of the skyscrapers find a foundation, the city extends deeper into more winter-beaten ravines, and bridges, and bridges, and bridges.

I turn from the city in shock. The frozen woman and her lizard sitting placidly on the edge of the short wall become figures representing millions in my mind. Is the whole city frozen like this? My eyes flick between her and the window.

I can't stay here, or I'll freeze to death.

"The flashlight has to work." I try to twist back around, but my shoes are stuck to the floor. I put more torc on my ankle, and the sole of my shoe breaks free. Standing in one place was a bad idea.

My cheeks and ears start to prickle with pain. I run to the flashlight and try to lift it off the ground. It's stuck. I have to kick it free from the layer of thin ice encasing it. I grab it, try the switch again. It won't work. An icy film begins to form on the flashlight. I drop it.

"Not good."

My throat is suddenly tight. How long can I stay here? I pace, rub my fingers and ears, trying to keep the blades of ice from creeping deeper into my skin. On one side of the room lies a row of massive double doors. The first set is locked. The second. The third. The fourth. At the fifth set, I ram my shoulder into the iron patterns woven into the wooden door. It quivers.

In another run, it gives way to darkness. My eyes adjust, and hundreds of upright forms become visible. My scream has no echo here, absorbed by the flesh of hundreds, no, a thousand victims. Only the light from the doorway shines in the room, but it highlights their immovable shapes far into the distance.

A few appear like the man in the last room, filled with terror. But others seem oblivious, posed like they're in the middle of some strange dance. I've walked into a frozen rave of Loamin mannequins. Normally, I would find it a relief to see so many people my height, but that was yesterday.

It's no warmer here, so I return to the foyer. I glimpse my reflection in the waterfall. Frost cakes my eyebrows, rims my upper lip. My ears and nose are bright pink.

"Reflection."

Andalynn's ring.

My fingers are tipped red now, but the blue-gray ring is there. Grabbing it with my other finger, I stare into the reflection, unsure if it will work. But it does. I'm glad the learning curve for using these things isn't too steep.

My sister's face appears distorted in the ice, flickering.

She squints. "Where....you?" Her voice is broken up.

"I don't know," I say. "I made a mistake. I left Rugnus, and—"

"....hear you....look cold."

I shiver out quick words. "I'm in trouble."

"Trouble?...but stay...father... not sure...out of this." The concern on her face deepens. "Mom is in trouble. The council... Keelcrawl Prison is no place for—"

Her face glitches and blinks out.

"No!" I pound the waterfall with numb fists. I try to will her back, twisting the ring in circles around my finger. But she doesn't return.

A high-pitched whistling fills the air. It's coming from the large windows.

The whistling heightens to a shrill shriek, and in a flash, the giant panes shatter to pieces blasting arctic air inward, instantly making the room twice as cold.

I'm not gonna live through this.

With a dull flash of red light, a human-like figure encased in lava, catapults through the opening. Swirling rings of white fire orbit the drooping mass. It lands, its feet hissing on the icy marble floor with each footstep. If it wasn't radiating heat, I would run away screaming.

But something stops me. The lava doesn't quite reach the thing's hands, a person's hands. There's a person inside the lava.

Even after everything else I've seen in the last few hours—if it's even been that long—I keep triple guessing what I'm seeing. The figure squares off with me; the lava around the front of its head becomes an opening. The first visible thing is a narrow face with crisp, easy-to-read eyebrows that say: seriously?

"Rugnus?" I say. "How—"

He flourishes a hand and bows, snagging the flashlight from the floor, and Icho, his go-to budge, from the back of the lava suit. He holds Icho forward. "It's my strongest relic." A quick glance at the women's body he passed, and he says. "Let's get you out of here before the fallout turns you to ice?"

We budge.

Back in the room with all the shelves, the lava recedes from his arms, legs, and head sucked into a chain-link girdle Rugnus immediately removes, folds, and returns to a middle column of the shelves. "Well, that was... something?" he says.

The chill isn't going away, even with the warmth of the room. "Fallout? As in nuclear?"

He procures a large blanket lined with gold foil and tosses it to me. I sit on a bench and bundle myself under it. After a few seconds, the cold loses its sharp edge, but my fingers are still red.

"There's still a brick load of active craft in places like Thiffimdal. Mithrium Fallout. We don't call it the Last War for nothing. The only true safe places are Tungsten City and Whurrimduum. Well, if you can call a place run by a monarchy safe. Whurrimduum, I mean, not my city."

"The whole city was underground. It had like, a miniature sun," I say.

Rugnus smiles. "Wait till you see Tungsten City."

"And Thiff-Thiffin—"

"Thiffimdal."

"It was destroyed by nuclear magic?"

"Craft. Mithriumcraft. Combine mithrium with any other craft, and—boom—you've got yourself a city-leveling event. Nearly wiped ourselves out. All across the world. Here, look."

My arms and legs remain in a dull icy grip, but the red color is retreating from my fingertips. Rugnus pulls me from the bench, and we cross the room to a large wall map of the Colorado Rockies. Dozens of yellow markers dot the bumpy surface. In large script near the top of the map, there's a single word: RIMDUUM.

I run a hand over the raised mountains. I know a few of the names of the peaks from planning my dream climbing vacation. "The yellow dots?" I ask.

Rugnus pauses for a long moment then extends a finger to a cluster of dots in the center of the map. "Only two cities left: Whurrimduum"—he taps a tall peak within the bumps—"and Tungsten City." His finger hovers over a lone peak in the eastern foothills. Pike's Peak. "Everything else was destroyed."

"Thiffimdal?"

He searches the board and taps a dot toward the bottom of the front range. "Gone. No survivors."

"Why didn't the people leave? I saw a whole room full of... It was like some people realized they were being frozen alive, and others didn't. People even seemed—"

"Oblivious?" he says. I almost sense he's seen the same thing before. "Some people might have had defensive objects that gave them a second's warning, but it's not like they could budge out.

The last hundred years, they started throwing up city-wide foilgrips."

"Hundred years? How long was the war?"

"Seven hundred years, give or take. When the three pieces of mithrium were first discovered, there was a lot of hope about the good it could to do to power our world. Then someone used one to attack a whole city."

"Three pieces of mithrium did this?"

"Yep. At first, it was years, decades between attacks. But the last fifty years have been terrifying. Well, until your Dad—allegedly—stole all three pieces of mithrium from Whurrim-duum. I think Thiffimdal was a hundred years ago."

"Who's responsible?"

"Tough question. Don't think there was a government that didn't use the mithrium. And terrorist groups. Our cities were destroyed—one, after another, after another. Government spies or revolutionaries would infiltrate a city and detonate the mithrium. Then the real fighting began. Teams in anti-mithrium suits, battling toward the center of the city in search of the precious metal, scrambling for control. It was the Last War, the Mithrium War, the end of the world. All over three pieces of mithrium. People just... went about their lives the best they could."

My head is numb. "That's the most horrifying thing I've ever heard."

Three pieces of mithrium.

My teeth chatter. The chill in my body refuses to leave.

Rugnus gives me a questioning look.

"Still cold," I say.

"Thought you might be. The mithrium fallout has receded over the years—that's why you didn't freeze instantly. It'll be about a day, but your body temp will normalize."

I cinch the blanket closer around me.

He sets the flashlight on the pedestal. "Why did you even pick this thing up?"

"You said light. I-I thought—"

"Ooh, yeah." He squints at the ceiling. "It was really bright in here. Not good for napping. Tried to change the light settings in my vault."

"Vault?"

"Right"—he sweeps his arms in a circle— "welcome to my vault. Ah, see... lights off."

The room becomes pitch dark.

"Lights on," he says, and I can see again.

He shrugs with the innocence of a child. "Sorry. Anyway, we're safe now."

Safe. How can we be safe in this world? I pull the blanket even tighter. "I spoke with my sister. She said something about my mother. And Keelcrawl prison."

His eyes grow large. "Keelcrawl? You sure?"

I nod.

"It's the highest security prison in Whurrimduum. Mercury locks, foilgrips, the works. Hard to break in. Impossible to break out. I don't think... well, they wouldn't—" Rugnus stares off to my left and blinks a few times. He gestures his hands apart. "Hold on. Breaking news." His eyes glaze over; the color of blue takes over his brown eyes as he watches the air next to my head.

"Uh, what's going on?" I ask.

He holds up a finger. "I'd share the footage, but you don't have a bluelink connection yet, and—get melted. Trollbrick. Who is that? For Ide's sake, I've never..."

Is this the same type of craft I used when those video-game style menus came up around the troll mech? The blue in Rugnus' eyes is the color of the blue beads on the bike chain necklace. He called it a bluelink connection. That has to be it. That's what's on the ninth shelf. The blue glass connects him to the news.

"What? What's going on?"

"One second, re-watching." Rugnus' only emotion is disbelief. He shakes the blue from his eyes and says. "Okay, good news and bad news. The bad news: everyone knows the king's been found. Some hacker found the footage from Bazalrak's body camera, broadcasted it all over bluelink. The good news: the concealer you had protected you. I mean, everyone is trying to guess who you might be, and your fake face is being analyzed by every political commentator under granite, but I think your identity is safe for now."

"Did it show my dad?"

He hesitates. "Yeah. Someone showed up to help him."

"Who?"

"Well, that's the crazy part. She was Dura. Can you believe it? Dura can't use craft, at least not like that. It was... overpowered. She faced all four ironheads at once."

"What does Dura mean?"

"The girl was a vacant. Dura. There's only a few dozen in the whole world... or well... could be more, some say, living on the surface... maybe. But I mean... Dura. The craft she used..."

"Wait, she?'

"She and your dad budged out."

"He's safe." I sink back onto the bench. "Wait. Was she tall?"

"Yeah, Dura. Vacant. What are you thinking?"

"His nurse, Ara. It could be her. She came to warn us before we, uh, budged to the RV park. She must've found him and—"

"You know this vacant? Your dad, he knows this vacant?"

"I'm not following. Is she vacant or Dura?"

"Dura. But a lot of people call them vacant, because..."

"What?"

"Clayson, vacants can't use craft like she did. It's impossible. And their minds are different from Loamin."

After everything I've seen today, I don't see why this is a big deal to him. Maybe I should tell him people can't control the elements, force you to see their memories, or teleport across the United States.

I remember Ara's hands on fire with lava and the earth rumbling at the cabin. "I'm pretty sure she can use as much craft as she wants. And she's no different than us."

He flops onto the beanbag. "Enlighten me."

DREAM BELOW GRANITE

RUGNUS TOSSES a small iron cannonball from hand to hand, something he picked up from the shelf as we've been talking. Every few seconds, the thing bursts into flames, but he doesn't seem to care. What did he say his strengths in craft were?

"You're not quite understanding," he says. "This girl—Ara—if she is a vacant, well, they only use simple craft: parlor tricks, cooking, performance, unlocking things, budging. Like I said, they don't even use metal, for that matter. None of them have an inner mind, like Loamin. They don't think for themselves."

"That ridiculous. I know Ara. She—"

"Clayson, they're a totally different race."

My mouth drops open. "Wow, okay, then what you're saying is not only wrong but completely racist."

Rugnus stills the cannonball in one hand. "No, I... I don't know. You're not hearing me. Dura have no inner mind. Maybe this Ara, maybe she's not Dura. If you'd have met a vacant, you'd—"

"Wait, I think I did. A man named Vor came with my mother."

"There! Then you know what I'm talking about. They can greet people, make a request, execute a request. Vor serves the royal family. Has for centuries, maybe even a millennium. It's documented."

"A millennium?"

"And did he make eye contact? Did he hold a conversation with you? See? There's a reason they're called the vacant."

I search my memories of Ara. She's not any of that. But one thing holds true. "They don't make eye contact?"

"No, and it's not by choice. And we don't force them to serve Loamin. They just do. You couldn't get a vacant to leave its chosen service for a million ferrum. They fixate on single, mindless tasks. It's their whole existence." Rugnus catches a glimpse of himself in the aquarium glass, straightens his back, and smooths out his shirt.

I shake my head. "Not Ara. She's thoughtful. Sure, she can be standoffish, but she doesn't take no for an answer, at least not from my dad. And, as we fled the cabin, she made some type of massive wall of earth and fire to block Bazalrak. Now that I think of it, there was this moment where she touched my dad. Yeah, why didn't I see that before? She must have healed him. He could breathe perfectly after that. But... no, wait... why not heal him before? I-I don't know."

He shrugs. "If this Dura on bluelink is Ara, then I don't know what to think. But I don't like being called racist. The work I do in Tungsten City... I help bring in refugees from all over Ide: Zal Kakraja, Himdem, Brimwok. Hatred against other people, against other kingdoms... that's Whurrimduum's game, not mine."

"Okay," I say softly, "I didn't mean to offend you. But you were talking about a person I've known for years. She's always been there for my dad."

Rugnus is thoughtful for a long moment, then he sets the cannonball on a shelf. "Getting late. Could you sleep?"

I almost laugh. "Honestly, I'm wide awake."

He leans in my direction. His right hand rakes over the thick black stubble on his head then extends outward. "Well met, by the way."

I reach tentatively to shake his hand, but he edges forward and clasps my forearm, a solid grip. "Better start learning the basics. We don't shake hands like humans. We test our strengths." His grip tightens, so I try to match it. His eyes, as brown as earth, search my face.

"No handshakes," I say. "Got it. Testing strengths." I release his arm and take in a deep breath. I still can't believe the air here is so dense, it has this warming effect on me. Which is good because the cold from Thiffimdal still rests in my bones. I gesture to the walls and the aquarium. "So, where are we exactly?

"My personal vault beneath Tungsten City."

"Under the city? How far underground are we?"

"Five tens or so, below the peak of the mountain."

I shake my head, confused again. "What's five tens?"

"Ten is short for tenbock. Uh, I don't think... I mean, don't have a leaf about basic measurement conversions for humans. Books. Humans put information in books, right? A leaf is like a book. But measurement's a topic for latchmages." He smiles at this—his attempt at reassurance.

I give him another confused look.

"Don't worry," he says. "Once we get you connected to bluelink you can look it up."

"That should be our priority," I say. "It's gonna take me a while to adjust to all this. I want access to information."

Rugnus is silent for a second. "Can't believe you lived up there so long...and without craft. Hate being above granite. Even for like...what was that...ten minutes? Blah. No thanks, humans. It fizzes my blood just thinking about it. All that sky making the air as thin as wraithspit. I'd rather melt myself."

"All my dad's health problems then?"

"Happens to every Loamin above granite...on the surface, I mean. But... hmm... didn't seem like you had any issues up there. And you never used craft to shield you from the effects?"

"Not that I know."

"And no terrible nightmares? Shortness of breath? Fatigue? Fizzblood?"

"Me? No. My dad had all those things. I guess that was after he gave up craft. If everyone has the same problems on the surface, why didn't you or my sister have problems?"

"We use craft—tungsten or lead—keep the effect out of blood and beard. Even that doesn't work completely for some people. But the real question is... you, wonder boy. How could you live up there for fourteen years and never have symptoms?"

I almost tell him about how my father took me to live on the surface so I would sleep, but it seems too personal, even if Dad wanted us to be friends. I change the subject. "So, when can you hook me up to the bluelink?"

"Not *the* bluelink, just bluelink. And it will be hard since you don't have an AMP."

"I'm sure my questions are getting annoying, but what's an AMP? And actually, what exactly is bluelink?"

His eyes widen, but he brushes away his worry with a wide smile. "Not annoying, just going to take more work than I thought. Bluelink is the same as the WideWeb or whatever humans call it."

"You mean the Internet?"

"Not sure. Anyway, it's the way we access information, communicate, virtual reality, gaming, things like that. Your sister's highly rated in bluecraft. The ring she gave you has access to a specific channel." He pauses there, thinking for a second. "Oh, and AMP stands for Accumulated Measure of Power."

"Why do I need an Accumulated..."

"Accumulated Measure of Power? Well, an AMP is the standard form of identification down here. Need identification to access budge ports, bluelink, vaults, game highlights, all that. Once we finish your summation, you'll get your AMP."

"That's why my dad wanted me to go to Gamgim? To do this summation? To get an AMP?"

He nods. "Every Loamin goes through an initial summation.

Usually at eleven or twelve, so you're a bit late, but it's not unheard of. Anyway, summation allows surveyors, like me, to make their assumptions. When it's over, you get a rating: one to a hundred. Therias, your dad, has an AMP of fifty-eight with peerless ratings in physical augmentation—that's goldcraft—teleportation—that's budgecraft—and animal domination—coppercraft—though a noticeable weakness in protective augmentation—that's shieldcraft by the way. Which is always great to have as a secondary craft, because it's a small degree stronger than other crafts."

"It's one to a hundred, so fifty-eight is—

"Ridiculously powerful," he says.

Rugnus strokes his chin. He crosses the room, stopping in front of the shelf loaded with blue glass. "Most people initially score between...maybe twenty and thirty AMP. Though to be fair, with some hard work and training, people can gain another fifteen to twenty points over their lifetime."

He pulls down a clear container filled with thin rods made from blue glass, then a metal skillet. He points the pan at me and says, "You, my friend, are bound to have a great AMP. You're the son of Therias Brightstorm. Not only that, but your mother—may she never find me worthy of being her enemy—has an AMP of sixty-one with a peerless rating in goldcraft, and zero known weaknesses. Scary stuff."

"Right. It's becoming pretty clear I don't really know who my parents are. So, what's the pan for?"

"Oh, right. Well, you can't access bluelink directly, but I may have a workaround. It'll take me a minute, but trust me, it will be delicious."

"It will be edible?" I should have guessed. They have drinks that can teleport you; why not food that can help you access the internet.

"Of course, the best craft is. But here, while I work"—he drags me over to the columns of objects—"you can test your strength. It's not like summation or anything official, simply a way to see what you might be good at. Start with the iron objects. Take a few into my testing room. Connect with some metal. You can't break anything—uh, mostly. And no budges—that's aluminum—and nothing sitting out on display, like the flashlight. That's my nice stuff."

"Your nice stuff? The flashlight took me to a nuclear wasteland?"

"Surveyors, like me, help with summations, but we also help reclaim crafted objects from the dead cities. That's hard work. I'm proud of my collection."

Without another word, Rugnus crosses the room, skillet in tow, and disappears under the arched doorway next to the aquarium. Firelight appears in the room.

I turn my attention back to Rugnus' collection of objects and see the etching above each column for the first time. He's labeled them not by metal type but by craft. It's a lot to take in, but I'm a quick learner. The only difficulty is some columns have two types of metal, not to mention all the alloys.

I shake my head. All the secrets Dad kept, but he taught me to distinguish between metals and to identify rocks. Something like resentment starts prickling inside me. He should've taught me about craft, about who we were. He should've trusted me.

The first three columns hold what are called enhancements. Also labeled as *ROYAL CRAFTS*. Gold equals enhancements to body and form. Silver, and to a lesser extent nickel, equal enhancements to the mind and spirit. Lead and tungsten equal protective enhancements. Goldcraft, silvercraft, and shieldcraft are written as secondary labels.

The next two columns read *ANIMATE*: copper for animal dominion and tin for plant dominion. Coppercraft and tincraft. Those should be easy to remember. The whistle hanging next to the aquarium was copper. It let me influence the crabs.

Hardest are the last five, labeled as manipulations: elemental, spatial, mechanical, field, and temporal. Elemental is also marked ironcraft. Spatial is aluminum—that's budgecraft. Mechanical is the same type of metal the bike chain is made from. Mechcraft. Field manipulation relates to bluelink, made mostly of clear blue glass but also of cobalt. Bluecraft. On the shelf of temporal manipulation, there are bottles of mercury and a bright shiny metal I think is chrome. Timecraft.

Though, if Rugnus tells me mercury is used for time travel, I'm gonna go back to the mountains to hide for the rest of my life. Or maybe I'll sell the cabin, buy a nice hiking bag, climbing gear, get a plane ticket to Europe, and travel the world. There've been enough revelations today. The possibility of time travel is not something I wanna think about.

Rugnus returns, a dishtowel over his shoulder. "Blow anything up yet?"

"Not yet." I point to the column with mercury. "What's with temporal manipulation? You guys can't like—"

"Travel in time?" he says. "Nope. Timecraft only allows someone to speed things up a bit or slow things down. Combine it with coppercraft, for example, and you can raise animals more quickly, if you run a ranch or something."

I breathe a sigh of relief. "Do some forms of craft have two metals?"

"Good eye," Rugnus says. "Yeah, some have minors and majors. Like silvercraft. Minor, nickel. Major, silver."

"And this one?" I point to the shieldcraft column.

"Lead minor. Tungsten major. And don't forget—shieldcraft is a pinch stronger—"

"—than other crafts. Got it."

"Right, anyway you can review all that some other time. Let's do some practical learning with ironcraft. Here, take this." Rugnus grabs a throwing ax from the elemental manipulation shelf. He drops it into my hands. "And this. And this. And... yeah, this one." He keeps placing things into my arms until, with a pile of iron objects, I follow him into the testing room, where I dump everything unceremoniously onto the diorite table.

As Rugnus combs through the pile, I ask, "How many objects can you use at once?"

"Best if it's just one." He sets a steel horn aside. "Though two often works, just split the power of each object."

I count off everything I've used so far. The glasses to open the camper, the camper itself, the concealer from my mother, the energy drink from my father, the bike chain necklace, the lead cat figurine, the copper whistle, the flashlight, my sister's ring, and the blanket lined with gold foil. Had I used any of those at the same time?

"I think I used three at once."

"Huh. Not impossible, but it would've split the craft. What objects?"

"Uh, the concealer"—I count them on my fingers—"a budge like an energy drink, and this." I show him the necklace.

He shudders. "Surprised the budge even worked. And from what I know of that type of concealer—bloodcraft—it should have lasted days. Bet none of those crafts are a weakness for you. Anyway." He picks up a ring, polishes it in his shirt, and hands it to me, "Try this one first. Its Total Object Rating—TOR—is eleven. I can explain how crafted objects are rated later. Dinner's probably ready. This ring was forged to let you control the wind. Point and shoot."

When I put it on my finger, nothing happens, but Rugnus jerks out of the way. "When I said point and shoot, I didn't mean at me." He grabs my arm and aims it at a pile of sand across the room. "Move the sand."

This object is simpler than the necklace I wear around my neck. "Do I need to take the necklace off first?"

"Bet it's only active around a mech unit but sure, to get the full effect. And might as well put your sister's ring in a pocket too, though the bluecraft in it wouldn't be active unless it was in use."

He helps me with the necklace, and I replace Andalynn's ring with the iron one. I extend my arm outward, and a puff of sand bursts into the air, swirling into a funnel cloud until I drop my arm.

I'm about to smile at Rugnus, but his face is scrunched in displeasure. "What?" I ask. "You told me to move the sand."

"Right, but a latchmage could move sand like that. And you don't need to raise your arm. Only mechcraft, bluecraft, and time-craft use gesturing. Guess I thought...you know what, just try this one instead." He hands me the horn he'd set aside. "Can pretty much drown your enemies with this one. TOR of eleven also."

I take the horn, face a boulder in the middle of the testing room, and blow out the only note the instrument can muster. Water pools around the base of the boulder but drains away.

Rugnus frowns. "Yeah, super, you made the boulder wet itself. Maybe iron is not your thing."

"Wait, give me another chance. What do you have with a higher TOR?"

"Fine, take the ax, smash it against one of the pillars, and think...I don't know...lava."

I take it from him, anxious to prove I can do more damage with a better object. I approach the pillar thoughtfully.

"Pillar isn't going to fight back, Clayson."

"Right." I square my stance, hoist the ax, and swing like a lumberjack. Surprisingly, a chunk of granite breaks off, the whole pillar bursts into flames, veins of magma running under the surface. It takes only a few seconds for the effect to wear off.

Rugnus hesitantly nods. "Not bad, but guess I'm just kind of surprised you need an object with a higher TOR. Here, back up. Let me show you what a Loamin with ironcraft mastery can do."

Rugnus puts the ring on his finger, the horn in his right hand, and takes the throwing ax from me as I walk past him. So much for using one at a time.

I haven't even made it to the table when sand pelts me from nearly every direction, only to quickly drain away from my cloth-ing, gathering in a thick ribbon, floating in the center of the room. I spin around, squinting. Rugnus hurls the ax to the right. It swings end over end and embeds itself in the wall, where a fountain of lava bursts, coursing under the sand.

It takes only a second until the sand crystallizes into molten glass, but by that time, Rugnus blows the horn, bringing water raining from every inch of the ceiling, except around the two of us. The lava cools into black ribbons, and when the downpour ends, the sand has been transformed into a table of transparent glass. He turns around, whistling smugly.

The hunk of glass makes me think of the colored glasses in Rugnus' collection of objects. I point to it. "Will that do something now?"

Rugnus gapes. "You just witnessed an amazing feat of iron-craft. That's what you go with! Will that do something?"

"Yeah."

Rugnus shrugs and smiles. "Nah. Just regular glass. But it's awesome, right?"

"No argument there. Didn't you use three at once?"

"Not technically. I started the sand going. Then, for just a little bitty second, used the ax to open up a lava portal. Though I did use the horn and ring together, it was only for a few seconds. Would love to pick up a nice iron relic, something where I could use stone and fire together. Expensive, though."

Rugnus retrieves his ax, and we leave the room, placing the objects back on his shelves. In the other room, I find the pan resting over the cooking fire, filled with roasted lemons, the blue glass rods he got from the shelf, and a single giant pale crab.

"Only way to give you access to bluelink," he explains, "is to have you connect to mine. I cooked dinner with cobalt glass... what type of craft is cobalt again?"

He's quizzing me now. "Field manipulation. So bluelink, bluecraft. Is it like magnets and electricity?"

"Now you've got it. Eat dinner, and it will tap you into bluelink. But we've got to eat everything, or it won't work."

The glass rods twinkle in the pan. "Everything?"

"What? Oh, no, not the glass. Who eats glass? Get melted. Just the crab and the lemons."

We sit cross-legged on the floor. This is ten times better than any fish or crawdad I've ever caught. The crab flakes away from the shell easily, and the lemon gives it a rich flavor, but it does something else too. Static electricity arcs from my fingertips and my hand seems drawn to the pan like a magnet.

As we eat, Rugnus reviews the qualities of each metal and rattles off as many questions as he can think of to see if I'm listening. He also wants to know all about my time on the surface, so I fill him in. I tell him about the first twelve years: going to a regular school down the mountain, taking the bus, playing kickball, and reading textbooks. The idea of a textbook fascinates him the most.

"Paper? Interesting," he says. "Loamin children just work with their parents, or other mentors, learn skills."

"My last two years were kinda like that." I elaborate on taking care of the property and Dad. How we made our own fuel and grew our own food. We both agree he must have stopped using craft about two years ago. But Rugnus, like me, doesn't know exactly why.

"Maybe he joined the conjurers. It's this group who swear off craft in the belief they can use natural magic without metal. But they won't be able to. He never said anything about them to me."

"I don't know, maybe there's something to that," I say. "Look what Ara did at the cabin and the RV park. As far as my dad... I don't know." I rip more crab meat free of the pale shell, dip it in the lemon juices pooled at the bottom of the bowl.

Rugnus leans forward, gathering a handful of lemon pieces. "Always has plans, your father, the king. Likes to surprise people, keep things secret until the last possible moment."

I squint at him. It's like he knows Dad as well as I do, if not better. "How did you say you met?"

Rugnus waves a hand. "Long story."

The bowl is mostly empty now. I sit back. "I don't mind."

"Well," he starts, "I went raiding Shadowsmith Dungeon when I was only eleven, right after my summation. Saw a cool technique on this guy's channel on bluelink, thought I could find a shadow cape all by myself, and get it out of the dungeon."

"You talk about it like it's a game."

"Kind of a game slash tradition slash sport slash religion. Dungeons are a big part of our culture. Wait until you meet Koglim. When he realizes how little you know, he'll talk your ear off. You won't even need bluelink to look up statistics and famous raiders."

He takes a long pause.

"So, you went into this dungeon..." I say.

"And I'm a moron. Your dad happened to be in the dungeon at about the same time. Found me curled in a corner of the Labyrinth of Obsidian, crying like a latcher. Saved me. Up until a couple of years ago, he'd take me into the dungeons for training."

The feeling of magnetism increases in my hands. I draw them closer. Dad had taken Rugnus under his wing. I get a picture stuck in my mind: him showing Rugnus how to use the ax, the horn, and the ring from the testing room. Every time he left me to tend the property, both when he was sick, and even before, he was coming to this world secretly.

For what? For Ara? For Rugnus?

A charge of electricity shoots across my scalp. There's a soft, electronic click, like a television turning on. Before my eyes floats an arm-sized magnifying glass in neon blue.

"Here we go," Rugnus says. He stands and taps the magnifying glass. "Access will last only a few minutes. What do you want to learn?"

"Is there any news about my dad?"

The name Therias Brightstorm scrolls into view inside the magnifying glass. Rugnus opens the results with a gesture, like reverse praying hands. Headlines and images fill the room. I stand, soaking in the information. There's a video playing in a few dozen places.

"Is that the video you saw?"

"Yep."

My disguise is good. I can't even tell it's me. Then I disappear. A few seconds later, someone appears next to Dad.

I look at Rugnus. "It *is* Ara."

They fight their way back to the camper and then budge. My shoulders relax. Even when we're apart, my instinct to protect him remains on high alert.

I open one of the articles:

THE FIZZBLOOD KING

The commenter isn't shy with his opinion. My father is dangerous. He's a thief. He has all three ounces of mithrium hidden away someplace, and he plans to use them to destroy Tungsten City.

"None of this makes any sense," I say. "Did he really do all that?"

Rugnus scoffs. "Don't listen to that trollbrick. Here, try something more positive."

He opens a simple biography. My father is the son of Drail Brightstorm and Seassa Tinseer. He grew up at the end of the Last War, as did my mother. He was close friends with a man named Theridal Silverlamp, now the keeper of Silverlamp dungeon, so his name has changed to Theridal Silverkeeper.

I find a portion about my mother. The word wedding is highlighted in pink. I touch it. Rugnus comes to my side. A night scene unfolds around us. The room changes to a rooftop garden with white wooden structures and neon plants. I think it's the same place Andalynn showed me from her childhood.

Instead of stars and the moon, a soft green light covers the world, casting a subtle aura of peace and contentment.

"What is this?" I ask Rugnus.

"Recording of their wedding, I think." He passes his hand through a ray of green light. "Must be somewhere in Whurrimduum." A crowd gathers around them in a semicircle, but I'm still at the front. They grip each other by the arm, smiling. My father takes a deep breath, but everything around me melts into particles, and I'm left standing over the empty pan in Rugnus' vault.

"Sorry," he says. "That's the most I can give us, but tomorrow we'll get you an AMP."

I nod slowly. I could become lost in the information available on bluelink. "Why can't we finish my summation now?"

Rugnus nudges me out of the room. "You should sleep," he says, pointing out the oversized bean bag chair squeezed between a short table and the aquarium wall. "There will be plenty of time tomorrow. Told your father I would watch out for you if he needed me someday. I'm going to keep that promise. And that starts with making sure you get enough sleep to face the rest of the summation."

I don't argue. Plopping down on the fluffy chair, I find the gold foiled blanket Rugnus gave me. The cold isn't as sharp now. In fact, I nearly forgot about it when I had access to bluelink. The image of a frozen underground city—and worse, the wall of ice-petrified people—returns to my mind. There's so much to ask Dad, but I can't be sure if, or when, I'll see him again.

Rugnus busies himself in the other room, and the lights of the central chamber dim, probably sensing a lack of movement. My pale reflection stares at me from the aquarium glass. I slip off the blanket for one second and try my sister's ring again, but there's no response.

Dark shapes slither far off in the murky water. My eyes droop as two large fish come forward to the glass then dart into the deep. The room darkens even more, turning my reflection into a shadow.

When my eyes close, I slip from reality.

My reflection in the aquarium wall stretches into a ribbon of light.

I budge somewhere. Or maybe this is a dream. I never have dreams.

In a flash, the ribbon of light bursts, shattering into tiny pieces. It's night. I'm in a canyon with smooth walls rising a hundred or more feet above me. My toes curl around sand, my feet submerged in a cool layer of rushing water. I've seen places like this on the travel channel. Is that where this dream comes from? The pieces of light linger in the air. It would be a terrible place to climb but a beautiful place to hike.

My reflection appears in the shallow water at my feet.

"Am I dreaming?" I ask.

My reflection winks at me and speaks in my father's voice. "You don't dream, Clayson."

I shake my head and step over my reflection. It stays in place. Why won't my reflection follow me? There are only a few strips of sand and vegetation along the sides of the canyon, so I hike through the river, against the stream, as the strange bands of rainbow light dance against the wall. The stream leads to the right for what must be a half-mile. When I stumble upon my reflection again, it's clear: I've gone in a circle. There were no side canyons, only a single long loop. I try going with the stream, but nothing changes.

Then the echoes start. Whispered conversations between a grumbling man and a dozen other strange voices, almost animal-like in their quality. I try to isolate a single conversation, one voice, which leads me back out into the loop and draws my attention toward a green ribbon of light. I try creeping up on it, charging it, but it always drifts away from me at the last second.

A butterfly net appears in my hands, and the rivulets of light scatter in every direction. I lose track of the green one. Eventually, when I can't catch any of the pieces of light, I close my eyes and follow the subdued voices.

"Mithrium..." Garbled words follow, but I catch the next one: "Brightstorm."

The conversation is coming from a small undulating ribbon of purple and blue light. I raise the net and swoop down over it. Dropping to my knees in the stream, I pull the net closer and reach inside, drawing out the ribbon of light. The garbled words become brighter, taking on a quality more like surround sound.

"Can it be done?" The voice is wary and rumbles as if someone has dragged the man's vocal cords over gravel.

A rushing wind answers him, filled with the voice of a younger man. "The universe is vast. What has yet to be done? Now that is a simpler question with a simpler answer."

Almost like it's a snow globe, I can make out the shadowy figure of the first man in the light. As I focus on the words of the second voice, my body pours into the vision.

The figure of the man becomes more distinct, with rich red hair, leather trousers, and a sunburned coloring to his skin. His hands and arms are pocked with old scars like he's worked shoveling coal into a hot fire all his life. The scene trembles at the edges. "If no coding or forge can make the mithrium a force for good in this world, then I will do everything I can to destroy it."

I search for another speaker, but the other voice isn't coming from another person. It's coming from a set of aged bones, large enough to be the main display in a natural history museum. Dragon is the only word I could use to describe them. I can't make out anything in the background, only the man and the bones.

The wind rushes around me again, and the bones speak. "Can anything truly be destroyed?"

"You haven't lived during my time, creature. The world may heal itself from the effects of these mithrium attacks, but things have been lost that can never return. In this, maybe I have answered my own question. Destruction is always possible. But if I could find the right code, a recipe to make it into something new, not a weapon, but something different. What is your answer? Is it possible?"

The bones answer with silence.

TEST MY STRENGTH

I SNAP AWAKE, echoes of the conversation rattling around inside my head.

Rugnus stands over me, still as stone. The smell of grilled meat is thick in the air. "Were you dreaming?"

"Yeah." I manage a whisper, then clear my throat. My body is sluggish. I rub my face and find the bristly start to a beard. Rugnus has changed into a black t-shirt, the same yellow beanie, white cargo pants. He looks rested. How long was I asleep? My eyes won't stay open, and my fingertips are still icy from my visit to Thiffimdal.

He blinks at me. "That's different. I've never heard of anyone dreaming when they're not on the surface."

I stretch, then shake my head to wake up. "Why? Loamin have dreams, don't they?"

He takes a bite of something, shaking his head. "Hate to break it to you, but no. Well, sometimes, but only on the surface. I mean, I've never had a dream. Maybe it's just a side effect of living up there." He feels my forehead with the back of his hand like I'm a sick toddler. "Did you dream a lot above granite? They say too much time up there can, you know..." He circles his ear with an index finger.

I rotate my neck and rub my eyes. "No. My dad did, though."

This brings sudden images to my mind, times when Dad would wake from a nightmare screaming, and I would insist on waiting by his bedside until he fell asleep.

"Really?" he says. "Therias Brightstorm had dreams? Weird. And you?"

I don't tell him Dad's dreams were nightmares.

It's hard to formulate a complete sentence when I'm still exhausted. I'm not sure how much to tell him about when I was small, about how Dad brought me to the surface to sleep. That I'm the reason he never returned. What if I'm still not able to sleep below the surface? That's what this feels like. I shake my head. "Uh, Dad said I slept like granite. He always seemed happy about it. But I can't remember ever dreaming."

"What was it about, just now?" Rugnus asks.

I stand and stretch, recalling the blurry vision. "There were these talking bones, and I had to catch a ribbon of light to hear a conversation. Is that weird?"

"Maybe not, but dreaming is. Dreaming is supremely weird. Anything else?"

Before I can answer, he holds up one hand. "Know what? Never mind. Don't need to know. What if you're cursed or something?"

I stop stretching. "Cursed?"

"Probably not, but that look on your face is worth a million ferrum."

"Okay," I say. "I'll add ferrum to my list of top ten things to figure out."

"Hey, that was very similar to a joke, Clayson. Maybe you're not as stoic as I feared."

I change the subject. "Is there any news about my parents on the, uh..."

"On bluelink? Yeah. Therias is on the run. The council is planning an inquisition for your mother—that's a trial. It will take place in four days, and you're sister's claiming she didn't know anything about their plans. The keepers may question her about why she left the castlestack last night, but the ironheads—" He stops. I must have a confused look on my face again. "Sorry, forgot you're new to this. The Keeper's Council is the business end of the Kingdom. Basically, they run the courts, the police, the military, all that. And ironhead is just a nickname for people who live in Whurrimduum. Anyway, all the ironheads love your sister. They won't let the keepers smear her with an inquisition."

"But my mother," I say. "I thought she ran the government."

"Ah, well, in a way. She's the steward since the King left. Only a Brightstorm can hold the throne. Or someone with Brightstorm blood. Still, she can only override a decision by the council that doesn't reach thirty-two cast—so she doesn't have much power. The cast for her inquisition was forty-five to ten."

Loamin politics gets added to my bluelink to-do list. Casts, kings, stewards, the council, the keepers. All these separate terms float around my head, banging into each other but forging zero connections. I can make a complicated flow chart comparing a presidential democracy against a parliamentary one, but I wouldn't graduate from kindergarten in this world.

"No mention of me at all?" I ask.

"Just that a random person was seen trying to escape with King Brightstorm. The media's presuming the two of you are in league with each other—which of course is true. But your gold-protected face is posted on bluelink pretty much everywhere. So, the concealer worked, besides the fact that without it, you are a mirror image of your father."

A thought strikes me. "How will that work when I get Tungsten City?"

"Got a plan for that, but one thing at a time. We'll do your summation tonight."

"We have to go back to Gamgim? Isn't that where the ceremony was supposed to—"

"We're not going back there. Now that we have the slate cubes you chose from the wall, I can complete the survey here and then on to one of the ninety-three dungeons to finalize your summation. And it's not just some ceremony. It'll help you understand your strengths and weakness when it comes to craft."

"Like the one my dad found you in? That kind of dungeon?"

His mouth drops open. "Yeah, that kind. Wow. Keep forgetting how little you know." Rugnus pauses, watching me rub my hands together. "Still cold?" he asks.

I clench my hands into fists. "A little."

"Well, it should go away by midday. You could get freshened up if you want." He strokes his chin, maybe pointing out my stubble. "Beards are out. Anyway. Left some chicken bites for you on the table, then test some other objects. Just stick to the stuff in those shelves, nothing from a display."

"Do you have a shower?" I ask.

He grimaces. "Gross. Know how much water is involved in a shower? That's for humans and nulls." He rummages through the backpack at his feet and produces a cast-iron flask, bound with a thick steel ring and topped with a golden cap. He tosses it to me. "It's a quick clean. You can keep this one. I have a personal cleaner, and I don't share it."

"Do I drink from it?"

"Just a sip will do. Keep the cap in your hand, though."

I unscrew the golden cap and take a sip of the liquid. Instantly, it's like I've walked through a human dry cleaner. My skin has been scrubbed and moisturized. It doesn't take away the fatigue, but it helps. I survey my clothes. My old undershirt looks immaculately white. My starter-beard is gone.

"Whoa."

He slaps me on the back. "And you expected a shower."

I weigh the small canteen in my hand. "Does it use two metals?"

"Good eye. Ironcraft for the water—does the actual cleaning—and goldcraft because it is a physical augmentation, of sorts. But you won't need any training about forging or coding objects."

I stand straighter, suddenly more interested. The man from

my dream mentioned something about coding an object with mithrium.

"No one forges their own objects anymore," Rugnus continues, "There are thousands of companies in Tungsten that specialize in various types of metals, coding them, forging them." Rugnus stares off to his left like he's reading words floating in the air. "Speaking of which, got to be at work." He pats the backpack at his feet.

"Work? Like a job?" I try picturing what Loamin do for work but fail miserably.

"Yeah. Work for a company called Quimdem. Harvest objects from the dead cities. Me and my team."

"That's right, you mentioned. And they let you do that?"

"Why wouldn't they?" he says, as if the idea of him being too young for a day job—one where he hangs out in radioactive cities—has never entered his head.

"You're only what, fifteen? What about school?"

"Whoa, your fizzblood is showing, Clayson. Loamin don't do that sort of thing."

"School?"

"If you want to learn how to do something, find a master willing to teach you. Sometimes they'll forge leafs for people to get a basic understanding of their craft. Some do live demonstrations on bluelink. They even take on official apprentices. Look at me, for example. I'm a master of ironcraft—controlling elements. Quimdem has loads of Loamin lined up to learn from me, but at the same time, I learn from one of only thirteen Loamin with a peerless rating in ironcraft. There's always someone better, and there's always someone less experienced."

"I guess that's true."

Dad must feel the same way. Once I was finished with grade school, I never went back. For about a year, I kept up with my friends the best I could. Eventually, being as far away from civilization as we were, I lost contact. Taking care of Dad and working on the property became my whole world—that and watching the news. The news has always been a way to escape.

"Is there any way to get me connected to bluelink again?" I ask. "You know, while you're gone."

"Nothing I could come up with quickly. Need to get you that AMP score. I have some leafs with other information. Those squares, on the silvercraft shelf." He points them out. "Nothing real current, but it's a start. Otherwise, feel free to mess around here. Just, don't —for Ide's sake—leave the vault. So, no budgecraft, uh, aluminum."

I nod numbly, physically tired and mentally drained. Worse, I don't have access to information.

Rugnus draws the club, Icho, from the holster on his back. "Should only be an hour at the office and then a few hours of training with my team. We have a big event coming up." He gives me a shrug. "Okay, see you later."

He leaves. Briefly, a shimmering tan outline pulses in his place. It's the first time someone has budged right in front of me. It's unsettling—like he doesn't exist anymore. I count the times I've traveled this way: once in the camper, then again at the RV park, then from Gamgim to Rugnus' vault, then to Thiffimdal and back. If I can avoid another aluminum object again this week, that would be great. But I know it's not possible.

The next few hours pass slowly. I have some chicken bites, which makes me wonder if all Loamin cook so well or if it's a talent Rugnus has. After that, I spend time using the leafs he pointed out on the silver shelves.

Each metal square functions like a notebook. When I hold one, my mind fills with new information about all sorts of topics. The Troll Wars, the Great Migration to the Rocky Mountains, and the slaying of the last three dragons. This last piece of information proves to be the most useful and confirms my suspicion about the talking bones from my dream.

They were dragon bones.

The information on the squares—or leafs as Rugnus called

them—lasts about a minute after I stop holding them, the information fades into obscurity after that. But the longer I hold onto the leaf, the longer I retain the information. About like reading a textbook: the longer you interact with it, the more you can recall. I hold on to the one about the dragons most of the day.

There's some information about dungeons, but there are so many other contextual roadblocks, and my mind has nothing to compare the information to. The best I can understand is this: a dungeon is something like a burial place for powerful Loamin. Each dungeon—and there are about a hundred—is named for the Loamin buried there. The man who slew the last dragon is named Harkus Bloodanvil—thus Bloodanvil Dungeon.

I take even more time rifling through Rugnus' shelves, but after Thiffimdal I'm hesitant to try my luck with much of anything. After a few hours, my exhaustion grows unbearable, and I find the bean bag chair, bundle up in the gold-foil blanket, and try my best to rest, half of the time staring at the aquarium, the other half dozing in a fitful sleep. I've never had any trouble sleeping before, so the whole process is frustrating.

When it's late in the day—a guess because I have no reference as to what time it might be—I discover a table with stacks of pieces of metal shaped like sticks of gum. Each rectangle is stamped with a lowercase, cursive letter f crossed through with one thick line and two narrow strikes. A stack of silver pieces teeters on the table's edge, and I stretch a finger out to adjust it, but suddenly half of them are gone. Then another pile disappears, a taller stack of copper pieces. After watching for a few minutes, more and more pieces start to blink away, until all at once, four small stacks of gold grow four times larger.

"Thought I'd get paid today." Rugnus' voice startles me, and I skitter into the table, knocking dozens of the little rectangles onto the floor.

"Sorry," I say, embarrassed.

Rugnus darts forward. "Didn't mean to sneak up on you." He

holds up his billy club. "This thing is a bit overpowered. It's a family relic. Here let's just…" he sets a brown bag at our feet—a whiff of barbecue rolling off it—and re-stacks the rectangles into painfully neat piles. "Not to worry. Needed to be straightened anyway. Here, put the tin and copper ferrum in their rows." I scour the table for every tin and copper piece I can find and set them into tidy stacks. Ferrum must be Loamin money. I guess Rugnus not only has a job but based on the stack of gold pieces on the table, it pays well.

He stands back from the table, judging the organization we've created, and adjusts his beanie. "Brought dinner," he says, nodding to the paper bag on the floor.

I unpack the bag, drawing out two lumpy shapes wrapped in butcher paper.

"Burgers?" I say. It smells good, whatever it is.

"Yeah. There's a taffy-themed restaurant down near Forge Center."

"Taffy?"

As Rugnus passes me one of the burgers, he says, "Right. It's a word we use for humans. Because they…well, they're kind of stretched out, and they're wizards with refined sugar."

"Taffy news," I say under my breath. "My dad, when he'd watch the news with me, called it taffy news."

Rugnus laughs. "Taffy news."

All of the human race distilled into a word. My connection to the surface continues to be swept to the side. I'm not actually human, but I'm still offended. "Derogatory," I say.

Blinking, he says, "Don't. I didn't mean anything by it. Besides, you're not human."

"Doesn't matter. Still insulting."

He glances at the ceiling. "Fine. You're not wrong. Sorry." He takes a bite of the burger. "Hey, tell me this: why do taffies—sorry, humans—call it a ham-burger when they clearly use bison meat?"

Now it's my turn to laugh. "Okay, there's so much wrong with what you said. They make hamburgers out of beef, and it's named for some part of Germany or something. I don't know."

"What's a Germany?"

I shake my head and tell him not to worry about it, then unwrap the butcher paper and find a bulbous loaf of dark bread. Lifting the top piece of the loaf, I discover a hearty patty of barbecue-spiced meat blotted with brown mustard, a few dark-purple tomatoes, pickles, and sauteed scarlet cabbage.

It tastes even better than it smells. For some reason, it makes me nostalgic for grade school recess and trips Dad and I took to the Grand Caverns during spring break.

I look at Rugnus. "Why do I—"

"A lot of food is made using silver objects, like spatulas, forks, knives, and stuff. Especially restaurant food—part of the experience. What're you thinking about?"

I tell him about our trips to the Grand Caverns because he's more likely to understand. Better than trying to explain grade-school recess. "What about you?" I ask.

"This recording thing my mother used to make me explore when I was a kid. All about the old mountains. My family comes from the Kingdom of Zal Kakraja. I guess she just wanted me to learn about everything that was lost during the war."

I slump involuntarily, glance at the map of the destroyed cities in Rimduum. It covers only one mountain range.

"How many more kingdoms were there across the world before mithrium?"

Rugnus sighs. "There were eight kingdoms: Rimduum, Brimwok, Hngaal, and Firas Andem on this side of the world. And Zal Kakraja, Bastlynd, Ras Dashen, and Himdem on the other side. But they're all gone. Tungsten City is home to so many cultures and people who managed to escape. It was a refuge during the war, and it continues to be a refuge."

We finish the rest of the meal quietly, but my connection to Rugnus is stronger than ever. I'm not sure if that's from the food or not. Did Rugnus want us to have this connection? Is that why he bought the burgers? I'm suddenly grateful to him for every-thing he's done for me. For a second, I try to make eye contact, but he's picking at his food, and with a nod, a certain under-standing passes between us that would be impossible without craft. It's similar to the wisps of silver in my sister's hair that brushed my face when I met her in Gamgim—how I knew her thoughts and hopes.

When we finish, Rugnus says, "It's time."

He urges me to a high table near where we first arrived yester-day. A large bowl woven from metal strings, filled with mercury, rests between us. It reminds me of the basins in Gamgim. I can't tell how the mercury stays inside. The two flat-gray, slate cubes I had grabbed the night before are stacked next to the basket-like toy blocks.

"This part is called the survey. And this is a summator. It will judge your mind and heart, then match you with one of the dungeons so you can complete your summation. It relies on all ten crafts and every metallic medium. And how many metals would that be?"

My mind races. This is something Dad might do, quiz me on new information. "Uh, fourteen."

"Correct. Don't ask how the mercury stays in a basket, a summator doesn't even hold water. A smith or coder might know how it all works, but I don't. I *do* know how to use it, though, which, honestly, is the only important thing when it comes to crafted objects. Here, take the two blocks, place them in the basket, make sure your skin has contact with the mercury."

I start to protest. "But—"

"And, no, before you ask, mercury is not toxic to Loamin, only humans. Once in the mercury, the two blocks will transform into two random types of stone. Let's go that far. Grab the stones and set them in the mercury."

I do as directed, making sure my hand dips into the silvery liquid. When I pull away, shimmering drops slip back into the pool. Instantly, the two plain blocks transform into other stones.

One is rough, almost grainy, with alternating red and tan layers. Limestone. I've climbed limestone cliffs years before a few miles down the road at a friend's house. The second rock is a brilliant black stone—obsidian. No, onyx.

Rugnus straightens and says, "Choose the rock in the summator that best represents power."

"Power?"

"Choose the rock that best represents power," he says again. It must be part of the survey.

I'm not sure how long I stare at the rocks, but after a minute, Rugnus clears his throat, so I pick up the red and tan limestone. My only reason is that I feel in control when I climb, powerful. When I lift the limestone, the obsidian splits, transforming into two different rocks.

Rugnus shoots me a questioning look, but it washes from his face quickly, and he maintains the decorum of the ceremony. "Place the power rock in front of you."

I set the limestone on the table.

"Choose the rock in the summator that best represents fear."

One is a dark gray chunk of shale. I would bet it's easy to break. The other one: radiant white quartz, only disturbed by hairline shadows. For some reason, my mind calls up the image of the cold sun hanging above Thiffimdal, and I grab the white quartz.

The shale cracks and forms two entirely different types of stone.

"Place the fear rock in front of you."

I line the quartz with the limestone on the table.

"Choose the rock in the summator that best represents hope."

Neither of these choices represent the idea of hope. The one on my right is like a piece of shattered peanut brittle: a yellow-colored conglomerate embedded with pieces of white. The other one is pure copper ore, like a ball of melted pennies, corroded with a dull green, gnarled in places.

Rugnus gives no indication he cares about my choice.

I reach for the conglomerate, but at the last second, change my mind and pick up the corroded ball. Ore can mean hope, the promise of something to come. The last rock vanishes, leaving an empty pool of mercury.

"Place the hope rock in front of you."

This last rock gets lined with the other two.

"Observe the three you have chosen. Which of these choices best represents freedom?"

I tap the limestone.

"Place this final stone in the summator and be judged."

I set the limestone in the mercury, where it melts away, revealing a single word: *WOLFSTAFF*.

"Cool," Rugnus said. The test is apparently over. Rugnus puts my other two rocks into the summator and dumps the metal basket, mercury and all, into his bag, throwing it over his shoulder. "You're a strange one. Somehow both thoughtful and reckless. I like that. Pickier than most. And you didn't go with the obvious. That concludes the first part of your summation. Change of clothes then off to the dungeon of Torlina Wolfstaff."

CROSS THE THRESHOLD

"SO, HOW DOES THIS WORK?" I ask.

Rugnus winds an aluminum ribbon around the palm of my hand. It's stamped with a logo that reads: *Troll Habit*.

"Just squeeze the wrap. Each time you squeeze, a different outfit will budge into place. Why are you so worried about this? It's clothing. Just... well, you can't go around dressed like a human. Flannel has got to go."

"The flannel's warm," I say, shrugging. But I know he's right.

When I squeeze the aluminum wrap, there's a half-second of extra gravity, but not as long-lasting as other budges. Instantly, I'm wearing something else. A simple hat has appeared on my head, and I'm now wearing a crisp dress shirt, a red vest with silver buttons, and a pair of heavily embroidered jeans.

I shake my head. "No."

"What's wrong with that?" Rugnus says.

I close my fingers around the wrap. Boots, golden corduroys, and a black shirt stamped with the picture of an exploding barrel. I try again. The more I change clothes, the more I realize this is Rugnus' style. The buttons, embroidery, and flat neutral colors, but with a single, brightly colored flourish that sticks out.

"You have anything less stylish?" I ask, giving the wrap back to him.

He frowns but searches the shelf. He hands me another wrap, this one stamped with a different logo—*NuFerrous*. Wrapping it around my palm, I give it a squeeze.

I like the first outfit: athletic shoes, white cargo pants, and a breathable silver t-shirt.

"Oh." A whisper of a frown forms on Rugnus' face. "You look fresh off the castlestack."

"Is that a good thing? Castlestack?"

"Means you look like you're from Whurrimduum. And... wait. You know what, we can use that. Refugee from Whurrimduum. I like it. And appropriate colors for Wolfstaff. It's a solid weave, and there are places to holster objects. Do you want a backpack? Or maybe... here, wait one minute." He disappears into the small dining room and reappears a few moments later, handing me a black canvas satchel. "What do you think? It's waterproof and essentially weightless, even when full. The gold buttons will complete the Wolfstaff color theme."

I sling the satchel over my shoulder, the strap lays across my chest. "Seems good. Will I need a lot of items in the dungeon?"

He lets out a breath, rubs his temples. "Objects, not items. And no, this is more for the look. Besides, only relics work in a dungeon. But it gives you a place to put anything you collect in there."

"Are relics and objects the same thing?"

"Uh, not exactly. An object is anything forged from craftable metal. A relic is an object raided from a dungeon. They're rare—I only have fourteen. But you can't use relics during a summation, anyway."

"You said there are traps and animals. Won't I need—"

"The dungeon provides. There will be objects you can use inside."

"Where's the dungeon? Tungsten City?"

"No, no, no. Most dungeons are far away from the cities,

carved out of the rock somewhere a bit closer to the surface. Wolfstaff is no exception. Ready?"

Claws of nauseousness gnaw at my stomach. It has nothing to do with budgecraft. In my mind, I see a side-by-side comparison between me and Rugnus in the training room. My mouth goes dry. "No other way to get an AMP?"

He shakes his head.

This is what I've gotta do to get into Tungsten City, to get access to bluelink. All of the things Dad hid from me are only a dungeon away. "Okay. I'm Ready."

We appear at the edge of a crowd on a wide, railed ledge behind a huge waterfall. Two bright lights filter through the crystal water. Now I understand Rugnus' comment about the color of my clothes. Most of the crowd is dressed head to toe in Wolfstaff's colors: gold, silver, and white.

"Are there this many people doing their summation?" I ask over the thundering water.

Rugnus matches my volume. "Probably only two or three, any one day. The rest of these people could be anyone. A scholar doing research, professional raiders trying to weaken the dungeon and build a reputation, paladins working security, watching over dungeon objects. Or just big fans of Wolfstaff. And look." He points to what can only be two knights, dressed the same as Bazalrak, standing over a girl of about eleven. "Whurrimduum won't let their citizens out of their sight. Even initiates. Ridiculous."

"What do you mean?"

"The citizens of Whurrimduum are oppressed by the Keeper's Council and the monarchy."

"You mean..." I don't say the words mother and sister, but I don't have to.

"Basically. Though your mother and sister have little say in anything. Anyway, there are always people trying to sneak out regardless of the anti-budge policies of the council. They use visiting a dungeon as a way to get out from under Whurrimduum's foilgrips."

We emerge from behind the waterfall. Two camper-sized chandeliers in silver and gold glimmer from the distant ceiling. It's hard to stare at the blinding white marble walls for more than a few seconds.

"Whoa."

Rugnus smiles. "Welcome to the lobby of Wolfstaff Dungeon. I've been here a few times myself, but never for summation. This should be awesome!"

We descend with the crowd down a wide stairway to the left, step by step winding our way to the base of the vaulted room. We wrap around the outside walls, passing under a second waterfall on our way. After that, a single gargantuan opening becomes visible in the white marble a few steps from the pool formed by the two colliding waterfalls.

The line stutters to a crawl, leaving thirty or so people between us and the opening. I spot a young boy staring at the waterfall with large eyes. Two women form bookends around him.

I nod toward them so Rugnus can see.

"Must be another summation. Cool."

I focus on the conversation between the two women.

"...and what do you think will happen," says a woman in gold leggings, whose fierce, narrow eyes are outlined with silver, "now that the King has been found?"

"Found? He escaped again," an older woman says, tugging at the white, drooping hat on her head and resting against the wall as the line slows to stop. "Did you see the torturer's leaked footage? A vacant. Though I'm still not sure I can believe that. More propaganda from Whurrimduum."

"Whoever's helping him, the council will make life there miserable if they can't find him."

Rugnus whispers, "Told you it was all over bluelink."

The older woman drops a hand on a boy's shoulder. "Other matters today, though. Are you ready, dear?"

The boy bounces on his feet in anticipation. "Wolfstaff is really awesome, and I know a ton about it. There's a sleep room, loads of climbing, lots of sacrificial doorways, and..." The boy trails off, eyes the waterfall, and gulps.

"And?" The woman with the silver eye makeup encourages him.

"Water," he says in reverence.

Rugnus shudders.

"Why is he afraid of the water?" I whisper.

"Loamin don't like being underwater," he says.

"They don't?"

When Rugnus' eyes go wide, I translate the meaning: another way I must be different from other Loamin. Besides climbing and working on the property, there's not much better than swimming the lakes of the Blue Ridge mountains in summer.

The line surges forward as a large group passes through the opening in the wall. "Is that the entrance?" I ask.

"Close. This door lets groups in one at a time. Wolfstaff was a private person. Dungeon entrances can be totally different from one another. Take Bloodanvil, for example, just a massive hole in the ground. You have to base jump into it."

"Hey, I read that on one of the leafs. Glad I didn't get that one," I say.

"You'd rather have water?" he asks, eyes wide.

I shrug.

The line moves forward again. "What will the dungeon be like?"

He purses his lips. "Tell you at the threshold."

We wait for our turn. As the line gets closer, conversations around us ebb away, and the water in the pool gurgles, draining underneath the floor into the dungeon. We move from the steps to the polished marble floor, and the doorway lets in the two women and the boy, leaving us waiting at the recess in the wall.

"What's to stop us from—" my arm hits an invisible shield at the opening. Rugnus leans against it casually, smiling. He must enjoy how little I know about the world around me, even though he hides it with a good-natured smile. There's a pride he takes in teaching people. I see it every time he tells me something new. Maybe he considers it a repayment to Dad.

Abruptly, the invisible wall vanishes, and Rugnus takes a dive into the marble. The group behind us laughs, and I can't help but join them. Rugnus catches himself in an amazing demonstration of balance. He holds out both arms. "Ta-da!"

We shuffle through the opening, along a narrowing hallway where the walls are flecked with glimmering silver ore. Soon, the stone presses in on us until the cold, smooth surface touches both of my shoulders like we're being squeezed into the dungeon. The hallway gradually darkens to an unnatural gray-green light.

We turn to our sides as the walls narrow further.

"Did we enter the dungeon?" I ask.

"No," Rugnus says, "still approaching the threshold."

We squeeze into a dim room, the same cereal-box shape as the last, aqueducts of water flowing to our right and left. Beyond the aqueduct to the left, there's no wall, only a rough opening like a cave, dark and ominous, but it's not the entrance.

A twenty-foot-tall copper-gilded doorway lies in front of us. "Here we are," Rugnus says, pointing. "Take your offerings."

"What?"

As we stop in front of the door, he hands me the two leftover stones from the summation test, first the copper ore and then the sharp piece of white quartz.

"The door will open when you lay them on the threshold." He taps a spot on the floor where a rectangular tile, like a massive doormat, is inlaid before the threshold—darker than the surrounding stone. Within the rectangle is another golden rectangle. "Remember, they represent your hope and your fear. Once you enter the dungeon, you can call for your hope or your fear to protect or aid you, but you have only those two to help."

"Call for them?"

"Yes, just speak a request out loud. I wouldn't use anything in the first room, but that's up to you."

I weigh the two stones in my hand. "What else should I expect? I mean, I'm not sure I'm ready. I—"

He waves a dismissive hand. "No one ever is. You're an initiate. It's your summation. Besides, Wolfstaff has a very low fatality rate."

"Fatality! You're not helping."

At that moment, a low growling comes from the left, and a hulking form shifts in the shadows of the cave. My body involuntarily tries to make itself smaller, and I glance at Rugnus, hoping he has some sort of an indication of what's happening, but his face is pale. "What is it?"

"It c-can't be."

A wolf, the size of semi-truck pads out from the cave, leaps over the aqueduct and bounds toward us. Rugnus says something unintelligible in a hoarse whisper.

The massive white-gray furred animal speaks to our minds.

I am Frrwelhst of Den Krrarn. Are you ready for the dangers of Wolfstaff? The voice is a woman's voice, both ancient and menacing as if she's wandered these caverns for an eon.

Rugnus inclines his head. "G-guardian, I p-present this initiate. I believe him worthy of the t-task."

None are worthy, son of Tignus Ironmace and Rusela Whitechin.

Rugnus raises his head, blood returning to his face and light to his eyes. He says, "We no longer bear the names of our enslavement in the Kingdoms. Our f-family is known by the name Rugnus throughout Tungsten City. A family of no small reputation."

The wolf grins cruelly. *Rugnus. Simpler names for a more complicated era. Very well, Rugnus. Your presentation of the initiate is accepted. Be silent or be eaten.*

For once, Rugnus is absolutely quiet.

Clayson, son of Therias Brightstorm and Azbena Bloodfeign presents himself as an initiate at Wolfstaff...interesting. Are you ready to face the dangers herein? You are no simple initiate. The way forward will be more difficult for you than for others.

"I don't know. I don't know if I'm ready." I dare to make eye contact with the beast. "How can I tell?"

Always willing, always trying, grasping, making plans. Gathering useless information. Spinning, spinning, spinning. We discern you. You may try, but know your fears and hopes are open to the dungeon. Torlina Wolfstaff is a shrewd champion. She will not let you get far.

Frrwelhst flips around and leaps into the darkness.

We both let out long breaths.

"What just happened?" I ask.

"Coolest friend ever," Rugnus says. "Never thought I would behold an actual dungeon guardian. And a Feral Wolf. That was epic!"

"What was that about?" I ask.

"Oh, I don't know, let me think. Pretty much only happens about every fifty years or so. And never during summation. The guardian of a dungeon shows up to judge the person entering. You know, look into their soul, see if they're worthy, stuff like that. I think you passed. A real Feral Wolf. Got to be the only one living. Can't believe it."

"I thought this was Torlina Wolfstaff's dungeon? She's not the guardian?"

A realization dawns on Rugnus' dimpled face. "Right. Wouldn't really know anything about dungeons, would you?"

"That's kinda what I've been trying to tell you?"

"Where to even start. Well, it's like this: the moment a Loamin's AMP rises over sixty-three, they're cursed—in a good way, though."

"How can you be cursed in a good way?"

"Ah, just the question. See, the moment they die, they become *this*," he gestures to the door of the dungeon.

I'm sure I'm missing something. "Okay," I say, shrugging.

"In the exact spot they die," he says, now pacing, "a dungeon is born. A changing, shifting, deadly, tomb. At its heart, the greatest, most valuable treasure forged or won by the champion—at least we assume so. No one has ever made it to the center of any of the ninety-three dungeons. This one is most likely the wolfstaff relic itself."

Bloodanvil had died along with the last dragon. That must have been the moment his dungeon was forged. "Wolfstaff is dead, though, right?"

"Very. She was peerless in coppercraft—animals—goldcraft—physical change—and silvercraft—"

"Intangible stuff. Thoughts. Like the threads in my sister's hair."

"Right. Anyway, this champion, Torlina, forged a staff in an alloy of gold, silver, and copper, allowing her to transform into a feral wolf. Could just speak to them, calm their fears about Loamin settlers. It ended our war with them over two thousand years ago."

The line of Loamin is adorned in gold, silver, and white. "People worship her," I say.

"Eh, it's more like they're her fans." He pauses briefly, a mask of expectation over his features. "Could invite the surveyor—in this case, me—inside the dungeon with you as a guide. It's always the initiate's choice. What do you think?"

I consider his words. "So, you could come in there with me?"

"Yeah, though the dungeon itself prevents a guide from doing much. But I could be there."

I take two more deep breaths. "I think... I think I wanna go alone."

Rugnus dips his head. "Choice is yours. Ready then?"

I shift toward the threshold and lay the copper ore representing hope on the inlaid rectangle. It melts into the floor the same way the limestone had melted into the mercury of the summator. If there is supposed to be some symbolism here, it is lost on me. Am I meant to feel as if I've lost hope?

Next, I lay the white quartz. The rectangle ripples, and it too is absorbed, the representation of my fear. It can take that one.

I'm not left to ponder the meaning of the stones for long. A loud crack splits the air, and light spills out as the door shutters open, the copper embellishments cut neatly in two.

Rugnus nods, his face like a kid with a thousand dollars to spend at a toy store. "I'll meet you in the exit lobby."

I creep into the dungeon, staring at my shoes, but the light is so blinding even my feet disappear for a moment. When I risk a few more steps, the doors rumble. I turn back to tell Rugnus I've changed my mind—he can come in with me—but it seals shut.

Even the door's seam tightens to the point where I can't tell the difference between the wall and the door. A smooth marble wall rises a few hundred feet upward, flawless and white. I spin around, trying to get my eyes to adjust to the light. The shape of the room is the same narrow box as in the lobby.

Opposite the smooth wall where the door was, a rough cliff face climbs to the ceiling far above. At the top of the room, a darkened smudge reveals the only thing resembling an exit. The smudge is some sort of cave. I know immediately I will have to climb.

As I scan the marble cliff, my confidence comes back to me. Finally, something I can do!

I can measure at least two moderate paths to the top, which I could free-solo, without climbing gear, in fifteen minutes, maybe less. I bounce on my toes to test my new shoes. They won't be bad for climbing. I've scaled a few places without a rope, without someone to belay, but not a cliff like this.

Even so, it draws me in, and I run a hand over the cool, rough marble. A shiver passes through me, along with some other dreadful premonition. It's too much of a coincidence. In the first room, a challenge to climb, evidence the dungeon knows me—Wolfstaff knows me.

Another detail pulls me closer. Barely a shadow rests on the wall. Even where large stones jut outward, the color of the rock underneath is undimmed. Unnatural light coats the room, like sunlight cast from every direction. I expect to glimpse some source—chandeliers, torches, a few crafted objects leaching light —but there isn't one, and the lack of contrast will make climbing more difficult.

I feel exposed. I take a few steps backward, but my footfalls are silent.

I look over my shoulder, expecting a hand to reach out and grab me. My eyes drift to one side of the room where a dark bird-bath sits. Did it just appear? Why didn't I see it before? It's situated as if someone had divided the floor into thirds and centered it in the last third. I march over to it.

Ornate metal vines cluttered with vicious thorns run from the base of the pedestal to the bowl, where the vines morph into an open flower. A demonic birdbath. It isn't as heavy as I expect. When I nudge the bowl, the water in the shallow saucer sloshes from side to side

It will obviously play into the challenge in some way, but what? Will I have to drink it?

Wolfstaff is daring me to climb the wall, but maybe there's some detail I've overlooked in the room. Some gold key chain that grants perfect balance and strength? As a precaution, I search every inch of reachable stone, pushing, pulling, and knocking on the surface in the hope that something will be revealed. I find nothing.

"Here goes." My words are swallowed in silence.

I find a perfect outcropping, a bucket-shaped groove that offers plenty of leverage. Handholds are almost prescribed for the first twenty feet, like a fabricated playground wall. After that, a narrow fissure zigzags upward. I find a hook for my heel, turn my body inward, and wedge my hands into the thin opening, swinging the other leg over to bring myself center. It's a little uncomfortable to find a grip without chalk, but the gap is the right size, and there are plenty of places to hold.

I look down, now thirty feet up. Next, I crane my neck back. I can't discern the ceiling from what I had hoped was an exit. The top of the cliff is still distant. I continue along the fissure until it branches left and right. When I reach the fork, I breeze right past it, as a large shelf above me presents an easier grab. One hand, the other, then I push upward like pulling myself out of a pool.

I rest for a minute, balanced on the ledge.

After a moment, I keep moving. Left hand upward, right foot, left foot, right hand—but only crimping the surface of a ledge— repositioning myself, hanging for a brief second—all of this a familiar, satisfying rhythm.

Halfway there, I find a long shelf. It tilts downward, but the tiny path leads to another outcropping where I can sit down. As I inch along, my back to the wall, a sharp fluttering breaks through the silence.

Bats careen toward the metal pedestal, a flood of wings and black fur. A thousand squeaking cries echo in the cavern. They fight over the brackish water, and in that moment, I understand something. Climbing the cliff was not the challenge. The bats are.

I can't be on the wall if they come back around.

The way upward is unknown, so I shimmy back down the path as the leading bats slurp water from the metal bowl, then swoop upward, aimed right at me. I move down quicker now, remembering the best places to put my feet. I skip a few footholds and drop onto the small ledge. It must be another forty feet down. If I could only get—

Bats swirl around me. I lose strength, amplified as my muscles tighten, forcing me to curl into a ball. Some magical panic enslaves me like the fright of a jump scare or the gut-wrenching of terrible news.

I need my parents!

What if they're dead?

I'm gonna die in this dungeon. Why do I wanna survive anyway? I can't breathe. My stomach flips inside out. For a moment, I wish the bats would kill me, tear the flesh from my bones. I begin digging my fingernails into my arm.

Wolfstaff is doing this to me. It's an unnatural fear coupled with control of the bats. The birdbath must be an alloy of copper and silver. It's the only moment of clarity I find. The bats torpedo me again and again, shrieking. Their translucent wings like thousands of fingers crawling over my body.

Bats that make you psychotic.

I fight the urge to throw myself off the cliff. They're doing this to me. Why did I come here? Rugnus. This is his fault!

I have to get to the water. I curse myself for not dealing with the fountain when I was on the ground. I scream at myself. "I hate you!"

Craft oozes off the bats, waves of paranoia ebb and flow into my thoughts. Doom. But no, if I could only get—I scream again. Sweat pours off my face and arms.

The pulsing flow of paranoia breaks here and there, but for only seconds at a time. It's enough to force myself to act. I use the tightening of my muscles to my advantage, making for the gap beneath me. I scale it as quickly as I can but open a large gash in the fleshy part of my left hand. Another wave of foreign emotions pounds into my skull.

My body shakes, but I cling to the wall. Suddenly my hands and feet are numb. I try to reposition my grip, squeeze my hand into a fist to fill the gap, but I don't have the strength.

I fall, but my foot twists sharply, catching in the gap. I dangle upside down, foot throbbing. Handholds. I need a place for my hands. Extending all my free limbs, I brace myself and dislodge my foot, but I'm immediately dizzy and disoriented. Unable to prevent my body from flinching, I drop downward, shredding my hands as I try to find any resistance.

I turn my head to the side at the last second, offering the floor my shoulder. There's a loud crack, and pain flowers over my body. Something deep in my shoulder crushes as I slide forward. It's broken. I'm broken. Alone. I should have let Rugnus guide me.

"Rugnus!"

Using my good arm, I drag myself across the floor to the

pedestal. The bats sense what I'm about to do and bombard me, a few of them biting as I try to push over the pedestal. I don't have the strength. I grip the bowl with my good arm and pull it down on top of me.

Two things happened at once: the bats send another wave—I'm choking, unable to breathe—but the water from the bowl rains over me, and through craft, the bones in my shoulder reconnect. The cut on my hand knits back together.

I lay still, detached from reality. I've been in shock before—trapped on a cliff face, Dad trying to calm me down—but now I separate from my body, ballooning above myself to watch as batwings bubble and writhe over my physical form. This is worse than pain or fear. Dad had once described what it was like to try to outrun something in a nightmare. I'm sure this is worse. I have no eyes to close, no skin to protect me, and I wish for the stark silence from before. Anything would be better than the fluttering of the bats.

An hour drains away, maybe two, but still, the bats continue to swirl around me, shooting the psychic fear into me with only their presence. After another hour, I start returning to myself—a pinprick of feeling in my foot. I blink a few times. The bats recede one by one, reluctant to end their persecution. But finally, my lungs pump normally again. I stand, legs shaking.

The bats are gone.

Besides any trauma this has caused me, I'm whole, and the room is quiet again.

Wolfstaff dares me to try the cliff once more.

With all the false emotions gone from my mind, I marvel at the dungeon. Wolfstaff created a formidable obstacle unique to me. No wonder the Loamin could only guess what was at the center of any dungeon. How many rooms and challenges would a person have to overcome to reach its heart?

Before moving on, I pick up the bowl of the fountain. It had detached from the pedestal. I examine it for a moment before smashing it against the wall. The petals of the flower bend out of shape, but I can't break or fold it beyond that. I leave the pedestal lying on its side, cross the room, and rest the bowl upside down on the floor.

I'll have to climb again. This time, I move faster, past the gap, up to the ledge, and onward. I approach the ceiling. What I had hoped was an exit is more of a cave. The opening is the size of a garage door, tapering to a point on one side.

Abruptly, a single bat blasts out of the cave. It glides in a small circle and dives toward the floor. A smile crosses my face. All he'll find will be—

"Trollbrick." It seems like a fitting thing to say at the moment.

The pedestal rests in its original location, filled with dark water. Not good.

Now a flood of bats exits the cave. Frantically, I find footholds and handholds as I race to the entrance of the cave. I heave myself over the lip of the entrance, slither forward, and stand, my legs shaking.

Here, the floor is made from river rock, yellow and white, shimmering under a few inches of crystal water. As the first of the bats return, despair expands inside my chest. The muscles around my heart tighten. I tuck into a ball as they flitter over me again.

A scream comes from my mouth. "Leave me alone!"

As the evil bats infiltrate my mind with psychotic messages of self-harm and self-hatred, I can only hope something will come to my rescue. Why did I tell Rugnus I could do this on my own? This will only prove what a coward I am. No. These are not my thoughts. These are not my thoughts. These are not my thoughts.

Hope.

"I need hope." The word comes out fragile.

I raise my head. As something encumbered by shadow and fire slinks out from the far corner of the cave, the cold dread produced by the bats is replaced by terror, real terror.

Something is here with me.

LOOK IN THE MIRROR

THE SHADOW GROWLS, and it's like metal scraping against asphalt. It paces in the dark, four furry legs, white flames flickering across its arched back. As it pounces, I curl inward to protect myself. There's warmth as it flies over me.

When it lands, I can make out its shape—a large lynx.

It tears through the bats in a feeding frenzy, smacking them from the air. The cat's claws pin one of the bats to the floor. With a yawning-hiss, the lynx bites the rodent's head clean off. It roars, sending a wave of panic through the cloud of manic bats. They knock into each other in an uncoordinated attempt to flee.

Arching its back lazily, the lynx finishes off the bottom half of the bat, then prowls toward the water, lapping up a drink before staring at me. There's a pulse of overwhelming calm, and every poisonous feeling drains off of me into the clear water at my feet. Even the dull restlessness from my inability to sleep the previous night vanishes. My mind is clear, and my body tingles with energy.

I know it's some power coming off of the lynx. "Thank you."

You are most welcome. Now you must move forward into the dungeon. Wolfstaff has tested only three areas of craft. I will grant you an opportunity to test one more. Nothing as volatile as the bats.

Maybe it's the fact I already talked to a wolf today, or perhaps it's the calm projected by the lynx, but it's not strange to have it speak to my mind. "Three already?" I say.

Should I find it this easy to communicate with animals? I remember for a second the copper whistle by Rugnus' aquarium, but this doesn't seem like that type of craft or craft at all.

The lynx narrows its eyes. *You are an interesting initiate. You have great power, yet you do not understand the basics of Loamin craft. Sorry to intrude on your thoughts, but... they are loud.*

I shrug. "I'm new to this."

Again, interesting. You seem secure in your identity and in your ability to face challenges. Confident even. Coping with the bats is a test reserved usually for professional raiders and other uninvited guests. No one typically escapes them without relics.

For a brief second, I almost wanna give up. That was only the first challenge. But I need to face this, then on to Tungsten City. An AMP will give me access to the information I need to sort things out about my parents, make a plan.

There it is again. Resilience. Well, you must continue. As promised, a simpler task. Find the gear in the water and open the door.

"What door?" I ask.

The lynx steps around me, and I swivel to follow his movement. An oaken door has appeared in the wall. I come to the door, scrutinize the lock. Instead of a keyhole, there's a single ring, like a gear. I search the water for anything out of place and find what must be the key—a larger gear.

It doesn't fit against the smaller gear on the door.

"What am I missing?"

It's a simple gesture to unlock these types of things.

The gears are metal, maybe titanium like my mother's bike chain necklace, but a gesture is needed. Maybe the gesture is intuitive. I stand back, holding the larger gear, and twist my wrist as if I'm turning a key. There's a soft click, and the door hinges inward a foot.

"Is that it?"

Push the door open and step inside.

Resting my hand on the door, I have a strange thought: I'm not in control of any of this. Craft doesn't seem to take much effort. You can either use an object, or you can't. Everything's based on a person's natural talent in craft and the strength of the object. I couldn't use the iron objects very well, not like Rugnus.

"I don't feel in control of the outcome of these tests. Is that typical?"

Why would you assume you could *control the outcome?*

"I assumed using craft would take focus, dedication, but it doesn't. If I can't have an effect on what's happening, then nothing I do will matter."

Doing and being are different things. The dungeon does not measure what you can do but who you are. Continue. Learn for yourself. The champions control their dungeons. Not you.

"What will happen when—" I glance back at the lynx, but it is gone.

In the next room, the walls are lined with stretches of reflective metal—mirror, after mirror, after mirror, only broken by slivers of white stone.

This room is shaped the same as the last, but like someone pushed it over onto its side and squashed it. A hundred ominous mirrors, made of some pale alloy of gold, line the way to a dim, vine-encumbered wall.

In the reflection of the left set of mirrors, a host of people appear, dancing in formal wear. In the right set, more guests, socializing noisily, eating little cakes, and sipping from goblets. Some sort of dinner party. At first, I'm disoriented, but the more I march forward and watch the crowd, the more their movements become indistinct from mirror to mirror.

A gaunt, dark-eyed figure with a pointed goatee is watching me. He leans casually against a pillar, drinking golden punch from a crystal goblet, feigning interest in the conversation of other partygoers. He keeps his eyes on me, almost smiling.

The scene draws me in. I'm a moth lured by the flame of

curiosity. My fingertips grace the closest mirror, and it accepts me greedily into the party. The crowd of bodies press against me, but I cut through toward the dark-eyed figure.

The gaunt man excuses himself and escapes through an adjoining hallway. I follow him, almost running, and as I skitter into the hallway, I find myself back in the dungeon, facing the wall tangled with vines.

The man is gone, but I know where I have to go next. The vines extend into a pool of lighted water. I don't like that the dungeon keeps giving me only one option. But without another choice, I remove my shoes and sit at the edge of the pool. Why does the water appear so much like light, silvery and opaque?

The dungeon changes based on the people inside it.

"Okay, time to get this over with."

I ease myself into the pool, breathe deeply, and plunge under the water. The vines provide a guide as I make my way down. The tunnel opens into an underwater cavern the size of a football stadium. I tread water. How large is this dungeon? How much longer can I hold my breath?

In the center of the cavern, a massive sphere of vines hangs suspended in the water. There are gaps in the vines, doorways maybe. Am I supposed to go inside of it? I blink rapidly, scanning the water for any new direction to go besides the sphere of vines.

I need to breathe. Kicking my feet, I shoot upward. My head meets a ceiling that hadn't been there a second ago, but there's no air. My mouth opens in panic, but I make a strong effort not to suck in any water.

Don't panic.

My lungs scream for oxygen as I follow the vines across the ceiling to a column of orange light. It could be another chamber. I kick over to the light. It's an opening!

I swim as hard as I can until my face breaks the surface of the water. I gasp.

How close was I to drowning?

Again, there's only one place to go: a small island in the

center of the room. I pull myself onto the elongated slab. Hovering in a pool of light, eye level, a chainmail shirt drips with metallic liquid.

Mercury.

This will test my strength in timecraft. I debate taking another plunge into the depths to search for something else. Timecraft makes me nervous. But what choice do I have? Wolfstaff—the dungeon itself—is driving me somewhere.

I remove my shirt and slip the chainmail on so it can have full contact with my skin. How weird I must look in cargo pants and chain mail. I throw the long sleeve shirt over it as the mercury trickles down my back.

"It isn't poison. It isn't poison. It isn't poison."

When I jump into the water, nothing happens.

I take the largest breath I can and plunge deeper, angling downward.

The obvious place to go is the sphere of vines. Then I see it. A billowing of unnatural smoke through the filter of water. It hovers near the darkened entrance of the sphere. Dozens of multicolored lights dance and spark within the cloud. It's a wraith. Even underwater, it looks the same as the one I saw emerge from the grove at Gamgim.

Rugnus' warning comes back to me: wraiths can take your craft permanently. The cloud drifts into the sphere, and I can no longer see it.

A current of cold water washes past me, along with a school of muted-neon fish. I steady myself by putting both hands together and using them like a paddle, but a long bubble appears where my hands cut through the water. Curious, I try to make the bubble larger. It works. I poke my head through and find a pocket of air. It's like being in a flipped-over canoe.

"Weird." My voice is muffled inside the bubble. It has to be the chainmail. It's the only object I have, the only way I can create anything as strange as this. But what type of craft can manipulate water and air? Iron is elemental manipulation. Is that what the chainmail is made of? What about the mercury leaching off of it?

The air might be thinning, so I take another deep breath and risk going closer to the sphere of vines. The pocket or air stays in its place for a second, then bursts in a reverse rain of bubbles.

Rugnus would not enjoy this part of the dungeon, but maybe he could use the iron of the chainmail to greater effect and create a permanent air bubble around himself.

At the sphere's entrance, I stop, make another air bubble, and catch my breath. "Still working." I pat the chainmail under my shirt. "Don't run out on me, though."

Another deep breath, and then I push into the sphere, through the darkened entrance.

The moment I enter, I understand the challenge. It's a three-dimensional hedge maze. I've seen garden mazes on travel channels before, but this one takes the victory. Three distinct tunnels stretch away from my location: down, right, or straight.

Sure, now there's multiple choice.

A tin watering can floats next to me, casting a pale green light into the surrounding water. When I grasp the handle, sunlight graces on my face. The watering can is anchored in place, but the vines to my right part just enough that I can see through to the other side. Another passageway of vines. When I release the watering can, the wall quickly knits itself back together.

This is tincraft, control of plants. I've tested six crafts now.

Using this object reminds me of my failure with iron in the testing room. Will tincraft be a weakness for me also? I imagine how easy the challenge would be if I could cut through the vegetation or control it using the tin watering can, leading me right to the end.

Now what?

Deja vu lances through my mind. The vines and the water, a particle of something floating in front of me; the details are as familiar as the cliff near my cabin. I try to shake the feeling off, but it clings to the inside of my skull. I suddenly glow purple.

Then, a ghostly outline of my body drifts in front of me, and I'm in two places at once. No, not two places, two times. A thin lilac outline floats around the second me.

I've been here before. I already went left—dead-end. And the tunnel downward, I've been there too. Maybe I can still work the maze without the help of tincraft. I touch the water can again, and again the area to my right—not one of the proscribed tunnels—opens. This would be the direction I would go if I could.

And I've already found a way to get there. The chainmail gives me a way—no, gives me extra time—to scout out every path, come to every dead-end, almost in an instant. Rugnus was right: it's not time travel, but it allows me to see multiple eventualities.

The path to the center of the maze is clear. And the wraith is waiting there. No other direction presents itself, no other outcome. I travel into the maze without another moment of hesitation. Every twenty seconds, I create an air bubble. Panic still grabs a slice of my mind every time I leave a new pocket of air, but I push the feeling outward with each breath.

When I come to the last turn, I catch a strange melody lilting through the water, familiar and inviting. It's a melody I've known since I was a child. Something Dad would hum as he worked or as he put me to sleep. A memory slips into my mind. I'd fallen off of something. My leg was scraped from ankle to knee, little droplets of blood welling up. Dad hummed this melody, deep in his chest.

I felt safe.

The melody oozes from every vine—another connection between Dad and this world.

Ahead of me, there's a break in the wall where blue light flickers to life—the center of the maze. I make another air bubble and pop my head inside for a breath. Seeing the light ahead. I'm being lured in again, like with the mirrors. I glance back the way I came. There could be another way.

But I'm tired of indecision. From the moment I crossed the

threshold, there's only been one way forward. I shake my head and swim toward the light.

When I'm within a foot—or however Loamin measure things —a crack of terrifying electricity sizzles through the water. I wait to be electrocuted, but nothing happens. Peeking around the corner into the next area, I see a rectangular window of pure light hovering in the center of an eight-sided room. In each corner along the wall, metal spheres—in turn—arc flashes of azure lightning into the shimmering window—each bolt making it crackle and glow all the brighter.

I'm not eager to approach.

The melody returns, but this time it's off-key, melancholy, droning almost like the thundering pipes of a church organ. The notes hang in the water. I open another air bubble and drink in the oxygen deeply. Each zap of lightning from the metallic ball into the hovering window of light coincides with a note in the melody. As the tempo increases, so do the bolts of lightning. The tune plays three or four times in a jumbled fever of sharp tones and light, then everything is still.

Eerie silence settles over the room. I wait a pulse, then swim over to one of the spheres and examine the metal. It's cobalt which means bluecraft, communication. What's this room trying to communicate?

When my fingers reach the gray metal, it takes on a bright blue aura. I swim to each ball, and each comes on like a switch. When the final sphere is turned on, the white sheet of light in the middle of the room vanishes, replaced with something like a screen.

The same dinner party from the hallway of mirrors plays out on the screen. The conversation echoes around me.

"Her son watches over her day and night," a man says.

The woman next to the man shifts uncomfortably, eyes darting from side to side. "He'll find himself turned to a wraith if he isn't careful."

A cheer rises behind me as hundreds of goblets clank against each other. I turn to see where the sound is coming from and find that I have again left the dungeon. I can breathe freely. I'm at the party with the other guests.

The man standing near me clicks his tongue in dismay. "Come now, don't be morose. Landred Wolfstaff, the mother's heir, wouldn't be so reckless."

A woman, younger than the first, swishes her golden dress. Smiling, she says, "He's practically a wraith already."

All around, people laugh to the point of tears. One woman, trying to impede her giggling, turns mistakenly to her drink. When she nearly gags, the crowd laughs all the harder.

But their laughter is cut short when the gaunt man with the pointed goatee appears from around a pillar on the staircase. He's dressed head to toe in gray. This has to be who they were talking about, Landred Wolfstaff. As he passes them, every person places a fist over their heart and inclines their head in respect.

Landred makes no pretense at greeting them. His eyes are rimmed red, but he meets their gaze in defiance. The sharp angle of his jaw leads to his twitching goatee. He leaves through a heavy door, but the whole mood of the group has soured.

The door is left open, and I slip through after him, the party vanishes.

I find myself at the threshold of Wolfstaff Dungeon, alone.

Is that it? Did I exit?

"Rugnus?" His name echoes off the unbroken walls.

A cacophonous group of voices startles me. "Dread, dread, dread you have come here."

When I turn, the wraith billows out, only it's Landred Wolfstaff. He's floating four feet from the ground, his lower half made of cloud and crackling lights. His arms, torso, and head are draped in cloaked shadows.

My brain suddenly assimilates the word wraith: this is what happens when someone is trapped in a dungeon with the death of a champion—immortality as vapor and light.

My voice shakes when I speak. "What are you? Are you—"

A myriad of voices respond, but Landred's is the clearest. "We, the imprisoned, keep our secrets fast."

The cloud swallows the man, becoming a twisted cyclone, then flattens into a bulbous disk. My body responds to the threat before I can process everything. I retreat to the edge of the room, but there's no exit.

The wraith approaches, and I raise my hands like I can stop a cloud. With a laugh, it pins me down—a crying howl assaults my ears.

I scream. "No!"

The mass of cloud and light covers me. I shrink reflexively, tucking in my arms and head. I know the cloud wants to feed on me, drain me of craft.

Then it stops.

I squint through half-open eyes, but the cloud is gone. The shadowy figure of Landred Wolfstaff stands before me, his face as sad and gaunt as it was at the party. His gray clothes billow as if in the wind. The red around his eyes grants him the eternal appearance of being enraged.

"What did you do to me?" I say.

He looks behind him to the door of the dungeon, inclines his head in thought, and vanishes. I can only assume something's been taken from me. Which one of the crafts did he drain? It's as if I've been taking care of someone's animals for a weekend before they were sent to the butcher.

Landred appears at the door, but he's different, more solid. This is the man I saw ridiculed at the party for his attachment to his mother.

Understanding finally reaches me: I'm watching something that happened in the past.

No craft guards the door, and though the marble itself is heavy, Landred pulls it outward. I follow him inside.

Beyond, I find a simple room, unadorned besides a wooden chair and slab made comfortably into a bed with a large cushion.

An old woman strains to sit up from the bed. "No, Landred. It is against my wishes. Leave."

I'm the intruder here. It's a personal moment between a mother and her son. "Sorry," I say, but neither of them responds. I'm only watching this.

Landred seizes her hand. "What of my wish? You are all I have. In our fame, we raided the dungeons of this world, tamed the wolves, but..."

He loses control, weeping. His mother, her old face puckered in anger, weeps with him.

This is Torlina Wolfstaff lying here. What had Rugnus said? Dungeons are made when champions die. Champions. The word seems wrong. I had pictured something more triumphant. But there's nothing triumphant in this woman's death or her son's pitiful cries.

Wolfstaff's body is racked with a fit of wet coughing. Her son tries to soothe her, gently patting her arm, lifting a napkin to her lips. Her breath catches. The awful sound of it trembles in the room. Her fists tighten upon the bedsheets, but only for a moment until her eyes roll back in her head and her limp form drops to the soft pillow.

"Mother." His sobbing goes on until he has no more voice. His desperation reverberates off the pale marble. He hums for her —the melody from the maze, from my own memories of Dad. This desperation connects us. I know this loneliness, what it's like to be without a mother. Isolated. If Dad used craft, would he become a champion? Would I someday find myself surrounded by marble walls weeping for his loss?

When Wolfstaff's son lifts his face from sobbing, he says, "I don't fear being like you."

I don't have time to process what he means. Is he speaking to me again? The walls expand, and the room grows to the size of a football field. When he reaches for the bed, his hands slip through it. His form is closer to a wraith. Suddenly he flies over to me and lifts me by the arm.

We sail through the dungeon, through walls, and out into a sort of black nothingness. It's there, in the void, where he drops me.

I plummet into an abyss for a full minute. Panic rising in my stomach.

But I hit a hard surface.

The fall should've ground me into pools of nothing filled with bits of bones. I stand upright in a stretching field of tall grass. My body is tangible again. The chain mail is gone. I'm left only with my sister's cobalt ring and my mother's bicycle chain necklace.

There's no sun, but the sky is an overpowering white, only a hint of gray-blue.

Another illusion inside the dungeon.

Something in the grass catches my eye—a wooden pail. A black metal rod sticks out above the rim. Tungsten. When I lift the rod out, the air fills with the reverberation of grinding stone. A second later, the horizon becomes a towering wall in every direction, squeezing inward, eating up the prairie as it comes. Even the sky flattens toward the ground, though the sun seems trapped above me.

I resign to being crushed. There's nothing else to do, the tungsten rod useless in my hand. When the walls are within thirty feet on all sides, the screaming starts. I swivel around. It's Dad. No, wait, my mother and my sister, too! I try to run to them, but the walls are collapsing on us. They're screaming for my help. Our whole family will die, and it will be my fault. I can't protect them.

As we huddle together, my mother says, "It's alright, Clayson. We're a family now."

"A family now," my sister repeats.

I know I'm in the dungeon, but everything's too real. My fear of losing them rushes in faster than the walls.

Fear.

The white quartz. "Okay, I'm afraid! I need help!"

My only job is to protect them. To face my fear of losing them when I've only just discovered the nature of our family: the craft hanging over my mother and I, my sister not knowing I existed, and Dad escaping to the surface to raise a son who can never sleep. But in this strange world, how can I have any power to protect them?

Out of instinct, I try.

I leave their embrace and extend the tungsten rod into the air, commanding the object to protect them. Far above me, the sun quivers turns a translucent white and plummets. It's not the sun. It's only light. Warmth and protection radiate from it. The walls close in on the sphere of light, and my family steps into the protective bubble. It scorches the grass, but we're safe. The light intensifies, not stark, but revealing and alive. The walls blast into white sand, rushing away into a void.

Each member of my family smiles at me and fades away. They weren't real, but my heart snags against the image. I float upward. The tungsten object in my hand transforms, curling around my finger and tightening into a ring. A white platform appears, and I follow it toward a lighted door—the exit.

Landred Wolfstaff is there waiting. This must be his true form. His face is opaque, stretched like paper over his swollen bones. His skeletal fingers point to the ring on my hand. "Mother grants you the ring—for now. Its name is Ergal. Few know of it. Two came for it. Two left it behind."

He vanishes.

MAKE A FAKE ID

RUGNUS LAPS up my account like a hungry bulldog. As he dances on his toes, the mercury threatens to spill from the summator he holds. "Keep going. What happened after you followed Wolfstaff's son?"

"Landred. He brought me to the threshold of Wolfstaff, but... I think it was... maybe before his mother died. If that's possible. Then he turned into that cloud thing."

Rugnus steps back, hand over his heart. "D-did he touch you?"

"I mean, the cloud came right on top of me, and then, yeah, a version of him grabbed me after we watched his mother die."

"Are you sure he touched you?"

Something in the way Rugnus won't meet my eyes tells me none of this is normal. Maybe the wraith did take something from me. "You're making me nervous, Rugnus."

"Just... not good. I'm sorry," he sighs. "Any loss of craft will be reflected in your AMP when the summator is finished."

"So, when Torlina Wolfstaff died, he was there?"

"Yep. Just like"—he snaps his fingers—"you're trapped with them forever."

"But the wraiths in Gamgim, are they—"

"Attached to a dungeon? No, but it's the only place in the world like that. Most think there's a connection with the forest. The fact one of them grabbed you...unheard of during a summation. Can I see the ring?"

I hold up my hand, and he examines the ring carefully. "This has zero imperfections, maybe pure tungsten."

"Tungsten is shield magic, right? Stronger than the other ones."

"Not shield magic, shieldcraft, but yeah," he says. "Though calling it stronger is an overstatement. Let's say it has an edge."

He draws the bubbling summator closer to his face. When he closes his eyes, the bubbling liquid calms. "Stone upon stone. Wisdom upon knowledge. May this guide you to self-illumination and clad you in the understanding of your place under the mountain. Take your record."

At his nod, I reach into the mercury, and my fingers land on something thin and cold. When I draw it out, the mercury flecks away in beads into the summator, revealing a teal, hexagonal ID card.

My picture sets at the center of the hexagon with my name printed under it in white sparkling letters against the teal of the card:

CLAYSON BRIGHTSTORM

Not Spangler. Brightstorm. Along its edge, various circles and squares are either punched out of the card or raised in tiny bumps.

"Mother's beard!" Rugnus snatches it away from me. "Wraith definitely didn't touch you. Peerless! I thought an eight at most. A perfect ten. Trollbrick. Can you believe this?" He shakes the ID toward me and clucks his tongue. "Sorry, just excited. Never done a survey for higher than a six."

I take the ID back. A diamond-shaped bump rises from the shieldcraft rating: protection and healing. Not only is it my highest score, but it's also peerless. Was it my life on the surface taking care of Dad? Or is it part of who I am? I imagine standing between my family and Bazalrak's ax. Ergal, the Tungsten ring, coils tighter around my finger.

There are five more symbols along the back edge. "What do the symbols mean?"

Rugnus shakes off his awe. "So, you have two punches. These open ones here. Tincraft and ironcraft—could have guessed the ironcraft—those are weaknesses."

"Ironcraft, uh, elements. And tincraft, plants, right?" My failure with the tin watering can at the entrance of the plant maze.

"Yep, those are weaknesses for you. Two points each. Then goldcraft, mechcraft, bluecraft, and timecraft are all raised circles, meaning three to four points each. Average. Though a three in timecraft is about as high as you can get, most people are nulls or one at best."

"Timecraft, right. There was mercury on the chainmail. It was like I had already been down every path in the plant maze."

"Yep, because you had been. But objects like that are extremely rare outside of dungeons. Anyway, where were we? Open squares. Looks like budgecraft and silvercraft are both exceptional. And then... apparently you have mastery over coppercraft, that's animals. Eight points is incredible for a summation. But this"—he points to the only diamond shape on the card—"that's ten for ten in shieldcraft, also called leadcraft when dealing specifically with healing. But remember it uses both lead and—"

"Tungsten," I say, holding up Ergal.

On the back center of the card, I find a large number: forty-five. It's my AMP score. "So, there are other colors?"

Rugnus digs in his bag. He holds up his AMP. It's bright white. "White means mastery, my highest rating. Started with gray—that's average—then moved up to mastery in budgecraft just last year with a lot of work in the dungeons."

More than a hint of frustration comes with his words. He's worked to improve his score over time. But I'm peerless in shield-craft without trying. Not to mention my mastery of coppercraft. My mind falls on his relationship with Dad. How much time has my Dad spent as his mentor?

The urge to show off my AMP score to Dad is overwhelming.

"So, what now? Tungsten City? Can I use the AMP to get on bluelink now?"

"Not yet. We need to connect you. Can't do that with your real name. It's just... didn't expect you'd forge teal on the threshold like this. And that ring." He glances over my shoulder to the narrow exit back to the lobby. "Getting a fake AMP is gonna cost more than I thought."

"Wait, a fake AMP? I have to get a fake AMP? Then why did we even come here?"

"Relax, Clayson. We need the real one, so we can imprint the fake one. But with a peerless rating..."

"It's harder to fake?"

A smile suddenly breaks on his face. "More expensive, but I know a guy." He dumps the basket into his backpack, slings it over his shoulders, and beckons me to follow.

A gnawing sensation lodges in my stomach as I tail him away from the threshold door, but I try to ignore it.

"Do we leave the same way we came in?" I ask.

Rugnus shakes his head. "Each dungeon has two threshold lobbies. The exit and entrance."

There's a difference when we squeeze through the narrow opening. This time, instead of two gargantuan waterfalls, we are greeted by a wide hallway crisscrossed by a glimmering maze of glass.

We scout a path through the maze of glass, and my worrying thoughts return. I wanna get access to bluelink as soon as possible. I look at the name on my ID—Brightstorm. That's real, but now we're gonna change my name again. Will I have to live under a fake name, miles under the ground? Never see the sky again?

117

Never see my parents? "So, we get a fake ID, head to Tungsten City, and then what?"

"Your dad gave me my instructions: keep you hidden. That's what we're going to do."

The walls of glass make it hard to find a way out. Though the exit is clearly marked, there's no sure way to know if we are heading in the right direction. The path twists and turns and sometimes backtracks, all the while heading for a stone-framed doorway in the distance where silvery light strikes out from the opening. It reminds me of the plant maze. Why would Wolfstaff put a maze outside the dungeon anyway?

Rugnus responds as if he's reading my mind. "The keepers of each dungeon—not the champion—build the tombscapes. Entrance and exit lobbies. Everything from the shrinking corridor entrance to the waterfalls is supposed to tell us something about ourselves and our connection to Wolfstaff."

What could a maze of glass tell me about myself?

We continue on our journey, and after my tenth sigh of frustration, we stumble out of the glass maze and into a beautiful courtyard lit with flaming silver fluorescent bulbs, their luminescent tubes snaking over the walls.

Wooden benches fill in the area between paved walkways and strange bushes with translucent bark and golden leaves. One group—who must be awaiting a family member—stands excitedly when Rugnus and I approach, only to sit back down when they see us. This must be a kind of waiting area, and for a moment, only a moment, I think of the possibility of my mother and Dad jumping to their feet, along with Andalynn, coming over to greet me after my summation.

"You hear me, Clayson?" Rugnus says, shaking my shoulder.

"Huh?" I blink back into what's happening here and now.

"Wait here a few seconds while I go to the vault. Got to grab some more stuff to barter with." He eyes the teal ID in my hand. "Put that thing in your pocket before someone sees it. Keep Ide."

He's about to put his hand on his club when he stops, nods

toward the ring, and says, "Maybe we should put that in my vault."

"No. I keep the ring," I say.

His reaching hand retreats. He thinks for a split second and smiles. "Not that you would know, but that makes sense. It's a shieldcraft relic, maybe even from before the Troll Wars. Tungsten City scanners won't even be able to pick it up. As long as we don't register it manually, you'll be fine. Probably the only one of its kind. I do think we should store your sister's ring and the chain, though. They're registered objects."

"Will I be able to go to your vault to use my sister's ring?"

"Absolutely."

"Let me try to contact her before you take it."

He looks around but nods.

I sit on a bench near a reflecting pool, trying to make contact through the mirrored surface of the water. Nothing.

He glances at the pool. "I'm sure she's okay."

I hand him the ring, then the necklace. With that, he's gone, a faint tan outline pulsing in his place.

I wait on the bench. The soft light around me, a degree brighter than moonlight, reminds me of the vision Andalynn planted in my mind when I met her in Gamgim. I'm still craving more information. I wanna learn about her life in Whurrimduum, about my parents and their role in the Last War—the Mithrium War.

Rugnus pops back into existence, his backpack bulging. "Ready? Last stop before Tungsten City. This one will be fun."

I sigh as I stand.

Rugnus chuckles. "Look," he says. "We'll get to Tungsten City. Get you patched into bluelink. Find you a way to make some ferrum while we plan our next move. We can search for your dad, find a way to communicate with your sister, and try to help your mom in any way we can. But still keep you hidden. Satisfied? Doing everything your dad wanted us to do." He lowers his voice to a whisper. "And think about the ring? Won't that glorious little circle come in real handy if we have to go breaking down doors and sneaking around Whurrimduum?"

This idea reaches inside of me and yanks on a cord. He's right. And in all honesty, I can't exactly guide myself down here. Thiffimdal proved that.

"Okay," I say. "I'm with you."

"Great," he says. "One teensy thing. We have to go above granite to meet this guy. He likes to do things leafless. You know, without making a record. Well, actually, he was exiled like twenty years ago. Which is both good and bad for us. Now, I have a few lead objects for myself, but I'm not sure what that ring can do. If you need extra help, let me know. I brought some lead roll on."

He holds up a tube of deodorant but stows it in a zippered part of his backpack. Stepping closer, he grins and grabs the handle of his club.

We budge to a muddy alley between two old wooden buildings, the scent of pine and pinewood smoke in the air. Rugnus takes two steps toward the street before stumbling and catching a wall. "My lead object isn't working all that great. I can feel the fizzblood," he says between clenched teeth.

As usual, the surface causes me no side effects. Crisp autumn air fills my lungs, and a line of stars peeps from between the rooftops. I step forward and rest a hand on Rugnus' shoulder.

He spins his head around, eyes wide. "Whoa! How did you do that?"

I step back, surprised by his reaction, and when my hand leaves his shoulder, it's like a ton of bricks settles on his back.

"Do that again," he says, a sickly look cascading over his face.

Almost before my hand reaches him, he recovers.

"That is a cool ring," he says, standing. "Try using it without contact."

My hand moves away, but I force it to protect Rugnus.

Rugnus' coughing laughter fills the air. "Works kinda like Icho. It's probably best to put that thing in your pocket. Don't want this guy seeing it. Lagnar Emberfence used to run an underground black market in Tungsten City. And let me do all the talking. He may keep to himself, but he likes to know everything about everyone who walks through his door."

I tuck the ring in my pocket. Rugnus shudders, takes a deep breath, and moves forward.

We exit the alley onto the street and knock mud from our shoes as we cross the wooden planks that form a sidewalk. The facades of the stores are like something out of an old western movie. Light spills from single-pane windows and the noise of a jingling player-piano greets us.

"Where exactly are we?" I ask.

Rugnus shakes his head mournfully. "Weird, ain't it? Supposed to be an entertaining, nostalgic environment for humans, but I don't get it."

We pass the saloon, and there's a sudden commotion of shouts drowning out the piano. A dozen grimy motorcycles balance on kickstands in the dirt. Rugnus gives the machines a quick glance, and I catch a smirk on his face.

"What's funny?" I ask.

"Just taffies. They're so goofy with all the ways they use to get around the mountains. Like steam engine trains. Have you seen those things?" He makes the sound of a train chugging along. "Trains are hilarious. Oh, and have you ever seen a minivan?" Laughter wheezes out of him.

Raised, angry voices come from the bar.

"Don't hurt yourself," I say. "And you might wanna keep your voice down. Offending this particular group of humans would be a poor choice."

"You and Winta are going to get along great."

"Who's Winta?"

"Taffy lover. Works with me at Quimdem. Anything to do with humans, she follows it like it's the championship of the Hundred Dungeon Games. And don't ever get her started on the complexity of mechcraft. Techno-babble."

"Hmm." Just like with the Dura, Rugnus is dismissive of

pretty much all of humanity. How many Loamin view the world this way?

A dull orange glow, punctuated with flashes of cobalt, emanates from a building ahead. The word BLACKSMITH is burned into a massive wooden sign swinging from cast iron chains, but the most impressive sight is the life-sized bronze bear standing on its hind feet, snarling at us from the side of the shop.

"This is it," he says. As we push through a long set of doors, he adds, "Remember, keep your mouth shut."

Inside, the walls and shelves are neatly arranged with metal artwork. Displayed off to the left, a family of snowmen made from old tire rims glistens dully in the strange orange light of the shop. Beyond them, candles hang from the ceiling by elongated wicks in a variety of shapes and sizes. Below the waxy creations, on a low shelf, silver bowls, lanterns, and decorative holders lay waiting to be paired with a candle.

A worker, half a foot taller than me, clad in an orange polo shirt, jeans held up with a buckle, and an authentic pair of cowboy boots, rushes over to greet us. "Welcome to Lagnar Metals. How can I help you today? We have a new line of wall sconces I'd love to show you."

"Sconces are nice," Rugnus says. "But we're looking for Lagnar." He shouts past the employee, "Lagnar, you old thief, is this how you greet me? With your taffies?"

A motorized whirring comes from behind a shelf to the right, and a disheveled old man, his neck and face peppered with gray and white scruff, appears in a wheelchair. The hair on his head is combed back, and he wears a robin's egg colored vest. The oxygen mask tightened against his face reminds me of Dad. "Rugnus, Rugnus, Rugnus. Mover of refugees. Peerless of smuggling. How's the brick smelling in Tungsten City?"

Rugnus contorts his face. "Hey now, geezer."

"Oh, alrighty," the man says. "How's the new world order y'all built for yourself in your little bubble down there?"

Rugnus bows low. "Democracy thrives."

"Well, fine, Rugnus." He says his name with a heavy dose of mockery. "What'll it be on this here fine evening?"

Rugnus juts his head toward the tall girl as if to say, 'not in front of her'.

"Right, right, right. Candy, why don't ya go check on the boys in the shop. See if they're finished with those fire rings—not what you think, Rugnus. For taffies to roast marshmallows and what-not. They love them some sugar."

The girl's facial expression tightens, "Only my grandmother calls me Candy, Mr. Emberfence."

"Right you are, ah, Candice."

She rolls her eyes as she marches over to a set of double doors, where splashes of blue light bullet the air through the little plastic windows.

When she pushes into the shop, Lagnar says, "Alrighty there then, Mr. Rugnus—"

"You can drop the cowboy inflections, Lagnar."

"Just how I speak," Lagnar says, muffled by the oxygen mask, "and may I say, I thought you were above the sort of transactions I offer up here. Must be in some dire circumstances. What is it this time?" He looks directly at me but squints as if he needs glasses.

"I need a washed AMP," Rugnus says.

"Is that all?"

"A good one."

"Those are the only kind I forge here"—he sweeps an arm through the sky—"at Lagnar Metals. Come on back to the real workshop, and we'll get 'er done for ya."

Rugnus rolls his eyes, but Lagnar pivots around without seeing it, and we follow in his wake. It's a small space, and metal objects protrude from every shelf. He leads us past all that to the rear of the store, where the vaulted ceiling descends into a single archway. Under the wide arched ceiling, in a small alcove, there are no shelves, no decorations, but sure enough, this is exactly where we stop.

Lagnar swivels again and squints at Rugnus. "Your friend here's not a gold null, is he?"

"Nope. Should be good," Rugnus says.

Lagnar's frown extends to his neck. "Shame. I've always wanted to see if I could get someone trapped in this drain. And by the way, Rugnus, can I point out the irony that you are apparently bringing someone into your utopian democratic—uh, transparent—society, secretly."

"Yeah, yeah. Off my back, would you please? Who's going first?"

"Not so fast. You know the drill."

Rugnus sighs but takes out Icho and rests it against the wall.

"You, too," Lagnar says to me.

Rugnus intercedes. "He doesn't have any budges. Been traveling together."

"What's he? A null? Near null? If he's got a budge on him, the foil won't work. He'd just clog the pipe. You gonna clog my pipe, Mr. can't-talk-cause-Rugnus-told-me-not-to?"

"Stop messing around," Rugnus says.

"Wait twenty seconds." Lagnar rips some gold-foil from a small roll hanging from a hook. He crumples it and stuffs it under his oxygen mask. His jaw works as he chews the paper.

Rugnus extends an arm, pushing me forward a foot or so. In the second it takes, Lagnar and his wheelchair become one fluid mass, a wobbling shape like he's been recently popped out of a jello mold. A sloping suction sound reverberates in the alcove. Lagnar is reduced in size until the last bits of his combed back, salt-and-pepper hair disappears down the golden drain.

"Okay, that happened," I say. "We're not—"

Rugnus gets that twinkle in his eye, the one he gets when he shows me something new and—at least to him—exciting. "Yep. Grab some paper. You're next."

"I've got to eat this thing?" I say, carefully breaking off another tiny sheet of gold foil.

"No. Lagnar was just being dramatic. I mean, he could use a

budge. Instead he chooses to use goldcraft. I don't claim to understand him. Hold the paper in your hand. Should be fine."

"Should be?"

"You will be. Now step on the drain."

My eyes fix on the drain, still gurgling from having sucked down Lagnar. I shake my head at Rugnus. "When this is all done, I'm coming back to the surface, and I'm gonna live a normal life. Me and my dad again, maybe my mother and sister."

It's the first time I've said this out loud, but nothing could be more true. It's the only desire I have left. Normal. I step over the drain.

Rugnus says, "You have a strange definition of normal," and his words echo around inside my skull. My elbows and knees send out rips of energy that make me cringe. The same as with my mother's gold blood, it's like hitting my funny bone except at every hinge in my body. My skin tightens. I become a liquid and melt toward the floor. Then all is black like I'm trapped in a darkened water slide until I land in a heap of goo on a warm surface.

My body reforms quickly, and I step from a massive golden disk wedged into the floor. Lagnar is waiting for me. "So why are you so important you have to hide? Or maybe you have something valuable. Information? A relic? Or are you the heir to one of the keepers, perhaps?"

As Rugnus reforms next to me, I resist the impulse to reach for my ring. Lagnar has something in his eyes like a viper waiting to strike, but only if we show weakness.

"Nice try," Rugnus says. "But you were right. He's under strict instructions to keep his mouth shut and his head down."

"Yeah. Yeah. The surface may have ruined my eyesight, but he looks... something's off here. I can sense it. Vulnerability." Lagnar sounds deeply reflective, but then his tone shifts. "Anyway, a washed ΛMΓ."

He scoots over to a messy table cluttered with wads of aluminum foil. The small room is the polar opposite of the shop upstairs. A soot encrusted forge and crucible surrounded with a circle of hot-white embers, a wall of jars and velvet bags, and a red brick floor. It reminds me of Rugnus' vault, except not hyper-organized. It's cluttered and well worn.

But Lagnar fits with the place. He grabs one of the balls of foil and unwraps it, revealing a gray ID card, another AMP. "Here we go. This oughta—"

"We need a master's AMP. Needs to show at least a seven for protective augmentation."

"Well, golly, Rugnus. That's a mighty big request for a little ol' blacksmith like myself."

"Can you do it?" Rugnus says, exasperation creeping into his voice for the first time.

Lagnar gropes around the table and pulls out a white AMP identical to Rugnus'. He drops the western accent for a second. "This one will cost you."

Rugnus removes the extra bag from his shoulder and dumps it onto the table, unloading four objects from his forbidden collection of relics. He only had fourteen to begin with. "There. My chips are down."

The way he talks about objects and relics—with an unashamed reverence—I can almost see the weight of the cost settling on him like a cloak. This is what Rugnus' relationship with Dad means to him. I'm not big on owing people, but I owe Rugnus, and I vow to find a way to make this up to him.

Lagnar folds his arms. He scrutinizes me again. "This must be real sensitive, real sensitive. Last time, we haggled for another hour, and I barely scraped a profit out of you."

Rugnus shrugs, and after a brief pause, Lagnar throws up his hands. "Fine."

He works quickly, rolling over to the shelf and finding a wide-mouthed blue jar. Pulling a handful of yellowish marbles from a bag, he combines them with the master's AMP inside the blue jar. With the lid in the other hand, he swings around to me. "All that's left is for you to drop your real AMP in the jar, seal it, and place it in the crucible."

Rugnus takes the jar and passes it to me, nodding. When I take my teal-colored AMP from my pocket, Lagnar laughs out loud, squinting. "Would you look at that? Peerless." he says. "How old are you?"

"He's sixteen," Rugnus lies.

Before much else can be said, I add my AMP to the jar, seal it, and cross the room. I take the jar with a pair of large tongs and rest it in the crucible inside the forge.

"Should only take about two minutes," Lagnar says. "You boys want something to eat?" There's a pile of heavily spiced chicken drumsticks on the table, resting on stoneware.

My stomach rumbles. It looks and smells like something Dad might barbeque. But after the burgers with Rugnus, I can't tell if there's some craft involved.

"No thanks." The words tumble out of my mouth, and I can't put them back.

Lagnar purses his lips, and his eyes—drained of all humor—find me. "You sound like...no. Can't be. Could it?" He grabs a pill bottle from the table, pops the lid, and siphons out a few pills, taking them without water, never removing his eyes from me.

"Blood thinners?" He says, offering Rugnus some of the medication.

"Does that really help with fizzblood?" Rugnus asks but shakes his head.

Lagnar reaches to his side. His fingers find the nozzle for the oxygen tank, and he cranks it open. He finds the chicken, picks up a drumstick, and points it at Rugnus. "I bet I never told you the story about how I got exiled, did I? It was all hush-hush. You can't even find it on bluelink. Ironic, seeing how I'd been next in line to be keeper of Bluebottle Dungeon. See, it was, oh, about eighteen years ago. The Prince of Rimduum got wind of something I had done, under orders, mind you. But it wasn't a good thing. Well, back then, people needed other people to take the blame for all that had happened."

In the darkened room, Rugnus takes a step to his left, then

another. He's a foot closer to me, his posture bristling like he's readying for a fight. I tense. Lagnar is still casually waving the drumstick at both of us. But his other hand picks up two large blue-glass spheres. He twirls them in his fingers, looks off in another direction, and squints hard. Is he reading something on bluelink?

"During my inquisition," he continues, "before they handed down the sentence, I told the prince—the prince of that backstabbing kingdom of trollbrick—I told him, I said: Therias, if you exile me, for following the orders given to me by your own dear old dad, the King—rest in peace—I'll never forgive you. And here I am, years later, the same poisonous wedge stuck in my heart, grown over like a splinter that ain't never gotten taken care of."

The glass jar shatters in the hearth. Rugnus nods at me to get the AMP, so I grab a pair of tongs and dig around in the embers. The only AMP is white. It bears the name Clayson Glintwheel and an AMP score of twenty-nine.

"Work of art," Rugnus says, almost too loudly. "Thanks, Lagnar. You have a good one."

"Oh, no, no, no, no, no," Lagnar chides us. "You're mistaken if you think I'm gonna let the very son—the prince's prince—leave my forgeside alive."

Rugnus throws an arm in front of me and reaches behind him for his club.

"Left that thing upstairs, even if you had a budge"—Lagnar lifts his oxygen mask, takes a bite of the chicken, chews, and swallows—"this here's my rodeo. My town. And I'm the sheriff. Not even I can budge out of this room."

Rugnus lets go of me. Flames burst along his spine and at his hands, ten times hotter than the forge next to me. I have to take a step back.

"Then we'll fight our way out," Rugnus says.

I slipped Ergal onto my finger.

An alarm blares from the back of the room.

"That'll be the knights," Lagnar says. "Just because they

kicked me out of the Kingdom doesn't mean I don't have friends. Many who are still willing to kill for me. I was a general, you know."

There's more slurping, and Rugnus and I both stop, angling toward the drain in the ceiling, where a red goop drips to the floor. Someone reforms upon the golden circle, blocking our only exit.

ARRIVE IN THE SKY

I BLINK A HALF-DOZEN TIMES, but even after the person reforms below the drain, I glance at Rugnus for confirmation. Andalynn, my sister, steps off the golden circle in a red velvet party dress, the same tin bracelets, the same flowing hair, the same fierce determination set in her features. Lagnar Emberfence squints at her as a grin spreads over my face.

"Andalynn?" I say.

Lagnar spins his wheelchair away from the table. "Wraithspit!"

"Don't be so surprised, Lagnar," she says. "I've had a trace on your contacts in the knights for years. They never got your message. You shouldn't have mentioned my family."

She's halfway to a smile when a bright ring of tan light pulses through the room. Lagnar vanishes from the table, his wheelchair left behind, only to reappear with the sound of crashing shelves in the corner of the room.

He was telling the truth. Even he can't budge out of the room.

There's a loud pop as one of the glass jars bursts on a shelf beyond the table, blue marbles drumming downward in a flood. Then another jar, and another, until marbles are raining from the shelves, gathering in pools on the stone floor.

"Clayson, the ring!" Rugnus gathers fire around his hands.

My mind whirls. "Right."

An air force of glimmering marbles rises in the center of the room. Rugnus sends a band of fire into the air, but when it fizzles away, the arsenal of marbles have become molten bullets, ready to fly.

My fist tightens around the ring, and it pulses with white light.

Lagnar growls, and as the marbles begin to spin, something else happens. A chain-link fence extends from both sides of the room, like fast-freezing ice, the ends meeting in the middle.

Rugnus raises his eyebrows. "A fence?"

Lagnar laughs, hurdling the marbles toward us. I flinch, turning my shoulder to absorb the attack. The marbles zip through the gaps between chains and bombard us. I glance at my body halfway through, expecting to see massive puncture wounds. Why am I not in serious pain? Maybe I'm in shock.

Rugnus is laughing. Yep, we're in shock.

His hands are full of something. The marbles? The small pieces are gathered around my feet. I grab a handful. They're crisp pieces of fluff.

"Roasted marshmallows," I say.

"Keep Ide," Rugnus says, peering at the fluffy roasted bits in his hands, eyes wide. "How'd you do that?" He pops one in his mouth. "Mm." His shoulders slump in pure bliss.

The fence dematerializes.

The second it takes Rugnus to sneak another roasted marshmallow, Andalynn crosses the room and seizes Lagnar by the collar.

There's a pulse of red light as Lagnar struggles against her. His hands turn into thick metal objects, one a hammer, the other a pair of sharp needle-nose pliers. But Andalynn taps her forehead against his, and he crumples into sleep. She catches him with ease, her arms glowing silver and gold. Rugnus nods admiringly as she drags his heavy body to the wheelchair and dumps him unceremoniously.

She shakes her head and huffs a breath. "You two seem to be having a lot of fun making my life more difficult."

Rugnus scoops up another handful of marshmallows. "Eat while they're warm."

I ignore him, shove past the table, and squeeze my sister into a hug. "I changed my mind. I know I'm supposed to go to Tungsten City with Rugnus, but I don't want to. I'll come with you and—"

"Hold on there," Rugnus says, swallowing another mouth full of marshmallows.

"Clayson." Andalynn hangs her head, her voice soft. "You can't. I was wrong. There's too much going on. It'll just complicate things. Our father—however foolish—is right to shield you from all this. I can help you better if you stay hidden."

My stomach lurches. Yesterday she wanted me to come with her. I start to protest, but Rugnus sniffs loudly.

"Very sensible," he says, looking at my sister in a way that makes me wanna lash out and punch him. "But what about Emberfence?"

Andalynn pats the man's shoulder. "In a few minutes, he won't even remember what he had for breakfast, let alone his encounter with you two morons. Ide keep us."

Rugnus eyes her, taking a step back. "Forgot you're kinda scary."

She inclines her head.

"In a good way," he adds.

Her demeanor is suddenly as hard as a stone. "Protect him, or you will have me to face."

"I-I like your face. It's very, uh, angular. I mean, kinda pointy. Don't get me wrong, pointy is good. I—"

I slap him on the back of the head. It's the only thing I can do. I didn't know I had a protect-your-sister reflex. Besides, he sounds like a complete lunatic.

"Right, anyway," he says. "See what your little brother did? You should know—peerless in shields."

"Really?" Her all-business mask drops away for a second but returns quickly. "Good. He's going to need it. This issue with my father...strange things are happening everywhere. Including in Helgrimral."

"Tungsten City," Rugnus says.

"Whatever you want to call the city, there are forces at work I don't understand. Dangerous things are happening. A business called Handler—"

"Yeah. That's the business hosting the Keeper's Social." Rugnus says. "Trying to make budgecraft stronger than foilgrips. They're a century away. What's so important about them?"

Andalynn lowers her voice. "A conversation I was not supposed to be privy to. It seems Bazalrak and Theridal Silver-keeper are working with the CEO of Handler on something. No one is supposed to know about Bazalrak's involvement."

"Then how do you know?" Rugnus says.

"I have good friends. Anyway, it has something to do with the lost mithrium."

"What?" Rugnus, and I ask.

"And Silverlamp Dungeon, where Silverkeeper is—"

"Keeper," Rugnus finished.

There's a weight to her words I'm unable to grasp. "Is that important?"

Andalynn's eyes widen. "It's like our father told you nothing."

Lagnar groans, breathing heavily into the table.

"You two need to leave," Andalynn says. "Rugnus, you'll have to tell him as much as you can. But keep Clayson away from Handler."

"I need to contact Dad," I say. "Then maybe we can sneak into Whurrimduum, help you both escape. Find someplace to—"

"You will do no such thing. Clayson, I don't think you understand how dangerous this is. Rugnus, please protect him from stupidity. We both know, even with a peerless rating, he can't go storming into Whurrimduum." She shoves me lightly. "Go."

Rugnus drags me beneath the drain and forces me to break off a small piece of gold foil. Before I step under the gilded pipe, I grip the fake AMP in my pocket. Something resolves inside my mind. "We'll have a normal life, Andalynn. I'm gonna make sure of that."

I'm nudged forward. As I transform into gelatin, my sister says, "I wish that were true."

I step off the golden drain into Lagnar's store. Rugnus grabs Icho, kisses it, and then smooths down his shirt. Candice comes from around a shelf a second later. She blinks and shakes her head like she's trying to get water out of her ears. "Where is Mr. Emberfence?"

"He'll, uh, be a moment—all that spicy chicken," Rugnus says.

We charge through the doors and along the street without a moment's hesitation. The sun is creeping into the sky. Rugnus asks for me to put a hand on his back. There are raised voices coming from somewhere, but we slip into the alley to catch our breath.

"I was hoping I'd have more time to prepare you for this," Rugnus says, "but we've got to go. There's the perfect budgeport at the top of the citybarrel."

"Prepare me for what?" I ask.

"For this."

The added gravity tells me we're budging—I like having at least that much warning—then, I'm jerked away from the sleepy western town, dropped into an entirely new world. Disorientation strikes me. The walkway at my feet is made from sheets of porous metal. Moonlight reflects off every surface. I crane my head past the handrails of the walkway.

The moon is below me to the right, a silver-green orb, hanging suspended beneath us in the sky, alive with waves of shimmering light, real enough to make me believe I could reach out and pluck it from the air. But it can't be the moon because above me, there's a mile of stone. My mind walks back to Thiffimdal with its ruinous underground sun, to the fallout and the bodies. I can't piece together all the elements of this world.

"Where are we, Rugnus?"

"See it?" Rugnus' voice echoes off the metal, off the stone.

"The moon?"

"No, no. Look past that. Down the barrel, to the bottom of the cavern."

I squint past the moon. This is the kind of view you get of a city only in movies, the perspective of a drone or helicopter. Despite the moonlight playing tricks on me, I find what Rugnus wants me to see. A crest of electric light. The stamp of a city, like I'm passing it in orbit...

"A city? That can't be right."

"Tungsten City. The future of Rimduum. Broke from the Kingdom of Rimduum at the end of the Last War."

"There's electricity."

"What did you expect?"

"And—are those skyscrapers? I can barely make them out from here."

"Yeah, that's why they put 'city' in the title."

This city itself might as well be from another planet. It's a distinct ring of electricity, a blur of rainbow colors. In the center of the ring, the fire of electricity gives way to dimmer lights and inky swells of asymmetrical blackness. What could fill those spaces? The walkway holding us up is suspended by corded metal columns attached to the rocky ceiling of the sky a few hundred feet above me. I'm both below the mountain and in the air.

Rugnus now gets to be the one to steady me. He places a hand on my back. "Hm? What do you think?"

My breath stalls. An entire city is hidden from all other life on earth, buried under miles of rock and dirt. A cold sickness spreads around my chest, and this image is replaced again, by Thiffimdal, with its icy sun, the vaulted room I found myself in, covered in thick frost. Mithrium created that horror.

That view was closer than this one, much closer.

I push away the images of the frozen bodies and focus on the vibrant city below.

"It-it's amazing," I say.

That smile—his default setting—hasn't left his face. "Thought the budge port here on Dolindur's Stairway would be the best place to orient you to your new home. Let's you get a sense of the size of the whole place. Every citybarrel has a different shaped cavern. Tungsten City is a cylinder. About two miles wide, seven miles deep. And just wait, swear you haven't seen anything yet, by silver. And we're right on time."

He scans the air as if he's reading something. "Perfect. Got five minutes until nightchange. Oh, and you'll need this."

From his bag, he draws a long rectangle of aluminum studded with blue glass. He slaps it onto my wrist, where it curls around. "Default budge, plus bluelink. You can go anywhere in the city now. Come on, let's get closer."

We budge inside a strange, brightly lit building where the walls and vaulted ceilings are made of ice-blue glass inlaid with pulsing veins of liquid metal. A sheen of light, the color of bell-flowers, glows all around. We're in the foyer of some massive skyscraper, alive with hundreds of people scurrying to places unknown. I shake my head.

"Sorry," he says, "Still strange, I bet, budging."

"Not that much."

"Fair warning: Icho has a unique rating, maybe not as strong as your ring, but as far as budgecraft goes, I haven't seen its equal —pure aluminum. But I think you'll find other budges to be much more jarring."

We move toward the center of the foyer, where there are large, polished sheets of aluminum embedded into already reflective marble floors. A woman in front of me, her shoulders wrapped with a foil-lined shawl, strides over one of the aluminum sheets, boots clicking noisily, and stops. As she adjusts a gold clip in her hair, she vanishes.

"Like these budge ports, for example," Rugnus says. "Pretty high-grade craft, but if your AMP in budgecraft is less than a three, it will make you a bit sick to your stomach."

"Wait," I say, thinking about all the strange physical sensations from the last two days. "I haven't asked this before, and I kinda guessed, but does each type of craft have a different sensation to it?"

Rugnus groans and slaps his head. "Sorry, forgot that part. Yeah, though the better the object and the higher your skill, the less you feel the effect. Your ring, for example. Shieldcraft. You should feel an ache in your muscles like you've spent the day lifting stone. But with your, uh, higher rating, and a relic like Ergal, you may not feel it at all. And I know Icho cuts back on the feeling of gravity and nausea connected to budgecraft, except for nulls and near nulls who have a score of zero to one in that type of craft."

"To get to Gamgim, my dad gave me this energy drink thing. That seemed rough."

Rugnus stops dead. "That's right. And those things are nasty. What was he thinking? If your budgecraft rating was less than two, you could've popped out missing a few parts."

"Sounds like my dad. He loves his surprises."

"Seriously. He waits until the last possible second to tell you anything." He pauses. "Well, if you've been through that, this will be easy."

As I'm processing the connection between Dad and Rugnus again, we step on the aluminum budge port. My calves are drawn down with the added gravity, my shoulders heavy, but the pressure wanes until everything is normal again.

We appear at the top of the same building, or at least I assume we have. It's constructed of identical ice-blue glass, pulsing with silver veins. Purple-lighted spires ascend into the dark sky all around us. Rugnus leads me up wide staircases and under looping archways toward the center of the building until we stop at the highest point along a stone railing.

"Behold," he says. "Your first nightchange."

We're inside the ring of city buildings I saw from above. The cityscape before me is a spectacular array of light and architecture. The moon, which I can only assume is made by craft, floats in the center of the long cylinder-shaped cavern. Directly below the moon, the land is flat and dark, but closer to me, it's alive with light and color, like the Las Vegas strip.

Rugnus must have chosen the highest building in Tungsten City. But it's the tallest jewel in the ring that forms the city skyline. Strange, almost living buildings lay huddled together, gathered along the rim of the cavern. Some appear as if they've been grown organically from crystal. Others are built of tough chiseled stone. Less than two miles away, the border of the city-sized cavern is carved directly into the walls. A few skyscrapers float lazily through the sky in vivid shimmering colors. Closest to me, thick, forest-green vines wrap around an entire brownstone skyscraper.

In a brilliant flash, sunlight bathes the whole city like someone flipped a light switch. I blink away spots. A breath involuntarily leaves my body. The night had hidden every detail from me, and my eyes soak it up hungrily. The flat, dark areas in the center of the city ring, directly under the city's light source, are sprawling agricultural fields and lakes.

Closer to me, the thick vines around the brownstone skyscraper erupt with flowers as large as houses. A flock of boney birds takes flight from a squat star-shaped building, joined by an even larger flock bursting from a canopy of trees, which must be redwoods or something as tall as them. A few building-sized flying machines in the distance click with gears while knitting together a new building as easy as putting together toy bricks. Glass and stone canyons beginning at the street level hint at urban development extending deep beyond what is visible to my eyes. They must have carved the city into the stone for miles beneath us.

In everything I've seen in life—or even on TV—nothing could've prepared me for the sight of such a place.

"There's so much life," I say, my voice a reverent whisper.

Rugnus squints against the sunlight, a finger stretched out toward the glimmering ball hovering in the sky miles above us. "The brightstorm."

"Brightstorm? As in..."

"Your great, great, great—well, however many greats—grandfather. The first king of Rimduum. That"—he nods toward the sun—"is your legacy, Clayson. It's how your family came by their name. The moment he forged the brightstorm, his new name echoed in the minds of every Loamin on Ide. The end of clans, the end of warfare, scarcity, hunger. Before the brightstorms, Loamin used all kinds of things to light the underground. But he forged hundreds of them—just had to find mountains with the right elevation. Combed over all of Ide to find them. Ushered in the Age of Discovery."

Warmth cascades through me. "Spangler."

"What?"

"My last name. Or what I thought was my last name. Our family crest is—"

"A sun. The symbol of Erikzin Brightstorm. His dungeon rests under the ruins of Kalisserl, but his legacy... well, look."

My wrist grows suddenly warm as a ringtone chimes. A pleasant male voice says, "Clayson Glintwheel, welcome to your new home in Tungsten City, the ancient site of the first intercontinental magma crossing and the cultural heart of the once-powerful, but now defunct, Kingdom of Rimduum. Please review the following Citizen Contract and make your mark with your record of Assumed Measured Power."

"Uh, Rugnus?" I say. "You hearing this voice? It wants me to—"

"Right, the Citizen Contract. Happens at nightchange every day. The city scans for new AMPs and sends out the contracts. Just follow the instructions."

A layer of augmented reality text pops up in front of me. I scan the fine print on the document, which scrolls naturally each time I reach the last readable line. There's no way to remember all of the terms of this contract. "Rugnus?"

"Don't have to read the whole thing, just scroll to the bottom and attach your mark. I'll summarize the Citizens Contract later. And here, I'm sending you a button to link me in."

A flaming icon of Rugnus appears above the words, and I press it to link him in. I keep scrolling and scrolling. In some spots, the words are actually changing as I read them. I find large flashing letters at the bottom:

HOLD YOUR AMP IN YOUR LEFT HAND.

Shaking my head, I free the AMP from my pocket.

TEST STRENGTHS WITH A CERTIFIED SURVEYOR.

"Oh," Rugnus says, "my part now." He extends his hand and grasps my forearm.

SWEAR YOU WILL BE FAITHFUL TO THE PRINCIPLES OF FREEDOM AND THE PRECEPTS OF COMMUNITY LOCATED HEREIN.

Not with much confidence, I say, "I swear."

The AMP becomes heavier in my hand.

The voice returns. "Thank you, Clayson Glintwheel. Again, we welcome you to Tungsten City. You now have full access to bluelink. We hope you will find peace and happiness in your new life away from the dominating control of the Kingdom of Rimduum. Congratulations to you for escaping tyranny."

With that, the voice retreats, but a string of blue words pop up in front of me. I'm not sure how to feel about having things in my field of vision all the time. It's not natural.

TO ACCESS BLUELINK, MAKE THE FOLLOWING GESTURE:

It shows a picture of praying, holographic hands. They gesture apart. I've seen Rugnus do this.

I complete the gesture, and suddenly my vision is crammed with three-dimensional objects. Off to my left spins a large version of the symbol from Rugnus' stacks of money, a cursive f with one large strike and two thin ones. In the center rests a tablet of dull-gray metal, scratched with a single word: *NEWS*.

"Hey, don't get lost in there," Rugnus says. "You're so easy to read. I've already checked the news this morning. No updates. Your mother's inquisition is still scheduled for Khalsday."

Rugnus' last word triggers something in my brain, and I start to mutter to myself. "If Monday was Zinsday, and Uulsday was Tuesday, then it wouldn't be strange to be followed by Lensday."

"What, in a troll's tilted beard, are you talking about?"

"My dad. He taught me the days of the week." I continue the nursery rhyme he used to recite to me. "And Dursday's the worst day, and Friday's now Alsday. The weekend's now here. Old names disappear. Silly words in our ears. It's brighter on Khalsday and Soonsday cartoons day."

"Oh, good, you know the days of the week, you'll pass as a latchmage. Until someone asks you how many bars there are in a tenblock."

"Wait. What's a bar?"

"About twice the height of a Loamin."

"Okay, so how many bars are in a tenblock?"

"Your dad didn't bother to teach you measurement, huh? You'll just have to fake it until you brush up a bit. Close bluelink and follow me."

I try the reverse gesture I used to open bluelink. It works; the words and icons disappear.

As we descend from the heights of the building, Rugnus' club bounces in his holster at his back. "Why didn't you use the club to bring us right to the top of the building?"

"Kinda frowned upon to pop up wherever you want. There are designated budge ports for most places, then you use their internal budges. Suppose I could, but it's technically a breach of the citizen's contract. Part of the precepts of community. No one would call the paladins on you for that."

We reach the budge port and appear in the lobby again. Rugnus scrutinizes my face. "Got to go to work in about thirty minutes. Maybe while I'm gone, you could get some rest, time to yourself. I... hold up." Rugnus opens bluelink with a gesture. He scans something. "Uh, let's make a quick stop first. This will be cool. Then you can have the rest of the day off."

Fighting against a crowd of people flooding into the lobby, we exit under arching ice-blue doorways. The courtyard outside is almost too normal. It could be any day in a city park on the surface, people bustling through their morning commute, though oddly appearing out of thin air. A fountain made of white crystalline cylinders shoots mercury into the air. Gnarled, silver-green willow trees form a snaking boundary around the courtyard, saturated with light from the brightstorm high above us.

"Ready?" Rugnus asks me.

A pair of doves, with ethereal florescent markings, settle on the side of the fountain close to us.

"One more stop," I say. "Then I'm gonna break the internet trying to figure this place out."

"Bluelink. But okay. I get you. Makes sense. If I got thrown above granite and had to make a home there, I'd be lost."

"Exactly."

He reaches behind him slowly and we budge, reappearing in a long, shadowed room, like an empty floor of a skyscraper, rays of emerald light striking through an exterior wall of windows. Industrial basins—like giant sinks without faucets—form long rows from one end of the room to the other. Black earth, heavy and wet, rests inside the waist-high basins.

"Where are we?" I say.

142

Before he can answer, a rich melodic voice with a hint of frustration says, "Good, you're here. Hold this."

A girl, nothing but curly hair and skin like deep-stained pine boards, brushes past me. I smell something like spring lilacs and motor oil. She drops a greasy gear into Rugnus hands, not bothering to look at him as she squeezes between rows of countertops.

"Just coming to check on everything before the Keeper's Social. Need anything?" Rugnus says.

"Nope," she says, crouching beside one of the narrow tables, fiddling with something underneath, still faced away from us.

Rugnus doesn't seem to mind that she isn't exactly paying attention to him. "Hemdi wanted me to see something."

A head pops out from behind another table, broad face, dark bangs down to his dark eyebrows. His eyes smile as he says, "That we did, my friend. And...wait, who is this?" His rich, almost Spanish accent hangs in the air. South America somewhere? Can that be right? Are there Loamin in South America? Rugnus told me the names of all the other kingdoms, but I can't remember them. A grin spreads over the boy's wide face as he stands and cuts around the table with an arm extended in greeting. He's shorter than all of us by a half foot.

We test our strengths, as Rugnus called it.

"Well met, ah, I'm sorry, what is your name?"

My mind goes blank. I can't remember the last name. "Clayson," I say.

Rugnus slaps him on the back. "Hemdi meet Clayson Glintwheel. Clayson, this is Hemdi. And that's Winta Brinzja. She's a master in both mechcraft and bluecraft. And the only person I know with a six in timecraft. Which is pretty much peerless. Not even your—" Rugnus stammers for a second. "Well, not even Therias Brightstorm has a six in temporal manipulation."

"Very nice, Rugnus," she says. "Another refugee. Where did you pick this one up?"

"Whurrimduum, for your information," Rugnus answers.

Hemdi views me with a new appreciation. "Winta, take it easy on the kid. I was new to Tungsten City not long ago. And your mother—"

Winta frowns and goes back to working on the mechanical device in her hand.

Seeing my discomfort, Hemdi chuckles. "If you hang around long enough, you will get used to Winta's, uh, tough outer shell. By the way, I have heard that breaking out of Whurrimduum is extremely dangerous. Rugnus won't tell us his secret. How many people have you gotten out of there now?"

Is that what Rugnus does? Sneaks people out of dangerous places? No wonder Dad sent me to him.

Rugnus clears his throat. "I've lost count. Anyway, Clayson has a very high rating in shieldcraft. So, it made it easier."

Winta is still working on attaching some metal gears to the underside of the table. "How high a rating?" she asks.

"Seven."

Now finished with her work, she spins around. Emerald light from the windows cast her in a strange, alluring light. Suddenly, I'm stuck in place. Usually, girls my age are taller, more intimidating. When she smiles, it's something simple and straightforward, and it makes me lightheaded.

"Okay, sorry," she says. "Suppose I'd try to get out of there too." Her hand brushes Hemdi's arm, and my back straightens involuntarily. "All fixed. Let's try this again."

"Watch this," Hemdi says. "All this talk of the Keeper's Social. I wanted to have something to impress a few of the keepers." He places his hands on the tin sides of one of the tables. The types of metal flash through my mind again, reminding me—tin is used for plants. The whole room makes more sense now. The earth-filled basins and strange light. It's some type of indoor greenhouse

Nothing happens.

Hemdi grunts, then removes his hands from the basin, crestfallen. A split second later and his optimistic smile returns.

Winta, however, looks like she might smash one of the tables to pieces. She blows out a breath of frustration, and a strand of her brown curly hair wavers against her forehead.

Hemdi puts a hand soothingly on her back. "It will work. It needs a little more care, that's all. So, it won't be ready for the Keeper's Social."

"If we use Linterna," she says.

"No, no," Rugnus says. "Don't use that. It's a relic."

"I would rather lose craft," Hemdi says. "My mother gave me Linterna."

Rugnus steps in to translate. "Been working on this project for a year now. Trying to start their own nursery with rare plants from other kingdoms. Dashen plants represent Winta's heritage and Hemdi here migrated from The Kingdom of Firas Andem. Figures some familiar plants will help refugees feel more at home. He has a nice relic that might help it work, but he would have to sacrifice the object to the project altogether."

"Sira got us those spots on level three of the Keeper's Social," Hemdi says, "We have a chance to make an impression. I intend to do so."

The Keeper's Social. That's what Rugnus and Andalynn had been talking about at Lagnar's. "Isn't Handler running it? What is it exactly?" The second I ask, Winta and Hemdi lean toward me as if they're waiting for the punchline of a joke. Then Winta's eyes squint, her mouth opens more, and I know I've just revealed I'm not from around here.

Rugnus clears his throat. "Funny. Anyway, you called, I came, but I've got to get Clayson settled somewhere for the night."

"Not Magmadew Court," Winta says.

Rugnus opens his mouth in protest. "How did you know I was—"

"You always take refugees there first."

Rugnus scoff. "And for a good reason. Affordable rooms, awesome craft, what's not to like?"

Winta points a finger at him, but Hemdi intercedes. "Tell me,

Clayson, what will you do now that you have joined the other side? Did you have an apprenticeship in the kingdom?"

I shake my head.

"A dream then, maybe? Something you have always wanted to do? There are no restrictions in Tungsten City to prevent you from charting a new course for yourself. Something in shields or healing? A paladin, maybe. Or helping Rugnus with the refugee crisis. Or you could always find work at Quimdem with our team, securing the world's relics and objects before Whurrim-duum finds them. It is an important task. And it is good ferrum."

Winta picks up where he left off. "Or there's working for bluelink... or helping in construction projects. Forging, if you're creative enough."

I think of the brightstorm hanging in the sky outside. "Forging? I would do that."

"Wonderful," Hemdi says. "You should head down to Forge Center, and—"

"When he's rested," Rugnus says.

"Right, sure. Get some rest. But welcome, Clayson, really. There are so many opportunities here in Tungsten City."

"Better get going," Rugnus says. "Clayson hasn't slept all night, and I want to get him settled before I head over to Quimdem for the morning report. You guys coming?"

Winta takes the greasy gear back from Rugnus. "We'll be there."

"Okay, see ya." Rugnus takes out Icho, but before we budge, I make eye contact with Winta and smile slightly. She only nods, but for a moment, her eyes are smiling at me. Tough outer shell, Hemdi had said.

Our next destination is a villa made of gray stone. Baskets of white flowers hang from braided hooks everywhere. Cobblestone walkways wind through lawns of thick grass, interrupted here and there by bubbling pools of mud. All the walls and stairs here remind me of a quaint medieval village I must have seen on the travel channel. Dozens of people lay on beach chairs, lounging in the heavy sunlight. Do they call it sunlight?

This must be Magmadew Court.

A few people stand from a nearby bench and move across the courtyard, entering a room through a yellow door. "Is this like a resort or an apartment building?" I say.

"Based on the precepts of community, living spaces are communal. Keep our things in the vaults and stay anywhere we want. This is one of my favorites—might have guessed from Winta's comment."

"What if someone chooses to stay in the same place or lives in their vault? We slept there."

"Too boring. Why stay in the same place all the time? I guess you could stay in your vault, but there's a limit to it, specified in the precepts. I think it's something like fifteen days in any spot, but people rotate from place to place, usually within a few days."

It's gonna take me time to adapt to living in Tungsten City. "What if I like living in one place?"

He shrugs. "Open bluelink, and let's find you a room."

He helps me navigate the map for Magmadew Court and find an open room on the top level. I follow him up a long flight of stairs to a plaza overlooking a large lake of mud. A few boats float tethered at a metal dock. More boats glide over the surface of the brown lake.

He walks me over to a closed door, grabbing my arm and holding my wrist to a blue glass plate set into the stone. The lock clicks, and we enter a room with a large bed and a stretch of silk curtains that let in yellow light. There's a single table and two low chairs facing the curtains.

"Okay. Relax your beard and bones for the day," Rugnus says. Then he strokes his cheek but points to mine. "And shave again, keep Ide. You look like some knight straight off the front lines of the Mithrium War." He rummages through my bag and sets out the quick clean. "Should be back late tonight. Got some leafs to record. I need to catch up from last week, and I dropped some ferrum into your account, by the way. So, order food if you get hungry." He nods toward an aluminum oval on the table.

We stand there awkwardly for a second. "Great. Well, see you," he says, fleeing through the door.

There's little to explore in the apartment. There's no kitchen. Only one room and a small bathroom with an aluminum toilet. Budgecraft. Figures. Back in the open area, I draw the curtains apart, greeted with a view of the hot mud lake and a stretch of grass beach where people stroll around in groups and lounge on deck chairs.

Inviting, but I have access to bluelink now.

I tap the blue glass on my bracelet, and floating icons appear across my vision. Curiosity leads me to a search about the Keeper's Social Rugnus and Hemdi were talking about. A few Keeper's Socials are held each year, where guests simply socialize with the keepers, or they can compete in feats of craft to gain notoriety and invitations to work for important businesses and high-ranking keepers. It's like a job fair and the Olympics had a baby.

Closing the search icon, I turn to another one shaped like a stone tablet marked: NEWS. The top story reads:

THE END OF THE MONARCHY?

I'm prompted to display the story on the large blank wall next to the bed.

In only a few minutes, I have multiple screens open. A few holographic three-dimensional objects float around the room languidly, which represent my bookmarks and favorites. I open a calendar, which apparently only has four months: Nox, Sol, Gem, and Stone. More like suits in a deck of cards than the names of months. Today's date is four-five Gem—not the forty-fifth of Gem as it would read to humans. Yesterday—or lastday—the day I received my AMP was four-four Gem. So, my birthday must have been three-something Gem.

The article is exactly what I expect it to be: a detailed description of my father's appearance and my mother's suspected involvement. Her name, Azbena Bloodfeign, blinks, shinier than the words around it. I open the link.

I scan a short biography, and I find myself overwhelmed by everything I didn't know. The shock starts sinking into my bones like it's never gonna wear off. My mother's mother, Glaris Everbloom, is presumed alive and well, the leader of the Conjures. They refuse to use craft and, supposedly, live in isolation somewhere in one of the mithrium wastelands. This is my father's world.

He swore off craft. That's why he stayed sick all that time.

I wonder for a second if that's where he and Ara went.

None of the reports say anything about my father's connection with them.

Besides her, none of my other grandparents are alive. But the picture of my mother's father—Yinzar Mithriumbane, whose name was once Yinzar Copperoath—catches my eye.

It's the man from my dream—the gruff red-haired man who spoke to dragon bones. Yinzar Copperoath destroyed a piece of the mithrium and became a champion—Mithriumbane. The only thing left of him is the chance that somewhere, hidden deep in the mountain, his death created a dungeon—like Wolfstaff.

A shudder runs over my whole body.

I push any remaining ideas of sleep far from me. Besides, I'm sure sleep would be just as unproductive as last night. This is my thing: learning, soaking in information from faraway places and foreign cultures. But this time, it's not another travel channel binging session. It's unraveling everything my father tied behind a shield of disinformation.

EXPLORE THE CITY

THE REST of the day is lost in a flood of information. I forget to order food until daychange when the brightstorm abruptly reminds me—like a light switch—I'm being kind of obsessive about information again. But there's a weight to this exploration into the histories of my parents and sister, a heaviness that never came with watching the news or following someone on TV as they backpacked through eastern European countries. This info binge is personal.

My father's parents were assassinated along with three and a half million Loamin in a city called Malguk, the capital of Hngaal Kingdom, a constellation of nine cities beneath the surface of Alaska. An operative of the Kingdom of Zal Kakraja had slipped into the cities ahead of them and set up a mithrium-powered bomb.

The catalyst was goldcraft, and like the blood my mother had put on my face, or the pipe system leading to Lagnar's underground shop, it changed the bodies of those affected. In this case, it's believed the mithrium-enhanced goldcraft reprogrammed everyone's cells, causing the atoms of their bodies to convect. They boiled away like a pot of water left on a hot burner. There's virtual footage of it happening. I didn't watch it.

Every story from every lost city is available, along with a time-line of the hundreds of years of conflict between the eight kingdoms. The heartbreaking story of Loamin pride and politics is not easy to watch.

My father took up the throne at twelve years old, at a time when his enemies held two of the three pieces of mithrium. Still, the Keeper's Council directed the war to its conclusion: the elimination—by mithrium—of every other Loamin city in the world. Only Whurrimduum and Helgrimral were left. Twenty years ago, in the last moments of the war, Helgrimral broke from Rimduum and rebranded itself a direct democracy—Tungsten City.

The three pieces of mithrium were locked away in Whurrimduum until, presumedly, Dad and my mother's father, Yinzar Copperoath, stole them. Yinzar destroyed one, and Dad escaped with the last two. The evidence makes it clear: my father was a thief. But many people think he did the world a favor by taking the mithrium from the council.

All this heavy material sinks like lead inside me, so I turn to simpler matters. I learn how to measure distances in loams, bars, and blocks. I learn about the ancient Troll Wars and the first champions. About the great migration to the Rockies, about King Erikzin Brightstorm and the Age of Discovery.

My mind is a sponge.

When exhaustion finally overtakes me, I don't sleep. I dream again. But it's more like a memory than a dream. Yinzar Mithriumbane, my grandfather, talking to the bones of a dead dragon. It's identical to the last dream until he looks right at me, his green eyes cutting through like hot irons. He says, "Opposite energy."

A kind, delicate voice draws me out of the vision. "You should wake up now."

Something grasps my ankle, jostling my leg. My eyelids part. and my body jerks away from the smiling teenage girl sitting at the end of my bed, cross-legged. Blond, perfectly styled hair drapes over her shoulders. Her eyes radiate an understanding that she's invaded my space, which she's apparently fine with.

"Don't worry," she says, "I'm not here to stab you in your sleep or anything."

I tighten the linen blankets closer around me. When she squints, it highlights a wispy smattering of freckles across the bridge of her nose. She pinches my ankle again and shakes my foot. "Everything's fine. Relax."

"Who are you?"

An even brighter smile breaks over her face, revealing immaculately white teeth bordered by pointed canines. There's something beautiful and unnerving about her at the same time.

"Only fair, seeing as I know your name. I'm Sira."

I rub the exhaustion from my eyes. "Sira? Like Rugnus' friend? You work for Handler?"

A glint shines in Sira's fierce eyes. "He told you about me? Great. Then you'll be happy to know I'm giving you an apprenticeship at Handler. Starts in about"—she finds a clock on the wall from an open bluelink display—"an hour."

"Wait, you can just do that? How old are you?" After Rugnus' stacks of money, Hemdi and Winta's flower shop, and my sister's skirmish with Lagnar Emberfence, I'm still second-guessing what teenagers in a normal society should be allowed to do.

"Handler needed someone with a young face and a lot of followers to do recruitment. It's a perfect fit for me. I love bringing people together and creating relationships." She winks.

Is she flirting with me?

"I-uh, does Rugnus know about this? Come to think of it, he said he would check on me last night. And I'm not sure I should really be—"

Sira stands and holds out a hand to help me from the bed. "I saw him last night. He kinda lied to you on purpose. He meant well. Told me you were exhausted and needed some time to rest."

"Did you tell him about the job at Handler?"

"No. To be honest, I saw a few pics of you—you know, the

public ones since you got here...that sounds bad...I—well, Hemdi mentioned your interest in forging. I thought it would be nice to help out."

Her words give me a category to put her in: aggressive, but nice.

I mull over the offer. Dad didn't trust me with all of the information he had about this world. And despite warnings from Rugnus and Andalynn, I feel drawn to the mystery of Silverkeeper—my father's closest friend—and the stolen mithrium. Maybe I can even help prove that Dad kept the mithrium safe by stealing it. Safe from men like Bazalrak. If Andalynn can clandestinely work to figure out the connection to Handler, and Bazalrak, and Silverkeeper, then so can I.

"That sounds great. Let me—" All of my bluelink searches are still displayed on the walls. I left off on a page about my mother's skill in Silverlamp Dungeon, something I thought may be important. But the most embarrassing thing might be all my notes on simple conversions from standard human to Loamin measurement. Hovering closest to us is a chart showing how many feet are in a bar. About ten. Ten embarrassing feet to a bar. "I, uh, can you see these?"

She stands and pushes one of the three-dimensional holographic icons out of her way. "Yeah, I kind of noticed your obsession with the royal family. I guess everyone needs a hobby. You can change your visibility settings, you know." She stops in front of a looping video of Dad giving a speech about governmental transparency. Seeing him so passionate and healthy has caused me to rearrange my perception of him.

"You know you look like King Brightstorm," Sira says. "Jaw's a bit softer, but the dimples are about the same. You must have Brightstorms somewhere in your ancestors. Did Rugnus tell you I came from the capital too?"

"The capital?"

"Whurrimduum. Clayson, you're a bit absent-minded, you

know? You might consider paying closer attention to what people are saying to you."

"Oh, yeah. Sorry," I say.

She squints at me again. "Anyway, my family lived in the largest castlestack near the Theater of the Keepers. And you? Did you come from a family loaded with ferrum like me? Where did you live? Did you still participate in your family's championation?"

I smile. My night of news and history binging has paid off. I know what she means by the word castlestack. It's basically another word for skyscraper. A lot of them are family compounds that house all of a champion's descendants. I learned about it when I did a VR flyover of Whurrimduum. It's a giant hive, a sandcastle made out of a thousand towers. So, her family's estate must have been in a building—castlestack—close to some theater.

Championation is unfamiliar to me. I know families in the old kingdom had been arranged in clan-like groups associated with the champions. Maybe it has something to do with that? I could try to fake an answer, but if Sira is from Whurrimduum then she'll be able to spot any lie I try to tell.

With a gesture, I close bluelink, and all the videos and holographic content vanish from the wall. "I don't like talking about my life in the capital. I came here for a reason."

She giggles and rests her hand on my knee. "Very mysterious. But I suppose I felt the same way when I first got here. You hungry?"

Glad she's changed the subject, I stretch my arms over my head, scrounge for a moment in a nightstand drawer for the quick clean Rugnus gave me, and unscrew the cap. "Yeah, food sounds good." I take a sip of the water from the little flask, and I'm immediately clean both body and clothes. It even combed my hair. Not a good night's sleep, but I'm refreshed.

Sira takes a step closer to me, and I squirm a little as she tousles my hair. "Let me... a part's not right on you. Messy looks better. There."

Next time I see Rugnus, I'll have to ask him about Sira. I'm not sure she understands the idea of personal boundaries, though I'm starting to warm up to her. And she smells like a cool summer breeze.

I check the time. It's morning, but it was close to morning when I started dreaming.

My stomach rumbles. "So, breakfast?"

I have enough ferrum to last about a month—well, a human month. Not only did Rugnus give me money, but many of the citizens of Tungsten City voluntarily contribute to a refugee fund that awards ferrum to new immigrants. It's not a bad system, but having a job down here will allow me to raise my own funds.

"I know a perfect place for us," Sira says, grabbing my hand and pulling me toward the door.

Planting my feet, I say, "Can't we budge there?"

"It's only a block. A little stroll together should be fun."

We leave the small room behind for the sun-soaked resort beyond the door. A small ringing tone notifies me I've paid for the room. Any objects left behind will be automatically transferred to my vault. Several girls lounging on benches near the bubbling mud lake stop chattering as Sira and I march past.

"Don't look now," Sira says, "but I think those girls are checking you out."

She shoots daggers at them and hooks her arm through mine.

Blood rushes to my cheeks as we hurry past them.

We slip under a canopy of large maple trees, grass underfoot. So far, there's been no indication Tungsten City has any streets whatsoever. No cars, trains, or planes. Though with travel all done with budgecraft, why would there be?

The weather is perfect. A slight, cool breeze coils around me, rustling the maple leaves. None of the recordings or images from my information binge revealed rain or snow, so the city might be like this twenty-four seven. But an uneasy cloud settles over me.

I've seen so many videos—perfect clarity, full three-sixty—in the last day that I know this short walk to go find breakfast might be recorded. Even Rugnus has a channel with a lot of viewers, who are upset he's been offline for a few days. There are not as many in Whurrimduum, but the people of Tungsten City pride themselves on being open and transparent, Zinsday through Khalsday.

Sira picks up on me scanning my surroundings. "Oh, by the way, I turned my recorders back on once we left your room." Sira seems to have an uncanny sense of intuition, and I wonder if it's silvercraft.

I knew I was being watched. Immediately, my posture changes, and I become as self-conscious as I usually am around Ara. A chill runs the length of my back. "You didn't record my room?"

"No. I'd need permission to record in your space, goofball. But my audience likes to know what I'm doing. There's already a ton of questions about you." She giggles. "I may have to unfollow some of these girls though, Ide keep me, the things they're saying."

"I don't even wanna know," I say. A thought—as invasive as the cameras in this city— strikes me out of nowhere. This has to be why Rugnus was worried I would be discovered. Luckily no one in this world has ever seen my face, but they've seen Dad's face.

"Isn't Tungsten City beautiful?" Sira draws in a deep breath through her nose as if it could relax her any more than she already is.

I nod, but a measure of caution still bounces around inside my head. I'm not gonna make any snap judgments about living here permanently.

We come to a path where Loamin jam the space underneath the maples. I catch the symbol of one of the champion dungeons plastered on the shirt of a passerby. It's a glittering spoon oozing with purple liquid. Every dungeon has its own following, like religion or sports. There are whole channels on bluelink devoted to what people call the Hundred Dungeon Games.

Further down the path, rows of Loamin sit opposite from each other, playing some kind of game with a globe of blue energy. The players take turns choosing random spots on the globe, trying to get lines to intersect with each other on the inside.

Sira sees me watching them. "You play maltobi?"

What do I say to that? It seems like something I should know had I lived here. "Not much," I lie.

Sira looks me over but pulls me past them. "I played a ton as a kid. Dad basically required me to learn. I didn't mind. We'll have to play sometime. Come on."

Past an algae-filled pond and a half dozen giant egg sculptures, we skirt by a street performer doing aquatic acrobatics within a floating sphere of water. The performer's long limbs stretch and grasp floating handles in the sphere of water until he hoists himself out and somersaults through the air. When he stands to face the crowd, he's a foot taller than everyone else.

"Is that—"

"A vacant? Yes, I believe his name is Sil. He puts on performances throughout the city. So kind of him to serve us this way."

"You mean Dura, right? Vacant sounds kind of racist."

"Oh, that's sweet of you, to care about how we label them. You're right. Dura it is."

Sira drags me forward to an enclosed staircase descending into the ground, like a narrow subway entrance. I don't have time to process why her comment makes my gut clench and my skin crawl, but I add it to Rugnus' beliefs about Ara, how she shouldn't have had the type of power she did to help Dad. Loamin don't think Dura are sentient.

"You're going to love this," Sira says. "You should go first."

The stairwell's dark, but I don't argue. She follows behind me, every few seconds resting her hand gently on my back. At the bottom, I find an oval room with a low ceiling. Purple and pink candlelight emanates from a wall filled with flowery ironwork.

We stop in the center of the oval, stepping on a large wood circle like the top of the roughly sanded table.

"Wait for it..." Sira presses closer against me. Suddenly, the wooden platform trembles and rises. A hole reveals itself in the ceiling. Short wooden walls build themselves around us, along with a circular picnic bench. As we float through the opening above, an umbrella flowers from the center of the wooden platform and pops open above our heads, blocking the sun, and we drift further upward like a hot air balloon.

"What do you think?" Sira asks, pulling me down to sit close to her on the picnic bench.

"I thought we were having breakfast?"

Sira frowns for the first time, but it adds another layer of cuteness to her face. "You don't like the booth?" She points to the large aluminum disk at the center of the table. It's similar to the delivery point for food in the hotel room. "The fruit and cheese will arrive in a minute."

"No, it's, uh, it's great." We're floating over the city in an umbrella-topped booth, waiting for breakfast. Sira bats her eyes at me. I freeze, suddenly realizing I'm on some sort of strange, kidnapped first date.

Who is this girl?

She's easy to look at, but there's a nagging thought in my mind, an irrational need to escape. Is there a way to send a message to Rugnus without gesturing or speaking? I'll have to ask him. For now, I sit across from her. The space under the table seems impossibly small for two sets of legs. My fingers rest on the table, and I find myself fidgeting with Ergal, which draws Sira's attention.

"That's beautiful. What kind of coding does it use?" Her words are casual, but I sense an increased interest.

"I'm not sure," I say. "Rugnus gave it to me."

This girl has a knack for being invasive, and briefly, I fear she's using silvercraft to trick me into revealing things I shouldn't.

The food appears on the table, and I forget everything in my hunger. Sira produces a silver knife and begins slicing things into smaller pieces. As casually as I can, I ask, "Is that a relic?"

She continues to chop a large strawberry. "This? No, just something that helps me understand people a little better. I didn't really grow up around many other kids, and... sorry, over-sharing. No, a simple piece of silvercraft. What about the ring? Did Rugnus tell you anything about it?"

"Simple shield, I think," I lie.

She nods, cutting into a ring of pineapple and passing it to my side of the table. I pick it up with my fingers. The fruit is better than anything I've ever tasted, sweeter, and like it's been picked only this morning, which may be true, given how easy it is for Loamin to transport things.

We float a long distance from the Magmadew Court. After the gnawing in my stomach subsides, I ask, "Do you know Winta and Hemdi?"

Sira comes up from admiring my ring for the third time. "Sure, I do. I helped Hemdi pick out balloons for their wedding."

A piece of ruby-colored fruit nearly falls out of my mouth. "They're married?" I say, swallowing hard, nearly choking.

"Rugnus didn't tell you?"

"No, I—wait, how old are they?"

"Same as us, I guess. Why?"

It takes every effort to keep the shock and confusion off my face. "No reason."

To help, I shove a large piece of white cheese into my mouth. My parents were married young, but I thought that could have been a royal thing. Why didn't I guess Loamin could marry so young? Rugnus has a full-time job. There aren't even any schools. What else can they do? Rugnus could even be married. Or, for all I know, Andalynn could be. I rub the shadow where my beard grows in too fast.

"Is this about Winta?" Sira asks, smiling. "She's pretty, right?"

This feels like a trap.

Sira giggles. "Oh, did you like her? Like, 'like her' like her."

159

She sets her knife on the table and reaches across. "Well, what can a guy do? She's gorgeous. You can tell me anything you want, you know."

My eyes catch the edge of our floating booth. We've wandered outside the dense ring of urban sprawl and into the center closer to the brightstorm. Below us lies an orchard of fruit trees. Would Ergal break my fall if I jumped out of the booth in embarrassment?

"Wait, I didn't say I liked her. Are you recording this? You're making it sound like... you're putting words in my mouth."

"Calm down there, big boy," she says. "Rugnus is right. You're too serious. Unwind a little."

I open my mouth to speak, but nothing comes out, so I stare at the skyline, watching with interest as a machine the size of a small parking complex tears down a building, reconstructing it at the same time. If we were a bit closer, I'm sure the sound could drown out our silence.

"You're more difficult to talk to than I expected. Don't worry, I kinda like it." She squeezes my leg under the table, and my ears become suddenly hot.

Gazing at a point past my head, Sira says, "Almost there."

"We're not budging to Handler?"

"No," she says. Tapping the slap bracelet on my wrist, she adds, "By the way, that generic budge makes you look like a latch-mage. We'll have to go shopping for some better craft after work. See, we're almost there," she says, and the whole booth swerves toward a ravine between a forest of oaks.

But the ravine, on both sides, is not stone but city. We're the only vehicle in sight, but people appear and disappear along a thousand balconies. We zoom past a suspended park where kids sail through the air, attacking each other with balls of water. There's something the shape of the Sydney Opera House that blurs past on the other side.

The light from the brightstorm is muted down here, but a

thousand shades of darkness devour us as we descend into neon pools of light in the Loamin underworld.

The booth lands at the entrance of a building. It's flanked by two giant brown flags that read *Handler*. Above us, the umbrella folds back. The table sinks into the floor, and the walls fall away. The moment we step off, the disk rises for the sky.

Sira takes the lead as we pass under a sizeable stone-carved sword at the apex of the arching doorway. The moment we enter, disquieting music fills my ears, almost classical, but with a thudding tempo and an overpowering, droning flute. Dull, tan light issues from recessed half-globes spaced unevenly in the low ceiling made of one unending mirror, wall to wall. The mirror reflects caverns of inky blackness at our feet.

I step back, clenching my chest, but Sira giggles. "It's not real. See?" She steps off the cliff. "Just art."

The whole lobby is an optical illusion. The cliffs painted on the floor are impossibly real. Even the strange music is designed to leave me off-kilter. Who was the architect for this place? My perspective shifts enough that I can move again, but the disorientation hangs over my first few steps toward the center of the room. As we walk, my senses return, and I begin to appreciate the detail of the illusion.

"Handler is all about creative budgecraft," Sira says. "The CEO, Filhrin Lonecharge, is obsessed with creating something that can overcome foilgrips."

Lonecharge's name came up during my bluelink binge yesterday, and so I find a small sense of satisfaction in knowing something before being told about it.

"Foilgrips," I say, "are made by passing craftable aluminum through a part of a brightstorm. It magnifies the budgecraft, but they say what Lonecharge is trying to do is impossible, and even if it is possible, it's still centuries away."

"Don't let Lonecharge hear you say that. Not if you want to keep your apprenticeship. Around here, it's all about trying to do the impossible. Silverkeeper himself is providing funding."

"Have you met him?" I say, hoping she can at least point me in the right direction.

"Silverkeeper? Hard to catch, very reclusive." She scans the room as we walk. "They say the year his wife and daughter died, he went into hiding. Afraid to show himself. Refused to use budgecraft."

In part, because he was my father's closest friend and in part because of his connection with the mithrium, Silverkeeper had been one of my other searches last night. He leads the Council of Keepers, a group of ten Loamin connected to the most powerful dungeons. Even after my Dad was accused of stealing the mithrium and fled, Silverkeeper defended him and protected my mother and Andalynn.

Then the accident happened. Unrecorded, it was never clear where it happened or what killed his wife and daughter, but from that moment, he began experimenting with radical forms of silvercraft, replacing parts of his body with relics and objects made from silver.

"Yeah, I read about that. But he's still helping in the research Handler is doing, right?"

"You know, if you want to meet him, I have an unused invitation to level three of the Keeper's Social tomorrow night."

"Aren't Rugnus and his team going?"

"They are. Also, by my invitation. You're welcome to—"

"I think I need a little more time to adjust to the city before something like that." Besides, if my sister and Rugnus find out I'm investigating Silverkeeper and the mithrium, they may just let Bazalrak find me.

"Well, alright. This way," Sira says, pulling me past the budge port. "You'll be starting in the basement today," she says, her smile deepening. "Logging failures is an essential part of the process of forging and coding."

When we stop at the far wall, I'm not sure what type of reaction I'm supposed to have. We're standing at the opening of a large yellow tube slide. I scan her face in search of any hint of a joke. "There's not an internal budge port to the basement?" I ask.

Sira's face reddens. She's embarrassed for some reason.

"What?" I say.

"I can't budge. Well, I can, but it leaves me sick for hours without good leadcraft. I'm a one in budgecraft."

"Oh... I-I don't know what to say. That's no big deal."

Her smile brightens, but she looks down at the floor. "Thanks for saying that." She shrugs. "It's not all bad. People like to watch my life. They're interested in how I get around."

"So that's why we took the booth thing?"

"Yeah. I'm surprised you didn't get that." She pauses. "You're a nice guy, Clayson. I've decided. And... oh goodness, my followers." She stares to the right of me, speaking to her followers. "Message him yourself. They want to know how tall you are."

"Me?" Unsure of where to look, I stare past her. If I'm being recorded by Sira, do I talk to her followers by talking to her? I suddenly have no place to put my hands, so I touch my face nervously. "I'm five-four."

"Not your birthday, silly. How tall are you?"

Loamin measure height differently, but the units refuse to come back to me. "Not sure."

"You're being modest. You must be three past a loam. Four past maybe. He'll fit in the slide fine. Ide keep me. I'm turning this off." She snaps her fingers. "After you, sweetness."

I climb in awkwardly, watching Sira, but she nudges me, and I slip over the yellow plastic, winding around five or six turns and then dropping onto a brown mat.

The new area is again windowless but brightly lit. Vines cover an entire wall. The bright yellow slide is the only interruption. The room is split between an upper walkway—encumbered with padded benches, rocking chairs, and squat tables—and a lower level, more like an industrial kitchen.

We're on the upper walkway.

A wiry set of stairs leads from the walkway to the inside of a giant mech that's been suspended from the ceiling by thick cables. Modern house music is bumping over invisible speakers. A woman's voice sings:

> *What's happenin' tonight?*
> *If you told me I wouldn't believe,*
> *I believe the night.*
> *'Cause she's wearing gold for me,*
> *Holding naught but bold with me.*
> *The moment has come.*
> *Well met by fire, son.*

The song drops into a mind-shattering, hard-to-follow beat. It's like music out of a nightclub. The whole room is oozing with a chill-out-and-play kinda vibe.

Then I see the Loamin. They're all younger than me by four or five years. One group has teamed up to control a pair of toy building mechs, similar to those I saw climbing through Tungsten City's skyline building skyscrapers. The toy mechs build their own miniature city, and the kids cheer as two buildings turn to fight each other.

Someone bumps into me, a dark-haired Loamin no older than eleven.

"Sorry," I say.

"He can't hear you," Sira says. "He didn't even feel that." She makes a gesture like she's slicing through enemies with a large sword, sound effects and all. "He's a total headslop."

I carve one more entry onto my mental "study later" vocabulary list. I can't ask Sira what a headslop is without looking like I've spent my whole life above granite. Though, to be fair, I have spent my whole life above granite.

"So, what does the failure department do?" I ask.

"They retest the codes designed upstairs where I work, research and development. Then confirm the results against the original test. You'll basically be double-checking our work."

The kids who had been playing with the toy mechs have devolved into bickering and one of the kids has a meltdown and stomps on the nearest building in the miniature city.

"Is it complicated?" I ask.

"Nah. We've got more experienced people double-checking the tests first. Then we send a few things down to the apprentices."

"So, what am I supposed to do?"

She rubs my shoulder. "Same thing as them, silly. Good luck."

"Wait, I have to work here with these kids?" I say, annoyed. If people my age are getting married, what's the deal with stashing me here with a bunch of pre-teens?

"Oh, aren't you just adorable," she says. "Must have been more sheltered than me as a child, huh. You're getting a late start on things. It's not uncommon. This is how things work: after summation, you go around to different places until you find something you're good at. Then you start working. If you want to do something else when you're, say, twenty or so, you start on the ground floor again."

There are maybe twenty kids here, none of them doing anything remotely similar to the work Sira was describing.

"I'll swing by at lunchtime. Bye, now," she says. She plants a kiss on my cheek and saunters away.

Stuck to the spot I'm standing on, I call after her. "Don't leave me here."

"At least they've got good music," she says and vanishes around a corner.

The gaggle of children playing with their robots has stopped arguing and are now staring at me, transfixed. One of them shouts, "That your girlfriend or your wife?"

All the other kids burst into giggles.

Ignoring them, I head for the stairs leading to the industrial kitchen, which might be the only actual workspace in this daycare. On my way over, I pass the headslop again. This time he's sitting on a bench, his head twitching in every direction, eyes an unnatural blue. Maybe headslop is the term for someone stuck on bluelink. He's some kind of junkie.

I make a mental note to take it easy on my use of bluelink. Even in the human world, I've been on some serious news-watching benders. The same thing could happen to me if I'm not careful. Even so, I open bluelink for a second to check if any of the news has changed in the last few hours. It's still only rumors and hearsay, which, over the years, I've learned to distinguish from actual news.

I shuffle through the headlines as I step down the stairs.

A voice aimed in my direction says, "Ho, don't tell me you're here to learn to forge at your age. I hope you bring a wealth of experience."

Closing the browser, or whatever I'm supposed to call it, I find a well-dressed boy, maybe eleven years old, in a bolo-tie and a crisp, purple button-up. His pink-brown hair is a mismatch but complements his almond skin color. He doesn't otherwise acknowledge me, sorting through a strange box of large square-shaped records, each album made of solid metal. Maybe they're leafs. The way he holds his head makes it look like he's constantly searching out every odor in the room, sorting them into categories based on their worth.

I freeze on the bottom step as if I need his permission to pass through his territory. He might be the only one working in the whole basement.

"If you are, then get off bluelink, and come work."

"Yeah," I say, "well, that kid's stuck in virtual reality or something." I point up the stairs.

"Dengor is an idiot. He'll end up spending his life on Dragonrock Island, fighting in imaginary dungeons, and getting paid in iron. And the sad thing is, he's good with that. Are you?"

This acknowledgment must mean I can enter his domain, so I take the last few steps.

"Okay then," he says, adjusting his bolo tie and pushing a hand over slick black hair. "You're my new assistant. Let's see how long you last. Put your AMP in the reader over in that workspace."

Every surface of the kitchen gleams, including the little kiosk he indicates. I can tell this kid is a bit of a go-getter. "What's your name?" I ask, placing my AMP in the hexagonal cut-out designed to scan it.

My information hovers over my kiosk like a banner, taken from bluelink. This boy considers it. "Brigklev. People call me Brig. Has anyone ever told you, you have a very traditional name, Clayson Glintwheel? Glintwheel sounds like a capital—wait, you're not..."

"From Whurrimduum? I might be."

"Impressive. Must have been hard to get out. Not that we don't have our share of ironhead refugees here in Tungsten City, but your breed is few and far between. Ho! And look at that score in shieldcraft. You know, my sister has a weakness for guys with a high rating in shieldcraft. I could introduce you."

"Uh—"

"Never mind that. Can I shoot you with stuff?" He nods toward my ring. "You've got the hardware."

"Shoot me with stuff?"

"My last assistant he, uh, he had a weakness in shields."

This kid is growing on me. "Maybe later," I say.

He hangs his head, but it instantly snaps upward again. "I have a perfect job for you. Perfect. Don't just stand there. Come over to the forge."

The glowing fire of a small forge appears only when I come around to his side of the table. He grabs my hand, the one with the ring, and jams it inside the forge. "Protect yourself!"

My elbow hits the shelf behind me the moment I recoil.

"Did you feel anything?"

My whole arm tingles from hitting my elbow. "Of course, I—"

"Not your arm. Did you feel the heat from the forge?"

"I... wait, no. It wasn't..."

"I bet you could reach your hand right in and grab the crucible out without damage."

"Really?" I say, incredulous.

"Try."

A cheer rises from the group of kids playing with the toy mechs as I reach my hand, inch by inch, into the forge. A foot away, I hesitate. I should not be sticking my hand in white fire, but I don't feel any heat. Even so, I flinch when a flame blooms out of the forge and licks the back of my hand.

"No way," I say. It doesn't hurt.

"Awesome, grab the crucible."

Don't overthink this. My ringed hand dips into the forge and seizes on the rim of a large, cup-shaped crucible, and I don't feel a thing.

"Okay, you're not allowed to quit," Brig says.

With that, we begin work. Testing the coding is relatively straightforward as we follow each formula.

We add a small cup of pearl-colored crystal beads to the inside of the forge. Then we heat the crucible, add two cubes of aluminum. While it melts, Brig heats a small amount of copper with a handheld torch. He mashes small cubes of drywall into powder—it's gypsum, I think—to which he adds the copper. Then we add the mixed copper with the aluminum. When it's a liquid, I reach in and grab the crucible, pouring the contents into a graphite mold under a sort of barcode scanner. A digital readout displays on the countertop showing the strength of the coding we've just created with an indicator that reads: *VITALITY*.

Vitality can range from one to four. Most of the variations we test display a vitality between one and two. An hour passes, test after test. Brig changes the amount of drywall powder and how much he stirs it, but the amount of aluminum and copper stays the same.

After each attempt, he places a few fingers on one of the metal leafs. When I ask what he's doing, he only says, "Taking notes." This must be the reverse of the leafs from Rugnus' vault, storing information instead of giving it out, more like a blank notebook than an encyclopedia.

An idea comes to me, almost like a strike of revelation. "Brig, that's gypsum, right?"

He smashes another small brick of the stuff and nods.

We've been using different amounts of the gypsum, but always crushed into a powder. "Maybe we could try not breaking it up as much. Leave it in more of a clump. Dissolve it that way."

"Not procedure," he says. He weighs something in his mind, his lips tightening for a second. "Okay. We've got plenty of materials. Can't hurt."

The larger piece of gypsum takes longer to dissolve, but when we pour the result into the mold and place it under the scanner, the vitality reading jumps to three-point-two.

"Ho. Look who has some skill. I am stealing that." He places a finger on the silver Leaf. "There. Stolen."

We've accumulated a small pile of thin metal tags that have come out of the mold. "What are these things?"

"Animal tags. They use them to budge animals to market. That little trick of yours will make Handler some serious ferrum. I'll log both of our names on the recipe and submit it to research and development."

A commotion erupts from the kids playing upstairs, and a familiar voice calls out, "Not a chance, latchers."

It's Rugnus' voice.

"Brig, I'll be back," I say.

"Take an early lunch. You deserve it. Best assistant I've had… well, ever."

I take the stairs two at a time and find Rugnus barreling toward me. "What in Ide's name are you doing here? I have news. Let's go."

Without another word, he grabs both Icho and my arm, and we budge, appearing in a darkened alley at the bottom of a chasm made from impossibly tall stone buildings. Budging so quickly and to such a different place leaves my head spinning. Pink neon lights shine over the street from grubby shops—potholes filled with grayish water litter the narrow alleyway. At the bottom of the closest hole, I see a black starfish adhered to the concrete but submerged in liquid.

After a quick breath, I say, "I thought you weren't supposed to budge inside buildings. The Citizens Contract?"

"It was an emergency," Rugnus says. He's breathing like we ran all the way here. "Besides, you weren't supposed to get anywhere close to Handler."

"Happened all of a sudden. Sira showed up and—"

"I don't care what Sira told you, I—"

"Where are we?" I ask. Only a sliver of the sky peeks between the walls of the stone chasm.

"Somewhere without cameras, where we can talk. Have you been on bluelink in the last hour?"

"No, I—"

Rugnus sighs heavily. "Clayson, I'm sorry...the steward, your mother. The inquisition was moved up."

"I don't understand."

"The inquisition, her trial, they moved it up. Happened already. Found guilty of treason against Rimduum."

A chill shudders over my whole body. My breath catches. "What does that mean?"

He doesn't answer.

"Rugnus? What does that mean?"

"They're sending her to permanent isolation in Keelcrawl prison for the rest of her life. I'm sorry, Clayson."

DEVISE A PLAN

A WRENCHING, stark emotion cascades from the middle of my body out to each of my limbs, out to the tips of my fingers. I'm numb, all but a raw tightening across my ribcage. I can't decipher the meaning of any of this. This news shouldn't have any power over me. I barely know my mother.

And that's it.

I've crashed abruptly into the truth. A few days ago, I knew exactly what to think about my absentee mother: nothing. Where there should be memories of her, there's a wound like a bullet hole. She was dead weight. But I was wrong. My mother didn't abandon me. She can't even see me, can't even hear my name from the lips of her own husband.

I'm nothing to her, but that's also a lie born of whatever strange craft keeps her from remembering me. And whatever craft makes me immune to the surface effects and induces these visions. I still have an arsenal of unanswered questions for her. Permanent isolation means none of them will ever be answered.

I almost feel her brushing my forehead with her warm blood. Her worry-filled face is before me again, and I can't shake it out. I squeeze my eyes shut, but the neon light from the nearby shop bleeds through.

Rugnus takes an audible breath as if he is winding up to say something. I hold out my hand. Whatever he has to say, I can't process it right now. "I-I need a second."

"Look, Clayson, I—"

"No, don't. I—what am I supposed to feel about this? I barely knew her." A sick feeling crawls through my stomach. "She wasn't even...what am I supposed to think, Rugnus? There's something not right about this. About everything." He tries to put a hand on my shoulder, but I step toward the wall. "I need to think. I don't even...I don't know what to feel."

"Don't feel anything, then," he offers. "You could—"

"No. I wanna be alone right now. I'll catch up with you."

Rugnus straightens up. "I can't leave you here. If you haven't noticed, this is a pretty sketchy place. I just wanted a spot where we couldn't be overheard."

I dangle my aluminum bracelet at him. "My budge—the one you gave me—it'll work down here?"

"Yeah, but—"

"Then I'll be fine. Leave. I'll find you later."

Rugnus shakes his head. "Yeah, no, I've got to stay. Can't just leave you here."

The strange emotion inside of me congeals my blood like snake venom. My hands are shaking as I take one more step away from Rugnus. I turn on my heels.

"Hey, come on," Rugnus calls to me. "Can't just"—he budges and reappears in front of me—"walk away from me. Trying to help you."

I stop before I run into him. The cold, invisible fingers around my chest tighten so firmly I almost can't force out my next words. "I'm fine."

"Yeah, you sound all peach lemonade and stormshine. Come on, let me bring you someplace safer, then I'll let you do whatever you want." He places a hand on the end of his club.

The idea of budging somewhere makes me sick. It's irrational, but there's something wrong about disappearing and reappearing

172

somewhere else. Fear works itself in between all my other mixed-up feelings. I won't do it. It's too much like an escape, which doesn't seem fair at the moment.

I turn the other direction. "I need to walk."

Rugnus appears again, blocking the alley. "No."

The moment he reaches for me, the concrete explodes from the ground between us. It rises in a wave, knocking Rugnus backward. In the same breath, a spiral staircase forms slab by slab. I jump back. The first step lies at my feet. A circular wall encloses me within a tower-like stairwell, but with long vines of neon light bulbs running along the walls.

I charge up the stairwell, stopping at a window cut out of the masonry, which gives me a view down to the alley. Rugnus spots me.

"Knock it off," he says, his voice a growling whisper. "That ring's blocking Icho and drawing attention."

My ring. Rugnus was gonna force me to budge. I had to protect myself, and the ring took over from a single stray thought. Ergal is as powerful as Icho. But Rugnus is right. People are gathering at the end of the alley, wandering out from the shops, curious about the commotion.

"We've got to go," Rugnus says, desperate.

It might've been a bit drastic—building a concrete tower in the middle of an alley—but I'm still not going with him. I need space to figure things out, and I'm tired of being told exactly where to go and what to do.

I climb the stairs, emerging on the top of the cylindrical tower. I glance over the edge through the dense battlements. Rugnus paces around the bottom of the tower a few stories below me, testing it for an opening, but the stairwell is sealed. He cranes his neck to glare at me and vanishes.

When he doesn't return after a few seconds, my shoulders relax, but a crowd starts to gather—a few burly Loamin step in front, stalking the area around the tower.

One of them, with hair the color of the blue-black stone buildings, points at me and shouts, "Ay! You do this to our street?" She kicks the tower with her heavy boots and the concrete rumbles under my feet.

A man, standing next to her, hands covering his ears, squeals in a high-pitched voice, "He did! He did! I heard him talking to the one with the club about a ring."

"By my blood," the woman shouts. "By my blood, I'll tear it down, you little latcher. Come down here. Give me that ring. Who's recording this? I'll have the paladins after you."

The crowd simmers with agitation. I back away from the battlements as the woman calls for others to help break the tower. The stone rattles under me more forcefully.

Whatever my feelings about budging right now, it's time to go.

An icon flashes in my periphery, working its way into my field of vision. I hadn't opened bluelink, but a small 3D pillar with the symbol for ferrum floats in the air. I swipe my hand over it.

In complete contrast with the poisonous, cursing language of those attacking the tower, the pleasant male tutorial voice is as warm as a tropical vacation—though I've never had one of those. "I see you haven't visited your vault yet. Why not get things set up now?"

At that moment, someone from a window above me utters something unintelligible. A figure descends from the same window, hovering in the air at the tower's edge, more a void than a man. Dull-green lightning crackles over the figure.

A lance of electricity stabs out for me, but the tower launches countermeasures in the form of massive slabs of concrete that tear away from the ground. Shards of concrete shower the battlements, defying the laws of physics by absorbing the attacking bolts of lightning and then exploding in the opposite direction.

Hastily, I grab the 3D pillar icon and open it with a gesture.

My calves strain against the budge, paired with a wave of nausea, and then I'm standing in near darkness. A dim red light reaches out from an arched doorway. A solitary table sits with a small stack of ferrum, and my quick clean. My vault is otherwise empty.

My vault.

This place under the mountains is my new home, but I don't want it to be. Living here in Tungsten City—it's what Dad wants. But I don't know what I want. There's always been the safety of the cliff near the cabin to work out my thoughts. Now I have only a hollowed-out room in a mountain of stone.

In the silence of the vault, everything catches up with me. Dad's left-over dinner in the fridge at the cabin. Icy bodies. The bubbling mud lake by the hotel where Rugnus brought me. Dad, breathing with the aid of his oxygen tank. A canyon rippling with shards of rainbow light. An abrupt, blinding nightchange. My mother's green eyes focused on something beyond me. An ax. A prison.

My hands ball into fists, but tears sting my eyes. I need a cliff to scale. Something for my hands to do. It's like all the pieces of my life—my parents, my sister, my home—can never be reassembled. But, of course, they've never been whole before, either. How did Dad expect me to start a new life here when it would mean he and my mother were either in danger or dead?

I would've been better off staying on the surface. I refuse to let tears stay on my face. I wipe them away and harden my feelings against emotion, blaming the tears on my lack of sleep. How long has it been since I slept without dreams? Or woke without exhaustion. Two nights?

A soft glow of blue behind me interrupts the single red light. I turn and find an icon shaped like a blueprint, clearly the outline of a typical vault: one large room and two side rooms. I click it open, hoping to find a distraction from my thoughts.

The icons multiply—*MESSAGES, FURNITURE, STORAGE, EXTRAS.* I wonder if I would find Rugnus' aquarium as a choice under extras. The message icon has a small number one attached. I open it.

The pleasant voice from before makes another announcement.

"You have two unregistered objects sent from another vault. Would you like to register them? If yes, say transfer and register. If no, say transfer only. You may also refuse the transfer request if desired."

The transfer is from Rugnus' vault. It's my mother's necklace and my sister's ring. Maybe this is Rugnus' way of apologizing.

"Transfer only," I say.

Both objects appear on the table next to the small pile of ferrum and the quick clean. I slip on the bluish-silver ring. Returning to the bluelink menu for my vault, I select the furniture icon. More categories appear along with pictures of items in a scrollable list. I find a mirror for three silver ferrum, which I hope is not a lot—still haven't gotten the hang of money down here.

When I tap PURCHASE, a dotted outline flashes on the nearest wall. I confirm the placement, and the mirror appears. "Easy."

I touch the ring, and Andalynn replaces my own reflection. She is surrounded by plant life in a large empty room. Vor, who I saw at the RV park, the one who attends the royal family, crosses the room and hands Andalynn a stack of leafs, then, with a nod from my sister, slips from the room.

Her earnest eyes lock onto me. "Clayson. You heard."

I bow my head. I didn't grow up with my mother around, but Andalynn did. Whatever motivation I had for calling her changes instantly. "I'm so sorry, Andalynn. What can we do?"

"The council made its decision. Silverkeeper now believes she helped our father steal the mithrium years ago and that she knows its location."

"Do you think she does."

Andalynn pauses, looks to her right and left. "Do you know the difference between a keeper and a seer?"

"I think I read it yesterday—lastday I mean—but I read a lot of things."

"A keeper, who adds the word into their name—like Theridal

Silverkeeper—is responsible for all the affairs relating to a particular dungeon. As the oldest living descendant of the champion, Challozil Silverlamp, it is his right to manage all of the dungeon's business. But a seer is the person known to have reached closest to the heart of the dungeon."

"What does this have to do with anything?"

"Mom's the seer of Silverlamp Dungeon. She knows its patterns and tricks better than any other living soul. Better than Silverkeeper."

"So, you think—"

"I think the mithrium is there, Clayson. In Silverlamp Dungeon. It's only a matter of time until they find it."

"Let me try to understand. Mother got further into Silverlamp than anyone else."

"Yes."

"But Silverkeeper can't find where she hid the mithrium, if she even did."

"But he will. He has a keeper's key, allowing him to move through the dungeon more easily than any other raiders."

"Why hasn't he gotten it already?"

"Because of his accident years ago. He won't budge. He won't enter the dungeon. But I think he is using Handler as a front. And Bazalrak is helping him."

"So, if we got his key, we could get there before him and—"

"That's not possible. I—my guards are here. I've got to go. Find me again. And stay away from Handler."

Before I can say anything else, my reflection returns in the mirror. Andalynn's hopelessness settles on me now. If I could find Dad, he would know what to do. And I've thought about where he might be, but the conjurers' location is currently unknown. There has to be a way to help my mother, or if not, to get to the mithrium before Bazalrak and Silverkeeper can find it. Maybe Ergal could help me protect it.

I pull up a short video about Silverkeeper on bluelink. He's half-man, half-machine, with a silver claw foot and various other body parts removed and replaced with metal. In the video, he knits his fingers together, and I catch a sliver of metal dangling from a leather wristband. It's the key to Silverlamp Dungeon. It has to be.

A sudden moment of clarity trickles to the end of all my nerves. That's it—the Keeper's key. Silverkeeper will be at the social. If I can get the key from him, maybe I can get to the mithrium first and protect it with Ergal. The idea is like a revelation. Maybe Wolfstaff Dungeon gave me the ring for exactly that purpose. What can a dungeon know? But these are all connections I can only guess at.

I open bluelink and find Rugnus on a map of Tungsten City. It really is too easy to track someone using the city map.

Something about the Precepts of Community leaves me exposed.

It's amazing how little they value privacy. The small orange dot representing him blinks inside an oval-shaped building labeled Kel's Lounge. I set my sister's ring back on the table, tap the lounge's icon on bluelink, and budge.

I appear in the entryway of a restaurant lit with a maze of cozy yellow and green bulbs strung across the ceiling. Through the window, I see desert landscaping. Strange, but at this point, I'm accepting what my eyes tell me unless an abnormal physical sensation goes along with it. The aroma of homemade bread sends pangs of hunger bouncing around inside of me.

It's crowded.

Crisp, holographic images hover over a handful of tables, blaring a sporting event, which I figure must be the Hundred Dungeon Games. A cheer comes in a wave, and, almost at the exact same time, a groan rolls out from another corner of the room. I crane my neck to search for Rugnus' face, but there are too many people.

"Is that my new man?"

It's Sira. A crowd of people part for her as she saunters toward me, the smell of her vanilla body spray briefly overpowering the food.

She smiles. "Yes, indeed! Back from the vaults."

My eyes widen. "I didn't say I was in my vault?"

Reading my horrified face, she says, "Oh, I forget what it's like to be new around here. Your icon shows everyone where you are at all times. You should get used to it. People are always watching, you know. And even if they don't watch you, Rugnus and I have quite the following."

No wonder Rugnus brought me someplace without cameras to tell me about my mother.

Tungsten City would make a terrible long-term home. Living in a cabin in the Blue Ridge Mountains spoiled me. I want more anonymity.

With a wave of Sira's hand, the crowd parts again. I follow her. Yellow and green light dances in her hair as she leads me to a center booth where Rugnus sits next to an older boy I don't recognize. He's taller than Rugnus by five inches or so, meaning he's taller than me. Here I was getting used to being the tallest person in the room.

The older boy sitting on the padded edge of the booth bolts upright when he sees Sira. A purple crystal pendant hangs by a thread of hemp over his skintight muscle shirt—but he couldn't hide his muscles even under a woolen sweater. Across the black skin of his cheekbone, gold paint frames the bottom of his right eye like a football player.

"Did you catch that last ejection from Bluebottle?" His voice is a high-pitched mismatch for his jacked-up physique. When I come around to Sira's side, his grin falters into an uneasy smile.

Rugnus sputters and pulls his face from a clear mug of brownish-red liquid. He clears his throat. "Didn't take long. Koglim, this is Clayson Glintwheel, a refugee from Whurrimduum. Clayson, this is Koglim Felsight, the last member of the team I work with at Quimdem."

"Last?" Koglim says. "More like, best."

"You two are too cute," Sira says. "Out rescuing refugees and saving artifacts from the ironheads. Here I am just recruiting for Handler."

Rugnus takes a long drink from the clear mug.

We haven't had time to talk about my visit to Handler. I can see it weighing on him. Rugnus promised Dad he would keep me safe. On top of that, Andalynn ordered him to keep me away from Handler. Not that he'd take orders from the princess of Whurrim-duum, but still.

Koglim grabs Sira's hand and slides back onto the bench, leaving only enough room for her. Rugnus scoots in on the other side, and I sit next to him. Another cheer rises from the crowd, followed by a chorus of groans. Koglim pulls up a yellow holo-gram shaped like a 3D bar chart. One of the bars flashes red. He taps the red bar, and the hologram is replaced by five tiny Loamin-like figures inside a miniature oval room without a ceiling.

One of the Loamin suddenly grows twice as big as the others. He hefts a long-handled battle-hammer. The four other figures fall behind him, and he swings violently at the wall. After a few seconds, the wall ruptures, spitting out a graveyard full of bones.

"Wraithspit!" Koglim says. Everyone else leans forward, examining the scene with wide eyes. "Down goes the room of solace. That will drop Doombeard's ranking by at least five. You think it will put them in Red Class?"

Rugnus nods absently. "Could be."

"And Grudgeleather fans are going to be unbearable. Someone lost ferrum on that one."

"Yeah," Rugnus says, but his voice is distant.

Koglim stares at him. "Oh, come on, that was the coolest incursion all of Gem. Even with an outrider. What's with you? Show up late. In a bad mood. Is it a girl?"

Rugnus shakes his head. I know I'm the reason for his bad mood.

We're interrupted. A woman, a foot taller than all of us,

arrives at the head of the table. "I'm happy to fill your orders." Her clothes, mostly soft leather, show no hint of metal. She's Dura. Her eyes smile, carrying a sort of faraway innocence I never saw in Ara's eyes. This is what Rugnus was talking about. But why do they all appear distracted, unfocused? All but Ara.

"Kel!" Koglim says. "You know what might help cheer up my friend here? Some of that prawn soup you make. The one in the cheese-lined bread bowl." Koglim moans. "So. Good. What do you say, Rugnus?"

Rugnus can't resist the smile forming on his face. "Okay, I won't say no. Make it two. If you're here, you should try some, Clayson."

"Oh," Kel says, eyes wide, "I'm so happy to make it." Then she retreats across the room, and no one makes anything of her strange behavior. It occurs to me I have never been around Ara below granite. Is that the difference?

"So, tell us more about yourself, Clayson," Sira says.

"Yeah," Koglim adds. "Where you from? What's your story? And"—his goofy grin widens—"more importantly, what's your AMP? Love the ring by the way."

Time to start weaving my cover story. "I—"

Rugnus clears his throat. "Not much to tell. Grew up in a backward family in Whurrimduum. You know the story. They didn't even let him complete a summation."

"The sheer brutality of these people," Koglim says. "Sorry to hear that."

"Got him taken care of. Has a master's rating in shieldcraft, but other than that, just trying to emerge from the gall moth cocoon of his former life."

A lingering resentment, or anger, or annoyance simmers in every single word Rugnus says. Even Koglim and Sira look uncomfortable now.

I look across the table at Sira. "Sira, tell me more about the Keeper's Social. You said Silverkeeper would be there. What do they do at a Keeper's Social?"

Koglim glances between Rugnus and me. "Did you really grow up in a gall moth cocoon? How do you *not* know about the Keeper's Social?"

Sira leans in close to Koglim and pats his cheek. "It's fine, sweetie. We're happy to educate you, Clayson. The Keeper's Social happens four times a year. Teams of people compete at different levels—mimicking the best craftsman—for the chance to impress the most important people: business leaders like Lonecharge, and keepers from every dungeon. Most people only go for the party. But Rugnus' team will be out to compete."

Sira bats her eyes at me. "Come to think of it," she says. "I know you said you wanted to get adjusted, but Rugnus hasn't picked a fifth for his team yet. Do you want to go?"

Rugnus kicks my foot under the table. He knows I'm fishing for information about Silverkeeper and the mithrium. "Sounds fun," I say.

"Oh great!" Sira says.

Koglim squeals with excitement. "Wraithspit! I can't wait for this!" Then he sobers. "The invitation better not be a joke, Sira."

"Sorry I couldn't get you level four."

Koglim still has a delighted look on his face. "Sira. Do. Not. Apologize. Level three is epic. This might be my steppingstone into pro raiding, huh? And with some luck, some hard work, we could move into level four."

Sira shrugs. "Don't get your hopes up, cutie pie. Moving a level is nearly impossible."

"Nearly," Koglim says.

Sira reaches across the table and jostles Rugnus' hand. "So, what do you say? About Clayson? His shieldcraft rating is a good compliment to your team. Could break a tie."

He takes a deep breath. "Sure."

Sira pulls her hand away, and for a second, I'm left feeling like she did something to influence his decision. There's no way he would let me go to this social.

Two bowls of soup arrive for Rugnus and me. He draws one

toward him. "Though I don't know. It would bring too much attention to—"

"No such thing as too much attention," Koglim says. "What's gotten into you? This is the Keeper's Social." Koglim scans the room but stops on me. "This isn't about you sneaking around getting refugees out because everyone already knows about that."

"It's not that," Rugnus says, taking his first bite of the soup.

"I'd like to go," I say.

Rugnus stabs the side of the bread bowl with his spoon, and soup oozes out.

Sira bats her eyes at Rugnus. "Please, let him come, Rugnus."

He sighs. "Yeah, okay. But we stay on level three."

"Uh, I'm not agreeing to that," Koglim says. "Besides, I already messaged Winta and Hemdi. Hemdi agrees. Winta wants to test Clayson tomorrow." He turns his attention to the center of the table again, where a new batch of dungeon statistics pop up. He's apparently done with the conversation.

Test me? I don't like the sound of Winta testing me, which calls back my failure with iron in Rugnus' vault. But if that's what I have to do to get closer to Silverkeeper, then I don't have a choice.

Sira grins from ear to ear. "You guys are going to be amazing."

Rugnus tries to patch the hole in his bread bowl with his spoon. "What did I just agree to?"

FOLLOW ALONG

Incursion.

That's the word Koglim uses to describe tomorrow night's Keeper's Social. The purple amulet hanging around his neck warns him of 'ill timing, bad situations, and dire circumstances'—his words. It's glowing softly.

"Rugnus," Koglim says, shaking the purple gem around his neck. "This thing would be burning a hole through my body if we were in any danger. And since when do you shy away from risk? Is this about your mother being there?"

We've left Kel's Lounge for the warmth of the late afternoon under the brightstorm.

Rugnus shakes his head, mouth scrunching up. "My mother has nothing to do with this. Make my own path in this town. Catch up with you tomorrow morning, though."

Rugnus drags me over a side path, through desert landscaping to an overlook. "Let's find a place for you to stay tonight."

As I look out over the city, I say, "Maybe back to Magmadew Plaza?"

He stretches and yawns. "Got to try something different, Clayson. That's how this all works. Look out there." He spreads his hands toward the city, then throws an arm around my shoulder. A long finger extends toward a floating construction mech in the distance. "It's exciting. Mechsmiths and ironsmiths are always redoing things, creating something new every day. Few places are truly permanent. Constantly inventing. Can't help it. I love watching them work. Winta does some mechcraft work as an architect on the side."

He's right about change. There's a whole building I saw around breakfast near the far side of the ring: it's been replaced, the stone traded out for glass and metal. I think back to a flyover recording I saw of Whurrimduum. That city hasn't changed for a thousand years. It's based around the keepers and their families, each family having its own tower in a hive of towers. Castlestacks. "Different from Whurrimduum."

Rugnus scoffs. "They have a saying: city is stone. But we say: people are stone."

A phrase floats to the surface of my mind. Dad so often tried to convince me of my mother's goodness and compassion. I was pretty dismissive, something I've only recently begun to regret. Dad had a phrase he would say every time I told him we didn't need her. "Family is stone."

"What?" Rugnus says. I can tell I've pulled him out of deep thought.

"Something my dad used to say: family is stone."

Rugnus smiles. "The king, your father is... well, he's an interesting guy. Principled. Powerful. But interesting."

"You have family here in the city, Rugnus? Koglim said something about your mom?"

"She's helping the council organize the Keeper's Social. That's her thing—parties, organizing, social standing, things like that. Brought us here from Zal Kakraja when I was young."

"That's the kingdom that sent a spy to kill my dad's parents, the king and queen of Rimduum."

"My mother was a political dissident. She left everything to come here, be free. Doesn't mean she's free from old traditions. Pretty connected. Just... rather do things on my own."

"Guess we share that in common." Something settles over me, a sort of assurance, a deeper trust in Rugnus. For once, the feeling has nothing to do with craft.

We both try to apologize at the same time.

"Shouldn't have—" Rugnus says.

"I'm—" I say. "Look, you were right to try to get me out of there. That place was nuts. The moment you left, a crowd of pretty angry people attacked my little tower."

"Little? It would take a hundred people—a thousand—to get you out of there."

"Pretty sure they had more than a hundred. Then there was the flying lightning guy."

Rugnus raises his eyebrows, checking me over like he might find some fresh burns. "But you got out. Where did you go?"

"My vault." I tell him about my conversation with Andalynn, about the mithrium and Silverkeeper, but I stop before telling him my idea about getting to level four and stealing Silverkeeper's key. He barely agreed to go to level three in the first place. I'm glad Sira and Koglim were there to persuade him.

He shakes his head. "Can't let you go to the social, Clayson. What I said in there... " The sigh he releases holds the weight of dozens of responsibilities. I know the feeling well. "Anyway, let's just find you a place for tonight."

Dad might as well be standing in front of me. I know what he said. I know he tasked Rugnus with protecting me. But standing still, doing nothing, is impossible. One look at Rugnus reveals his desperation. His eyes are wide with the expectation I follow his lead.

"Fine," I say.

"Not going to argue with me?'

The sensible way Rugnus denies me freedom is something out of Dad's playbook. "Would there be a point?"

"Guess not. By the way, you look exhausted." As he opens bluelink, I get a connection request. He watches me with half of his attention. "Dreams?"

186

I nod.

"I may have a solution, but it will take me a bit to figure out."

"That would be great." There's an edge of hope in my voice.

We join our bluelink feeds and sort through some options for where to stay.

I settle on a group of white stone and oak cabins in a grove of pines near the center of Tungsten City called the Tin Bluffs.

My room has a view of a wide river. After Rugnus leaves, I exhaust the rest of the day scrolling through bluelink, soaking in the city's culture and the rules of the Keeper's Social. At daychange, the trees and cabins are enveloped in inky shades of deepest purple. Lanterns alight almost instantly, adding a layer of royal blue, which calms the low buzz of a million insects.

After an hour or so, marveling at the expanse of Tungsten City, I retreat to my room and lose myself in another tide of information. This time, I dive into the virtual histories directly: The Age of Discovery; my name sake's construction of the first brightstorms; the hundreds of years of mithrium attacks on all sides.

In less than ten minutes of research, it's clear who was at fault in the destruction of the world: everyone.

Extremists from Zal Kakraja used it first in Bastlynd—a kingdom once under the Swiss Alps. Then rebels from Himdem got a hold of one of the pieces and used it against Brimwok in the Sierra Nevada. Then Rimduum recovered it, kept it in a vault for fifty years before someone stole it—Rimduum ex-patriots. They attacked two cities in Hngaal.

And it goes on, and on, and on. There are five hundred years of this history.

I take a deep breath and move on to something else.

As a way to push the mithrium from my mind, I attend my parent's wedding and the announcement of the birth of my sister, along with the respective royal celebrations for each event. I sit in a half-dozen decades-old Keeper's Council meetings as Dad argues with them about the fate of the mithrium. He's so young.

Everything recent is sealed behind a firewall, so I can't watch my mother's inquisition.

When the glut of media tires me, I close my eyes, trying to imagine sleep.

But sleep isn't the right word for it. Visions maybe, but not sleep.

The canyon in my vision is the same as before, but the ribbons of light are more concentrated this time. They fly through the air, gliding in and around each other, echoing whispered conversations. No butterfly net appears, but it doesn't matter. I chase after a pink ball of light dripping echoes of three distinct words: mithrium, destroy, create. It's more difficult to catch than last time, but after almost a whole turn around the circular canyon, I pin it to the wall, and it allows me entrance into another scene, Yinzar Mithriumbane at the center.

His surroundings, this time, take on greater detail. We are deep under the mountain. A plain of blue-black stone stretches behind him. He balances at the edge of a ravine, lamp extended in one arm, his other converted into a mass of writhing brown vines, like serpents.

"Where does it come from?" Yinzar's words rumble across a ravine toward a stone cliff.

The whole of the cliff across from him quivers, and a mystic voice says, "Yes, good, good. Is he here with you now?"

"I can only guess so. Answer my question, Devourer. Where does it come from?"

My mind racks, trying to understand who they are talking about. Who is the 'he' they are referring to? This must have happened decades ago. But no one else can be seen in the darkness.

"Good. Yes. Yes, he is here."

"The mithrium where—"

"Yes, good, very good. It has no beginning, no end."

The light from Yinzar's lamp doubles, and the vines making up his other arm blacken. Again, the cliff on the other side of the ravine shifts. "Speak plainly. You say it has no end. Does this mean it can't be destroyed?"

"A good—yes, a good question. Eternal things can change, though they have no end."

Yinzar shifts his weight. "Then it can be changed."

"Yes, yes, good, a sacrifice, though. Change requires this."

Yinzar's eyes flash in the light, but the scene darkens and fades into nothing.

Pounding fists rattle against a wooden door.

I wake. Someone's knocking.

Moving from the bed is a mistake. My legs almost give out. I haven't slept well for the third night in a row. Opening the door reveals a smiling, mischievous Koglim, Rugnus' dungeon-obsessed friend from Kel's Lounge.

But his face transforms the moment he sees me. He whistles. "You look like you just crawled out of a hot, fresh pile of trollbrick."

I don't respond. My eyes are heavy with fatigue, and my mouth is dry.

Koglim digs in his bag and hands me an armband; basically a replica of the gold foiled blanket Rugnus used after he had to drag me out of Thiffimdal. "From Rugnus. Put this on one of those little biceps of yours. We've got work to do."

I put it on. Instantly, it's as if I have slept the whole night, went for a run, and had a hot breakfast. Exhilaration.

"What's in this thing? Pure adrenaline?"

"Magic," he says, tinkling his fingers in the air.

He pushes me into a chair, grabs the quick clean from my nightstand, and motions for me to drink. "I just saw you last night. How did you grow half a beard in less than twelve hours?"

My chin is like coarse sandpaper. Then I drink from the quick clean, and it's gone. Maybe I'm not a hundred percent refreshed, but Koglim's right. The armband is magic.

"Thanks for this," I say, tugging on the armband.

He nods. "Rugnus asked me to bring it to him during our

practice this morning. Said he wanted to bring it to you... but guess what?"

My back stretches involuntarily. "What?"

"I'm here instead. Meaning you're coming with me to practice. Don't care what Rugnus has to say about it. When I looked over his other choices for the Keeper's Social... keep Ide, no way I'm going with any of those pilgrims and runners. Unless... you're not a pilgrim, are you?"

"I—"

"Nah, you don't look"—investigating my face—"jumpy. Not going to back down from a challenge, are you?"

I smile. "Not that I'll admit to."

And like that, the day brightens. This is my way into the Keeper's Social tonight, my way to get that key, or at least see it. See him—Silverkeeper. Though I can't imagine Rugnus will be happy with Koglim or me when we show up to their practice.

"Good." A dull glow sparks in the heart of Koglim's necklace. From what he said last night, it only glows when there's danger in the future. "And see? Every time my brain thinks you're coming with us, Elbaz gets excited. Bigger the trap, bigger the treasure."

Elbaz must be the name of his pendant relic. "I thought if it glowed—"

"Small glow good, big glow... well, certain death... or something like that. I've always canceled my plans if it's too bright. Now let's move. The others are expecting us. Though Rugnus doesn't know yet, so yeah, prepare for that."

The moment we're out of the cabin, we budge. Then, below us, I'm greeted by a checkerboard of buildings. Each must be fifteen stories high. Koglim and I step from a budge port, and he hauls me over to the edge. We're standing on the roof of the corner of the checkerboard.

"The Lead Flats," Koglim announces with a sweep of his arm. "Most businesses have a practice arena here. And look," he points up. "You can see why Rugnus likes it."

Above us, light from the brightstorm casts glimmering ribbons through gently rolling waters. A snake-like river pythons around the checkerboard buildings, suspended in the air. A bright orange school of fish races by on the interior of the nearest loop.

"Rugnus tells me," Koglim explains, "the river has chain-link bypasses made of aluminum. The loops are wide enough to let through most fish, but anything big enough to eat will contact the chains and appear in Rugnus' favorite restaurants all over the city. What do you think?"

"Yeah," I say. "Uh, cool."

Koglim giggles. "Don't let Rugnus hear you minimize the river's glory. He takes his fish love to an unhealthy level."

"He did buy me a hamburger once," I say.

Koglim raises an eyebrow, impressed. "Seafood and taffy food. So, he's broadening his palate a little. Set me in front of a cow-roast with an unending supply of creamed onion soup, tuned into the seventy-six dungeon finalcount...that's my happy place." At this, he groans a stretch and rolls his head to one side. "Can't remember the last time I was up this early."

As we move across the roof toward another budge port, Koglim starts spewing more information about the Keeper's Social. Last night, I spent a brief moment reviewing footage from the last one. From a wide-angle, it's a party, but listening to Koglim now, I realize it's more like a sporting event, which explains why Koglim is obsessed with it.

"We'll have to find the highest-ranking keeper, or whoever happens to be representing that dungeon, and copy their use of craft. Some things are obvious but difficult; other things, hidden. It's all about seeing things as they really are. If we can find and copy the most difficult challenge on level three, they will give us the key to level four. Rare, but a guy can hope. Other than that, the more we impress people, the more contacts and invitations we'll get. This could be my shot to break into professional raiding."

There's the social aspect of the event. Impress people. Move up in the world. Many people go to the Keeper's Social for enter-tainment, food, and music, but others group together in teams of five and complete against the keepers to win fame and glory. We're the second type. The potential for instant fame is why Rugnus doesn't want me going. But besides looking for Silver-keeper, I'll keep my head down.

My mind returns to Koglim's mention of a key, and I turn inward, trying to make a plan for what I will do if we make it to the fourth level, if I make it before Silverkeeper. He may not even have his keeper's key on him, and I may not be able to get it if he does. If I did, what would I do with it? I shut off the part of my brain that's screaming about how reckless this is, telling myself if it was that dangerous, Koglim's necklace would warn all of us. Koglim hasn't stopped gushing about the social. "...which is why it's best to have a master of each type of craft. That's where you come in."

This jars me from my thoughts. "Me?"

"Master of shieldcraft is pretty rare. Speaking of which, Hemdi and Winta are probably already here. And Winta insists on forcing you through a test. Let's get over to Quimdem's training floors." Koglim rolls his head in my direction. "So, our team has been together for... well, a long time. You think you can keep up with us?"

"I'm a quick learner."

Familiar sheets of aluminum pockmark the rooftop—budge ports. We step on the one labeled seventeen and budge to the top of an identical skyscraper somewhere in the middle of the checkerboard of buildings. Koglim veers over to another group of budge ports and takes one labeled Quimdem A3-E3.

He vanishes, and I follow him. We budge inside. Every wall, ceiling, and floor are formed from rough concrete, just like the testing room in Rugnus' vault. It's made to take a beating. Hemdi and Winta await. I thought I would be the center of atten-tion the second I arrived, but Hemdi has three chocolate lab puppies on a leash. The knot in my stomach loosens. The sight brings the first genuine smile to my face I can remember in the last few days.

Rugnus stands with his back toward me.

Koglim goes right for the puppies. "You brought them!" He kneels and scratches one under its chin. The two other blobs of chocolate fur vie for more love and attention.

"They didn't want to leave the park this morning, and—" Winta spots me. "Koglim, what did you do?"

All of Koglim's bravado melts away. He finds a concrete post extremely interesting. "What do you mean? I picked up our fifth."

Now Rugnus turns. His mouth drops open. He blinks. Then he blinks again.

I offered a clipped, "Hey."

Rugnus' expression hardens. I feel everyone's eyes flicking between us until Rugnus marches toward me and snags my elbow, pulling me away. Koglim calls after us, "Just let the guy come, Rugnus. What's wrong with you?"

Rugnus drags me around a corner. He crosses his arms and waits.

"Koglim invited me," I try.

"But what did *I* say to you." He lowers his voice. "It will be too many eyes on—"

"The whole city is filled with eyes. I can't—"

"You can. That was the whole point of this." He rakes a hand over his stubbly hair. "What was I thinking. I should have never introduced you to Koglim... or Hemdi... or Winta, now—"

"Rugnus." I hold up my hands. This is my only shot to get close to Silverkeeper. "You're the one putting a spotlight on me... by treating me differently. Besides Koglim's necklace, Elbaz, or whatever... there's no warning about the social. I think it's safe for—"

Koglim peeks around the corner. "Hey, Mr. Openness-and-transparency. What's the deal? Come on, man. Winta's ready with the kid's first task. She brought the puppies. And we both know you can't control them."

Rugnus shakes his head. He points a finger at me, breathes, then throws his hands up, his resolve crumbling. "Ide keep me, Clayson. Fine. Just... okay, fine." He spins around, stalking past Koglim.

"I'll take that as approval," Koglim says.

Koglim leads me back to the group like he just convinced his parents to let him keep a kitten. As we turn the corner, Hemdi loosens the leash holding back the puppies, and they charge us, mobbing our feet. I find the nearest one and scratch its head, but I can tell instantly it has an unquenchable desire for attention.

We play with the puppies for a few minutes until Koglim says, "I've got to meditate."

"Now?" Winta asks. "There are puppies. Puppies can be your meditation!"

"Meditation is serious business. Proceed with Clayson's test." Koglim stalks over to the other edge of the room. When a few of the puppies break off and try to follow him, he jump-scares them with a high-pitched, "Boo!"

They retreat, scurrying over to the safety of the larger group, paws clicking on the concrete floor. Winta throws her hands up in protest, but Hemdi says, "Better let him. He isn't wrong. He's more focused after a bit of meditation."

Rugnus takes a deep breath, passing me one more look, but then rolls back his shoulders. Which I assume means he is gonna let me go to the social. My argument worked. Or maybe Koglim's insistence. Either way, it worked.

"Wipe that smile off your face, latcher," Winta says to me. "You still have to pass my test."

Rugnus' face transforms. "That's right. Don't know anyone who can control the puppies."

"That's the test?" I say. "Controlling the puppies?"

"It's a start," Winta says. "If you want a spot on the team, you'll have to prove you can—like taffies say—punch your weight."

"You mean, pull your weight?" I ask.

"Whatever," Winta says.

"So, Winta," Rugnus says, seemingly back to the cheerful version of himself. "What's the challenge?"

"Did you bring the whistle?"

Rugnus smiles, adjusts the hem of his shirt, and pulls a copper whistle from the pocket of his embroidered vest. It's the same whistle I used to control the crabs in his aquarium, but he was under the effects of napcraft when I used it.

Hemdi takes it from Rugnus, scrutinizing it closely. "I thought this was used on small animals, fish, and stuff. I mean, maybe it could work."

"Sure, sure," Rugnus says dismissively. "But that's the challenge. Can he use it to control these adorable, out-of-control little puppers?"

Hemdi appraises me, detaching the puppies from their leash again. They bolt, reckless, for Koglim on the other side of the room. "He can try."

Rugnus shoots me a quick look. "He won't be able to."

We both know my rating is not a five, but a seven. The fake AMP didn't erase my skills; it just covered them up.

From across the room, Koglim's thin sigh is audible as the puppies yap at his knee. His eyes still closed in concentration, one hand still massaging the strands of his necklace. He grabs one of them by the back of the neck and lifts it to his lap, working his hand across its fur. The puppy wiggles onto his back, and Koglim—with another nasal sigh—scratches its belly.

"I can do it," I say.

"Inspiring," Winta says.

Koglim's hulking figure rises from his cross-legged position on the floor. He marches over, puppy in his arms, apparently abandoning his meditation.

"Let's prove it," Rugnus says.

Hemdi bends down, tussling the ears of one of the puppies. "Shouldn't we test his shieldcraft?"

Koglim waves a hand. "Nah, latcher's a natural seven. What

we don't know—that Winta kindly pointed out to me—is if his rating in animal craft will be useful. You know how many dungeons have coppercraft as a secondary, if not primary, focus? We need a tamer. Let's see how he does."

"We need a goldmage," Rugnus says. "They always use royal crafts in the key."

Royal crafts. I know this one. Gold, silver, and tungsten.

Koglim slaps his own chest. "I've got silver and gold."

"That's a learned seven in gold," Rugnus says.

The hulking form of Koglim pivots directly in front of Rugnus. "A seven you helped me earn after Bitteriron. And don't forget what happened there."

Rugnus' face cools another fifty degrees. "Don't bring Ifra into this."

Koglim takes a step closer to Rugnus.

Winta points a finger at them both. "We're not going there, again. Valifra is out of bounds."

Hemdi must find my face wrinkled in confusion. He leans closer to me. "Valifra Hollyhelm was the fifth member of our team. She was killed in Bitteriron Dungeon."

At the mention of her name, all eyes fall on me.

Haunted ripples of grief echo out from each of the members of the team. Not only is Rugnus trying to prevent me from revealing my identity to the world, but he truly doesn't wanna fill this open spot on his team, even temporarily.

Taking a step back, I say, "I didn't know. Maybe I should—"

"No," Koglim says. "We need a fifth. Winta, let's roll this show onto the road."

Winta groans. "Koglim, don't try to use human expressions. Its 'roll this show *on* the road."

"It's 'get' this show on the road." The words exit my mouth before I can think better of it.

Rugnus shoots me a look, but Winta scoffs. "What would you know, latcher? Get. That sounds so stupid. You roll on a road.

Keep Ide, the brains on these ironheads nowadays. It's like Whur-rimduum keeps them locked in a bubble."

"They kinda do," Koglim says.

Dropping to one knee, Hemdi flips his bag around and draws out a small stack of leafs. These ones are about the size of sticky notes but thicker, and made from mesh instead of solid metal. Winta takes the batch, delivering them around the room, pausing at each person to make sure the leaf is right.

One for Hemdi, three for Winta, two for Koglim, two for me, and two for Rugnus. Ten in total.

My best guess? They have something to do with our strengths. Everyone chooses one and bends the mesh over a few fingers. When I separate the two squares, the familiar revelatory sensation of silvercraft tingles my mind. The skin around my ears goes numb, and a minor electric charge cascades through my head.

The charge jump starts my intelligence about both shieldcraft and coppercraft. As a test, I mold one of them around my fingers and place the other in a pocket. The knowledge about shields flees my mind, but I still know a lot of extra stuff about controlling animals. Eager to prove myself, I ask Rugnus for the whistle.

"Good luck," Hemdi says.

The moment I grab it, the puppy in Koglim's arm leaps for the floor, and together, the excited dogs scurry toward my toes. Winta takes a step forward. Confidence floods my veins, and I smile. I've got this.

I whistle once, long and slow, close my eyes, and will the puppies to make a line. I wait for a breath and ease my eyelids open. Everyone is staring at me, and then Koglim bursts into squeals of laughter. Two of the dogs have buried their heads in their paws. The other one is draining its bladder on my sneakers. If they weren't so ridiculously cute, it would make me upset.

Winta shakes her head at me. "Just try the first task listed on the leaf. Don't improvise."

The weight of the leaf hangs on my fingers, the metal

pinching my skin. I search my mind for some trick to perform, some way to show I can command a few puppies, that the team can rely on me. There is a sequence to the information, but I skip ahead, settling on a complicated set of notes that will produce an adorable tumbling routine bound to get everyone's attention.

Without any concentration on my part—and maybe that's the trick with craft—the notes come flowing out of the whistle, long and bright. Two of the little chocolate Labradors stand on their hind legs and beg, while the other one weaves through and around them in a figure eight. The effect on the team is instantaneous. Koglim jumps up and down as excited as one of the puppies, Rugnus blinks and takes a deep breath, and Hemdi claps. Even Winta can't help but smile, which only encourages me.

Next, I have them jump over each other in turns, each barking when they hurdle sideways to take the center position.

"Wow!" Hemdi says. "I believe we found a dog sitter."

Winta narrows her eyes. "And you're only a five?"

This is Rugnus' cue. "Okay. He's proved himself. Let's split up and practice individual challenges. In an hour, we can reassemble and try some combos."

"Wait a second," Winta says. "I want to test his shieldcraft against my timecraft."

Hemdi raises his hands. "No, no. Winta. Put the bracelet away."

Loops of mercury have already spun outward from Winta's wrist but retreat just as quickly. Winta growls. "Yeah, fine. You're probably right."

Koglim has come to my side as well. "Good call."

Slowly, everyone breaks away from the group except Rugnus. "Nice job with the puppies." He leans close to me. "Maybe ease off a bit, though, when you use your ring. We don't need you making massive stone towers today. Some simple energy shields oughta do."

"Rugnus—"

"Let me finish. Wanting to participate with us makes sense, and it's partially my fault for even telling Sira about you. She can get kinda obsessive. And yes, Elbaz hasn't warned Koglim of anything bad associated with the night. But I'm still worried. You look just like him."

I pat the pocket with the leaf about shields. "I get it. Low profile."

"Exactly," he says, leading me to an empty corner of the room. Clearing his throat a few times, he says, "Here." Concrete bubbles from the ground and the walls, forming into knee-high stumps, gymnastic-like bars, and dog-sized rings like a mini obstacle course. He kneels by the puppies, which have followed me.

"You little doggies be good," he says, ruffling the skin folds of one of their faces and scratching another on the back. He stands and leaves.

I play with the puppies for the first few minutes, getting them to balance on concrete stumps and jump through the rings. One of them even hops from stump to stump on its back legs. All thanks to the whistle and the leaf providing the instructions. After fifteen minutes, I swear I can see through the eyes of one of the puppies like I'm jumping through the hoops myself. When I discern a sense of hunger from the smallest one, I let them all rest.

I switch from the coppercraft leaf to the one about shields. The first task is easy. Did Winta or Hemdi code it that way? I'm supposed to throw something in the air and create an energy field above me to prevent it from smacking me on the head. I throw the whistle up in the air and block it easily.

The next tutorial is more intimidating. I'm supposed to jump off of something higher than ten feet—in Loamin measurement, that's a bar or two loam—and use the same type of energy shield to break my fall. But if the ring can construct a massive stone tower and a chain-link fence that turns speeding marbles into roasted marshmallows, a drop of ten feet shouldn't be difficult.

199

I spin around, searching for someplace to drop from but find Winta staring at me from the other side of the room. A mass of liquid metal circles her head in a stream—mercury. Droplets of the mercury break from the larger mass and form a semi-circle in front of her. With a gesture like she's adjusting a nozzle, my body's pulse simmers to a slow drip. When I step forward, it's like I'm stuck in molasses. My thoughts are as slow as my movements. She smiles.

Sending everyone off to do their tasks was a distraction. She had always intended to test my shieldcraft.

But I have my ring, and the moment I ask it to protect me, a white light glows on my skin. Winta freezes in concentration, but my speed has returned to normal, and I make a point to jog over to the staircase nearest to her, smiling.

Before I reach the first step, Koglim, Hemdi, and Rugnus thunder down the stairs.

"What happened?" Koglim said. The purple pendant around his neck is glowing with a sharp light.

I look from Rugnus to Koglim. "I—Winta tried to slow me down or something."

"Snitch," Winta says.

"It's an omen," Koglim says. "Winta won't be able to use her mercury band."

"You sure?" I say.

Rugnus stares at me. "The hard part is connecting the premonition to something concrete. In this case, it might be Winta's mercury band. We all felt her slow time, and then the pendant started to glow. But it might be something else."

Winta draws the mercury into a sweatband on her wrist. "Hold on. Clayson blocked it."

Hemdi blinked, stunned. "Is that possible?"

Winta puts her hands on her hips. "I'm telling you, he blocked it."

"Did you..." Rugnus looks at my hand.

"I used my ring."

Winta points to my hand, "That thing blocked my timecraft? Where did you get it?" She's more interested than annoyed now.

Rugnus sighs. "If you insist on going to the social, you'll have to use something else. Can't take the chance. Lead. I can get you something high-rated. It—"

"Hold on," Winta says, stepping closer. "I asked where he got the ring. Seems pretty powerful for some low-rated refugee. Spoil the beans, Rugnus."

"What does that mean?" he asks.

"It is a human phrase," Hemdi says.

A short laugh jumps from my lips, but I quiet myself. Rugnus did say Winta was into human culture, but her misuse of the phrase "spill the beans" makes her look suddenly more vulnerable, and unfortunately for me—though I know she's married—more attractive. I give myself a command not to think about her that way anymore.

She stands waiting for me, or Rugnus, to explain.

"Okay, fine," Rugnus says. "It's a relic."

Koglim, in some sort of celebration, gives a massive flex of every possible muscle in his body. "Yeah, buddy!"

"Where did you find it?" Hemdi asks.

"Wolfstaff."

Koglim stops his celebration. Winta and Hemdi share a quick look.

"During his summation?" she says, surveying me with wary eyes.

Rugnus nods.

"Well, one thing's for sure," Koglim says, shaking his glowing beads at me. "There's no way he can use that thing during the social. The omen is law. No doubt it would prevent us from getting to level four."

My mind spins with another possibility. Koglim has no way of knowing what the omen means. If I try to use the ring to shield myself from Silverkeeper—steal his key—I could be caught. Or something even worse, something unknowable. I glance at Rugnus, who, without craft, seems to read my mind.

"Agreed," Rugnus says. "He *won't* use the ring."

"But," Koglim says, patting me on the shoulder, "with a man who can summon a relic during summation, getting into level four should be as simple as budgecraft."

Nods and smiles greet me all around, but Winta grants me only a vague, unreadable expression.

MIMIC THEIR CRAFT

As FAR As dressing for the social, Rugnus refused to leave me to my own devices. But at least I match everyone else. Even with the party split between socialites and fame seekers, everyone is dressed in crisp colors and flowing fabrics. I settled on a coffee brown collared shirt with yellow and white neon accents and a simple pair of slacks.

I've never had to wear anything this uncomfortable in my life. I'd rather gear up to muck out a goat barn.

Two girls in denim blouses, one lined with strings of light, one lined with fur, eye me from across the room. I take another drink from the floating serving trays, but Rugnus grabs it from my hand and sets it on the table. "Not that one. Got to keep your head in the game."

The room is already spinning, thick with bodies and music and conversation. Keepers are spread out over the whole floor of the building, waiting to demonstrate their craft to the handful of teams who've 'come for glory'. Koglim's words. Screens everywhere show the scores of the competing teams. Though the score has nothing to do with finding the key. It's more about the notoriety the teams gain as the night progresses. Anything under one thousand points and none of the headhunters for businesses and keepers will even talk to you.

Most of the partygoers are of the social variety, ignoring the challengers altogether, preferring the company of their friends and the keepers. Rugnus tells me there are many people from Whurrimduum in attendance. And Sira has said, more than once, that Handler installed the best foilgrips for the occasion. No one can budge away at will.

"This better work," Winta says, gazing at thousands of kinetic spheres dancing with the music against the reflective black ceiling.

Eating appetizers, dancing, and greeting strangers has me numb.

The swinging, digitized tones and brass instruments of this Loamin music—like something out of an 80's spy movie—must be lulling away my senses, or maybe it's the stiff collar smothering me. Either way, we're not making any progress toward the fourth level. Rugnus is happy about that, but Koglim is as determined as ever.

Rugnus flashes yet another smile, a trait that's gained him even more followers on bluelink in the last few hours. The decadence and pomp breathe life into Rugnus. Every arm he grasps to test strengths, every joke he tells emboldens him to greater heights. In short intervals, he checks in with his followers through his bluelink connection, sometimes talking to the air as if they might be listening.

To say the least, I strongly dislike all the added attention. Everyone but me seems able to act naturally, but I'm as rigid as an oak. More than once, someone from the group has had to come search for me in the crowd—I've been using them as camouflage.

"Koglim and I can duplicate this craft in our sleep," Rugnus says. "Our audience agrees."

Winta lowers her voice, and it's almost drowned out by the music. "If you can deal with the heights."

I shift my attention to the balcony's edge. Silver-iron disks form a flagstone path out over the side of the thirtieth floor of the Handler building into the darkness.

"You really think this Magmakeeper has the key to the next level?" I say to Koglim, holding my hand up to a floating aluminum tray of pineapple meatball skewers.

"Got to be," Koglim says. He's spent half the night obsessing over dungeon numbers, held up in some secluded corner trying to meditate. "Magmakeeper is both keeper and seer of his dungeon, and it's the second-highest-rated dungeon on this level. No one's got past this tonight. But we can do this. We copied Gaintkeeper to the letter."

"We?" Winta says.

Koglim rolls his shoulders and stiffens his spine. "Okay, you and Rugnus."

"And look what it got us," she says. "A lousy two hundred points. To get noticed by anyone, we need to be above a thousand. At this rate, we'll reach that by next Khalsday."

"Have faith," Koglim says. "And points won't get us the key, just more notice."

Winta opens her mouth to protest, but Hemdi intercedes. "Faith is Winta's second nature."

Shaking his head, Koglim says. "Faith in machines doesn't count."

Magmakeeper swaggers at the edge of the balcony. "Unless there's another challenger, I'm going back to the party." His slurred voice is tied into the sound system.

Rugnus makes the decision. "We challenge you!" He's been two different people all night, sometimes apprehensive about taking a challenge but also drawn in by the keeper's alluring craft.

Koglim wolfs down what's left of his skewered meatballs and trundles behind Rugnus. The crowd cheers, and Rugnus pumps his fist into the air with the rhythm of the music. Taking a position at Magmakeeper's side, Rugnus shoots a wink out to his followers on bluelink.

I call up his feed through my own connection, and for a few seconds, I slip into an augmented reality where I can view the world through Rugnus' perspective. My heartbeat accelerates. I'm him now. There's a rush of euphoria. I scrape my hand over my stubbly hair, and I smile—the whole crowd cheers.

But an image comes to my mind, the boy from yesterday, the one with electric blue eyes, who didn't realize I had bumped into him. What had Sira called him? A headslop. The term makes perfect sense now that I've had a few media benders over the last couple of days. How many people in this city are lost in a different reality?

Fingers snap right in front of my face. "Wakey, wakey, Clayson," Sira's sing-song voice brings me back to reality. I shut the connection, my mind returning to my own body. There's a gap in the crowd where her presence parted them like a boat through water. She's batting her eyes at me.

"On my channel?" she asks.

"No. Rugnus'," I say.

Sira leads me by the hand as we follow Winta and Hemdi through the crowd toward the edge of the balcony, the other side of the city cavern glimmering across the open distance. The five of us stand shoulder to shoulder. Sira announces the challenge to the whole floor with an amplified voice.

All night, each challenge has quickly drawn attention. Still, Sira is Handler's representative on this floor, making official statements and giving announcements. There are also holographic displays hovering over all the tables and even a few larger displays along the walls. I feel a few thousand eyes on me, but there could be hundreds of thousands of people watching through bluelink.

For a second, my hand reaches for the ring in my pocket. Could it stop others from following me through bluelink? I don't know the total count, but Rugnus has been checking my followers, and the number is growing. There's no way to block them. Maybe I could use the ring to censor my image across the whole network? Instead, I squeeze my hands in front of me to keep them still.

Magmakeeper—a bright-faced man with rose pink cheeks and a close-cut beard—frowns, unimpressed with us. He exudes a certain nonchalance as if he's been to a lot of socials and couldn't care less what happens tonight. But holding a long metal rod, he steps right off the balcony onto a floating silver disk. If he slips, there's a tenblock between him and the bottom of the city cavern far below. A bar is about ten feet, a block is ten bars, and a tenblock—well, it's a long way to fall. He'd be only a red smudge to be power washed by the cleaning mechs if he does. There's no budgecraft allowed on the floating flagstones.

Rugnus whispers to Koglim, "He'll shield with crystal this time."

Koglim isn't listening. He's trying to draw Sira's attention by forcibly crossing his eyes. And it's working. Sira slips him a coy smile, controlling a giggle the best she can. He plants a massive paw on top of her head, and she nudges him with her shoulder. She can't see it, but Koglim gives me a smile. Translation: he is interested in Sira, and I'm not allowed to be.

Okay by me. I have other worries tonight. Forget about winning the key to the next floor, which is hidden behind layers of craft. I've gotta figure out how to sneak a completely different kind of key away from the head of the Keeper's council. And I've been watching. Many keepers have their keys visible on their person—a badge of pride. I'll have to get close.

Rugnus slaps Koglim on the shoulder. "Koglim! The challenge. Pay attention."

There's a slight grunt, and Koglim straightens. He's probably five seven—seven past a loam—meaning he's about a head taller than most Loamin. I'm four past, which makes me stick out more than I want to, but Koglim uses height to his advantage as he peers out over the balcony to study what Magmakeeper is doing.

The heavyset man leaps from the first disk to another, which appears a couple feet away—half a loam or a quarter bar. The moment both feet are on the platform, there's a pulse of red light, and a column of white flames engulfs him. Rugnus nods and points to the flames. "Look through the fire," he says to the rest of us. "I'm right. He went with crystal to defend."

I squint at the mass of flames. Inside the fire, I make out a growing lump of geometric patterns. Encased in crystal, Magmakeeper waits out the attack, impatiently tapping his foot. When the flames die away, the crystalline growth shatters like tempered glass. Magmakeeper shakes the sandy material off and, before I can even process what's happening, jumps to the next disk.

A whirlwind erupts from the new disk. He shields himself by adding a layer of heavy stone to his skin. Disk after disk appears. For each one, Magmakeeper leaps, balances, and defends. I can understand why this is a good challenge for Rugnus, but what is Koglim's part?

"I don't see the silvercraft he's using," I say to Rugnus.

Hemdi answers. "The disks are silver and iron. You must predict where they could appear. Watch him."

At last, I see what's happening. Magmakeeper jumps to the next disk before it even appears, and the disk he'd been standing on vanishes. "Whoa," I say. "His timing has to be—"

"Perfect," Rugnus says.

From a distant point beyond the balcony, the heavyset, nimble man makes jump after jump, which goes on for an impressive amount of time. With what seems to be a final effort, he leaps and snags something shimmering out of the air. In a flash, he vanishes but reappears, standing beside us. A serving tray floats up as everyone cheers. He releases an aluminum foil bird from between his fingers, and it takes flight, circling out to where he grabbed it seconds earlier. He takes another large foggy glass of ale from off the tray, raises it to the sky, greeting even more cheers, and gulps it down.

The crowd quiets as Rugnus and Koglim step toward the edge of the balcony. Koglim slaps Rugnus' back with a meaty paw. Rugnus pulls an iron file from his bag like he's gonna try to break out of prison. Rugnus scrutinizes the first disk over the edge. He nods to Koglim and jumps.

The purple gem laid over Koglim's black dress shirt glimmers for a second, and he yells, "Left."

Rugnus leaps into the void, but a disk forms and catches him. Ice snakes up his leg, but Rugnus uses the iron file, and lava cascades from the crown of his head down to his toes, counteracting the ironcraft from the disk.

The crowd surges around us toward the balcony's edge for a better look.

"Left," Koglim shouts.

Rugnus leaps and lands. With a crack, lightning rips from the sky and strikes out at him. In a swirling mass, he catches it with an open palm, redirecting away from him, into the side of the building below, where a wall of glass explodes outward into the night.

The crowd erupts in cheers. Rugnus' face hardens in grim determination as he leaps forward under Koglim's direction.

There's a tug on my shirt. "You're with me, handsome."

It's Sira.

"What?" I say over the deafening cheers.

"Come on. Let's show you off to some influencers."

"Wait, what about this challenge?"

"You can't tell they're going to win? They've crossed the threshold on this one. And if you're worried about the points, don't. You came as a team; you win as a team. Besides, maybe you'll find another challenge out there that plays to your strengths."

I hesitate for a second, but now the crowd pushes me from my spot near Hemdi and Winta. I don't have the greatest view from here anyway, so I shrug and follow her.

We wind through a throng of people, her hand gripping my forearm. Past the crowd, we close on two people sitting in armchairs across from each other. A tall Dura man stands with a food tray behind them. I stop when I see his face. It's Vor. One of these people must be connected with the royal family or the Keepers.

My feet start dragging, but Sira pulls me forward. The best I can hope for is that Vor doesn't reveal me, but he's staring at the floor.

The conversation between the two people barely reaches my ears above the din of the clapping behind me.

"...but think about what we are doing. This city is something new, powerful, with the potential to transform our world into something beyond clans and kingdoms. Beyond wealth, surnames, and factions." The man scrunches his pockmarked face, his hands placating.

The woman, probably the shortest Loamin I've seen yet, says. "New means it hasn't been tested." Her words are slow, calculating.

"Oh, you two," Sira says.

They break off their conversation. Both of them smile broadly. The man with the pockmarks gestures to Vor, and the tall, lean Dura man bends forward with a tray of what looks like fruit tarts. "Ah, Sira, just in time. My favorite advocate of pure democracy."

"Not so hasty, Fenquick," the painfully short woman says, "I have personally heard Sira defending tradition and eschewing the pace of life here in Tungsten City." Vor plies his tray toward her. "Not now, Vor." She nudges him back a little bit.

If Vor is offended by being shoved away, he doesn't show it.

Sira releases my forearm and gestures to them one at a time. "Clayson, let me introduce you to Ha'da Fenquick and Orangal Tinkeeper. Fenquick is a local businessman, to say the least of him, and Tinkeeper—of course—is the keeper and seer of Tinseer Dungeon."

Tinkeeper cranes her neck to look at me. Her voice rises when she says, "By Ide, you know who this boy looks like?"

Sira smiles, but I guess what Tinkeeper will say. I'm as exposed as a raw nerve. With this many people visiting the social from the courts of Whurrimduum, I must play a careful game.

"This is surely a Brightstorm."

My attention snaps into focus. They must see Dad's features on my face. I need an excuse to walk away.

Fenquick laughs. "You see something of Whurrimduum in everything."

"Clayson recently fled Whurrimduum," Sira says, which only solidifies the confused look on Tinkeeper's face.

"Good for you, son," Fenquick says.

"Have you truly?" Tinkeeper says. "And how did you manage that? The foilgrips can't be bypassed."

Fenquick takes another fruit tart and waves Vor over to me. I'm not hungry, but the way this conversation is going, it's a good idea to keep my mouth full. I turn my face from Vor and slowly reach out, taking one.

"My old friend"—Fenquick slaps Tinkeeper's arm—"would a border stop you from obtaining freedom?"

The woman closes her eyes and shakes her head. "Freedom? With a mob as your king? Please, Sira, explain the danger to the man."

Sira touches each of their arms and says, "Oh, I wouldn't dare interrupt your musings. You two are the most entertainment I have had all night."

"Then you, Clayson," Tinkeeper says. Her eyes slice through to the truth in my bones. Could she have guessed who I am? Maybe it was a mistake to come out in the open. But no. No one could possibly know my real identity. Still, my heart is about to jump out of my chest. I make every attempt to keep myself faced away from Vor. "Tell me your thoughts. Are you free now that you have no true government? Are you free with your every action recorded and your privacy destroyed?"

"So dramatic," Fenquick says.

Behind their heads, I catch a glimpse of neon hummingbirds as they dive from the ceiling. Brig, the boy who works logging failures in the basement at Handler, stands next to a girl about his age. Her eyes are closed, her arms moving like the conductor of an orchestra.

I swallow the rest of the tart. "Please excuse me for a minute. I see an opportunity for my craftsmanship." I use the same phrase Rugnus has used throughout the night to interrupt conversations. It indicates to others you need to find ways to get points.

Fenquick claps his hands in front of his face. "You've been holding out on us, Sira. He's here for victory tonight."

"And," Tinkeeper adds, "he is no doubt on the same team as your other friends."

Sira nods.

As I move to leave, Tinkeeper holds up her hand. "What is your family name then, Clayson?"

"Glintwheel," I say.

Her pupils shift as if she's searching files in her brain for some mention of my fake last name. I'm not gonna wait for her to ask any more questions. If there are Glintwheels in Whurrimduum, I know nothing about them. It would be a dangerous conversation. I stride toward the girl, who's looking at the hummingbirds.

"Can I attempt the challenge?" I ask. There's more confidence in my voice than I expected.

"Clayson," Brig says. "Ho, no call, no show today, I should have guessed you were prepping for the Keeper's Social. I'll introduce you to my sister. She's around here somewhere."

"Hi, Brig. So, can I complete the challenge?"

The girl has an ethereal glaze over her eyes. Her orange hair lays in a braid down her front left side, and freckles dance across her face when she speaks. "I doubt so, but I certainly won't stop you from trying. No one yet has had the wisdom to do it."

Brig smiles at me encouragingly.

A large copper coin stirs in her hand, and she rubs it between her fingers. The hummingbirds, which had been hovering in a circular formation, seamlessly break for the ceiling, merging with the kinetic spheres. Against the gloss-black ceiling, their bright yellow feathers reflect in the spheres, giving an effect like the whole sky is a kaleidoscope. They race and weave, switch positions like trick planes, always coming back in line with the spheres, even though the shape of the cloud of kinetic balls morphs into different patterns every few seconds.

The dance of the birds—colorful, silent, beautiful—warms something inside of me. In contrast to the power of ironcraft, coppercraft—animal dominion, as it's also named—puts me into a sort of trance.

Dominion.

The words stick somewhere inside my head. It's an unnatural word that doesn't describe—at all—the connection I have with the girl, with the hummingbirds. I wanna tell her what I think about the craft she's performed, but I guard against my natural reaction. I still can't tell what is supposed to be simple and pedestrian and what is supposed to amaze me.

"That's cool," I say.

Without making eye contact, she blinks in confusion. "Cool?"

"I didn't... I mean, it's amazing."

The hummingbirds whiz into place in a circular pattern over our heads. With folded arms, she juts her chin to the hummingbirds.

I sigh. "My turn?"

She nods.

I remove the whistle, which for the first time breaks the little girl's dazed look. "A bit on the nose," she says, "a whistle."

She has an air of being older than her years.

The moment I blow into the whistle, the hummingbirds change formation, climbing as a group toward the vaulted ceiling, not as seamlessly, but a decent copy of what the girl did.

Sira, Tinkeeper, and Fenquick draw closer from behind. Vor has left their side. Thank Ide—if that's the right way to use that phrase. I can almost feel Sira breathing on my neck. Fenquick cheers me on, and Tinkeeper nearly bores a hole through my face with her eyeballs.

But I don't let her steal my focus. I take the hummingbirds

through a maneuver I imagine on the spot. They dive and roll past one another. After a few seconds, I'm connected with them—as I was with Hemdi's puppies—as if I am looking through their eyes. I finish with a sort of free fall into a hover and park the birds over our heads. I hope for some approval from the girl, and I'm not disappointed. Her whole demeanor has shifted.

"Hm. Cool," she says.

"Cool?"

"I didn't expect anyone to—I'll have to make it more difficult next time." The girl floats away without another word.

Sira crashes into me, excited, ruffling my hair. "Bearcloak Dungeon is tough. Rugnus will be as giddy as a latcher. Check the team's points."

I open bluelink and stare. The feat earned us twelve hundred points. It's not like I found the key to the next level, but it puts us in the spotlight. Behind me, there's a loud cheer, and our points double. Rugnus and Koglim won their challenge against Magmakeeper.

Fenquick is jumping out of his skin with excitement. "What a show tonight!" He makes a few tight gestures in bluelink like he's signing something. "Being new to Tungsten City, you must be searching for an apprenticeship. Please consider coming to work for me, young man. You or anyone in your team would be welcome at Fenquick."

A notification dings over bluelink with Fenquick's contact information. I copy what Rugnus has said and done a few times tonight. We test strengths, grasping each other's forearms. "I'm honored."

"This is why," says Tinkeeper, her voice now as dangerous as a flame, "we have tightened up the boundaries. Your talent and service should be given to your kingdom, son of Glintwheel."

"Oh, don't be so sour, Orangal. Let the boy enjoy his new life." He leans over to me. "And from what I've just seen, you have a bright future ahead. Go with all Ide." Fenquick spins around and goes back to the armchair he'd been lounging in, Tinkeeper following him slowly.

"There you go impressing a girl again," Sira says. She checks something over bluelink, "Brig, my cute little guy, could you head to level four? Tylith went home for the night."

Brig shakes himself out of a trance and nods. "Ho! I should have guessed you were no latcher, in coppercraft. Well, got to go. See ya," he says, disappearing. The foilgrips must allow Handler employees to move between levels.

As I make my way to the balcony with Sira, Koglim's voice sails over the crowd, "Clayson, you gooey piece of trollbrick. Good for you."

He plows over to me, the rest of the team in his wake. A tray floats by, and he grabs a silver mug of something frothy. He gulps it down, leaving a sizable foam mustache across his upper lip.

Hemdi throws an arm around my shoulder. "I didn't know Fenquick was here. He's the largest plant distributor in the whole city. If we can get our flowers producing..." He squeezes Winta's hand. Her shoulders tense up, but Hemdi places his other hand between her shoulder blades and smiles.

"That's a big if," she says.

"But if we can," he says, "it could make all the difference. We could get our flowers planted all over Tungsten City. Wouldn't it be beautiful?"

Winta's resistance collapses under Hemdi's optimism. "It would be beautiful."

Something, almost like a sad memory, hangs over Winta. Everyone else senses it too, it's written on their faces, but no one says anything. I wonder if it has to do with their friend, Valifra Hollyhelm.

The belonging of seconds ago is gone. They're all strangers to me again. They share a common history I don't. Just like that, I wanna be back in the cabin with Dad. It's only been a few days, but the leaves must have taken on even more brilliance, and the cliff at the western part of the property calls out to me.

But my old life is gone.

"What's next?" I ask, breaking the somber mood of the group.

Hemdi speaks first. "I have one idea. I took another look at the guest list. What about Sternripper?"

This snaps Winta out of her thoughts. "Absolutely not."

Koglim strokes the chain of his necklace, and the purple gem hums softly, a dim light glowing deep at its center. "Unclear," he says. "It is more dangerous than other challenges, but Sternripper has a low rating, and the keeper isn't in attendance, only the seer." He looks at Sira.

"Don't look at me. I work in recruiting." She touches Rugnus' shoulder. "What do you think, Rugnus?"

His attention had been focused elsewhere, but he says, "Maybe they planned the key to be with someone unlikely. We could try Sternripper. With Koglim's sight, it may be easier than we think."

Rugnus' eyes flash to a screen that displays our point total, and a picture of me and my fake name. If he's concerned, he's buried it deep under the excitement of the night.

Hemdi tries for some approval from Winta. She blows out a breath of air in frustration. "Fine, but Koglim can stand on the sidelines. My husband and I can do this challenge together. That way, I can slow things down if I need to save him from his own stupidity."

Koglim flicks a finger against his necklace. There's only a glimmer of purple. He shrugs. "Risk seems low."

"Let's do it," Rugnus says.

It takes Sira a while to weave us through the maze of people who wanna congratulate us. I grasp a lot of arms and accept another dozen contacts before we can make it to the other side of the room, where a plump older woman sits crossed-legged on a triangular carpet, her eyes closed, her dark skin absorbing the surrounding orange light. She sits at one point of the triangle. A large plant bulb grows from out of the floor in front of her, its fleshy limbs tangled over the carpet, flowering here and there with red-purple pedals.

"Ah, I thought I might be seeing all of you tonight," the woman says. "I am Vulenzar Sharpboot. Seer of Sternripper. Welcome. Though I must give you a warning. This challenge is not what it seems. There'll be a price to be had."

The statement stops the whole team in their tracks.

Rugnus holds up his index finger. "Maybe we'll take a minute to look things over." He brings us into a huddle. "Let's pull up the feed for this challenge."

A hologram flickers in the center of our group with a miniature version of Sharpboot and two flanking challengers surrounding the plant bulb. One of them, a woman with pink hair, stands and steps around the plant's limbs like she's trying to avoid tree roots. She stops at one of the red-purple flowers and plucks it out. The plant reacts so quickly, I can't follow it.

We watch it again in slow motion. The plant grabs the woman with one of its tentacles, bursts open to reveal a half dozen rows of pointed teeth. and spits a glob of acid into her face. She falls to the floor, and a healer comes to drag her away, white light pulsing over her wounds.

"Brick," Koglim says. "Did you see how fast that thing moved?"

Hemdi plays the hologram on a loop, frowning.

"Yeah," Winta says. "We're not doing this."

"Hold on," Rugnus says. "I admit, it's a wraith's cradle, but—"

"A what?" Instantly I know I've asked a question every latcher in Tungsten City can answer in their sleep. Rugnus raises an eyebrow, telling me my life on the surface is showing. Before anyone can say anything, I try to cover. "Oh, a wraith's cradle. Sorry, I couldn't hear you over the crowd." It's true enough.

People are flocking around us, abuzz in conversation. A handful of wagers are murmured between onlookers: will we meet the challenge, or will the man-eating plant cover us in the flesh dissolving acid?

Sira shakes her head, a look of concern on her face. "Every one of you is just wonderful. You don't have to do this. My followers agree. You've shown your worth, made plenty of new connections." She rests a hand on Rugnus' back.

None of the extra noise bothers Rugnus. "But we're so close." There's an unnatural greed in his eyes I haven't seen before.

In the two days I've known him, he's never been this reckless. It's like he's starstruck. The attention on bluelink. Being surrounded by the most powerful Loamin out of both cities. He's lost on a sea of possibilities, chasing a glimmer of fame in the distance. Yesterday, he was determined to stay on level three. He knows as well as I do who's on level four—Silverkeeper. But, for some reason, he doesn't seem to care.

Though I need for him to be thoughtless, reckless. Or I won't have a chance to see Silverkeeper, let alone sneak his key off of him.

"Try the next clip," I say.

Only two teams have even attempted the challenge tonight. This time when the challenger picks a flower, the plant remains passive. It even purrs softly, like it's a giant cat that's had its belly rubbed. Sharpboot rises and picks a flower. Again, nothing happens, only purring. They go a few rounds like this until the last flower is picked and the challenger is asked to leave.

"Did he fail?" I ask.

"Weird. The challenge is not about getting through safely."

"So, Hemdi will need to get hurt?" Winta says. "If you think—"

Rugnus holds up a hand, impatient. "No. I think we're still missing something. What do you say, Hemdi?"

"I imagine, to win, there is another task you must do without being hurt and without ending the game. I am not sure I will be able to tell until I touch the plant."

"I don't think that thing wants to be touched," Koglim says.

Winta blinks at him. "Finally, you say something that makes sense."

Hemdi scratches under his chin. "Winta. Do you think you could slow the plant's reaction?"

"That's not the point." Winta waves an angry arm through the hologram, and it vanishes. "Why do we even need level four? Sira's right, for once. We don't have to do this."

Sira put a hand over her heart. "Oh, thank you."

"Don't mention it," Winta says flatly. "We've got good contacts. It's been a fun night. Let's call it here. Relax and enjoy the party.

Koglim and Rugnus roll their eyes so near the same time they might as well have synchronized it.

"Fine," she says. "Fine, we'll do it. But if this is not the key to level four, we're done. Agreed?"

Everyone but Koglim nods, even me. But something tells me this is the right challenge. Silverkeeper is within reach.

Rugnus shrugs. "We don't need to get to level four, but I-I just need to see how this challenge works out."

Koglim sniffs and flexes toward no one in particular. "This is the right challenge. I'm going to level four."

This comment loosens everyone up. Hemdi leads Winta to a place on the carpet opposite Sharpboot and takes a seat crossed-legged on the final corner, eyeing the plant more with curiosity than fear.

"Good," Sharpboot says. "I didn't think you were cowards. I hope you enjoy this sweet little game I've created." She extends a fleshy finger toward the closest flower. "And as always, I serve my guest first, my dear."

INVADE THE SOCIAL

HEMDI KNEELS in his corner of the triangular carpet, hands resting in his lap, head bowed, almost like he's praying. In front of him rests a tin lantern no larger than a fist, his mother's relic, Linterna. Green light leaks through the swirling pattern punched out of the tin. Winta's eyes are fixed on him. Linterna absorbs the light again, and Hemdi opens his eyes.

My heart's pounding. If he chooses the wrong bulb, we all saw what the acid did to the other challenger.

A transformation moves over Sharpboot's features. The menace which has clung tightly to the lines of her face melts away. "My dear, but that is a beautiful lantern."

"Linterna connects me with the plant," Hemdi says, smiling. "It wants my help. I have to choose a flower that will take away its pain."

Sharpboot hangs her head, frowning. "I had family and friends in Firas Andem. They made beautiful objects like Linterna."

Hemdi rises to his feet, readying to make a choice. "May Ide keep them safe and well-fed in the life beyond."

"Yes," she hisses. "Yes, I hope that is true."

The exchange is brief, but for a moment, it leaves an exposed image in the back of my eyes, as if these are the only two people left from the Kingdom of Firas Andem beneath the Andes Mountains.

Hemdi strides with confidence over to one of the purple-red flowers and plucks it. A shudder lurches through the tentacles, and the plant purrs with satisfaction. The woman takes her turn with the same result. Winta doesn't have to choose a flower. We can work as a team, but only one of us has to take the risk in this challenge. Her foot drums the carpet as she watches Hemdi choose his next flower.

This time, he's more confident, stroking the vines affectionately as he approaches. I shudder, positive I would fail this challenge. The tin can in Wolfstaff's underwater hedge maze wouldn't respond to me. This might be something my sister would be good at. I recall the intimidating way she drew the trees around her when we first met in Gamgim.

Hemdi succeeds again, and it dawns on me: this is not the way to win. I display the holograms again and quickly re-watch them one by one, searching for any other hints about what we could do differently.

Rugnus and Sira flank me.

"What is it?" she says.

"He's gonna lose. It happened with the second challenger. He's gonna get everything right, and we won't win."

Rugnus nods. "Been thinking about that. Sharpboot said there would need to be a sacrifice, which is about as clear as hot mud. He can't exactly let the plant eat him."

I pause the first hologram at the moment the plant spits greenish acid into the challenger's face, fighting not to turn away from its sheer violence. An idea washes over me, cold and sickening. I rewind and un-pause. The challenger screams and falls to the floor, but the healer approaches and casts a white light over her wounds.

"Rugnus," I say, pointing out the healer. "Can two dungeons work together to create a challenge?"

"Yeah, remember. Our first few points were from Coldhearth

and Gearvine. Why?" He follows my finger to the healer. "Oh. No, they…would they? That's sick."

The woman has already taken her second turn, and Hemdi stands again, eyeing one of the flowers.

"Wait." Rugnus storms over to the side of the carpet nearest Hemdi. "Got a slight problem here."

Winta scowls. "What do you mean? He's doing great."

"Think you might actually have to pick the wrong one."

Hemdi considers the center bulb of the plant. "It would be too painful."

"Clayson could heal you right away," Rugnus says. "We think that's the real challenge."

"I don't mean for me," Hemdi says. "The plant feels something like pain when you take the wrong flower. That's why it defends itself."

Koglim joins Rugnus at the edge of the carpet. "That can't be what you're worried about."

Sira pouts a little. "Ah, so sweet, Hemdi."

He shakes his head. "I can't deliberately hurt it."

"And you don't have to," Winta says, coming to his side.

"Come on." Rugnus puts his hands together in a plea. "This kind of thing, we face it every time we go on a survey mission to some mithrium infected city in search of relics."

Koglim clears his throat and rubs a palm at his neck. If possible, his voice pitches higher than normal. "Can't say I've purposely let my face get burned by acid, though. That's another level of stupid."

"It's not that," Hemdi says. "I-I can't do harm to this plant." His voice is firmer now. He's made up his mind. He takes two quick steps and plucks the third flower.

It's over. The crowd groans. I guess they were hoping for a more violent ending.

The woman stands and nods. She steps carefully over the plant limbs until she's face to face with Hemdi. "Well done. As you have already figured out, I cannot award you any points, but nonetheless, I am still the seer of Sternripper Dungeon. I want to invite you to work directly with me, not as an apprentice, but as an equal."

Winta's mouth drops open. This is something more than the offering Fenquick made me earlier. Being an apprentice is one thing, but working directly with the seer must be something much more significant. There's a notification in bluelink, and we've been granted another contact.

Hemdi takes a slight bow and says, "Let me consider over a few days."

"Of course," she says.

Sira nudges Rugnus. "I guess that's it? You did so well tonight."

My heart sinks. Any hope of reaching Silverkeeper drains away.

As Hemdi steps back, Rugnus fills his corner of the carpet. "We challenge again."

The crowd murmurs. Half of them open bluelink with a gesture, in what I guess is a confused attempt to check Rugnus' AMP score in tincraft. I think it might be as low as mine. What is he thinking?

Hemdi tries to prevent Rugnus from sitting but can't. "Rugnus, no."

"Sorry, Clayson and I have to get to the fourth level."

I shake my head. Something's wrong. He wouldn't willfully help me get to level four. It's in his posture and his eyes. His whole demeanor has shifted. His wide pupils scan the plants, calculating what he has to do.

"Rugnus?" I say.

"Hey, don't count me out," Koglim says. "You know what dungeons are on the fourth level? Runearmor, Shatterkeg, Silverlamp. I mean, come on, this is the chance of a lifetime."

Winta's eyes are daggers. Hemdi's face firms into something hard, as if Rugnus plans to burn the plant with ironcraft.

Breathing deeply, trying not to think about what happened to the challenger in the hologram or about the lust for power Rugnus is exhibiting at the moment, I step to his side. "I think it will hurt us more than we can hurt it. And that's the point. We can do this."

"You don't get a say in this, latcher." Winta grabs Hemdi by the elbow. "Come on. I think they can do this one without us. Besides, I want to check on the nursery."

"Don't go," Koglim says. "We're about to find the key. Breach level four." Koglim raises his voice over the crowd, but Winta and Hemdi are lost behind a wall of people. "Well, that's some brick."

"This is a bad idea," Sira says.

"Forget it," Rugnus says. "It was the same in Raldirkfar. He's a sensitive guy. We'll smooth things over tomorrow."

The woman, Sharpboot, has resumed her spot on the carpet, her mouth cut into a permanent frown. "Guests first," she says, gesturing to the flower closest to Rugnus.

Eyes wide in excitement, Koglim gives him space. Rugnus grits his teeth and strides over to the purple-red flower. The crowd smothers every sound, not a single foot shifts out of place; not a single throat is cleared. The kinetic balls above us soar to the highest possible point.

I panic. "Rugnus, maybe we should—"

"You'll be fine." He says this more to himself than to me. His hand stretches out slowly. "We'll be fine."

The second his finger twitches against the flower, the center bulb screams open, baring its prickling barbs. Instinct kicks in, and Rugnus' arms fly upward to guard his face, but too late. A jet of steaming green goo erupts, volcanic-like but more focused, enveloping not only his face and head but his whole upper body. Its veiny tentacles pulsate dull green light, lashing out for anything to grab.

Sira jumps back.

I spring onto the carpet as quickly as possible, but the plant's limbs find Rugnus like a strike of lightning, and he falls like a stone to the ground. Whether he's in shock from the burning acid, or maybe the vines have some paralytic effect, I can't tell. The gasps of the crowd struggle to compete with Rugnus' painful cries for help. My name gurgles from his lips. White bone appears in gaps in the flesh of his face.

And it's over. The tentacles retreat, leaving Rugnus crumpled on the ground in a green pool of liquid. Koglim moves first, dragging him out of the puddle, ignoring the small amount of acid that makes contact with his hands and arms. Maybe it's harmless now.

My name enters my ears, muffled. Then again, more clearly. "Clayson, now!" Koglim is pleading with me.

The healer in the white cloak moves out of the crowd, angling for Rugnus. My chance will be gone soon. My feet move under some power, not craft but instinct. I grope in my pocket for the spool of malleable lead Rugnus gave me to perform shieldcraft. Lead, the weaker of the two metals. My fingers find Ergal first, and before I even think about what I'm doing, it's on my finger. I commanded it to protect Rugnus, to heal him.

Two things happen at the same time. First, Koglim's gem, Elbaz, glows so brightly many people in the crowd turn away, blinking. The blood drains from his face as if he has never witnessed his own power of precognition. It must be a seriously bad omen. Second, fiery blue scales crystallize over Rugnus' face, down his arms. The blue, lizard-like skin flashes like metal in places where the acid had burned away his shirt.

His eyes snap open. "Whoa!"

Koglim and I lean over him. I catch a small patch of the same scales on Koglim's palms.

"Are you okay?" I breathe.

"Better than okay. That was—" his voice trails off as Koglim's necklace burns with purple-white heat. "Tell me you didn't."

"I-I just thought the lead wouldn't have worked. I-I knew it wouldn't. Somehow I knew."

The scales disintegrate into dust, and Rugnus stands, shaking blue powder from his skin. I healed him. Two words ripple through the crowd: dragon scales. We round the carpet, and even though we're ten feet away—a bar—the whole crowd stutters backward. Even Sharpboot moves away. The healer presents himself in front of us.

"That was powerful. With your skill in shieldcraft, Lighthealer would welcome your service, young man. If you are so inclined, I could—"

"Just the key," Rugnus says, holding out a hand.

"Very well. Our door is open to you, Clayson." The man pulls a small key from his pocket and floats it gently over to us.

Koglim shrugs apologetically at Sira. "It's a budge. We don't—"

She brushes him away. I forgot she's a null in budgecraft. "You boys go. I can meet you there in a bit. Besides, the comments are pouring in. You three are way better, and cuter, than any recruitment ad I could ever create."

We all grab it at once, budging into a tight stone stairwell facing rising steps. Wooden torches are spaced evenly along the wall, throwing Rugnus' face into deep shadows.

Rugnus scrapes a hand over his bristly hair. "That was crazy. Something's not right about this. Did you use silvercraft on me, Clayson?"

"What? No."

"Then how did you talk me into doing this?"

"Me?" I say. "Hey, you wanted to get to this level more than any of us. Don't blame me."

Rugnus points a finger at me. "It was something. Silvercraft maybe. I—none of this would be a problem if—"

"You guys cool?" Koglim says. "Why are we upset we got to the next level? I mean besides the ominous warning not to go up. Though, was the light really all that bright? We could—"

"No," Rugnus says. He brings out Icho. "No. Clayson and I are leaving right now."

I look from Koglim to Rugnus, who is nodding agreement. "We can't. I can't. Rugnus, you almost died for this. We have to take the chance. If I leave empty-handed…" But I don't finish the sentence.

"What do you mean empty-handed?" Rugnus' eyes narrow on me.

My mother's prison sentence hangs suspended on a thread as if the next few seconds could seal her fate even further. Taking Silverkeeper's key is the only play I have. I can use it to bargain for my mother's life. Or find the mithrium myself.

"Cameras off," Rugnus says.

Koglim winces. "You know, nothing good ever comes from ignoring the omen," Koglim says. "I'm going to find someplace for a late snack. You two work out whatever this is. Bye."

He budges.

Rugnus frowns. "I was tasked to keep you safe. With that warning… with Elbaz… what have we done. Trollbrick. This is all your fault. You shouldn't have—"

"I'm going on," I say. "Leave if you want. There's too much at stake." I step past him, taking the stairs two at a time.

"What are you talking about?" He pauses, and I swear I can hear the gears turning inside his head. "You're trying to get to Silverkeeper, aren't you?" But his voice fades behind me.

The stairway spirals around, and I make out a dim gray light ahead. I enter the room without any hesitation. Where level three was a vast ballroom with vaulted ceilings and techno-swing music, here there are only swirling brown walls of agate, warped and shadowed. The small room has two exits. The pounding of pitched drums echoes against the low ceiling, accompanied by a haunting ballad and a crisp bassline, like a Gregorian chant laced with acid. A hint of moisture coats the first deep breath I take. The whole place is like some beautified, medieval prison.

There are footsteps on the stairs behind me, and Rugnus emerges. "So, what's going on."

"My mother hid a piece of the mithrium in Silverlamp Dungeon."

I can almost see Rugnus' brain making all the connections. "Silverkeeper and Handler. They're looking for it?"

"We can't let them find it."

"How do you expect—"

"The keeper's key. Silverkeeper won't be able to get the mithrium without the key."

"That's the stupidest plan I've ever heard."

"You have a better one? Maybe, let them get the mithrium?"

"No." He smooths out the hem of his jacket.

"We can do this."

"No, we can't. But you're right. We can't let the ironheads get the mithrium. Just wish you would have given me some time to think about this. Lead the way. You're the tank armor. I'm the missiles. Ide keep me. This is such a bad idea. The king's going to melt me." His spine and hands take on a dull red glow. To Rugnus, this is the same as flexing.

A green light appears in one of the adjoining rooms, and Rugnus and I stand there, unsure of what to do. The light grows stronger until, at last, someone bursts into the room, as if from out of the stone. And it's the second time in two days my sister leaves me shocked.

Four royal guards—covered in lead body armor like x-ray technicians—flank her, weapons of metal glimmering in their hands. I've seen the royal guard in old recordings with my parents.

In a swirl of strawberry blonde hair and brown satin, Andalynn charges. "Dragonscales! I told you to keep him safe." She yells this at Rugnus, but her feet don't rest. She's a blur, bolting past us for another doorway. "Well, come on. No time."

We chase after her, the royal guard following behind us.

"What's going on?" I ask.

"Bazalrak."

We sprint through a maze of narrow rooms. A few guests here and there dive to the side to avoid getting bulldozed.

"Then he's here?" I say.

"He's been watching you over bluelink all night. He's guessed it. The dragonscales put him over the edge. He knows who you are, Clayson. He didn't know where the key would cause you to appear on this level, but he's intent on capturing you. Luckily, I found you first."

"He can't do that!" Rugnus says. "Not here in Tungsten City."

"You think a few laws and principles will stop him? By his beard, he's out to wipe out our whole family."

"Then we'll just leave." Rugnus grabs me as we run and snags Icho at the same time. Nothing happens.

Andalynn doesn't even glance back. "The foilgrips, you fool."

Shadows curl around the edge of the stone behind us. Bazalrak. He's only around the corner. We sprint along the next corridor, people shouting questions at us. The darkness behind unfurls like groping hands, searching for something to poison, to torture.

Another turn.

Andalynn skitters to a halt. Two different hallways branch away from us.

"You know where you're going?" Rugnus says.

Andalynn huffs. She's searching the air with her hands—bluelink. "The map keeps blinking off. Bazalrak has someone trying to scrub our connection to bluelink."

Rugnus spins around, hands flaring in red heat. "Then we face him."

"Bad idea," Andalynn says. "Silverkeeper is with him." She gets a firm grip on Rugnus' back and yanks him toward her.

We take the left corridor and wind through more narrow hallways until suddenly the walls are gone. We're standing in a spacious room—emerald and gold—packed with dozens of people. Every eye is on us.

"Rugnus?" A woman says with a majestic tone. She's about my parent's age. A fur hat tops her dark glossy hair, and gold strands of jewelry drape her ears. She steps into the space between the crowd and us, wearing a pair of golden jeans.

"Mom?" Rugnus shakes his head. "Forgot you'd be on this level."

Andalynn switches her stance so she can see both of them at once. "Rusela Whitechin is your mother?"

Rusela squints at my face. "What have you gotten yourself into, Rugnus?" Her voice carries something Eastern European. Rugnus did say his mother was an immigrant. Is that where Zal Kakraja was located? Russia maybe? Russian mountains? She points to me. "Is that who I think it—"

But she's cut off—a loud clap echoes around the room.

Then another. And another.

"Well, well." Bazalrak's smooth voice rises directly behind us.

As I whirl around, the crowd shifts at the same time. A few dozen people slink across the room noiselessly, assembling around Bazalrak, who stands, as always, leaning on his ax. The royal guard tighten behind us, apparently willing to fight against the keepers for the princess of Whurrimduum.

The man now standing closest to Bazalrak can only be Theridal Silverkeeper. I recognize him from bluelink. His hair is a rich blond. A hundred surfaces all over his body glimmer in bright silver. Besides his face, nearly every body part is covered with metal or entirely replaced with it. His only foot sits in a heavy silver boot. Where his other foot should be, there's a robotic claw extending all the way to his knee.

The keeper's key hangs on a leather strand at his wrist, but now that he's standing before me, I know Rugnus is right: this was the stupidest idea I've ever had. Silverkeeper's face is unreadable. This was my father's closest friend, but I can't get a read on his intentions toward me.

The other knights who had been with Bazalrak to capture Dad lurk behind him. The insect man, the gold woman with disproportionate arms, and the young man with the heavy rail gun. Apparently, they're allowed to have weapons at a Keeper's Social. Though that shouldn't surprise me when a silver bracelet can be a weapon.

Bazalrak clears his throat, and my eyes are drawn to him. His lip ring twitches before he speaks. His eyes lock on mine. "That was a performance worthy of a fair amount of adoration. Clayson, is it? Are you using your true first name, or have you concealed that as well? And look at you, the spitting image of your father. And no one guessed it. And they call us ironheads." He bows to me over his ax. "I present to the citizens of this city, Clayson Brightstorm. The once-heir to the glorious Kingdom of Rimduum."

Murmurs fill the air. Rugnus' mother tries to edge him away from Andalynn and me, but he shrugs her off. Dozens of hands in the crowd gesture open bluelink. They're recording. Now there are hundreds of thousands of eyes on me, and tomorrow—on instant replay—millions.

"And wonder overtakes me," Bazalrak says, taking a wide step forward. "What doomed mission has your father sent you on? Or is it simply a vacation from the surface you're after? And where is he? Hm? Who's helping him? Where's he hiding? And so many more questions. I suppose we can sort that out back in Whur-rimduum."

Rugnus steps in front of me, but I react first. At last, I have a target for all my frustration. "What am I hiding? How about you, Torturer? What are you hiding? Have you and Silverkeeper found the mithrium yet? What will you do if you do find it? Destroy Tungsten City, like Thiffimdal and all the rest?"

"Clayson." Rugnus places a hand on my arm, but I shake him off.

Bazalrak's face hardens. I sense wide, curious eyes on both sides of the room, and then I get it. I understand what divides the two groups. Supporters of Whurrimduum have lined up on Bazal-rak's side. And behind Rugnus and his mother, the people of Tungsten City are readying various metal objects. The only discrepancy is the royal guard. I have a feeling like I'm standing between a den of snakes and an angry nest of hornets. I'm not sure which is more dangerous.

Whatever the risk, I want answers. I ignore Bazalrak and speak to Silverkeeper. "What are you planning to do with the mithrium?" The sharpened toes of his clawed foot tap against the stone, but he says nothing. "My parents were right to hide it from the council. I thought you were my father's friend. It's Bazalrak that wants her dead. Don't let him do this."

Finally, he speaks. "Someone has to pay the price."

"For what? The war went on for centuries. Who isn't to blame? And now you're planning on using the mithrium again, aren't you? But you're too afraid to go into Silverlamp yourself; that's why you need Bazalrak and Lonecharge."

"Th-that's enough." This voice comes from behind me. It's Lonecharge, emerging from the crowd of undecideds at the side of the room. I recognize him from bluelink, bright blue silk suit, slick blond-pink hair. Unlike Bazalrak and Silverkeeper, he wears little metal.

Out of the corner of my eye, I see Sira slip into the crowd of people behind me, lending me her support with a wave.

"It's time for you to leave, Clayson," Lonecharge says, risking a glance at his partners on the other side of the room. He will need to play a delicate game here, balanced between his supporters in Tungsten City and the two men of Whurrimduum. But I'm not in the mood to be delicate.

"I'm not going anywhere until the Keeper's Council agrees to let my mother go."

"As presumptuous as your father," Bazalrak says. "Your family has brought nothing but shame and death to the Kingdom. But don't worry. Maybe you can share the same cell with your mother. Though with this revelation, I can get the council to agree to a stiffer punishment. Bring my ax down on her neck."

My hands curl around Ergal. Bazalrak's fingers turn red on the handle of his ax.

"He's a citizen of Tungsten City," Rugnus says. "He signed the contract. You can't legally detain him."

Silverkeeper responds to this, his voice almost amused. "He

232

signed under a false name. The contract is void. He's a citizen of the Kingdom."

Bazalrak's eyes survey me greedily. "How right you are, Theridal."

"I'm not leaving here with you," I say.

"A lawful execution can occur anywhere, even at the Keeper's Social."

In a single motion, he catapults toward me and swings his ax. It ricochets against a solid wall of white light from Ergal. The room bursts into chaos. Rugnus launches a quick succession of fireballs at Bazalrak's head, but they're snuffed out the moment they come within a foot of him. Growling, Rugnus shoots a shaft of lightning at one of Bazalrak's goons instead.

The ironhead with the rail gun unleashes a barrage of sharp metal gears against my shield. Rugnus' mom crashes toward the line of ironheads. The skin over her face hardens, becoming as thick as a rhino's, and she bowls over the man. As he tumbles backward, the gear-spitting gun clatters to the ground, shooting the star-shaped bullets in all directions. I move to protect anyone in danger, but Ergal is way ahead of me. Extensions of my ring disintegrate every bullet with white light until the gun splutters to a halt.

Rugnus' mother circles around. "Leave now, Rugnus!"

"We've got this. Don't need more advice."

The mother and son stand back-to-back, whipping rings of fire at the ironheads like lion tamers. I take in the whole scene. A third of the crowd has fled. But the other two-thirds are locked in combat. Bazalrak hacks away at my shield with his ax. The calm-faced expert ironheads are more experienced in fighting, blocking nearly every advance, but the Tungsten City citizens have faces painted with fury. Bazalrak has broken the peace of their beloved city, and he will pay. Nowhere does this intention appear clearer than on Rugnus' face.

One of the Loamin from out of the ironhead crowd wheels his arm and throws a glass vial. It spins toward the edge of my shield, but Andalynn snaps her fingers. A puff of gold smoke nudges the vial toward the wall using some type of telekinesis. The vial cracks against the agate walls and rock explodes across the room.

A jagged boulder tumbles through my shield, aimed straight at my face. Rugnus pushes it out of the way without effort.

"Get to protect you for once!" he yells over the destruction. The aggression edging his voice sinks like a rock in my stomach. How eager the two sides are for each other's blood. For me, disgust is the only emotion that cuts through the visceral fear and adrenaline rush. In a few terrifying seconds, stretched as long as a lifetime, I've learned how capable each side is for mutually assured destruction.

No wonder they destroyed all but two cities.

From out of nowhere, Brig comes charging toward me. "Sister's coming. She's a Paladin."

"Paladins are coming?" Rugnus says. "We have to leave."

"The council will have my head for this," Andalynn says. She whirls on her guards. "Do not follow me." They protest, but Andalynn cuts them off. "Return at once to the castlestack."

The blast from the vial opened a gaping hole in the exterior wall. Silverkeeper has vanished, taking with him any chance to get the keeper's key to Silverlamp. Rugnus signals he understands with a shrug.

"If we get outside the building, we can get past the foilgrips," Andalynn says.

"You're coming with us?" I yell.

Her eyes burn into me. "I can't go home. The council."

Rugnus chases after us, his mother yelling something unintelligible.

We arrive at the breach in the wall near the top floor of the Handler building, the canyon of the city below us in glittering lights.

"Three..." Rugnus yells.

"Wait, we're jumping?"

Behind us, someone's trying to keep Bazalrak tied down with thick chains, but his ax slices through the wrought iron like it's string cheese.

"Two..."

Andalynn grips the club strapped to Rugnus' back. "Can your budge handle plus two and reverse momentum?"

He smiles and nods. "One."

Right as Bazalrak breaks free of the final chains, we jump. Cherry blossoms from Andalynn's tin bracelets fill the gap in the wall, turning to stone as we plummet.

STAY IN THE MUD

"WE'LL HAVE the people to fear," Andalynn says as we pace across the walkways of Magmadew plaza. "What were you thinking, coming to the social? I told you to keep him safe, Rugnus. I thought my father wanted you to hide him."

It's still night, and because the brightstorm has only two settings, I can't immediately tell the time. I keep looking over my shoulder, expecting Bazalrak. Everything is dark stone and hot mud. Heat radiates from a brown, bubbling stream as we cut across a lawn spiraled with two different colored types of grass. The earth smells almost medicinal, like eucalyptus.

Rugnus has been quietly listening to Andalynn lecture him since we budged from Handler. "Don't know what happened," he says. "My team had planned to go to the social. Clayson hijacked it."

"I was invited," I say.

"How many times did I say it was a bad idea?"

"Clayson didn't know any better—maybe—but you, why did you do it?" she says.

Rugnus shakes his head and shrugs. "That's what I'm trying to figure out."

Something occurs to me. My feet slow to a halt. "Wait. How

powerful is Silverkeeper? I mean, he can do mind-control-type things, right? What if he wanted us there? *Me* there."

Rugnus pulls me, and we keep walking. "I would have felt the silvercraft."

"Not if it was a powerful relic, right?" I hold up my ring. "Like Ergal. Using the lead, I felt the shieldcraft, like sore muscles after a workout, but with Ergal, I never feel it. Or with Icho. Your club doesn't leave me feeling sick. It doesn't have the same heavy gravity effect as a lower-rated object. So, could Silverkeeper have used a really strong relic?"

Rugnus stops along the path where two bridges go in different directions. Mud bubbles in the river beneath. Glossy, footlong toad eyes peek from the mud. "Very unlikely," he says.

Andalynn spins him to face us. "Where are you taking us, Rugnus?"

"A place next to the lake. In case we need protection."

"Protection from Bazalrak?" I say.

Rugnus and Andalynn both respond. "No."

Andalynn looks around the plaza. A few people stroll the lawns, but it's mostly empty. "From the whole city."

"It won't come to that," Rugnus says shortly. "And as far as Bazalrak, if the paladins started showing up, he's gone."

"What are paladins?" I ask.

"Vigilantes," Andalynn answers.

"They're not vigilantes. Everyone in Tungsten City can cast opinions about the conduct of another citizen. Paladins legitimize the effort through investigation. It's part of the citizen's contract. Besides, they also serve the dungeons."

"Unorganized, mass confusion," Andalynn says, tagging on her own definition.

Rugnus whirls on her. "And the council is better?"

I make an attempt to head them off before they start an eye-rolling political discussion. "When's daychange?"

"You mean nightchange?" Rugnus asks.

"Yeah, that. When does it change to day?"

Rugnus calls up bluelink. "About an hour."

"I had forgotten how much earlier nightchange is for you," Andalynn says.

"Better than eighteen hours of darkness," Rugnus says.

Andalynn sighs. "Whurrimduum is a beautiful place. I don't expect you to understand." I sense a weariness in her voice. She's tired of defending herself to Rugnus.

He must sense it too. "Sorry, didn't mean to be insulting."

"Yes, you did," I say. "But can you two please stop?" Neither of them meets my eyes. "We didn't get the key from Silverkeeper so—"

"That's why you came?" Andalynn says.

"Don't look at me," Rugnus says. "I didn't even know about his idiotic plan until we reached level four."

"You should have never gotten to level four," Andalynn says.

Rugnus' voice becomes louder. "I get that. Trying to tell you, I don't know what happened."

"But could it be Silverkeeper?" I ask again.

They both respond. "No."

Rugnus points to a spired castle on a rise at the bank of the mud lake. A drawbridge over the mud leads to the only entrance. "Let's get settled for the time being. Need rest, time to think. And we have another problem to deal with. Lonecharge has announced he will be forging an opinion about the situation in the next hour. If he does, it will give the people something to vote on."

"Will he deny working with Bazalrak and Silverkeeper?" I ask.

Andalynn shakes her head. "Their work together has been well documented by both the council and the people of Tungsten City. He's not going to be the one on trial."

Steaming mud surrounds the structure. The heat becomes dense, and moisture enwraps my skin, like the dewy condensation after a hot shower.

Rugnus comes to the entry pad and swipes his wrist across the sensor. The drawbridge lowers. The stone shakes, and the large oaken doors swing outward. We follow Rugnus across the bridge and into an open hall. A table sits at the center, nearly half the length of the bridge. Huge flags with Magmadew's logo hang at the sides of the room. At each wall, dark orange flames flicker in obsidian fireplaces.

Rugnus reaches one side of the table, stops, and spins around to face us.

"Cameras and mics are muted. And you should both see this." He flings out holograms with a waving motion. At the center of the table, our fight at the Keeper's Social is displayed in perfect detail. It's all there. Bazalrak threatens me, and I accuse him right back. My face is a mask of anger, more than I would have guessed. Rugnus dials down the speed right after Bazalrak realizes I'm not technically a citizen of Tungsten City—I was fair game.

We watch the fight play out. But a bell sounds, and Rugnus pauses the video on the part where the exterior wall explodes. "Lonecharge already has his opinion ready." He projects the words onto a wall.

A cool dread cascades down my neck. "My name's on this."

Skimming the text helps clarify what it means for someone to cast an opinion in Tungsten City. There's been a decree of sorts. He wants me banished from the city.

"Great," Andalynn says. "See. Exactly what's wrong with this place. You have no leadership. No king or queen. No steward. No elected officials. No police. Anyone can make their accusations over bluelink, and that's it—the court of popular opinion."

"We rule ourselves. I trust the people to make the right choice. They'll let us stay."

"They're a faceless mob," Andalynn says.

I've had enough of their political bickering. "You two need to stop. Are they kicking me out, or not?"

"Depends," Rugnus says. "If the opinion reaches consensus, then they could. Technically. But I don't think that's likely. There's not much evidence against you, and no one likes Silverkeeper. Besides, this video is a good indication of your opinions."

"If they even watch it," Andalynn says.

Rugnus un-pauses the hologram. "How could they not?"

Tiny versions of the three of us leap from the opening in the wall. The moment after this, Bazalrak smashes his ax on the ground. Sira emerges from the background and grabs Lonecharge by his shirt. I adjust the hologram to zoom in on them.

"What did you do?" she says.

He gestures, and a second later, half of the room disappears along with Bazalrak and Silverkeeper. The loop starts over. A speech bubble icon floats near the edge of the scene. It allows comments. "Maybe I should say something," I say.

Rugnus rakes a hand over his head. "No way."

Andalynn agrees. "You've said enough. You accused him of searching for the mithrium and basically admitted our family stole it from Whurrimduum. What were you thinking?"

"He's the one planning to use it. It's pretty clear Dad took it to protect everyone."

Rugnus sits on the table, thoughtful. "Then he did steal it. I always thought it couldn't have been him. Maybe Lonecharge is right, though. Have we thought about that? Mithrium could be used to create something that benefits society."

Andalynn laughs. "You think Bazalrak will be leading us to some peaceful utopia? Even if he was out of the picture, can we trust Lonecharge or Silverkeeper with the mithrium? No way. Maybe I finally understand why my father did what he did."

She's ignoring the fact our mother and grandfather were both involved, but I don't bring it up.

A moment of silence encases the three of us until Rugnus takes Icho out. "I'm running to my vault to switch objects out. Best to be prepared."

"Are we safe here?" I ask.

"Absolutely," he says, but this earns him a skeptical glare from Andalynn. "Be back soon." Then he blinks, scrunches his nose, and shakes his head. "What kind of trollbrick is this? My vault is under review?"

"What does that mean?" I ask.

"How's that possible? The opinion didn't reach a consensus. Blocking my vault isn't legal without consensus."

I scrunch up my face. "I'm not following."

"Sometimes, when a person is convicted of a crime or found to be dangerous, they get locked out of their vault. But not until after a consensus is reached."

Andalynn opens her mouth with what I assume is a prepared I-told-you-so. Instead, she pauses, shakes her head, and says, "That's odd, even for Tungsten City."

A few different emotions—surprise, confusion, worry—cross his face as he considers what to do. "There's no opinion. This is a mistake. Winta can break through this illegal review in no time."

Andalynn tucks a strand of hair into place. "The girl from the team you came with to the Keeper's Social?"

"Yep."

"Do you trust her?" She asks this of me, but Rugnus answers.

"With my life." He turns away from us, talking to the air. "We need help. Bring everyone. I'm sending the location. Oh, hey. Yeah. No, no, no. Totally exaggerated." With an acknowledging wave to us, he crosses the room and continues his conversation, leaving Andalynn and me alone.

Neither of us says a word, but Andalynn steps closer to stand beside me at the table. She leans her head on my shoulder, the silver strands of metal in her hair brushing my chin. At that moment, neither of us is alone. The tension in my shoulders falls away. Something passes between us as if the strands of her hair are tendrils of her thoughts and emotions.

Like in Gamgim, I find myself in a moonlit garden with neon purple flowers. I stretch out my hands and catch her hope on my fingertips. A tangible hope that I'm the same as her, that we share a common worry for our parents. Hope for a world where we can live together in peace.

My mother is before me, balanced on the edge of an impossibly tall building, the surrounding stone gilded in silver, muttering to herself. I'm terrified she'll jump. She screams, and I find myself holding her, comforting her. But this is Andalynn's life. Our connection deepens. It had been the same with Dad. Times when he awoke from nightmares brought on by the surface, or the dozen times in the last two years that he collapsed, out of oxygen, having wandered too far into the woods.

Andalynn leans away from me. "Our separate lives only appear different on the outside. But...I tried to ask her about you, you know, before the trial. It's strange craft. It's like she can't acknowledge you even exist. I'm sorry, Clayson."

"It's okay."

Rugnus' voice interrupts us. "Got visitors."

A silent understanding passes between us as Andalynn steps away—we both took care of fragile parents, and we will do what it takes to protect them and each other. I still need answers from my mother, and Andalynn wants answers from Dad.

The oaken doors swing open. Winta, Hemdi, and Koglim file into the room. I had expected Sira to be with them, but she must still be at Handler trying to clean up the mess we made or trying to commute here without a budge.

Andalynn and I stand off to the side as they all test strengths, except Winta, who's not interested in greeting anyone. She casts a hard stare at us. If she didn't like me before, now it's much worse.

Koglim marches over to me and clasps my arm. "A Brightstorm! By my bones. This is crazy stuff. And you fought off General Stonedoom himself, the old torturer. Keep Ide." He pushes me and taps on his pendant. "Even royalty must respect the omen. Bad stuff happens."

Winta slows everyone down with the band of mercury at her wrist—everyone except me. "Are you right about the mithrium?"

"What?" That's what this is about for her. Like everyone else in this world, somehow, she's been affected by society's fight over the mithrium. I place her in the group of people who wanna protect the world from its danger. "Oh, yeah. I am. And we still need to do something to stop them, regardless of what the people of Tungsten City decide about me."

She taps her fingers against her thigh, considering this. "Fine. I'll help."

Everyone returns to normal speed.

Koglim growls. "I've told you not to—"

"Rugnus," Winta says. "Give me access to your vault so I can check into the problem. There shouldn't be a block if there is no opinion against you. It's probably something in the code like red stitchers, golem vials, or the strands."

Hemdi clears his throat.

Koglim says, "There she goes again, techno-babble. You know none of us understand all that bluelink trollbrick."

Winta's band releases the mercury again, but Hemdi's able to talk her down.

Rugnus must not be used to opening his vault controls to anyone because Winta has to show him the correct gesturing. Once it's open, she retreats from the others to the table and begins some complicated gesturing work I can't follow, tracing the air with nimble fingers.

While she works, Hemdi is the only one willing to talk. He asks Andalynn about the blossoms she used to obscure our exit. She compliments Linterna. Then he asks me about life on the surface. I don't go into detail, but he's fascinated by everyday life.

It only takes a few minutes, then Winta claps her hands. "Done. It should stay unblocked for a while. You were right, Rugnus. Lonecharge had someone at Handler process the review illegally. Though, to be fair, it is only a matter of time before there are repercussions, seeing how you helped Clayson get his fake AMP."

"Guessed that, did you?" He says.

"Doesn't take a genius."

"Okay, I'm going to my vault. I'll be back soon."

Winta's eyes harden. "What if we choose not to help you?"

"Winta," Hemdi says, an edge of pleading in his voice. "They can't go to Whurrimduum or the surface. Not now. Bazalrak will only hunt them down."

"Fine," Winta says.

"Great, glad you've decided," Rugnus says.

Another bell sounds near Rugnus' display of Lonecharge's opinion.

Koglim is the one nearest to the projection. "Bones and bricks," he says. "He's forging on all of us. The whole team. Sira included."

"What?" Winta pushes him out of the way and scans the words. "That's ridiculous. They can't exile us for knowing someone."

"They can if the consensus is large enough," Andalynn says.

"No one asked you, princess." Winta glares at her.

"What if we try to talk to him," I say. "Or make our own comments. Or wait, Brig told me his sister was a paladin. We could talk to her and—"

Koglim holds up a hand. "Stop right there, my little latch-mage. That's not how it works. Trying to influence the investigation of the paladins looks, well, bad."

Now everyone tries to talk at once. Andalynn explaining how people are easily influenced, Winta interjecting about how stupid the Keeper's Social was, how it should be abolished in the first place, Hemdi trying to calm everyone down, and Koglim enjoying the chaos of argument.

"Okay, okay," Rugnus yells. "I'm going to swing by Quimdem, see if I can get them to cast an opinion in support of our team. Then I'll stop by my vault. But we should all be prepared in case we have to leave the city. You two"—he points to Andalynn and me—"stay here. And the rest of you change, get any objects you need, and come back."

Rugnus nods with finality but then doesn't move. "I can't budge."

Koglim looks at Rugnus' club. "Not possible."

Winta spins up something on bluelink. "We have company."

The overhead holographic map she displays shows the island castle off mud lake's coast with our locator dots inside. They're a strange neon-orange color. Past the drawbridge, a thousand more locator dots have gathered.

Something heavy and ominous settles on the group. Koglim's amulet takes on a dull gleam. "That's a lot of people," he says.

"They must have a foilgrip," Andalynn says.

Foilgrip. I'm beginning to hate the stuff.

It's the type of craft that kept me from budging at the RV park. It stopped us from leaving the Keeper's Social, but those were minor things compared to what I know of its history. During the Mithrium War, out of fear, the cities used it to keep people from entering in the hopes it would prevent an attack. In the end, they all failed.

"I know what a foilgrip does, but what makes it so powerful?"

Winta growls. "Why do we have to keep explaining simple things to you?"

Hemdi places a hand on her arm. "It is budgecraft, passed through a brightstorm. It makes the object thousands of times more powerful but in a negative sense. So far, aluminum is the only metal we can get to work that way."

"And it stops everyone from budging just like that? How did people sneak past it during the war?"

"Usually through a loophole," Rugnus says.

Koglim speaks with a sort of stunned reverence. "Or with tens of thousands of knights pushing on it with their own craft."

"Okay," I say. "Then how do we get out of here?"

"We don't," Andalynn says.

Another notification bell rings. This time it's Koglim's. We all look at him, expecting the update. "Uh, well, do you want the bad news, or the really bad news, or the really, really bad news. Maybe—here watch this."

He throws his hands outward like he's casting seeds into a

garden, and suddenly we're standing beyond the drawbridge on the shores of the mud lake, inside augmented reality. Bluelink media personalities, some I recognize from my news binging, others I don't, line the shore speaking to their viewers. Koglim is focused on a man with a blindfold, a purple silk suit, and a blue glass sword at his back. His voice is as coarse as a bag of rocks dragged over asphalt.

"An outpouring of updates from my sources say Clayson Brightstorm and his team from the Keeper's Social have taken up residence here in Magmadew Plaza. We've also confirmed Princess Andalynn Everbloom from Whurrimduum is with them. In her absence, Silverkeeper—the head of the council—has moved to close Silverlamp Dungeon. In addition, in light of her family's clear involvement in the theft of the mithrium, the council has sentenced Azbena Bloodfeign, steward of Whurrimduum, to death. She will be moved from Keelcrawl prison tomorrow morning to an undisclosed location for her execution."

Andalynn stumbles backward toward the table. I catch her, help her steady her hands on the firm wooden surface. I search for her eyes, but they're hidden behind green-shadowed eyelids. No. Hidden behind an entirely new Andalynn. One without power, composure, friends, or contacts. All her confidence and poise evaporate, leaving behind only this: a daughter—my sister.

That's when the idea of having a mother strikes me through my chest, a cold spear of regret and disbelief. Only now, in seeing Andalynn's reactions, does my blood thicken. The line connecting me to my mother was once drawn with chalk, but it's now inked harder into my DNA. My mother will be executed tomorrow.

Ide keep me. There's no way I will let that happen.

But the pot of trouble I've stirred up down here boils over the sides as the newscaster continues.

"And—breaking news— the opinion has been cast. Clayson Brightstorm and his associates are indeed being exiled based on the recommendation of the people. They will be apprehended and forcibly budged to the surface. They must turn themselves over to the people within the hour. They may not budge of their own accord as that would be in violation of the Precepts of Community for those convicted by the people as dangerous."

Winta scoffs. "They're about to see how dangerous I can be."

I spot long blonde hair moving through the crowd toward the castle. Sira emerges, but she's held firmly by a group from the angry mob.

"It's Sira," I announce.

Koglim has to look twice. "Oh, time to melt some fools. She's totally helpless."

"Turn off the stream," I tell Koglim. Something's simmering in my blood.

Everyone turns toward me, the inside of the castle now oddly quiet.

I don't ask for permission or think about what I'm doing as I move over to the door and swing it open. Andalynn and Rugnus are on my heels. Koglim is right by my side. I step onto the bridge, only three bars between the mob and me, but the whole crowd simmers into quiet anger.

Heat rises from the mud under the bridge, and that earthy, almost medicinal smell hits me once again. The group that has Sira comes forward at the other side of the bridge, pushing her to the ground. I recognize her. It's the woman who commanded the people in the underground to attack my tower. I can see in her eyes she's already connected me to that event.

"This your null?" she asks.

"Let her go," Koglim says, his voice amplified by craft.

"The people have spoken," the woman says. "You're not welcome in our city."

Koglim's face purples. He taps his necklace ceremoniously as the light from his amulet glows brighter. "Give. Me. My. Friend."

An icy wind swirls around us, and the bridge trembles. I don't even flinch. Ergal will protect me. At the thought, the bubbling mass of mud rises from under the bridge in a wave, slathering the shore. The crowd panics. I expect some of them to budge, but the foilgrip must be keeping them here. There's a stampede as people retreat.

The mud spills everywhere but the end of the bridge where the woman still holds Sira to the ground. I rush over the bridge into the chaos, the massive Koglim at my side.

Thunder splits the air, followed by a streak of blinding sand-colored light. It didn't come from any of us, and it didn't come from the crowd. Behind me, Rugnus gasps, grabs onto me for support. When I can see again, I tip my head to the side. A smile leaps to my face, and a laugh of disbelief exits my mouth.

"Ara?" I say.

The word vacant ripples through the crowd, and a thrill of satisfaction warms my blood as I see everyone's disbelief. Now they'll see how stupid they sound when they call any Dura a vacant.

The woman holding Sira is frozen, either in shock, or fear or by some craft I don't understand. Ara tosses the woman aside and helps Sira to her feet. "We need to go," Ara says.

"But the foilgrip," Rugnus says. "How did you—"

"We need to go," she says. I see the same hesitance, almost embarrassment, I saw in her every time she visited Dad. "Is this everyone?"

Winta and Hemdi are behind Rugnus and Andalynn.

"Yeah," I say. "Get us out of here."

TRAVEL BETWEEN WORLDS

ARA BUDGES US INTO DARKNESS, and Rugnus immediately produces a bright flare of hovering light. Far above, there are glimmers of wet stone. A few more people add lights against the dark—orange, green, and white.

Sira gags, trying to hold back vomit, but she's unsuccessful. Liquid splatters against the concrete. Around us, massive slabs of road, shattered and ruinous, provide witness to some unholy destruction in this place long ago. The broken road is wide enough to allow a fleet of fifty semis to drive side-by-side. It goes on for as far as I can see. This world should have no roads. Where are we?

"The crossroads," Koglim whispers.

Hulking shapes lurk barely out of the light's reach.

I shuffle toward Sira in the near dark and find Winta there with a hand on her back. Sira bends over, and loses it again. Her legs are shaking and sweat glistens on her face and arms.

"It's alright," Winta says, helping Sira sit on a raised piece of broken concrete. In the shadows, the strange, colored lights play over her face. She looks almost kind. Or maybe it's some trans-formation, some softening of her features as she helps Sira.

Hemdi watches her admiringly. His love for her is written on his face, as always.

Andalynn produces a tin cup from who knows where. Rugnus fills it with steaming water, delivering it to Sira. "Sip it slowly."

My sister's regal demeanor has returned, but I still see the cracks in it. Close up, she's wilder, more desperate, and dangerous

Sira tries to take a small sip but can't. She can barely breathe.

"Ara," I say. "Can you do anything?"

She shakes her head. "Sorry, it doesn't work that way. I only borrowed some of your father's craft. No shieldcraft."

Is that how it works? Is that what she did at the cabin, borrow Dad's craft? All the elemental power she displayed was his.

Sira retches again.

Ergal. How could I forget?

I move to Sira's side and extend Ergal's healing powers to her. Her skin, already without much pigment, becomes translucent. White light shines from her pores. A large clear, breath passes into her body.

She stands, leaning into me softly. "Thank you, Clayson."

I let her stay against my shoulder but glance as far as possible into the gloom, trying to discern if the hulking shapes are moving. They look like charred metal and gears.

"What are the crossroads?" I ask. "Why are there roads at all?"

Rugnus angles his light differently, so it extends further down the massive road. "You remember I showed you that map in my vault?"

"Yeah."

"The three main mountain ranges contain all of the old cities. The largest group is to the north." He points his light over the road. "Whurrimduum lies that way. The other two main groups are southeast and southwest."

"Okay," I say.

"Right, well, after the first mithrium bomb went off—"

"We've got company," Koglim hisses.

A swirl of headlights appears in the distance.

"Ara, what is this?" I demand.

Everyone else steps even further away from her.

Ara's face is pointed toward the distance. "She wouldn't let me budge you straight to the settlement."

The roar of engines reaches my ears. Rugnus looks at me. "What do we do?"

I study Ara and the approaching vehicles. "She'll take us to my Dad."

"Is that what this is?" Andalynn says, squinting against the blaring headlights.

"She's Dura, though." Koglim tightens his arm around Sira. "This is a bad idea. And typically, I *like* bad ideas."

I glance around. Besides Ara, the whole group has their eyes glued on me. She's the unknown to them, and they're looking to me for answers. "I have no problem following a *vacant*." I say the word with as much dismissiveness as I can summon. "It's Ara. I know her, and I trust her."

Ara is looking away from all of us. "As you should."

That doesn't stop Koglim and Rugnus from preparing craft against whatever's coming. Soon a dozen trucks and motorcycles surround us. With caged cabs, jacked-up tires, and billowing vertical exhaust pipes, the vehicles are like props from one of Dad's post-apocalyptic 80s movies.

Something claws over the top of one of the larger trucks. I register long teeth and a flicking tail before it leaps through the air toward us. Sira screams. I hold up my arms, expecting it to pummel Ergal's shield, but it skirts over my head and lands at the front of our ragtag group.

Up close, the pale, almost transparent lizard is nearly the length of our long bed truck back at the cabin, but only half the height. A bridle cuts through its mouth, and in the saddle, on its back, a gray-haired woman leers at Andalynn and me. She wears a simple tunic, stained with dirt along the rim.

Andalynn shines a light directly on the woman. "Grandmother?"

Can it really be her? I saw her in the histories, but now living, breathing before me, she's different, maybe less real, less alive.

"You've grown. I've missed you." Her words to Andalynn are flat, perfunctory even. She gives the lizard a quick pull to keep herself facing us. "Not how I would have preferred a reunion. And Clayson, you look just like your father." Her tone reveals some distaste for Dad. "And seems like you have about as much sense. I've kept your secret for a long time."

"The council's going to execute Mom," Andalynn says.

The old woman focuses her attention elsewhere, frowning.

"Glaris," Andalynn says. "Did you hear me? I said—"

"I heard you fine, Andalynn." Glaris shakes her head. After an intense second of scornful eye contact with me, her lizard slips over to a heavy truck. "Load 'em up!" she yells.

A half dozen people, dressed in simple linens, tumble from every vehicle. Two of them haul a huge wooden chest from the back of one of the trucks. A swaggering man with a thick belt, sunbaked skin, and a red tunic inspects us. The men open the chest. It's empty.

"I'm Nasur Lavalock. Your, uh, new warden. All metal's gotta go," he says. "No craft allowed in Geum Ide."

Koglim's eyes bug out of his head. "No craft? Are you serious? Wait, so you guys are—you must be..."

"Conjurers." Lavalock spats. "Here's the deal. Not everyone is sold on bringing you in. Not even Glaris"—he points to Andalynn and me—"and that's your own grandmother. So, ditch the metal and get in the truck bed. It's not a debate."

He whirls around and returns to the driver's side of the nearest truck.

"We really doing this?" Koglim asks.

Wherever they're taking us, I know who it might lead to. "Ara, is my dad there, in Geum Ide?"

"Yes, he sent me to check on you."

"Not a moment too soon," Andalynn says. "Put all your objects in the chest. These people are dedicated to ideals, to their oath to swear off craft. It doesn't seem like they want to take us in. I can only imagine our stay with them will be temporary."

She removes her bracelets and rings.

We follow Andalynn's lead, placing all of our crafted objects into the chest: Rugnus bitterly parts with Icho, Koglim with Elbaz, Winta with her mercury bracelet—after she forces the liquid metal inside a small compartment. Sira leaves her silver knife, Hemdi, Linterna, and me, Ergal. And that's just our prized objects.

Rugnus sets his whole bag inside the chest, and Koglim does the same. The only thing difficult to part with is the gold, foil-lined armband that kept the exhaustion at bay. Without it, the recognition of lost sleep overwhelms me. Ready to faint, I wave and bend like a reed. And with the physical weariness comes a second wave of guilt about my mother. I caused this. I squeeze my temples with my fingers.

"Are you going to be okay, sweetie?" Sira asks, rubbing my back. "You look awful. Have you not slept?"

Rugnus slips his arm around me and walks me to the truck bed. "He'll be okay."

Andalynn helps him. Like me, she's dealt with a parent that can't sleep. If she guesses anything about the visions and my dreaming, she keeps it to herself.

When we're ready, the trucks peel out, tires skittering over the broken concrete. My grandmother takes the lead, and the lizard scrambles away at an incredible speed, followed by the bikes, then trucks.

But we don't make it a hundred yards before every vehicle comes to a stop.

"Something's wrong," Rugnus says.

Koglim waves a hand. "I don't even need my pendant to tell you that."

I stand and peer over the cab. Ahead of us, my grandmother

struggles to reign in her giant lizard. It screeches and claws at the ground, throwing a shower of concrete behind it. Large, beastly shapes move into the pool of light formed by the conjurer's trucks and motorcycles.

Andalynn comes to her feet at my side. "Feral wolves. There must be a whole pack."

"Rugnus," I say, "is it the same wolf from the threshold of Wolfstaff?"

He opens his mouth but nods.

Koglim's high-pitched voice comes from behind me. He reaches to rub his pendant, but it's not there. "Ide keep me safe. Ide keep me safe. By silver and bones. Are you telling me the guardian of Wolfstaff Dungeon appeared before your summation?"

In answer, the ancient, womanly voice of the guardian sounds in all of our minds.

I am Frrwelhst. I would speak with the Loamin named Clayson Brightstorm.

"Your cue," Rugnus says, nudging me off the truck bed.

Lavalock glares at me as I come around the cab. "I-I'm here."

My grandmother backs the lizard away from the closest feral wolf, disbelief plastered over her face.

Clayson, there is a place we must show you. We believe this to be Torlina Wolfstaff's desire.

"You need me to come with you?"

Yes.

Frrwelhst pads over next to me, lifting a paw to form a sort of step.

Our pack is faster than yours. We know how to locate their den. We will return you.

"Clayson?" Andalynn says.

I don't hesitate. I climb onto Frrwelhst's broad shoulders. "Guess that means I'll catch up!" I shout. Frrwelhst's muscles gather under me, and she leaps. We bound into the darkness over the broken road.

Frrwelhst flies from the concrete, pouncing on a burned-out shell from some war machine, and then back to the concrete on the other side. It's such a fluid movement. I barely have to hold on. Dry, cold air pummels my face, and I squeeze my eyes shut. Engines roar behind us, but after a few minutes, we've left them behind.

I can't track time, but we move quickly. I open my eyes every few minutes, but it's pitch dark. Mile after mile of the broken road falls away behind me. We blur past a machine, still smoldering with active lava. How that's possible? A few stories tall, it lights our path, resting behind a massive pile of rubble. It's a bulldozer, destroyed in the act of tearing up the road. I can't come to grips with the scale of death and destruction during the Mithrium War. I close my eyes again.

If I'd been raised under the surface, maybe I would've done the same thing as Dad—take the mithrium, hide it, or better yet, destroy it like my grandfather. Yinzar Copperoath. The man the world calls Mithriumbane. Though something doesn't sit right about this legend told on bluelink. It had been a process for him, searching for knowledge about the mithrium, whether it could be used for good or if he would have to destroy it.

We turn a corner, heading deeper underground into pure darkness like I imagine the bottom of the Mariana Trench would be.

More miles. A half-hour, maybe an hour.

Suddenly to my right, the wall is gone, replaced with a ledge lighted with a muted blue-green. Beyond, a bottomless abyss. Black water glimmers on the horizon. A sheen of light grants me sight enough to judge it for what it is—an underground lake. A rock wall replaces the view of the lake, but only for a second. We continue this way, always downward, but weaving through tunnels and out onto the ledge again. The sliver of oily water grows each time it comes back into view until we emerge from a tunnel, and I get a good look at it.

Endless. More like an ocean than a lake.

Do you know this place? Frrwelhst says to my mind.

"No."

Loamin call it Onthratia. Yinzar Mithriumbane spent many of his last days here. The wolves call it by a different name. It is called Drwworra—lair of the Great Smoke. We fear this place, but you must know its secret. Frrwelhst stops, and the pack behind her waits in the dark as we move closer to the shore. *You will find this in Yinzar's memories, in your visions.*

"How do you know—"

The memories circle like you are a carrion. Yinzar came here to speak to the Great Smoke.

"What is the Great Smoke?"

A low growl rumbles through the feral wolf. *In the water, the eel lives—trapped here. The water grows dense with its filth and wickedness. The dark energy here. That is why Yinzar came to ask the Great Smoke about this power, but in our fear, we persuaded him to abandon his forge deep under the water. That is what Wolfstaff wants from you. You must find Yinzar's forge under the water. Continue his work.*

"Yinzar's forge?"

He spoke with the wolves, and this eel—the Great Smoke—and the dragon bones, even the mountain itself. If I can believe my visions, could this be what needs to be done? A way out? Could I forge something powerful enough to save my mother? To help Loamin from both cities find lasting peace?

"I have no way to the bottom. I mean, maybe Rugnus could... or with the right craft, but I have other priorities right now. I've got to save my mother."

Then I have delivered the message.

The wolf's shoulders tighten, and we take off. The road transitions into dark sand as we travel along the lakeshore. The rest of the pack disappears. Greenish light glows from a point in the wall ahead, and we veer to the left into a bright tunnel, where I can't help but stretch my hands into the air to soak my arms in brilliant ribbons of light. It's not tangible, but there's a warmth to it. The shimmering effect is the result of pools of water here and there beneath our feet. Frrwelhst even dips her head for a drink.

She shakes her body, spraying me. The cool droplets rain on my skin as I cling to her.

Along the walls, large dark leaves sprout above the pools, until the whole cavern is covered in plant life, and the light becomes duller and more ominous. When we burst free of the tunnel, I'm dazed once again. It's another mithrium-destroyed city. In Thiffimdal, the mithrium had been combined with iron-craft to make nuclear, elemental craft—ice. In this place, the mithrium must have been combined with tincraft.

Mountainous vines hang like stalagmites for a couple miles outward. Through their thick vegetation, I catch flashes of a yellow-green brightstorm. The stone and glass of dozens of sharp-angled skyscrapers peek out through a carpet of plant life. Could this place have been as deadly as instant winter? I strain to control my imagination. A single plant had nearly killed Rugnus. It must have been terrifying when the mithrium bomb went off.

My grandmother, on her lizard mount, emerges from the tunnel, followed by the trucks and motorcycles.

We must part ways here.

Frrwelhst kneels, and I step off hesitantly.

Good hunting, Clayson Brightstorm. Remember the gift you bear in Ergal.

The lizard hisses as the great wolf bounds over it in a single leap. The oncoming procession of vehicles parts to each side to let Frrwelhst into the tunnel. The closest truck zips around me and screeches to a halt. Winta faces me directly, flanked by Rugnus and Hemdi, who crane their necks to bring the over-grown cityscape into view. Rugnus, wide-eyed, unbuckles himself from his harness and steps out of the truck. Hemdi unbuckles next. He kisses Winta and jumps from the truck bed with the same excitement as Rugnus.

A chain of sharp popping—like someone has weaponized a few hundred helium party balloons—erupts from somewhere out in the jungle. I'm not the only one who jumps at the sound. Our whole crew from Tungsten City fixates on the jungle while my grandmother and a few of her conjurers glance our way with satisfied looks. Our worries are justified—they seem to want us to feel on edge.

"Where are we?" I ask Rugnus.

"Gythanstyan. Without a doubt. The evil lake just outside the city gives it away."

"Onthratia," I say, repeating the name Frrwelhst had used.

Rugnus grunts. "Is that where the wolf took you?"

I nod and turn my attention back to the jungle. "We're not actually going in there, are we?"

Before he can answer, a growling white noise approaches like a semi barreling down the freeway at high speeds. It fades with an unnerving echo, stretched out, and slowed down. At the same time, humid air curls up around me, only to be sucked away with the sound.

My grandmother skitters over on her mount, careful not to get too close. The lizard's hungry eyes flicker between the three of us as if choosing which will be its next meal.

"Welcome to Geum Ide. Besides Ara and your father, we haven't had visitors in more than a decade. I forget how disturbing the jungle can be." It's the right word, but she says 'disturbing' with a smile.

"What's in there?" I ask.

"Mostly things that will kill you." She smirks. "But we'll guard you to your final destination."

"Is it wrong to think this place is beautiful?" Hemdi says to no one in particular.

It's an odd comment, but I understand him. Mithriumcraft devoured the entire city. Frightening and beautiful. A similar awe and terror came to me the few minutes I spent in Thiffimdal. But none of the beauty of the jungle competes with the weight in my heart. The scale of death and destruction in this world is monstrous. It leaves a film of disgust on the inside of my skull.

"Perhaps not," my grandmother says, "but there's more to see. And first..." she gestures to the truck, where Nasur Lavalock waits for us, tapping his foot, holding a small wooden box. Inside lay a dozen stemless daisies with delicate white petals and sapphire centers.

Lavalock holds out a box to me. "Take one, but don't smell it."

As I remove the flower from the box, similar instructions are given to our whole group. I get buckled into a harness opposite Sira and Koglim, who each take a flower when the box comes around.

My grandmother's lizard comes to the end of the truck bed. "Okay, eat up."

"The flower?" Koglim says.

"We can't let you in any other way."

For some reason, everyone looks at me. "If I can eat a crab that connects me to the internet, and a bison burger that makes me nostalgic, then a flower's not that bad."

I shove the whole thing in my mouth and chew.

A pulse of heat, like a habanero pepper, attacks my mouth. There's a Chinese buffet Dad used to take me to before he got sick, and I swear the flower tastes like the sauce on their hot ginger chicken, which usually makes my eyes water. I guess that's why I'm not surprised when I have to blink away tears. But after a few blinks, I open my eyes to darkness.

There are murmurs of concern all around me.

"I'm blind," Sira says.

My grandmother says. "The effect will only last through the hour."

"That's some spicy brick!" Koglim wheezes.

"What type of craft?" Andalynn asks. "I can't see a thing."

"Goldcraft?" Rugnus says.

"No, tincraft?" Hemdi says.

"Both," Rugnus guesses.

"Come now, we don't use craft here," my grandmother says. "These grow wild."

With that, I sense her leaving. The trucks rumble over the path, and—I can only assume—we enter the jungle. The ride is terrifying. Every tightening snap of a vine, every screeching animal, every explosive pop—from Ide knows what—is magnified. At first, we try to talk over the noise, but then a horrifying sound will bring us back to the jungle, and we collapse into nervous silence.

Every time the truck lurches over some huge bump, I'm almost happy to be tossed around like I'm on some old roller coaster. At least it's something else to interrupt the screams of plant life, or animals, or whatever else might be out there. There's nothing of craft about the truck, at least nothing I can tell, which for some odd reason, makes me nervous.

I lived my entire life without craft, but at this moment, I return to the place in my mind that holds Thiffimdal in ice. The transformation and the hosts of people frozen to death in a nightclub. I feel a paralyzing need to be aware, to have my ring ready. But I don't have that protection.

After what seems like almost an hour, we slip onto a smooth stretch of road. I welcome the silence. I don't dare break it to ask a question.

But Rugnus does. "Everyone good? The noises stopped, yeah?"

Andalynn and Koglim confirm this with an audible, "Yep."

The trucks stop, and the conjurers work in silence to unbuckle us, refusing to answer any of our questions. We're dragged over dirt floors and sat around a rough wooden table.

My grandmother speaks. "I'll return when the effect of the flower wears off."

Her footsteps cut softly away.

"Okay," Rugnus says, "Say 'here' when I say your name. Hemdi?"

"Here."

"Sira?"

"Here?"

"Koglim?"

No one answers. Sira asks again. "Koglim?"

"Oh, sorry," he says. "Trying to meditate."

Andalynn and Winta acknowledge their presence next.

"Great," Rugnus says with finality. "Now that's done. Let's summarize. Clayson officially got to ride a dungeon guardian, which is beyond amazing. We are obviously in the hideout of the conjurers, which is…"

"Bad," Koglim offers. "I don't think there's anywhere to watch the Hundred Dungeon Games around here."

"We can't stay here long?" I say.

"Great timing," Winta says. "So where would you like to go? Maybe a vacation in Hawaii?" Now that she knows I lived on the surface, I have a feeling she will keep trying to use her knowledge of humans against me.

"Tomorrow morning, my mother will be executed. We have to stop that from happening. There has to be a way."

Feet shuffle toward me, and a hand rests on my back. "There is." I would know the sound of Dad's voice anywhere. He spins me around and pulls me into a hug. "But none of you have to worry about that anymore. You're safe."

LOSE OUR CRAFT

MY SIGHT RETURNS SO FORCEFULLY, I have to squeeze my eyes shut. After a full minute, I ease my eyelids open and step back from Dad. Life under the surface has brought color to his face again, hope to his eye. He smiles this lopsided smirk I haven't seen for years.

We all stand in a rough circle in a large room with a dirt floor. Half of the room is constructed of cobblestone, but along the other half, hundreds of mismatched windows have been stitched together to form a sloping wall. Winta and Hemdi have moved to the windows, drawn by the light.

A second passes, and that's all it takes for me to remember he kept this world hidden from me for fourteen years. "Why didn't you tell me who we were? Or at least prepare me in case—well, in case of this exact thing. That we'd have to run, have to hide. Why didn't you get me ready?"

Dad recoils. "Clayson, I—we had more time. I didn't mean to keep it from you. It just happened. I kept waiting for the right time and—you know what, it doesn't matter. I had hoped you could live in Tungsten City for years to come, but you're here now. And everything's going to work out."

Rugnus steps forward. "I'm sorry I didn't keep him safe."

"By Ide, you did everything you could." Dad and Rugnus test strengths with accepting smiles.

"What about mom?" Andalynn says.

"I'm going to take care of that," Dad says.

Andalynn tilts her head. "What does that mean?"

My fingertips find my temples. "More secrets, Dad?"

"No, I'll tell you, just"—he glances at the room full of people — "not here. When we're alone, I'll explain everything."

Andalynn comes to our father's side, and we look through the windows. The vision through the glass rekindles my desire to return home to the Blue Ridge Mountains, to our cabin. They've carved this place out of the fallout of a mithrium bomb. It's nothing I would have expected.

Down a long road, in a valley of brilliant green grass and blooming, terraced farmland, squat pentagon-shaped buildings wrapped in flowering ivy cluster around a ravine. At the edge of the low buildings, a courtyard of stone holds a towering fountain. A bright tractor chugs along in one of the terraced stretches of farmland, trailing a harvesting machine. A group of conjurers follow behind the tractor with another truck. They comb through the hewn-down plants and toss pieces of it into the truck bed.

Koglim slaps my arm, "Look, Clayson. This must be exactly like what you did on the surface."

"Get melted, Koglim," Winta says. "They do more than farming above granite. There are a lot of other jobs too."

Rugnus squints against the glare on the windows. "It's so primitive. So…"

"Human," Winta says, and a genuine smile blossoms on her face.

"The land was ruined," Rugnus says. "Uninhabitable for the next two thousand years. What—"

"Ara," Dad says. "She made all of this possible."

I find Ara standing at the back of the room. She looks away when we all turn to her.

"How?" Rugnus says. "Dura can't use craft like we can."

Dad shakes his head. "She's different. She can assume my craft, and it's more powerful than anything I've ever seen or heard of. Makes it safe for her to approach the brightstorm. That's how we're healing it. One touch from her using a Loamin's craft and—I don't really understand it, but it pushes back the effect of the mithrium fallout."

Koglim's pupils are saucers. "Wow."

Rugnus narrows his eyes. "So, craft is bad, but not if a Dura girl does all the work for you?"

Ara speaks, her voice calm, but her eyes still averted. "That's not right. I want to help. These people deserve a home. Something safe. Where they can live their beliefs. They're willing to let me help."

"Metal is the source of craft," Rugnus says. "Try all they want; these people will never conjure it out of Ide itself. It's not possible."

"Regardless," Hemdi says with placating hands, "it's a beautiful home. Thank you for sharing it with us in our time of need."

My grandmother speaks from the doorway. "That's yet to be determined. All of you should change. Some of your clothes still have threads of craft woven into them."

Next to her stands the tall, unmistakable form of another Dura. He's as young as Ara, wire-thin with fair brown skin, coarse hair, and a hunched-over posture. His fingers work over a mass of knotted twine, and though his eyes tell a story of grief and sadness, his mouth plays at a vague smile.

Humming parts his lips, then he rambles. "Just everywhere. Solve the puzzle. Connection. Solve it. Ide. I'm sure I'll never reach the bottom. Never reach it? The first and the second and the third. Connection. Solve the puzzle."

He's not like Kel or Vor or the Dura I saw doing acrobatics in the park. And he's certainly not like Ara. None of them speaks nonsense like this.

My grandmother catches me looking him over. "That's Tas. Ignore him."

Koglim frowns, his attention drawn to the window again. "I'm not down for living here."

Sira nudges Koglim's massive shoulder. "Things work out, dear. Trust."

Another conjurer comes through the door, handing each of us clean, earth-toned linens. I notice now that my father, grandmother, and Ara already wear them. They're different in color but styled the same.

We're directed through a series of hallways, passing smaller rooms here and there. Two men walk by, carrying our chest of crafted objects down another hallway. Koglim stares longingly in that direction, even after they've turned the corner. Sira pulls him along.

"Here," Glaris says, coming to a stop in a large room with a machine-shed sliding door at the far wall. Nasur Lavalock is waiting for us. She points to a few animal stalls.

"You got to be kidding me," Koglim says.

"They're clean," she says. "We haven't used this building as a barn for years. Change. Then Nasur will take you on a tour of the settlement."

"A limited one," he says.

Sira skips to her stall. Rugnus and Andalynn take stalls on either side of her. Hemdi and Winta take the last one.

"No need to wait," Dad says, leading me back down the hallway to a small room. "Go ahead and change here." He lets me in and closes the door.

Distillery equipment—coils and stills, flasks heavy with greasy liquids—clutter a long table. I've used these objects before to help Dad make biofuels out of household scraps. It was one of the weird things he used to make me learn. Now I understand where his obsession came from. A jungle-like the one outside these doors could make a lot of biodiesel. My hands fumble as I pick up a small glass hydrometer. Did Dad teach the conjurers how to make fuel for their machines? Or was it the other way around?

I set the hydrometer down and switch my clothes.

There's a knock on the door.

"I'm dressed. Come in," I say.

Expecting Dad, I blink when my grandmother steps into the room. She looks nothing like my mother or sister. There's an openness about them she doesn't share. She crosses the room and picks up the hydrometer. "I want to make things clear to you."

She's direct, exactly the opposite of Dad.

"I appreciate that."

"Don't. You're here for a single reason: to keep your father happy. His connection with Ara makes this settlement possible. Without her, the poison of the mithrium fallout creeps back into our land. He sent Ara to check on you without my permission. When he learned what was happening in Tungsten City, he forced my hand. Said we would take you in, or he and Ara would leave. Do you see the situation my people are in?"

"Yes, but it's not like we wanna be here."

"That's the problem. Everyone here, they chose this life. Besides your father, no one has ever left."

"Seems a bit cut and dry. He left because of me. I wouldn't sleep. You're treating him like it was his choice."

She narrows her eyes at me. "From those bags under your eyes, it seems as though that hasn't changed."

"It hasn't."

She frowns at the biodiesel equipment behind me. "His leaving was less of a choice than he makes it out to be. Everyone was scared of whatever curse my fool of a husband put upon you and your mother." She turns her frown to me. "I can't persuade the people here to welcome you."

"Is it really a curse?"

"I call it like I see it. He did whatever he did to you two and then goes off and gets himself turned into a dungeon. He was always reckless. Always foolish. I can't welcome you knowing you're still under whatever craft he placed upon you. It's dangerous."

266

"Look, I'd rather return to the surface. At least I could sleep, but what will everyone else do? And how would we stay hidden from Bazalrak? We can't. This is the only place for us. I can deal with dreams. What I can't deal with is putting everyone else at risk by forcing them into a life on the surface."

"Dreams?"

I hesitate, but she might be able to help me understand what's happening. "I keep seeing my grandfather. I think he's trying to tell me something."

"Yinzar? You see him?"

"Every time I fall asleep down here, I see him."

Her deep-set eyes cut into me. "Was it the forge? Under Onthratia? Is that what you're seeing?"

"A forge? I don't know. I've seen him talking to weird things. Debating about the mithrium. Searching for secrets. I don't understand what I—"

"Those aren't dreams. They're memories." She yells for my father, and he appears at the door. "Tell him what you just told me."

"Uh, Yinzar... I see him in my dreams—or memories. I haven't told you yet. I'm not sleeping down here. But you knew I couldn't sleep."

Koglim bounces through the door. "Look, Clayson, I'm a conjurer. Watch me use craft"—he raises his arms with the flare of a street magician—"Oh, wait. I can't."

Nasur's sharp voice says, "Is he mocking us?"

Everyone else shuffles into the room. Andalynn comes to stand next to me.

"Clayson." Dad snaps his fingers. "What is Yinzar doing in these dreams?"

I find myself rambling about the cliff thing he spoke to, his arm made from plants, about the dragon bones, Onthratia, how the feral wolves convinced him to avoid it. "He was trying to find a way to use the mithrium to create something. Not unlike what Lonecharge and Silverkeeper are doing.

267

"He couldn't figure it out?" Glaris says.

I shake my head. "But he did figure out how to destroy a piece of the mithrium, right?"

There's a crowd at the door. Koglim's mouth is wide open. "So, he only destroyed one of three pieces?"

Dad twitches toward the crowd, looking mortified. "We need privacy."

"Dad," I say. "They all know. We know my mother hid another piece of mithrium in Silverlamp. Silverkeeper wants it, but he won't enter the dungeon. So, he's trying to use Lonecharge and Bazalrak to get it."

He opens his mouth, stunned. When he looks to Glaris for help, she scoffs and says, "Secrets always come out."

My father squares his shoulders. "It doesn't matter who knows. They won't find it."

"How can you be sure?" Andalynn says.

"They have Silverkeeper's key," I say. "Won't that—"

"A keeper's key," Dad says, "is not a license to grab anything you want. Challozil Silverlamp—the consciousness of the champion herself—controls the dungeon. Your mother left it in Silverlamp to protect everyone. The dungeon would kill them if they tried. Ide keep me. The dungeon would even kill her if she tried to get it back."

Something crystalizes in my mind. "An undisclosed location. What if they try to force her to get the mithrium? What if that's what this is all about? Maybe they still think she can get it out of Silverlamp." I say.

He recoils from this. "No. I..." glancing around, he says sharply, "Can everyone give us some space, please. I want to talk to my son alone."

Glaris shrugs. "Fine. Everyone, let's go. We'll get you bicycles so you can get around the settlement and find someplace temporary where you can stay tonight."

Everyone but Andalynn moves. "I want to hear what my father has to say."

"Of course," he says, gesturing to her closer. Something sad and broken rises to the surface of his eyes. Andalynn is the child he had to leave behind to give me a better life. The regret is as plain on him as I'm sure the exhaustion is on me.

Once everyone is gone, my father takes a deep breath. "I did steal the mithrium with Yinzar's help. Your mother was furious when she found out. But Yinzar didn't share the recipe code with me. After he destroyed his piece, I had no idea how to destroy the other two. Even so, it would have been foolish to try. Yinzar lost his life, even though he became a champion and spawned a dungeon."

"Allegedly," Andalynn says.

I nod. "Mithriumbane. They still can't find his dungeon."

"Right. So Azbena convinced me to hide the other two. Which leads us to the dreamwell."

"Wait," I say. "Where is the third piece?"

Dad's jaw tightens. "That's too dangerous for you to know."

My hands curl into fists. Why is he still clinging to his secrets? "No. Everything needs to come out in the open. Right now."

Andalynn extends a hand toward me, but I pull away.

"He's not wrong, Clayson," she says. "It's better if the last piece stays hidden."

"Clayson," Dad says, desperately trying to get me to make eye contact. "I don't think it's your mother they're after. I'm worried Theridal is trying to lure *you* into Silverlamp dungeon. If he knows about your dreams—"

"The dreamwell," Andalynn says. "That's where she hid the mithrium. It's brilliant."

"Someone tell me what a dreamwell is?"

Dad starts to speak, but Andalynn is quicker. "Not many people can even reach its entrance deep within Silverlamp. And those that do... it's believed it can only be accessed by someone who can dream under granite. But no one can."

"No one except for me," I whisper. "What happens to people when they go inside the dreamwell?"

"Traps them in their worst nightmares," Dad says. "They come back catatonic. Within a few days, they start having seizures. It doesn't take long before... Clayson, you can't go into that dungeon. I won't lose you. I've made up my mind."

This brings both Andalynn and me to attention. "About what?" Andalynn says.

"I'm leaving Geum Ide. It's the only way to rescue your mother. Either they *are* planning to execute her, or if they're bringing her to the dreamwell... it's a death sentence either way."

"We can go with you," I say. "And Ara should be able to—"

"Ara can't come with me. I've made an agreement with Glaris. You and your friends get to stay here—so you can be safe—but Ara will have to stay as well. She's not happy about it, but she's willing to continue the work we've started."

"But without craft—"

"My oath... it's not worth your mother's life."

Andalynn and I must come to the same realization. We look at each other, then at him. Andalynn says, "And the conjurers won't let you back if you choose to use craft."

"I wouldn't expect them to. We live by certain principles here. Besides, Ide keep me, this will bring the wrath of the council down on me. I can't return here."

We're all silent. My future in this world keeps shifting. Before I reached Tungsten City, it seemed like I would be on the run with nowhere to call home. Then I began to feel like I could live there permanently. For the first time in my life, the world was more than trees and mountains—it was invention and millions of new ideas and places to see, millions of people.

But always, in the pit of my stomach, I knew it couldn't last. My name is not Glintwheel. And it's not Spangler. It's Brightstorm.

"I'm going to catch up with the others," Andalynn says, shifting toward the door.

"The guards should be able to find you a vehicle."

Before she leaves, he says her name. "You should know how proud of you I am. You've taken such good care of her, my Azbena. The day you were born—I've never been happier. You were my reason for wanting to make the world safe. You're so beautiful. You treat the people with such love and kindness. I just—"

Her face falls. She half shrugs. "Alright."

It's such a small word. I can't translate it. Maybe she means for him to stop. That being told how he feels about her hurts too much. I can see that on her face. It's how I feel about my mother. My sister hurries through the door.

Dad glances at the distilling equipment, then at the walls and floor, as if each thing is an old friend. He dusts off his hands.

I can't let him give up his whole life again. He has his oath to the conjurers. It binds him to this place, but I can make promises too. His sacrifice of fourteen years—years I slept like a baby as night terrors plagued him—sits between us like a challenge. He's not the only one who can free my mother. I have Ergal, and I have friends.

"When will you leave?" I ask.

It's like I wake him from a daydream. "Oh. Uh, early, very early. It's the perfect timing if I play things right. Besides I need another day here, a day I can spend with you and your sister. Speaking of which... I brought you to this room for another reason." He moves over to the cobblestone wall, searching the surface. "Here it is."

Dad wiggles a loose stone from the wall and reaches into the opening, taking a second to glance behind me to the door. "I have something for you," he says, unwrapping the piece of gray cloth in his hand. "It was your grandfather's. My father's."

"Is this an object? I thought—"

"The single thing I kept hidden from Glaris. I've always wanted you to have this."

The small diamond-shaped lapel pin he hands me is heavy, a

sun carved into the iron—the symbol of Erikzin Brightstorm. The Spangler family crest. I laugh softly.

"What?"

"Ironcraft is one of my weaknesses."

He scrunches his face. "Truly? And this is metalcraft, a more challenging use of ironcraft, which would make it even more difficult for you."

"Conjurers took my AMP, or I'd show you." He seems disappointed, so I say, "But I'm peerless in shieldcraft. Rugnus had to trade a few relics to get me a fake."

The blood drains from his face. "Only a few people could make a fake with a peerless AMP." The look on my face must confirm what he's guessed. "Lagnar made your AMP?"

"Yeah. That was a fun surprise."

"I'll have to talk to Rugnus about that. How did you get out of there alive?"

"Andalynn caught him sending a message to someone in the Knights."

"I'm glad she did. Anyway, here, take it."

"What if you need it?"

"Ironcraft won't help me break into Keelcrawl prison. Do what you want with it."

I pocket it and follow him out of the room. Outside the building, a cool breeze sweeps in from the jungle. Strange, because it should block the wind. We check for another bicycle, but they're out.

"Should we take a truck?" I say.

"I've got a better idea," he says.

On our way out of the building, I see Tas again. Sitting idly in a corner, working on his knot. Mumbling to himself. "Ice then fire then ice then fire then ice... the first and the second and the third...the first and the second and the third." His words don't make any sense.

"Is he okay?"

"Not really sure. His mind isn't vacant like other Dura. But he's not like Ara either."

I shake my head. "Even you use that word—vacant."

"I didn't call him a vacant. I said his mind isn't vacant. There's a difference. I've been around Ara enough to believe maybe all Dura will be like her someday. Or maybe she will become like them. I really don't know. I hope not."

Around the building, we pull open the hanging barn door revealing a gray and white four-wheeler. "Where do you guys get all these vehicles?"

He shrugs. "Ara's been known to budge a junkyard down here a time or two."

"So, it's okay for her to use craft, but..."

Again, I'm met with a shrug.

While it's not clear how often he rides this four-wheeler, it is clear how much he's gonna enjoy it. Everything around us—from the machines to the biodiesel distillery to the barn to the cobble-stone walls, everything—fits. He can't abandon this life. The faster we get back to Andalynn, the sooner I can try to convince her we need to break our mother out of Keelcrawl prison ourselves. And we need to do it tonight.

"The faster, the better," I say.

REND THE MOUNTAIN

THE FOUR-WHEELER RUMBLES over the gravel road, irrigation ditches to our right and left as we travel the length of another terraced stretch of farmland. There are signs of my father's presence everywhere, in the tidy rows of corn, in stacks of wood strapped down with waxed burlap against cobblestone houses. A single long greenhouse edges this side of the settlement, made from windows they must've stripped from a thousand dead buildings hidden in the jungle. His distinct world view of self-sufficiency doesn't belong only to him but to all conjurers.

I consider asking about some foreign plant life sprouting from long lines of PVC pipe in pale shades of cactus-green, but it might slow us down. Fascination needs to take a back seat to necessity.

I have a prison break to plan with my friends.

We slow down when the street transitions into a blacktop. Where did they find the materials to pour blacktop roads?

Clay tiled roofs hint at a kiln somewhere among the shops. Short, vine-woven fences border the tarred road. I crane my neck to take in the large water tower pinned with narrow pipes, leading to a few waiting ground tanks.

Dad yells over the roaring motor. "We'll try the scrap house!"

We bump into a part of the city that was functional in its previous life. Every wall we flash by, every tunnel we dip under, is peppered with thousands of faded patches and bolt holes, as if the conjurers removed, by hand, hundreds of thousands of attachments. We skirt the edge of the ravine I saw from the main barn. Dark vegetation grows entrenched along the sides and into the depths.

We zip into a longer tunnel with evenly spaced shafts of light. It looks as if they live and breathe, not adhering to typical laws and properties of light.

Dad shouts back to me. "Beautiful lightfalls, right?"

Lightfalls. That's a good word for it.

With a sharp left out of the tunnel, the road pitches upward, wrapping around a pentagon building—made from the same stone—with at least ten gaping garage-sized openings. A group of bicycles is parked against the side of the nearest stall.

Hemdi steps from the building, calling to us. "In here."

I jump off the four-wheeler, but Dad stays on. "Doesn't look like Ara stayed with the group," he says. "I'm going to go find her."

"Is she okay?"

"She likes to use any leftover craft to push back the fallout in a few places. I'll find her. Should only be a few minutes."

The four-wheeler takes a wide loop and heads back the way we came.

Each opening is some type of large hangar bay. My friends are huddled around a monster truck. Winta's closest, getting a crash course on human engines and biofuel from a rail-thin conjuror wearing grease-stained overalls. Nasur Lavalock is holding up a pillar off to one side of the hanger, rolling his neck from side to side.

I get Rugnus' attention and call him over. Andalynn tears away from the tutorial at the same time and makes straight for me. For some reason, I can tell she's prepared for what I have to say.

Lavalock is only on the other side of the group, but the engine's noise and Winta's even louder questions conceal our whispered conversation.

I lean over to them. "I've got a plan. Well, the start of one."

"Good," Andalynn says, "I have one too."

Rugnus, who's already found a food source, takes a bite of a yellow apple. Switching his focus between Andalynn and me, he says, "Great. Great, great. One thing though—these plans? Do they involve us leaving Geum Ide?"

"Among other things," I say.

Andalynn agrees.

He swallows and leans in closer. "Is this going to be like your plan to steal the key from Silverkeeper? Honestly, I don't want to see what will happen if we try to take our stuff back and sneak out. I'm pretty sure Lavalock will... what do humans say? Shoot first. And this latcher version of me can't absorb bullets."

"They won't try to stop us," Andalynn says.

"You sure?" Rugnus says. "They've kept this place a secret. How do you think they've done that? No one leaves. Ever."

I ignore this. "My dad's leaving. Tomorrow morning he's leaving by himself. He's gonna try to break my mother out of Keelcrawl."

This sobers Rugnus. "And use craft again. Wraithspit. Okay, what's your plan?"

I shrug. "Leave tonight, for Whurrimduum, before my dad leaves."

Amusement touches the corner of Andalynn's mouth. "Hmm. Forgive me, but Clayson, you can barely pronounce Whurrimduum, let alone find your way through the foilgrips."

Rugnus agrees with this but says, "They probably blocked your access too, though, princess, how do you... oh."

Andalynn leans into Rugnus playfully. "Hypothetically, do you know how people are leaving Whurrimduum?"

Rugnus blushes. "Nothing hypothetical about it."

"If you can sneak people out," I say. "Then you can sneak people in."

"Sure." Rugnus takes another bite of the apple. "Getting to Whurrimduum is the easy part. Keelcrawl will be impossible unless..." He fixes Andalynn with a questioning look.

There's a fire in her eyes. "Our father has been absent for fourteen years. There's no chance he can break into Keelcrawl. That's why we will have to do it ourselves. I have a way in." She glances at the conjurer teaching Winta. "But we're going to need serious craft to get my mom out. It's the strongest Chainbearer prison in the whole kingdom. Transparent aluminum cells, temporal locks, the highest-level encryption, and the best gold binders available, made in Harthen's forge."

"Brick. Okay then, how far in can you get us?" Rugnus says.

"We won't be seen by anyone. But I can't pick locks like those."

Rugnus points to Winta with a slight lift of his hand. "She can. But I'm not sure we can get her away from the trucks."

Winta's giddy words flare over the revving tractor engine. "So, it's like hundreds of controlled explosions?" she asks the conjurer man.

"How long do we have to convince the others?" Rugnus says.

Andalynn says, "I can't get us into the prison during the day."

"And we have to leave before my dad—"

"Why not just include him?"

"One," I say, "he's adamant we need protection."

"Of course," Rugnus says.

Andalynn picks up where I left off. "And two, if he breaks his oath and leaves the protection of Geum Ide, he'll be hunted down and executed."

Rugnus rolls his shoulder back. "Right. Then we'll need a plan that stops him and Ara from just following us the moment they figure out we're gone."

"I have the start of an idea for that, too," I say.

We spend the rest of the morning getting a tour of the valley.

Most of the conjurers are generous and quick to help us, which makes me sick at the thought of having to force our way out of here if we need to. Every now and then, I catch the glimmer of Nasur's assault rifle, and my hand wants to search for the lapel Dad gave me. Metalcraft.

They roast a whole goat for lunch, not only for us, but half the settlement comes for the meal. I hear someone in line say Ara budged a herd of goats down a few days ago, which makes it pretty clear we're eating my goats. Which is fair. They were due to the butcher at the end of October.

The other conjurers bring vegetables both strange and familiar as sides for the meal. Most things are roasted or boiled and seasoned with fresh herbs.

Dad returns at lunch and continues the tour with us, taking the time to show us specific problems he solved for the community and anything else he finds interesting. Strange seeing this type of excitement from him. I try not to think about what I'll have to do tonight to prevent him from following us.

In the afternoon, there are still more buildings to tour, but we're able to bring Sira and Koglim into the circle about our growing plan. Koglim is eager—breaking into the highest security prison and sneaking around Whurrimduum will give him another unique experience to use when he applies for his license as a professional raider—if he lives through it.

Sira asks for time to think about it. She will have to budge again, but as long as I get Ergal back, I can cure the effects from the budge, mostly. As we transition over to a citrus greenhouse—which Rugnus miraculously gives his complete attention to—she slides over next to me and squeezes my arm. "I talked to Rugnus. I'll go as far as your next stop. I should have access to bluelink from there. I can start an appeal for all of us. My fans weren't happy about my exile in the first place."

Her massive following in Tungsten City might help us find our way back there when this is all over. Everyone loves her.

Hemdi and Winta are eating up the conjurer lifestyle. It's a perfect place for them, a blend of plants and machines. None of the rest of us wanna spoil their time here, so we wait to tell them our plans.

Hours later, we pile into the back of a truck, and Dad drives us out to a smaller wooden barn only a hundred yards from the edge of Geum Ide. The jungle beyond, still overtaken by the mithrium fallout, groans with terrifying noises and animal calls.

Dad tries to apologize for the accommodations. "This will be temporary. Glaris and Nasur are still discussing some permanent housing for you."

I fight the urge to tell him we won't need it.

On one side of the barn, the conjurers have set up cots for each of us. On the other side, I find all of my goats from the surface—all but two. Now I'm sure we ate one this afternoon.

"They're really treating us like royalty," Koglim says, spreading himself out on one of the cots. His feet stick out at the end.

Without a true sunrise and sunset, it's hard to tell the time, but as Dad and I tend the goats, the light outside dims to a shadowy orange, and he brings us outside for everyone to watch, where we find seats at a single picnic bench and a group of boulders.

This brightstorm is different. In Tungsten City, the change from night to day is abrupt, enough to jar you from whatever activity you're doing. But this is more like a sunset.

"It is a paradise," Hemdi says.

Dad seems pleased with everyone's responses. "I bet none of you have ever even seen a sunset. Well, besides you, Clayson."

Sira nearly comes to tears. "When I was a girl, my dad and I used to vacation in Rhelmirfar. The brightstorm would change slowly like this. It was beautiful."

We all watch as the color of the brightstorm slowly deepens to a shade of red, then magenta. After it turns purple, it starts to lighten to the shade of the moon, becoming pale and silver. Even the city jungle quiets.

Dad stands first. "I'll come say goodbye before I leave in the morning."

Andalynn doesn't quite meet his eye. I stand and follow him back to the truck. Once he's sitting in the driver's seat, I come to the open window. "Dad?"

"Yeah."

"This is a weird request, but can you come back in a few hours and check on me? The dreams..." I hate lying to him like this but, I have to get him back here some way.

"Sure, anything. I'll do anything for you. And hey, I'm working on getting that armband back to you as part of the deal."

I take in a breath. "Love you, Dad."

"I won't be able to return after this, but you'll be safe here," he says.

"I know."

He starts the truck and zips away. No one else is back in the barn yet. I run my hand along the rail separating us from the goats and find one of them with her head sticking out. I scratch her between the horns and help coax her head back through the slats.

I yawn. The cot closest to me is inviting, so I sit. I count seconds in my mind. Somewhere around a hundred, I slip into Yinzar's memories again. Back in the canyon, I chase after a golden butterfly trembling with the word Onthratia. I catch it and open the memory.

My grandfather's muscular form stands before me, barebacked and sweating, hunched over a forge in the center of the room. The rough walls are slick with oily water. Stalagmites drip from the ceiling. A semi-circle of molten lava swirls at the base of the wall, which provides his forge with an unending source of heat.

Yinzar works cautiously. He pulls oakwood from a barrel of mossy liquid and stokes it with a lambskin bellows until the forge is white with heat. Then he sprinkles dusty peat and chunks of gypsum over the white coals.

Is this how I knew the best way to use gypsum when I was

with Brig at Handler making those animal tags? I hadn't seen this vision before, but was the knowledge somehow part of me?

Once he sets a crucible inside the forge, he unwraps a leather bundle, revealing a metal cube as bright as a hundred-watt light bulb. The mithrium. He holds the bright cube with massive tongs and places it into the crucible. When it's melted, he adds onyx stones to the fire under the crucible. The mithrium glows silver-white. Finally, he adds amethyst dust right into the liquid metal.

Sweat drips off of him in the intense heat—his fist tightens around a small object. "Once I pour this into the mold and add the other metal, I'll either die or create something beyond anyone's comprehension."

He's answered with a noise as if someone is screaming into a pillow, a hissing yell. The cavern shakes, and droplets of water sizzle into the lava. Yinzar swallows, and I can read the worry and questions on his face as he sets a triangular mold next to the forge.

Almost imperceptibly, he shakes his head.

"What if you're wrong?" He's talking to the cavern. No. It must be to the eel. The Great Smoke.

Yinzar opens his hand, rolling a black metal coin between his fingers. The ceiling shakes again, followed by the same strange, screaming murmur.

He shakes his head. "All my other advice points to the mines, to potential energy. And you tell me it has to be opposite energy. I can't trust you, worm. This will not work."

And he tucks the coin away.

Someone shakes me awake, and without the armband to counteract things, I'm greeted by a new wave of exhaustion.

"Clayson?" The voice is mild, too soft to force my eyes open. "Are you awake, friend?"

It's Hemdi.

I expect a crowd behind him, a train of people trying to get a glimpse of the dreaming Loamin, but it's only him. His broad, kind face absorbs my worry.

281

"You okay?" He sits on a cot next to me.

I rub my eyes. "Just exhausted."

I try to stand up by myself, but Hemdi forces me to remain where I am. Our eyes meet.

"The others are outside. Rugnus explained what you're planning."

"What do you think?"

"Did you know there were only two cities powered by bright-storms in my home kingdom, Firas Andem? Much fewer than the Kingdom of Rimduum."

Were—past tense. The mithrium destroyed them. Not a soul I've met doesn't have a connection to the mithrium war. Hemdi's family were refugees, Winta's mother, Rugnus' mother. The war ended more than twenty years ago. But the fallout is wide and deep. I haven't even begun to process what life had been like in the war-torn areas of Hemdi's past. Had it looked like the Cross-roads, with burned-out machines and mass destruction? How did he even get to Tungsten City? Did he have to walk from South America all the way to the Rockies?

"I guess it's not something I've thought about," I say.

"It's not surprising." He plays with the linen trim on the hem of his shirt, twirling it between his thumb and forefinger. "Com-pared to Whurrimduum, Firas Andem is very small. In fact, many of its people didn't live under the brightstorms. My family once had a simple cottage, miles away from Castillogar."

"Were they safe there?"

"For a time, but no one was truly safe. My mother told me about the day the ironheads came. They collapsed the farm and the cottage. Took all the metal."

"I'm sorry."

"I was born after that. After Castillogar was destroyed, they stayed in the area, searched for food and helpful objects, but there was very little. In Castillogar, the mithrium had been combined with silver."

In Thiffimdal, the outcome of combining mithrium with iron

had been eternal cold. Here in what's now called Geum Ide, it was tin. Why is he telling me all of this? "What happened?"

He stops twirling the trim on his shirt. "Waking nightmares."

I don't ask him anything else. A whole city lost in nightmares sends a shiver down my back. Dad said the dreamwell can trap someone in their nightmares.

"I'm sorry I got you and Winta kicked out of Tungsten City. I made you a refugee again."

"Not true." He breathes the cool air deeply. "You've led us to a paradise."

"So, what? You and Winta would want to stay here?"

He smiles. "I couldn't give up tincraft."

"And now you and Winta are outcasts because of me."

Hemdi bows his head. "I want you to know something," he says. "I don't hold you responsible for what your father's father did during the Last War. And if your parents are truly trying to rid our world of mithrium, then I'm with you to the end."

Winta enters the room. "Good, our fearless leader is awake. You have us in quite a wraith's cradle."

"Would someone finally explain that one to me?" I ask.

"A wraith's cradle," Hemdi says, "is a situation where it's difficult because it is literally impossible—a phrase unique to this kingdom."

"I don't live in a kingdom," Rugnus says. He and Andalynn enter the barn from the other door. "Truck's coming. Time to show me that lapel pin you've been talking about."

For the first time since my father gave it to me, I take it from my pocket. Rugnus gasps.

"King Erikzin's seal. Wow! Does it have a name?"

"I didn't ask," I say.

Rugnus nods with a laugh. "Of course you didn't."

The truck rumbles over the gravel road

"Everyone, get ready," Andalynn says.

We move to our places, half on one side of the door, half on the other.

"I hate this plan," I say.

Rugnus raises an eyebrow. "I don't really like it either, but it's your plan."

"I know. I hate it."

Whistling.

Dad is whistling when we ambush him, pushing him to the ground. Maybe with craft, he could have put up a fight. Koglim does half the work for us. Once my father is pinned down, Koglim digs a knee into his back.

"Koglim, careful!" I say.

He wipes the smile off his face. "Right, your dad. Sorry."

Hemdi ties his legs and hands, and we roll him over.

The red rims of his eyes cut through my flesh. "W-what are you doing? Clayson?"

"Sorry, Dad. I'm not gonna let you throw your life away."

"Sorry," Sira says, "so, so sorry. Oh, guys, this is terrible."

He forms a few words but can't settle on a sentence. He shakes his head, but then the color drains from his face. "You're going to Keelcrawl."

"You guessed it, Papa King," Koglim says.

"And Dad, you're not," Andalynn says. "We can do this."

"I-I can't let you," he stammers. "Please don't do this. It's my job to take care of you."

Rugnus pulls him up, tying the gag around his mouth. "Sorry, Therias. Really, sorry. But they're right. And we've got this. But you're just noble enough to try and follow us, so this is the way it's got to be. You get to keep your life here, and we get to leave."

I'm glad Rugnus can tell him our reasoning because I'm being torn into a million pieces. Here's the man I took care of the last two years. A week ago, getting roughed up like this would have killed him.

We tie him to a pole and leave him there, yelling mutedly.

From this moment, my mood shifts from sadness to anger. When Koglim starts arguing about who should drive the truck, I yell at him. For a few minutes after, as we pile in and speed toward the large barn in the distance, no one says anything. Sira starts humming, and I try to intimidate her with a glare.

Her nose wrinkles, and she says, "You are doing the right thing. Your dad is going to thank you someday, sweetie."

I shrug off her comment. I don't wanna be made to feel better. I want this world to stop punishing my family for something they are trying to do right. I want my mother free. I want her to see me, to know who I am. I want Dad not to have the weight of the world on his shoulders for once. And I want my sister to have a kingdom willing to be led into better times.

Being Loamin is total trollbrick.

As we roll to a stop, two guards come out of the barn holding metal in their hands. At first, I think they're big hypocrites—they're using craft—but I'm wrong. We tumble out of the truck, leaving the headlights on and the driver's side door open. The night carries the same breeze in from the jungle as the day.

"Stop!" one of them says, leveling an assault rifle.

I start toward them. "I'm not stopping. Rugnus."

Their guns glow bright like embers, and the two men drop them to the dirt. Koglim growls, and Rugnus brandishes the lapel pin. The guards scatter.

Winta helps me pull open the sliding barn door. We don't meet any more guards inside the barn. As we follow the hallway back to where we last saw the chest with our objects, Andalynn steps beside me.

"You okay?"

"Fine." I've kept my exhaustion from the surface for a few days. I can push back a few emotions while I'm at it.

We turn a corner, and Glaris bars the way. She tilts her head to the side. "I thought you might try something like this."

"Don't try to stop us," Andalynn says.

Rugnus waves the lapel pin.

"No need for that." She sighs. "I knew I wouldn't be rid of Therias that easily. Follow me." Glaris turns and disappears around the corner.

"I don't get it," Koglim says.

I lead us down the hallway, around the corner, and into a lighted room, where Glaris stands next to an open chest. Our objects are waiting for us. Koglim is the first one to respond. He retrieves Elbaz, puts it on, and waits for an omen while casting a glare at my grandmother.

"Checks out," he says.

We all reequip ourselves. The moment I have the armband, I breathe a sigh of relief. Even getting Ergal back takes second place. Once we're ready, Rugnus kisses Icho and holds it out.

Glaris clears her throat. "Don't ever come back here again."

"We won't," Rugnus says.

We're greeted by both intense cold and searing heat. Hard, black stone forms the battlements I'm standing next to. No. It's a wall, rivaling China's Great Wall, disappearing in both directions along the horizon. Made of obsidian, the wall divides two distinct worlds. An ocean of lava rises and falls in swells to my right. To my left, a never-ending field of blue, rainbow ice.

How can two things so opposite exist so close to one another?

Before Sira can vomit over the polished obsidian, I extend Ergal to her. She takes a deep cleansing breath and thanks me.

Andalynn gapes at Rugnus. "The Foundation? Rugnus, why did you take us to Edium Fiarie?"

He points along the wall to where an impossibly long building made of the same black stone juts out over the churning lava. "The House of Ide."

"What's in there?" I ask.

Winta's mouth opens, but she can't get out any words.

"Death," Sira says, wide-eyed. "It's where we send our dead to return to Ide."

Koglim squeezes her shoulder. "But there's a bluelink connection for you and a public budge."

"That's how you're sneaking people out of Whurrimduum." Andalynn says.

Rugnus eyes glaze over with lavalight. "Yeah. In body bags."

PEER INTO WHURRIMDUUM

LOAMIN LINE their body bags with aluminum foil.

When the zipper on a bag is engaged, a body is immediately transported to the House of Ide, where the caretakers prepare it for incineration. The families arrive with a few final craft objects, which they tuck inside layers of a body wrap like the ancient Egyptian pharaohs. Then the pallbearers attach ropes to the corpse, drag it to the edge of the void, and inch-by-inch, lower their dead headfirst into the molten lava. Both Koglim and Winta have told me to get melted. Now I know the origin of the phrase.

If we screw this up, we're straight melted.

Winta helps Rugnus track his contact over bluelink in a way that makes his presence untraceable. Rugnus gives us no other details about the individual who provides him access to the body bags. Andalynn presses him about whether the person is native to Tungsten City of Whurrimduum.

"Has to be anonymous," Rugnus says. "Anonymous and... very expensive."

We budge right into the room, and there's no sign of whoever let us in.

The height of the room must be under six feet.

"Cozy," Koglim says, who's the tallest of us.

The House of Ide has no doors or windows, only a maze of openings cut into the polished obsidian. This room runs along the edge of the building, and the openings on one side let in both heat and light from the ocean of lava.

Koglim gets close enough to look. "I wonder if the people who work here chuck all their lunch wrappers right into the lava."

"That's a weird thought," I say. It makes me think of the aluminum toilets in Tungsten City. Somewhere I read that all the garbage and sewage gets transported to the lava flows.

At the center of the room, six body bags await us.

"This is weirder," Winta says.

Rugnus orders us to get in, and everyone but Sira chooses a bag, climbs ups, and shimmies inside like we're snuggling into sleeping bags. Thinking that makes the lava light appear more like a campfire.

"Remember," Winta says, her feet tapping against the inside of the bag, "stay off bluelink until I can get us set up with a false signal."

"Got it the first time," Rugnus says, still as a corpse.

Winta moves her feet around more quickly on the inside of the bag. "Did you, though?"

Hemdi laughs. "She has a point. You can't just charge in cannons firing, like when—"

"I understand. This is not a surveying mission. We're entering the dragon's lair. I'll be careful."

Koglim shrugs. "Those cannons were cool, though."

Andalynn shifts her weight forward in her bag and lays back. "Okay, let's do this. I'm first."

"Then me," Winta adds.

"Then Rugnus. Then Clayson," Andalynn says.

I shift into my bag and take a deep breath. "Right. So, you can use me as a human shield."

"Correct," Winta says. "See, Rugnus. He listened the first time."

Rugnus chooses to ignore this. "Then Koglim. Then Hemdi."

Koglim sits back up. "Sira, take care of yourself. I'll find you the second we get back."

Sira pushes him into his body bag. "I'm a latcher at this heist, prison breakout thing. All you cuties are better off without me. But take good footage. I'm sure you'll look amazing rescuing Clayson's mom. Oh, and I'll check on the puppies."

Hemdi smiles. "Thanks. Their food and water is automated, but still... they'd like the company."

I lean into my bag as Sira walks over to Andalynn. "Ready?"

There's a loud zip.

"One down," Koglim says.

Sira counts out sixty seconds and zips Winta's bag. It disappears.

Then Rugnus' bag. Gone.

When she starts the count again, she's standing at my side. She doesn't even reach thirty before she stops. "Just like when I met you."

Her eyes smile at me. I swallow. I can't tell if she actually likes me or not. She talks to everyone like this. As if, with a bat of her eyelashes, I'll be hers forever. I don't wanna hurt her feelings, but her disregard for boundaries makes me uncomfortable.

"Instead of waking me up," I say, "it's more like putting me to sleep."

Her face changes subtly. "You were having a dream when I woke you up, weren't you?"

"Yeah."

"Well, you'll have to tell me all about it when I see you again."

I nod, and she zips the body bag closed. A weight presses so hard it knocks the breath out of me. This budge is worse than the generic one Dad had me use from that energy drink. My soul itself disintegrates. My body itches furiously, but I don't have a corporeal form to scratch. Stuck in a void. Scattered into the cosmos. I'll never be reformed. Someone takes all my atoms, scrapes them across the floor of some old warehouse littered with glass, puts them in a vice, adds water, and tries to mold me into hard clay.

I turn and vomit inside the bag.

Wait, did I make it out?

Andalynn's voice is muffled. "You're being stubborn."

"Not this again. I—" Someone unzips my body bag—"Ew, Clayson, gross." Rugnus pulls me out of the bag, trying to help me avoid the mess. I take a sip from the quick clean. The stubble on my chin is gone, my clothes are clean, but the smell of my puke lingers in the room. If you can call it a room. It's a half-circle with two tables stacked with empty body bags. A buzzing force field in an arched doorway blocks our only exit.

Winta laughs as I scoot further from the bag. Why does she delight in my embarrassment?

"That was the worst budge I've ever been through," I say.

Winta says, "You can't go through a budge. You just use it."

"Through it, use it, whatever. It was awful."

Rugnus sniffs the air near my bag. "Yeah, Sira was smart to stay behind."

"Okay," Winta says, handing Rugnus and me our slap bracelets that connect to bluelink. "You should be good to go. I've wired us together on a secured network and hidden our individual signatures from the ironheads. But I can't get any of the budge ports to come up."

"That was nice and succinct Winta," Rugnus says.

"Shut up," she says.

"Very little cobalt techno-babble."

A body bag suddenly appears on a table next to me. Koglim is squeezed tightly inside like a bear struggling to get free. Andalynn grabs the zipper and lets him out.

Koglim groans and checks his pendant. Nothing foreboding. "You didn't say it would feel like making a fiery exit from a dragon's rectum."

"More like into the dragon's rectum. We're in Whurrimduum now." Rugnus says.

Andalynn fires off a withering look.

"Guess I had a few clients who said it was bad. Just didn't think it would be *that* bad."

As Koglim closes his eyes for a moment to meditate, Hemdi appears. Once we get him out of the bag, he sits for a while to steady his breathing, hands on his knees.

"Where are we?" I ask Andalynn.

Her eyes search the air in front of her, and her hands manipulate some 3D objects. She activates an unseen button and points to everyone in the group. A blueprint map pops up in front of her. A ghostly outline of Whurrimduum hovers in the air, but she's moving through the image so quickly I can't get my bearings.

"Okay." She squeezes her thumb and index finger together a few times, and the image zooms out. "We're here. Since we don't have access to budge ports—"

"Right," Winta says.

"—as soon as we can get out of this storage closet, we can make our way down this corridor and out onto the roof. From there, we should be able to use Rugnus' club to reach the royal garden. It will be within view."

Hemdi eyes flash wider. "Everbloom Garden?"

"Yes. And from there, we are only two stacks away from the entrance of Keelcrawl prison."

"Stacks, I know that word," I say. "Each keeper has a castlestack, the royal family has multiple stacks, industries devoted to each specific craft have multiple stacks."

"We're so impressed," Winta says.

Andalynn points to a pair of stacks near the center of the city. "Keelcrawl prison is attached to Chainbearer's stack."

Rugnus wrinkles his face up. "I get everything up to this point,"—he sticks a finger right into the hologram of Keelcrawl prison—"But how do you expect us to get into the prison?"

"I sent a message," she says.

"That's pretty vague," Winta says.

Andalynn shrugs. "Let's concentrate on what's happening now." She gives Rugnus an expectant look.

"Absolutely not. You can't use it."

"Use what?" I say.

"She wants to use my club. Says she can budge us to the garden directly."

"He imagines me a spy, thinks I might be working with Bazalrak," Andalynn says.

"What?" I say.

Rugnus holds up his hands. "That's not what I said. Well, not exactly. I—"

"So," Winta says, "you let us get all the way to Whurrimduum…"

"…and then tell us you think Andalynn is a spy?" Koglim says.

Hemdi stands from the table. "I trust her."

Rugnus shakes his head. "I trust her. I just don't want to give her my most powerful object. Brick, I wouldn't even let you use it, Koglim."

"True," he says.

"Then how do we get past the shield?" Andalynn says.

Shield. The word forces me to appraise our situation differently. I'm not sure how the force field works, but the light is bright white, meaning shieldcraft.

I walk straight for the doorway. Rugnus calls out a warning, but I march through. My muscles tighten. I'm denser. The ring works to get me through. I linger in the empty corridor for a minute and return to the storage room to find everyone staring at me.

"That was dangerous," Andalynn says. "You could have set off an alarm."

"Alarms?" Rugnus says. "He could have been shredded into atoms, just melted. You can't do stuff like that without asking anyone."

I shrug. "I got tired of listening to you two argue. It works. Let's go."

Winta slaps my arm. "There you go, Mr. In-Charge."

I take everyone through one at a time, but I don't feel any increase in the sensation, so I'm sure I could take more through at once. No one wants to risk it. With Andalynn at the lead, we sneak down the corridor. There are shields everywhere. When I ask about how they work, Andalynn tells me only certain people can pass through certain shields. It's the reason no one thought of the morgue as the source of the refugee leak.

Rugnus never asked them how they got to the body bags.

"Compartmentalization," he says when I ask him why.

A budge at the end of the corridor takes us to a rooftop access, but I'm not prepared for the skyline view of Whurrimduum. I take comfort in the fact that everyone, excluding Andalynn, stands on the edge of the wall peering out at the city in shock.

The soft green moonlight from the brightstorm blankets a thousand towering stacks of carved stone, a hive of rectangles of varying sizes. They could be identical but in varying degrees of maturation, making them look as organic and geomorphic as sea coral. It's not like the VR flyover footage from bluelink I viewed my first night in Tungsten City. There's something forlorn about it. The square shape of the citybarrel contrasts with Tungsten City's circular one.

Rugnus clears his throat. "I didn't realize it would be so…"

Andalynn makes no effort to address him directly. "Empty?"

Half of the stacks look abandoned. Though the other half light up the night in bright neon color. That's how I spot the fluttering cloud-like mass crossing the sky.

"What's that?" I say.

"Police swarms," Rugnus says. "They enforce the curfew."

Andalynn verifies this.

"If you could have seen it in our parents' days," she says to me, her face sad. "It survived five hundred years of war, only to be drained by a mob of ungrateful zealots. No offense, Rugnus."

Rugnus stiffens. "Offense taken."

"I saw it in old footage on bluelink," I say.

No one speaks for another few seconds. The police swarm crawls through the cavernous sky, casting grotesque shadows on the city as it blocks out the green light of the brightstorm.

If Tungsten City represents the paranoid future, Whurrim-duum is the paranoid past. Stone-yoked. Another word from my searches on bluelink. The destiny of the last two cities, locked together, marching toward some unknown future—two opposing sides of the same ferrum. The only alternative is to swear off craft and live in seclusion.

Andalynn points out a dull rainbow light coming from the top of a distant stack. "Can you budge us there?"

Rugnus grins. "Easy."

He extends the club, careful not to take his eyes off the target rooftop.

"Here we go."

Rugnus' budge is starkly different than the one we used for our terrifying trip to the morgue. There isn't a hint of extra weight. We appear in a garden, which I immediately recognize. It's the moonlit garden my sister shared with my mind the night we met in Gamgim. A sharp, clean smell charges the air with energy, tangible and light, like we've stumbled on some misty valley filled with static electricity.

"Everbloom Garden," Hemdi says, breathless.

To our right and left, plants and vines ensnare every wall, bursting in neon colors: bright pink, lime green, and ice blue. Above us, lemon-yellow vines snake over a golden trellis. Anda-lynn leads us around a Loamin-sized tin flowerpot, the sides dotted all over with holes. Gold-webbed leaves poke through every circular opening.

A drop of golden liquid pings in the soil beneath one of the flowers. It reminds me of my mother's golden blood that protected me on the surface. "Can that stuff change your appear-ance?" I ask.

"Not like Mom's concealer, but yes," she says.

Rugnus' forward motion stutters, and he scans the garden again, with what I assume is an eye for what powers each of the plants holds. "We'll have to come back here."

Winta's holding Hemdi's hand now, admiring his bewildered face. "Definitely."

When Andalynn smiles, Rugnus adds, "But probably not until the ironheads stop executing their own citizens."

Someone behind us clears their throat, and we all spin around.

It's Vor.

Andalynn smiles, though her hand is over her heart in fright like the rest of us. "I knew you would be here. You always come this time of night." She moves away from us, taking Vor's hand and resting her forehead against it.

Vor, though he never looks at any of us, smiles. "Yes, Your Highness." Then he vanishes.

"What was that about?" Rugnus says.

Andalynn brushes past us with increased purpose. "Our way in."

Without another word, we weave through the garden until we come close to the edge of the stack, where the skyline peeks through the foliage. Andalynn takes us to the edge and points to a narrow, brown-glowing appendage on a taller stack. "There's Keelcrawl. There's a top door. That's the main entrance. If this works, someone will be waiting for us at the bottom entrance."

"Should we budge there?" Rugnus asks.

"No, the outer foilgrip prevents that. We'll have to jump down to the bottom entrance from here."

"Jump down?" I say. "If that's Keelcrawl then I think you mean, up. Right?"

"That's the fun part," Andalynn says.

She leads us back from the edge. We turn sharply to the right and march down a set of stairs straight into a clump of bamboo. Andalynn raises her arms, trailing the shafts of bamboo with her tin bracelets. We push deeper into the grove, my arms brushing against the bark of the bamboo. The angle of the ground is changing. Warmth soaks into my skin like the height of summer in the eastern meadow. When we exit the bamboo grove, I blink, disoriented by the upside-down world before me. No one else must find it strange because they keep walking.

My foot slips forward, and for a second, my foot comes unglued. "What's happening?" I say.

Koglim slaps me on the back. "What a latcher. I mean, I've only used reverse gravity a time or two, but... oh wait, what's your rating is tincraft?"

"Complete brick. Are we upside down?" I ask.

Koglim puts an arm around me. "Nice use of language. Andalynn! Will your brother be okay with a weakness in tincraft?"

She looks me over. "Should be okay. Let's get to the next part."

I straighten and brush Koglim off. My feet cling to the ceiling as we cut toward the ledge, but it's more like the adhesiveness of a lousy bandage. We're standing on some reverse balcony looking over the city, the stacks above us and the brightstorm below us.

Andalynn glances to the floor, which had been an overhanging balcony, and says, "Grab a flower. The floating effect will split fifty-fifty with the reverse gravity. We'll have about thirty minutes."

Above me, the original floor made from a patch of sand specked with bits of gold foil holds green desert plants with white, iridescent flowers.

"Yucca flowers," Hemdi says.

Rugnus plucks one off and hands it to me. Andalynn holds hers carefully as she motions for us to gather around her.

"So, the plan is to just jump down to the prison?" Rugnus says.

Andalynn nods. "Yeah. Then we'll use the floating effect to navigate all the negative space inside the prison. Though if anyone sounds the alarm, it may reinstate gravity."

Rugnus agrees to this with a nod. "And if there's a guard?"

"That's why I sent Vor. There won't be," she says. "Or rather, we'll get past him."

We all wait for more explanation, but nothing comes.

"Trust me." She pops the white flower in her mouth, chews, and swallows.

Koglim and Hemdi devour theirs. Winta growls a complaint but gets her down. Rugnus and I trade looks, shrug, and eat. My stomach growls, and I'm suddenly hungrier than I've been in days. I think it's an effect of the goldcraft combined with the tincraft from the flower.

"Follow me," Andalynn says. She walks to the edge of the balcony, climbs onto the rails, and leaps into the night.

"Okay," Winta says. "Now that we ditched the princess, we can go home."

"You wish," Koglim says.

"Sira would love this part," Hemdi says, then he climbs the rails and plummets. Winta follows him, muttering under her breath. Koglim half-covers his eyes and steps off the balcony, peeking through his fingers, falling away with a girlish squeal.

"Just you and me again," Rugnus says.

He digs into a pocket and finds Dad's lapel pin. He holds it out. For me, its power is insignificant, but for Rugnus, it would be a force worth reckoning with. I push it back to him. "You keep it."

He steps back a foot and looks at the object. "You want me to have this?"

I shrug. "I suck at ironcraft. I figure you could make better use of it."

"True, but...Erikzin Brightstorm. I can't—"

"Yes, you can. How many other relics did you sell to get me that fake AMP? It's a gift. Besides, I-I cost you the life you had in Tungsten City."

"A life I wouldn't even have without your dad. I don't know what to say."

"Tell me breaking my mother out of this prison is possible."

The smile that breaks over his face is infectious. His eyes harden into a cold dark fire. "We will." Pulling me to the edge, he counts down. "One...two—"

"Three!" I toss myself into the void, angling toward the building Andalynn pointed out. Rugnus follows me.

I don't need to eyeball my landing. Winta's network is working, and the four other team members are outlined in shimmering gold ahead of me. I can make out Koglim landing like some superhero, sticking to the side of the tall gray granite building digitally labeled Chainbearer. The entrance of Keelcrawl passes underneath me, a single square hole cut into the top of the pyramid, bleeding brown light.

I land flawlessly next to Koglim.

"Sick, right?" he says.

"Yeah," is all I manage to spit out.

Rugnus lands, crawling over to Andalynn like a spider. "Okay, where did you send Vor?"

"Well," she says. "Let's just say he's talking to the guard for me."

"Only one person is guarding it?"

"That's all it needs. The prison is a trap. Every layer we break through will seal behind us, making it all the more impossible to break out. But I'm banking on the power of your club."

"The craft? It's all spatial manipulation?"

"The layers, yes, but the locks are temporal."

Winta spins a band of mercury around her wrist. "Pedestrian."

"Now we deal with the gatekeeper," Andalynn says.

Rugnus affixes the lapel pin to his shirt. "Which means?"

"Which means I go talk to him, and he lets us in."

"What?" Koglim, Rugnus, and Winta say at the same time.

"No one follow me," she says.

Before anyone can argue, she jumps. Her form becomes a black outline when she enters the square opening, swallowed up in the light.

"Well, that's it then," Koglim says. "We're wraithbait."

A purple ray flashes against the glowing brown light.

"Is that supposed to happen?" I say.

Winta stares at the square. "I don't think so. That was time-craft. Not budgecraft."

Something's wrong.

My feet are already loose on the building, so I jump, ignoring Andalynn's orders. I call Ergal awake, and a white energy shield appears around me. The square of earthen light swallows me into Keelcrawl prison.

SEE THROUGH THE FOILGRIP

EVEN THOUGH I'M faced the wrong direction when I come into the room, Lagnar Emberfence's drawl is unmistakable. "...and, get melted, my memories came right on back. Imagine that. And then—Clayson, so nice of you to join us."

I touch down next to Andalynn on a floor of thick glass pulsing with veins of mercury. She steadies me as I turn around. Under the surface, Lagnar doesn't need the oxygen or the motorized wheelchair. The brush of color in his cheeks reminds me of Dad's returned vitality. Lagnar and one other figure stand on the ceiling above us.

No, wait. We're the ones on the ceiling.

My fists tighten, and I extend my shield around us. I wonder for a second if I could use it like a whip to lash out at Lagnar, wipe that stupid smirk off his face.

"I said not to follow me," Andalynn whispers.

"There was a flash of light. What's he doing here?"

"Wowie!" Lagnar says. At least everyone's eyes are at the same level. "Out to rescue everybody. You rescue him. He rescues you. Y'all rescue your mom. It's the family business."

Next to Lagnar, a stout figure I don't recognize holds a ball of purple static energy, his body wound by lengths of chain. His rough hair is braided in long strands, knotted with red glass beads, but his beard is trimmed neatly, gray-black against his brown skin. With deep blue, almost purple eyes, he takes us both in as if judging which to fire at first, but the purple ball shrinks, and his hand falls to his side.

"Lagnar, please," he says, and his voice has a layer of falseness to it, words pretended more than believed. "Let me conduct the council's business first. As I was saying, your Highness, Vor brought me your message."

"Drop your shield, Clayson," Andalynn says to me.

I scowl at Langar but reluctantly follow her lead.

"It's alright, my dear." Again, his voice carries something fake along with it, as if he wants us to believe he cares. "It's good he's come. Both of you standing before me; it brings my mind to an older world. I can recall the royal wedding like it was lastday. You look so much like them."

"Who are you?" I ask him.

"My apologies. I am Reftik Chainkeeper, both keeper and seer of Chainbearer Dungeon, warden of Keelcrawl prison, and the second of the ten keepers on the council."

"We need your assistance," Andalynn says. "I have always had your ear, so please believe what I am about to tell you. Bazalrak is conspiring with Silverkeeper and a man named Filhrin Lonecharge—"

"Stop right there, my lady. You don't have to convince me of this. I am well aware. Lagnar dug up all their secret communications over bluelink. General Stonedoom thinks me loyal to him. And I have played that part to the finest particle. But he's not the future of our kingdom. I am here at your request, though I also have ulterior motives."

"Yep, now we get down to business," Lagnar says.

Andalynn narrows her eyes. "And?"

"I will let you pass with two promises, sworn in silver. First: the reign of your parents comes to a complete end. You, and you alone, assume the throne."

"Me?" Andalynn says. "I'm too young. Not to mention my inheritance is as an Everbloom, not a Brightstorm. And my mom deserves—"

"Your mother is not royal by birth. And you are of age. There are precedents in our history. Besides, who else will rule us? Your father? The rumored conjurer. This boy, raised above granite?" He points to me. "No. Though you hold your grandmother's name—Everbloom—you are a Brightstorm by blood, if not by craft. And your line still has the potential to bring another Brightstorm to the throne. You command the adoration and respect of all of Whurrimduum. If they could elect someone, it would be you anyway."

Andalynn lifts her chin. "Hardkeeper's opposition..."

"That's where I come in," Lagnar says. "Hardkeeper is a close friend. End my banishment, and I can influence him to accept your new position."

My sister takes a deep breath. "I see. And what's the other promise?

Lagnar smiles. "Well, here it comes."

Chainkeeper clears his throat. "We redraft the Contract of Keepers and Kings. The monarchy will only be granted the power to review decisions under thirty-five casts. All higher decisions from the council will stand."

"What's he talking about?" I ask.

Lagnar unsuccessfully stifles a laugh.

"Giving the council more power," she says.

Lagnar clicks his tongue. "Less power, my dear. Without a lawful descendant of Brightstorm on the throne, the council would have full authority to run the kingdom how they see fit. So, what do you say?"

Chainkeeper bows slightly. "Without your leadership, the council may well devolve into chaos and clans. You are respected. Will you make the promise?"

A moment ticks away. Andalynn stares at the floor as she searches her own thoughts. The conflict in her face is clear. She reaches trembling fingers upward and plucks out a silver filament from her hair. As she loops it around her hand, Chainkeeper steps toward her, reaching down from the floor. They clasp arms, the silver strand makes contact with a purple tattoo on the keeper's forearm.

"I promise to accept the throne. I promise to redraft the contract as you have stated," Andalynn says.

Chainkeeper smiles through his salt-and-pepper beard, pumps her arm once. "Good luck breaking into my prison."

"You won't help us?" Andalynn says.

"I won't hinder you. The guards will not be notified. I have the integrity of this office to uphold. But... go with all Ide."

He vanishes with Lagnar.

"That will have consequences," Andalynn says.

Four more figures drop to the ground from the entrance above us. Winta lands on all fours like a cat. Koglim scans the room.

"We couldn't follow you," Rugnus says. "Something barred us from entering."

"Chainkeeper," Andalynn says, "He came to negotiate."

Koglim presses his hands to the sides of his face. "Chainkeeper? No wonder. Man, I've always wanted to meet him. He wasn't at the Keeper's Social. Sent a proxy."

Rugnus smiles. "He could turn your blood into cold molasses and send you back to the Troll Wars."

"I'd let him," Koglim says with a grin. His necklace flashes with purple light, and the humor vanishes from his face. He takes a deep breath and buries it under his shirt. "I'm going to ignore that in the understanding we're all in mortal peril at this moment."

Winta surveys the locked door at our feet. "I could take Chainkeeper craft to craft."

"He's letting us in?" Rugnus asks.

"He's an old family friend," Andalynn says, brushing away a wandering strand of her hair. "But this is still his prison. He won't actively try to make this more difficult."

Winta squints at her suspiciously. "Just like that?"

"I talked to him, and...yeah."

"Talked to him?" Rugnus says, doubt creeping into his voice.

She breathes in frustration. "Yes, Rugnus, talking reasonably with people is a thing. You should try it. It could open a lot of doors for you."

"Not that one," He says, pointing to a small square spot in the center of the floor.

I move closer, squinting at the spot in confusion. No matter what angle I take, the area appears blurry, like someone tried to erase it from existence.

"Move," Winta says, pushing between Rugnus and Andalynn. The band of mercury uncoils from her wrist. She spins it above her head and whips it downward where it adheres to the square —a hard, electric purple light streaks down the mercury. An unseen hand tries to yank Winta toward the ground, but she plants her feet. The stream of mercury slips toward the floor, but she catches it and winds it doubly around her wrist.

Another flash of purple and the fuzzy spot becomes clear, glaring now with tan light.

"Your turn," she says to Rugnus, her teeth gritted.

Rugnus, already prepared with his club, leaps into the air and smashes down on the glass. He flies backward, and the reverberation sends a shock wave toward the rest of us like a sonic grenade. Ergal's white light flashes in my vision. My ears instantly feel as if someone jammed them with cotton. But that vanishes when the pulsing mercury veins in the walls freeze and the square of tan light splits down the middle.

A door slides open like an inviting jaw.

"Easy," he says, but disquiet settles on the whole group. I think we'd all feel better if we had to fight our way through the entrance. First Chainkeeper and now this. It's like scaling that cliff in the first room of Wolfstaff. I should know better than to trust something that doesn't require a sacrifice on our part.

I shake my head, confused. "I thought this was supposed to be the most secure prison in the world."

Winta shrugs. "If it makes you feel any better, that was the hardest temporal lock I've picked in...well ever. I made it look easy. And if these doors shut behind us, we'll be trapped in their forever."

"She's right," Rugnus says, "Nobody else could have gotten through. Now let's get down there and get your mom out."

We jump through the door, the gravity shifting the moment we do, and we're pulled to the side. The yucca flowers' effect allows us to orient ourselves however we want, but the room is an empty void, and I don't know which direction to go.

Andalynn takes the lead, guiding us as we fly through the void, weaving around a maze of transparent glass boxes—prison cells suspended in mid-air. There must be thousands of prisoners, but I can't see the edges. There could be tens of thousands. I'm reminded of the swarm of police drones sweeping the city.

Each glowing box pulses with bars of mercury. Some boxes hold more than a dozen people. The prisoners are tethered to the floor with gold bands, but on different interior sides of the many cubes, leaving me unsure about which way is up or down—which way we came in. They move in slow-motion, faces stricken with horror, and I turn away from a man whose features are frozen in rage.

"Awesome," Koglim says, short of breath.

Not sure that's how I would describe a prison. But as always, Koglim means the craft is awesome. He's not thinking about the people it affects.

We streak along through the dim space. As we round one of the cells, Andalynn points out a larger wall. We land on the glass, but I'm careful to avoid a ribbon of mercury, even though it is trapped inside the interior of the transparent aluminum.

It's curious: aluminum, mercury, gold. How do they work together to make this prison function? The mercury must keep the people paralyzed in time. I'm not sure what the gold chains do, but the only use for transparent aluminum is as an anti-budge —foilgrip.

There's another lock to break, which Winta and Rugnus clear as quickly as the first. Andalynn rushes us through the gap, and we continue the descent. Or ascent? This door remains open behind us as well. The layers of protection make it seem like we're cutting to the interior of Russian nesting dolls. If these doors shut, I don't think Rugnus can budge us out.

Four more walls, four more doors.

Something's off. Andalynn's promise, Koglim's glowing pendant, the open doors at our backs. Then I see my mother, and I push all these thoughts away from me.

"She's here," Andalynn says.

My heart sinks. She's alone in the cell, still wearing the brilliant white dress from the night at the campground. Her body is rigid, her back toward us.

Andalynn and I race for the door. There is an initial lock Winta and Rugnus must break through first. Her cell is a cube within a cube. We find the lock to the inner cell at eye level, and we're facing my mother now. I sense a shift in her eyes. Can she see us? How much can she still perceive? I'm right about the mercury. They use it to freeze her movements, lock her in a single time.

Winta snaps her silvery liquid band to the lock, tensing and pulling, and the purple light snakes downward, searching for its target. The lock comes into phase, and at that moment, my mother sags to the floor in a heap.

Rugnus pounds on the square with his club and the glass door parts and hisses open, like every other door so far.

Andalynn rushes into the cell, collapsing to the floor with our mother. She strokes her hair, plants a kiss on her head. This action brings me to a halt. As Andalynn helps her to her feet, Rugnus, Winta, Koglim, and Hemdi march into the cell, but my legs refuse to move. For some terrible reason, my thoughts are the horrible type, the ones from before I knew about the curse.

She would never even look at me. She couldn't acknowledge my existence. The few times she showed up, she'd toy with my father's emotions, leaving him frail and depressed for weeks. I've resented her for so long. I can't break myself out of the cycle of anger. Her face has only ever been a picture on the mantle, but now she's unfrozen. When I step into the cell, my fear crystallizes. Her face levels off.

She looks right through me.

"Mom," I say.

Confusion stirs in her face. Nothing has changed. Why did I expect it to? Her eyes stop on everyone but me. I'm nothing to her. I don't exist. Then Andalynn and Rugnus move to the side, trying to give me a clear view of her, but she strokes Andalynn's arm and asks. "Did you get me released? Who are all these people?"

Andalynn looks from my mother to me, and her eyes cloud with sadness. "Then it's true. She can't see you. Mom, can you see Clayson? He's here. He's right there."

"Don't bother," I say, tears forcing their way into my eyes. "It's the curse." My jaw seizes up as if it's trying to lock in my words.

My mother pulls away from Andalynn. "You're trying to free me from Keelcrawl? Now who's taking risks? I tried to keep you out of this." Water brims in her eyes.

That's when something inside of me breaks apart like the shattering of a boulder that, for years and years, has blocked off a flood of water.

I don't care if she won't feel my arms around her. I run to her and squeeze her into a hug, burying my head against her. In that second, in a plume of white light, Ergal flares to life. Its power courses through my blood, extending beyond me into my mother, who at first tenses with shock against what she can only guess is some unseen craft.

But her tension fades. "My boy. My little boy," she whispers.

My heart nearly bursts. "Mom?"

I step back, keeping my hand on her shoulder. I find her eyes, and for the first time, she sees me.

With a soft shake of her head, she says, "This can't be real. Can I really speak to you? Can you hear me? This must be some dream?" She holds me back, searching every part of my face.

Everyone else in the room fades away. "I'm here, Mom. I won't leave."

Both of her hands grasp my face, tracing my dimples with her fingers. She doesn't have to say it: I look like Dad. I see the words in her eyes.

"Is your father... did he... where is he? No. You two shouldn't... w-we tried to keep you safe."

I don't know what to tell her. For the last few days, I've been intent on getting her free. But like Dad, she had hoped to keep us in the dark. She knows this means we will be dragged into her conflict with the keeper's council, pulled into my father's secrets about the mithrium. She's not wrong.

"You did," I say. "You did keep us safe. But now we're gonna keep you safe."

Andalynn nods fiercely. "Mom, I made a deal with the Chain-bearer, with the council."

Confusion sets in. "A deal? What did you do?"

"What I had to do," she says. "But let's get out of here. We're bringing you to Geum Ide."

She steps back from us. "No, wait! Clayson. I can see you now. And every time I have seen you in the past, every time your father has spoken to me about you, I-I wanted to scream out loud. I wanted to explain how this happened. Explain the craft your grandfather and I used. You're in danger, Clayson. You need to know about—"

A sonic blast hits me from behind, and we're all shoved to the ground.

I groan to my knees and flick my vision in the direction of the blast origin. Silverkeeper stands in the doorway. As he steps backward, his silver-clawed leg taps against the glass floor of the outer cube. The gears and pistons in his body pop and hiss. His eyes stay eerily unfocused as he engages the lock and seals us in.

A shudder cascades over my entire body—deja vu. I can't move. In front of me, Rugnus' fingers had already been tightening on his club, but he's as frozen as I am.

Even Silverkeeper appears to freeze on the outside of the cell. But no. We are the ones stuck in this. It's as if we stand on an event horizon, time slipping away on either side, but I'm stuck in a single frame as if captured in a picture.

How can the prison be so powerful? Stronger than Rugnus' club and my ring. But I know the answer. Each foilgrip has sealed behind us, every layer adding strength to the craft trapping us in. Maybe if I can slowly get to Rugnus, we can combine our strength. The ring and the club. But I can't make any progress toward him. My mom stands next to me, her eyes fixed permanently on a point in the distance. Has our connection been severed? What was she gonna tell me?

We wait for an eternity. Until a thousand things happen at once as time catches up. We're free of the enchantment. I can move again. In a flash of light, Sira appears inside my mom's cell. She vomits, then straightens up. She nudges between Koglim and me, marching over to Rugnus.

We're saved.

He grins, "How did you get in?" He glances to Silverkeeper, still standing in the same place he had been moments before, a glazed-over look on his face.

"Oh, you know"—she stops in front of my mom—"just waiting for the right moment."

In a blur, she rips Rugnus' club out of his hand, grabs my mom, and vanishes, reappearing on the outside of the cell, bent over holding her stomach. What's happening? Sira is almost a null in budgecraft. Why is she doing this? When the shock wears off, Rugnus bolts for the cell door, but the lock is engaged again, this time only the anti-budge. We're free to move around.

Sira stands straighter.

I struggle with what my eyes report to my brain. In the outer cell, my mom tries to break free of Sira's grasp. Sira slams the butt of Rugnus' club into her stomach and knocks her to the ground. My mom has no metal to defend herself, and I can only watch in horror as Silverkeeper takes two quick steps and snatches her, locking her against him in a vice-like grip with his mechanical arm.

Sira pulls her silver knife from some hidden pocket and pins it against my mom's throat. Then my mom's face goes as blank as Silverkeeper's.

"Oh, Clayson," Sira says, her voice still lovely and singing as it always is. "I'm going to send my father in there to get that price-less little ring of yours. Okay, sweets. If you move an inch, I'm going to slash your mom's throat. And don't think you can protect her with your shield. Onrix"—she wiggles the knife at us — "is its equal, so who knows what would happen first. And I don't need her anymore, so if she dies..."

It's Koglim who speaks first. "What are you doing? Your father? Silverkeeper? I—"

"Koglim. I really do like you. I'm not sure my dad does, though."

"You expect us to believe he's your father?" Andalynn says. "Silverkeeper's daughter was killed years—"

"I started that rumor. Since the accident, I've had to control him with silver to keep him alive." She yells at her father, jokingly. "Stay alive! It's not easy, but Onrix is powerful. It got Rugnus to go to the Keeper' Social and made him want to break into the fourth level."

Winta has a moment of realization. "You did make me do stuff. I knew it!"

"No," Rugnus says. "I-I would have felt the craft."

"Like Icho's craft? Or Ergal? No, Onrix is like them. Ancient. I'm glad I found it during the accident, or my father would've died, me too probably." She turns to Silverkeeper. "Dad, can you please go get Clayson's ring for me. And

Clayson, no cheating or…" She pricks my mom's neck with the knife.

Silverkeeper transfers my mom into Sira's care. The sleek weapon hovers there against her neck for a moment but travels downward. Sira pricks my mom an inch below her collar bone, deep enough to draw blood. A red blotch grows over her spotless white gown. Sira commands her to walk to the door of the outside cube.

"I have some simple requests," Sira says. "If you choose not to obey me willingly, I'll make her jump. It's a long drop without craft."

Silverkeeper unlocks the inner cell, and Rugnus tenses beside me.

"Don't!" The word flies from my mouth. "Rugnus, please."

His chest expands with a deep breath, and for a second, I think he's gonna get my mom killed, but he exhales. Whatever fight is left in him remains seething under his skin.

Silverkeeper removes Ergal from my finger. I have a reflex to tighten my fist—I can protect everyone, get us out of this—but Sira is watching me so closely I'm afraid to blink.

When Silverkeeper steps backward, Sira says, "Out of the cell."

"Me?"

"Yes, sleepyhead. You and that dreaming brain of yours."

It's her. She wants the mithrium. It's sitting in the dreamwell, and she knows it's there. Maybe she's even controlled the council this whole time. Dad was right about one thing: I was being used, but not by Silverkeeper. By his daughter.

I step out of the inner cell, my eyes darting from Silverkeeper to her, and I see it, the resemblance. "You *are* Silverkeeper's daughter. It's you who wanted me to go into the dreamwell?"

She places a hand over her breast as if she's embarrassed. "So smart. But I just told you the first part."

"Theridal Silverkeeper was my father's friend," I say.

Sira smiles, barring her flawless white teeth flanked by

pointed canines. "We changed that, didn't we, Dad? His friendship was a weakness. I was only four. I told him not to go to that dungeon, but he didn't listen. So, this is what he gets."

"Yes," Silverkeeper says. "That is what I get."

"Now he's pretty much all silver. Anyway, let's go."

Andalynn's voice floats out from the cell. "It's you?" she says. "You're controlling Silverkeeper. And everyone on the council. Why?"

Silverkeeper grabs my wrist.

Sira's eyes smile. "What I'm doing is important. Once I have the mithrium, I can combine it with Onrix. Forge something that will help everyone be kind. Be good. It will end all the fighting. All the hate."

"Wraithspit, Sira," Rugnus says. "Even if that works, you can't force people to—"

Sira huffs, rolling her eyes. "Bye."

Silverkeeper seals the inside door. My friends' bodies freeze in boiling anger. Andalynn's eyes storm with rage.

We budge using Icho, appearing in a cylindrical room like the inside of a subway car. Sira retches, but nothing comes out.

I step forward to grab the knife from her, but Silverkeeper pushes me further into the center of the room, toward the only exit. The open door exudes darkness as penetrating as any light. Silver lanterns hang from the wall near the door.

"How did you get us out of Keelcrawl?" I say.

Sira shrugs. "Keep up, Clayson. I can do anything I want. My father is the head of the council. You don't think he can unlock a few doors?"

"Where are we?" I ask, but I fear the answer.

A group of dangerous looking Loamin appear near the door, and a smooth voice answers. "Silverlamp Dungeon. The entrance lobby to be exact."

It's Bazalrak and the three ironheads who follow him around.

Sira wanders between us, her knife dancing in her hands.

"You're using them too?" I say. "Did you send them to my cabin? How did you even find out about me and my dad?"

"Oh, I've got to keep some secrets, Clayson."

"And Lonecharge?"

"Ready with the coding I need to make the mithrium into what I want."

"So, everything in Tungsten City and with my mom, why go through all of that? If you can control people, why put her in prison? Fake her execution?"

"Well, Clayson, I didn't think I could get the one in the dreamwell. Thought that piece of mithrium would be lost forever. I was trying to drive out Therias, make him turn over his piece. Well, until we all got to Geum Ide, and I realized something."

The truth of her words grabs the jumble of my thoughts and shakes out an idea. "Until I told you I could dream."

Sira ticks her tongue. Smiles, almost blushing. "Smart, handsome, powerful. You're the whole package, aren't you, Clayson?"

Bazalrak grabs my chin. "Enough. Lonecharge is waiting. Time to find the mithrium, prince. If you give us any trouble, we'll kill her." He nods toward my mom, who at the moment still stands obediently at Sira's side.

"You could've forced me to get it for you."

She passes the knife gently through my mom's hair like a brush. "I did try. But that ring. It's the knife's equal. And shield-craft always has a small edge in craft. Now I just don't want to. There's only one way to control you, Clayson." She grabs my mom's hair violently. "Now get a lantern and move through the door. The dungeon is waiting."

FOLLOW THE FEAR

THE SILVER LANTERN Sira makes me carry has a single purpose—to induce fear.

The moment I take a lantern from the wall, a prickling worry begins to gnaw on my bones. Silvercraft. Dark thoughts fly at me from the doorway. I buck against Silverkeeper's grasp, recoiling in terror. Something outside this room has the power to destroy me.

Is this thought real?

No one else moves. The lantern is only affecting me.

I glance at my mom for help, for some reaction, but she's still under Sira's power, knife to her neck. I struggle against Silverkeeper's control, but he edges me closer to the door.

Bazalrak laughs. "You will guide us to the threshold despite your unwilling disposition."

He helps Silverkeeper drag me forward. With a grunt, he pushes me, and I topple through the inky darkness of the door onto a path.

The fear leaves me. It must have been temporary until I passed the doorway. This area is also cylindrical but more like a tunnel than a subway car. Three doorways sit along one side, filled with the same inky blue-black clouds from the first door.

"What was that?" I ask.

"That's what I love about you, dear," Sira says, emerging through the door, my mom in tow. The three ironheads follow her without the slightest hesitation. Now that I know to look for it, I can tell they are under her control. "You know very little about our world. It's just so...cute. Like you're a lost puppy."

"Follow the fear," Bazalrak says. "The fear will lead you through the correct doorways. The threshold resides in the terminal room."

Unlike the lobby of Wolfstaff, Silverlamp's lobby is empty of people. Then I remember why—Silverkeeper closed the dungeon.

I have three openings to choose from. At first, I try fooling them—take my time, make things drag on—but Bazalrak is too clever. Anytime I'm willing to enter a doorway, he shakes his head and pulls me to a different opening, searching instead for the door that causes the strongest physiological reaction. There's nothing I can do to conceal the palpable dread cutting into my flesh each time we find the right direction.

We work through the maze. I know the fear isn't real, but that's the thing about silvercraft: I can't tell the difference between my own thoughts and the effect of the doors.

After the sixth room with multiple doors, we emerge into a well-lit domed room. The floor is polished marble, ornamented with an asymmetrical design like someone took a tangle of silver vines and pressed them into the floor.

A loose end of one of the decorative vines pulses silver. I understand exactly what I'm supposed to do. I hesitate only briefly. Would Sira do it? Would she hurt my mom if I don't enter the dungeon? I can only hope there will be a way to stop them. If I'm that important, then maybe I can find some leverage inside Silverlamp.

Sira hands my mom over to Silverkeeper and steps closer to me. "Did the lantern reveal the pathway?"

I scowl at her for a long moment. "I thought you were my friend."

She lifts the knife. "And I thought you were smarter than that."

With a glance at my mom, I follow the lighted vine etched into the tile. Each step I take lights a new section. It's like I'm untying a knot. The jumble is so difficult to follow that I wouldn't be able to unravel it without the light.

I keep my eyes on the ground until I reach the end of the glowing vine. In a flash, all the other vines disappear, leaving only a single winding path on the tiled floor. It snakes off to the side of the dome and skirts along the wall, forming into an oval archway. A hook appears, and Bazalrak orders me to hang the lantern.

The moment I do, the inside of the archway billows with the same blue-black fog.

This is the threshold of Silverlamp Dungeon.

"Strange." My mom leans away from Silverkeeper, staring at the archway. "How did we open the threshold without following the correct path in the vines?"

She didn't see me. It's the curse again. Ignoring the recurring feeling of being passed over, I make for the doorway. "Let's get this over with," I say.

When I turn around to Sira, she's eyeing the threshold warily, like it might strike at any moment. Stepping closer to her father, she says, "Everyone into the dungeon."

As her eyes narrow, something Rugnus said about dungeons comes to me. "Your father can't go in. Only relics work in the dungeon. All the craft keeping him alive..."

"You think that matters?" Sira snaps. "I can have Silverkeeper give Bazalrak an order to force you in the dreamwell and then give the mithrium back to him."

Silverkeeper's voice blasts the cavern. "Take the knights in the dungeon, General Stonedoom. And make sure Clayson brings out the Mithrium from the dreamwell."

Sira smiles. "See?"

Bazalrak orders the knights forward, but before they take even a few steps, a bulbous shape zips out of the threshold door. It whirls around the room. For a moment, I'm afraid it's a wraith.

Then I catch sight of the creature's tentacles.

More creatures come swimming from the threshold door, swirling around the room. One stops in front of my face only long enough for me to see dark, watery eyes and slick skin.

Then it smiles, revealing cruel, sharp teeth. In a high-pitched voice like some demonic dolphin, it screeches, "Here's the one!"

The rest of the squid-like creatures echo the words.

"The one, one!"

"He's him!"

"He's *the* he!"

Bazalrak takes a swing at one with his ax. "What is this?"

More squids come through the threshold, filling the room. From a high corner of the dome comes another squeaking declaration. "It speaks!"

"Says him!"

"Words, words, words!"

The echoes bounce from one squid to another but begin to happen all at once.

Bazalrak growls and swings again.

They all speak as one. "Shut him up!"

Three of the squids create a blue-black vortex over Bazalrak's head. The edges of the vortex curl and flap like a cloak in a windstorm. His shadow ax is pulled from his hands, careening into the vortex. His feet lift from the floor.

"Stop this!" he yells. Then, in a heartbeat, he's gone, sucked in after his ax.

All the squids laugh.

The ironhead with the gear-spitting machine gun, the same one who came to capture Dad and me, fires off a round of gears. The squid closest to him erupts in a shower of goo.

But the squids only celebrate. "Yeah!"

"He did it!"

"Kill us!"

"Kill us all!"

Two of the squids closest to the ironhead duplicate themselves, giving us a hands-on science lesson in mitosis. We couldn't kill them all if we tried.

To prove this, three more of them create a vortex and suck up the ironhead with his machine gun.

"Stop!" Sira says. "I know what you are: guardians."

She has to be right. We're not in the dungeon yet, and like Frrwelhst came to judge me at the threshold, these things have come to prevent our entrance.

They stop swirling, and all their marble black eyes settle on Sira.

One of them whispers, "Keeper's spawn!"

"Baby silver!"

"Oh, how ugly!"

Half of them chitter in high-pitched laughter.

"Challozil Silverlamp welcomes you!"

"It's time."

"Play the game!"

For the first time, I see fear in Sira's eyes. She stomps her foot. "You're ruining everything, you stupid things."

"We're so dumb!"

"Idiots!"

"Piles of brick!"

"Brainless!"

A dozen of them swing down to the center of the room and create another huge vortex. I step backward. The pull is so strong it knocks me off my feet. I dig my hands into the floor, but there's nothing to grab onto. I look up. The two ironheads who were closest are gone. I could shout for joy, but then I see a ripple of white fabric. My mom is pulled through, leaving only me on one side and Sira and her father on the other.

In desperation, Sira grabs his arm, trying to keep him from the vortex. His silver claw foot touches the tip of the blue-black void.

Sira screams, "No! He can't go in the dungeons! He can't. He'll die! Stop it! Stop!"

The guardians squeal in delight.

Then he's gone. Sira rages. Then her body slackens, and she's pulled in after her father.

The vortex closes, leaving me sprawled over the marble floor, panting for breath. The squids fall silent. Standing, I eye the little squids nervously. Why did they leave me behind? Once I stand, they gather on the other side of the room, chatting noisily.

"Did you feel that?"

"More have entered!"

"What was it?"

"Dura?"

"That's cheating!"

I step over to them. "What's going on?" I say. "What Dura?"

They all laugh. "Dura cheat!"

"But how?"

"She's not allowed!"

"Gather the rest!"

A few dozen swim through the door we came through, echoing outside the domed room.

"The newcomers!"

"Late for the game!"

"More for the game!"

"Bar all Dura!"

"Set the timer!"

I raise my voice. "Hey! What's going on?"

"To the threshold!"

"Shut him up!"

"But he's the he!"

I yell again. "What does that mean?"

"Don't care!"

"Through the door!"

"Push him!"

They swarm, ramming me toward the threshold with their

slimy heads. Tentacles grab my arms and legs, and they hoist me into the air. There's an echoed countdown starting from ten. When they reach six, they send me flying through the door.

I flail through the fog covering the threshold and land with a hard drop, air shooting out of my lungs. My eyes dance with tiny pinpricks. I roll to my stomach, trying my best to breathe. The floor is made from bright green grass, freshly cut.

Why am I suddenly so tired? I grope for the gold armband on my bicep. It's there. Why isn't it working? Then I remember: only relics work inside dungeons. I flip over to my back and lay on the grass, staring into... nothing. There's no ceiling. The room ascends forever and ever.

Exhausted, without any objects to help me, I'm trapped in Silverlamp Dungeon.

Then, Sira's screaming enters my awareness. "Dad!"

Only relics work in dungeons.

Her shrill cries wake me enough to stand.

The hexagonal room is split in half by a wide chasm, green grass on one side, yellow grass on the other. I come to the edge of the abyss. Bazalrak and the other three knights stand on the opposite side, waiting by Sira's side, standing over her father. She cradles him in her arms.

"Sira?" My voice carries across the room. "What's happening?"

Bazalrak and the others come to the edge. It would be stupid to try jumping across—it must be thirty feet.

"You're dead Brightstorm," Bazalrak says. The calmness in his voice reverberates like a stone dropped in a well. "The moment I find a way across. I'll kill you with my bare hands if I must, but you will not make it out of here alive."

Sira's voice is soft now, but I hear it clearly. "He's dying. I need—I need silver." She stands up, frantic. "Help me." She wrings her hands through her hair. "Help me!"

Bazalrak turns back to her. "You're searching in vain. The dungeon took our relics."

"There has to be something." Sira pauses, then abruptly screams at the top of her lungs.

Silverkeeper groans. "Rensira. Sweet girl, please. Where... I can't—I can't see you." He hisses in pain.

His voice is more distinct now, not as far away and ethereal like it was at the Keeper's Social. Sira's influence on him has lifted. I keep reframing each of our conversations in Tungsten City, like our breakfast together, when she must have tried to use the knife on me and failed. Was our friendship all an act for her?

Without the aid of silvercraft, her father is dying. Dad's closest friend is dying.

Sira kneels next to him, almost sobbing. "No one will listen. No one's listening to me."

He strokes her face. "How long... but you're older. Where... my daughter... my daughter." He takes a huge breath, letting it out in a stuttering wave. "Therias. Go to Therias. Bring him the knife. He'll take—he'll take care... of you. Sira..." Silverkeeper's head droops backward.

Sira pushes her face into his body, wailing. Her father's dead. Something tries to break through the betrayal I feel. Is it pity? Can I pity this girl who has put my family in so much danger?

A hand touches my back.

I turn. My friends are all behind me. "How—"

"Ara and Dad," Andalynn says.

"Sira," Koglim says, eye narrow. So many emotions play across his face I can't read any particular one.

Andalynn's eyes stare at the girl and her father. "We must have played together once. But I didn't—we were so little. I had forgotten. Our fathers—"

Bazalrak shouts. "That's enough! Get her up. He's dead."

The ironhead usually carrying the railgun hoists a weeping Sira to her feet.

Bazalrak storms back to the wall and grabs Silverkeeper by his hair. He drags the lifeless man to the edge of the cliff. "If you don't cease your crying, I'll throw him over the edge."

Sira begs. "No, no. Please. I need him. I—"

"Then shut your mouth!"

She goes silent as if Bazalrak has slapped her. I suddenly see how she's still a child, the same little girl who lost her father in an accident years ago.

"And you!" Bazalrak says, his finger spinning back toward me. "I'm sure your mother is here. When I find her, there will be no bringing her back for a trial. She's dead."

"Don't you get it?" Rugnus' words echo off the walls. "Sira's been controlling everyone. She used you."

"Regardless, I find myself in an advantageous position. I know where the steward hid the mithrium, and I have perhaps the one person under granite who can get it for me. And, thanks to Lonecharge and Silverkeeper, I have a way to make something powerful out of it. Something Whurrimduum can use, I can use, to get back everything that belongs to us."

"There's no way I'll help you," I say.

"No? Of course, you will." He sweeps his arms around. "Don't you recognize a race when you see one, Brightstorm? If I was a betting man, I'd say your mother is at the finish line. So, first, I'll kill your mother. Then, if you don't help me, I'll kill each of your friends one by one."

Winta laughs softly. "I really want you to try that. See what—"

The sound of stone scraping against stone drowns everything out. A wall rises from the ravine between us, filling the gap and closing the two groups off from each other. At the same time, a massive stone table rises from the floor behind us. A purple-black cloud door opens on the back wall.

Rugnus comes to the table dragging Koglim away from the new wall separating us from Sira and the others.

Andalynn squeezes my hand. "I'm glad you're okay."

"So, Ara and Dad, they—"

"Followed us into Keelcrawl," Rugnus says.

Hemdi's eyes widen. "She broke us out single-handedly. The

foilgrips did nothing to stop her. I've never seen anything like it before in my life."

"Where's my Dad? Where's Ara?"

Winta huffs. "Those squid things—"

"Floaters," Rugnus says.

"Yeah," she says, "those—they dragged us all into the dungeon. Your dad included."

Rugnus nods. "Not Ara, though. Dura can't enter a dungeon,"

"Same with our group," I say. "They forced us in. Even Silverkeeper,"

Koglim stares at his feet. As much as he protected Sira in the past, he must be feeling more betrayed than any of us. Did she mean to lead him on as a ploy? I don't know what was pretend with her. Maybe all of it.

Rugnus starts looking over the pedestal in more detail. "Bad things happen when dungeon guardians get involved."

The solid table in the center of the room is topped with a miniature dungeon. On one side, there's a dollhouse maze of hexagonal rooms, holding miniature trees, steps, and dividing walls. On the other side, raised to a second story, there's a single bridge leading nowhere.

"Koglim, have you seen this before?" Rugnus says.

If Koglim hears Rugnus, he doesn't acknowledge him. "None of this is right. I can't tell what I'm supposed to think or feel. She betrayed us. But she doesn't—that was her father."

Hemdi nods and moves next to Koglim. "We're all confused, betrayed. The best way to help is to teach us about this dungeon, about this challenge."

Koglim brings his head up and looks around like this is the first time he's seeing the room.

"We need you in this game," Rugnus says. "Lives depend on it."

Koglim clears his throat and says, "I've seen this before. History documentary. Silverlamp hasn't run it in a hundred years. We have to get the board ready." He places his hands on an iron knob on the side of the model. Twelve oval stones appear inside a closed-off hexagon—six green and six yellow. "Green grass, green team. That's us. The other team is yellow."

"What about my mom and dad?" I say.

"My best guess?" Koglim circles to the other side of the table, pointing to the far end of the bridge. "They're stuck here. Bazalrak was right. They're the prize for the winner."

An echo projects around the room. I don't see any of them flying around, but it's the floaters again. "No! They guessed it."

"Rules are rules."

"Tell them."

"Show them."

Sand pours from the bottom of the pedestal. We all jump back, but the tiny grains shift across the floor, accumulating into the shape of a dome about waist high. Part of the dome erodes, revealing the sand-shape of two people backed against a wall.

Andalynn takes a quick step forward. "Is that—"

"Our parents," I say.

More details emerge. They're past the bridge. The wall to their backs can't be scaled. They try and fail to climb it. Small bricks of sand keep falling away at their feet, making the ledge where they stand more and more narrow.

The floaters start again.

"Better hurry."

"No, please don't."

"Die, die, die."

"This really is a fun game."

Koglim raises his voice. "Back to the table, quickly."

I stumble away from the sand as it crumbles and retreats beneath the pedestal. I follow it as long as I can until every grain is gone. I almost fall over, but Rugnus puts his arm around me to hold me up.

The dungeon will not hesitate to kill my parents. I know this. Silverkeeper is dead. The dungeon, the long-dead champion, was his executioner. These places are like forces of nature. They're tornadoes, and fires, and mobs out of control.

How do we stop a force of nature?

"Until we find more keys, only one of us can enter the maze," Koglim explains. "There are three types of keys, leading to different things. The first type will call another teammate into the maze. We need those quickly. Another type will unlock a hidden relic. Remember, everyone's relics are in the dungeon. Elbaz, Clayson's ring."

"Sira's knife," Andalynn says.

Rugnus nods. "And Bazalrak's shadow ax."

"And Icho," Koglim says. "The last type of key unlocks the finish line. My guess is there are two of those. So, who should go in first?"

Rugnus and I nominate each other at the same time.

I try to argue, but he cuts me off. "You're the only one with a peerless rating. Get in, use the keys, find some object, and get your parents out. Nothing else matters."

Still staring at the model, Andalynn says, "Mom told me something about this. The keys mimic natural things: a twig, a beetle, a patch of grass. Each key gives off different emotions. That's how you find them."

Like following the fear toward the threshold. "Got it."

"Alright," Rugnus says. "Then I think maybe Andalynn should go first. Find as many of the keys as you can. And—this might be a bit of a downer, but Silverlamp had three brothers who came into the dungeon with her."

"Three wraiths?" Hemdi says.

Andalynn moves to the door, a flame in her emerald eyes. "Wraiths or not, those are my parents out there. We're not going to let them die. And we are not going to let Bazalrak and his goons get there first."

She runs through the door.

"There she is," Koglim says, pointing to the model.

The green stone marked with a number one disappears from

the group of stones and reappears in the dollhouse maze. Our whole team crowds the table studying the layout, watching the green marker shift quickly through two of the rooms. A yellow stone appears in one room, and in less than a minute, the stone edges with light, and another yellow stone appears next to it. They split up.

"Who do you think they sent in?" I ask.

Rugnus lifts his finger from where he was following Andalynn's stone. "Bazalrak. Then anyone but Sira. She's in no state to play the game, which gives us an advantage."

"I don't think she will leave her father, even if he's..." I don't say dead.

Koglim suddenly leans over the board and claps his hands. "She got something."

The edge of Andalynn's piece glows a soft green. She moves quickly to the next room, her marker skirting along one wall. Two rooms later, she stops altogether. Behind me, the doorway reopens.

"She's found one of the keys to let us in."

The doorway reappears. Rugnus slaps my back. "You're up."

Adrenaline moves me to the door, and I step through. The moment I exit the cloud, Andalynn pulls me toward her onto a large patch of grass. "Off the stone. It leaves footprints for the other team to track you."

My feet have left clear tracks on the polished stone floor, the same type of grass in the room with the model. If I didn't know it was part of a deadly dungeon, I would say we were in a garden courtyard of some Irish castle. A few tall trees crowd one vertex of the hexagonal room, and in another, vines snake up to the cathedral-style ceiling. Silver light fills the room.

"They have two players in. They're about five rooms that way." I point past the vines.

"I found this, and it helps." She waves Hemdi's lantern in front of her, and the grass we're standing on grows outward, taking over more of the polished stone. She steps on the new grass. "We can move pretty fast now without leaving grass prints."

I'm relieved we have at least one object, but I need my ring. "Should we split up? We need relics to defend ourselves."

"Okay, but stay in the grass as much as possible. I don't want them tracking you."

I nod. "I know where you've already been from the board, so I'll head into new territory."

I jump to a patch of grass leading off in the other direction. Andalynn calls after me, "Any emotion that feels strong, follow it. Hemdi's lantern was a feeling of peace, but the key that let you in was like watching a lakeshark eat a puppy."

"Good to know."

A long winding patch of grass leads to the next room, where a dais surrounded by stairs sits spotlighted in the center. As far as I can tell, I don't sense any magically strong emotions, only my own. My heart's racing. Bazalrak could be around any corner.

In the next room, there's little grass, but where I can, I jump from one patch to another. I don't wanna leave anyone a trail leading to me, but I can't help placing my feet on the stone to reach the next door. I settle for walking backward, hoping I will confuse anyone following me, but the footprints match my direction. I can't fool the dungeon.

As I come to the doorway, I spot yellow grass footprints for the first time. Someone from the other team is close by. Each room has three doorways, so without any relics to protect myself, I take a different route.

At the doorway, I sense something, still far away, but a feeling of power. It's the only way I can describe it. If I can find where it is hidden, I will be invincible. Must be the craft talking. Could it be my ring? I've never felt this kind of thing when I've put it on, so I doubt it.

I trace the power into an adjacent room, and it grows inside of me. I know exactly which door to take. The power takes on an

327

edge of malice. This is not Icho or Ergal. Bazalrak projects those types of feelings. I know what relic this is: his shadow ax.

Then, all at once, the strange power is smothered like a hot poker submerged in ice water. That can only mean one thing: someone found the relic.

A shadow crosses the floor, and I'm struck by how dark and disconcerting the shape is. My breath catches in my throat. Something rustles the leaves around a hedge of tall bushes, and the shadows grow darker on its branches. Bazalrak steps out from behind the long row, his ax resting on his shoulder.

I duck out of the room, but my heart is pumping so loudly Bazalrak might hear it. I peek around the corner in time to see him turning in my direction. I sprint back the way I came, heedless of the tracks I'm making on the floor.

A smooth, sing-song voice calls after me. "Clayson."

He's toying with me.

I run harder, searching for Andalynn, or waiting for a strong emotion to catch me so I can get a relic to defend myself, but suddenly everything becomes muted and gray. Bazalrak calls out, "Can't locate that precious ring of yours, I see."

Bazalrak won't kill me. I have to tell myself this to slow my breathing. He needs me to get into the well. I stop and turn around, ready to face him, but hands grab me from behind.

It's Andalynn. "Run." She pushes me behind her.

"I can't leave you," I say.

Hemdi's tin lantern—Linterna—swings in her grasp, dispelling the darkness around us. The surrounding plants become luminescent, absorbing more of the shadows.

"There's something else in that direction." She points behind her. "I think it's Ergal. I'll hold off Bazalrak. Go. Straight, left, left, right."

Bazalrak comes into view across the room. Bolts of light from Linterna strike out for him from out of the nearest bushes. At his feet, a pool of light grows like a flood of water. His boots hiss against the glare, and he takes a step back, growling.

A grim smile cracks Andalynn's determined face. "Go. I'll be fine."

I run toward the door, flying through each room. Straight. Left. Left. Yellow footprints skirt the side of the third room. A strong emotion draws me forward—safety. Like a comforter thrown over me, or like I'm sitting on the porch swing at night. I go the only direction it could be, but the feeling is duplicated when I get through the door. Two relics?

A large tree with glittering leaves rises in the middle of the room. There are two relics in here, and they both send out waves of security. What else could produce the same emotion as my ring? No other shieldcraft relics were brought into the dungeon.

It has to be Onrix, the knife. The first thing Sira used it for, so long ago, was to keep her father living, and command him to do so with the power of silvercraft. Then she learned to manipulate people to get the things she wants. It must have created a life free of fear and retribution. I can see why it would have made her feel safe.

I'm halfway to the tree when someone emerges from the opposite doorway.

Sira.

SEARCH IN SILVERLAMP

SIRA'S EYES are rimmed red, but her tears have dried. She runs a hand over the leaves on the closest branch. Like me, she knows the two relics are in the room. I can sense them both in the tree. This is what Silverlamp wants, or her soul, her presence, whatever runs this dungeon. She wants us to fight our way up the tree, clawing for these objects to control each other.

The souls of the champions, the dungeons, are sadistic.

"I'm sorry about your father," I say. "That shouldn't have happened."

Her lips twitch into a frown. "I hate the dungeons," she says. "I hate craft. You're lucky, Clayson, to have lived on the surface, free of this world."

Thousands of images and video clips of violence and strife crop up out of my memory. For my part, I lived in isolation and peace, but the surface is far from what she thinks it is. I watched too much news to think otherwise.

"Sometimes," I say, "things are out of our control."

"That's why I need the mithrium. If I combine it with Onrix, no one will have to suffer again. Everyone would be kind and helpful. They would listen to each other. Help me, Clayson. This is the right thing to do."

"My grandfather thought he could make something useful with the mithrium. It killed him."

"Mithriumbane was a visionary. My father thought so. That's what we were looking for, but then—the accident."

"But my grandfather was wrong. He—"

"I heard what you told your dad about the dreams. Mithriumbane chose to use potential energy to destroy the mithrium. What I'm doing at Handler will use opposite energy."

I think back to the last dream I had, the one I haven't told people about yet. Yinzar's conversation with the worm in the underwater cave. Potential energy versus opposite energy. Yinzar had chosen to leave the cave. He had gone to the mines in search of potential energy, but what if he had completed the process using opposite energy? Could it have created something as powerful as a mithrium bomb that could be used by an individual?

"Controlling everyone isn't the answer," I say.

"Then what is? How else can I stop people from hurting each other? Clayson, sweetie, please, I need you to help me get the mithrium. We can make sure no one is ever mean again."

It's the dream of a child. She's the same girl who had to save her father during his accident so long ago.

"I can't help you," I say. "I'm gonna get my ring and save my parents."

"No!"

Sira launches toward the tree, and I'm right behind her. The first branch is eye-level, and I catapult off a large stone and grab it. I pull myself up, but Sira stomps at my fingers. I scoot closer to the trunk, and her foot misses.

The emotion, that feeling of safety, surges as I make my way up. Sira must be closer than me. She'll reach one of the relics in just another few branches. I grab onto her foot.

"Let go!"

She tries to shake me free, but I clamp down.

Suddenly, a barb of hot metal pierces the tree next to my face.

A flicker of fire ignites the bark. Both Sira and I look down and find one of the knights, the woman who used to have massive arms, standing to the side of the tree. She hurls another piece of hot metal at me.

She has Erikzin's lapel pin. It has to be.

"Stop it!" Sira yells at her.

"Get out of the tree or burn with it." She sends a wave of flaming metal flying at the tree.

A sharp pain cuts my side. I reach for my stomach expecting blood on my hands, but the barb only scratched me, hitting the tree trunk instead. Sira cries out. The flames spread quickly. Cutting around to the other side, I climb the next three branches as fire engulfs the tree. The heat reaches my skin, and ash from the leaves above floats into my face.

A single leaf in the branch above shimmers like a ripple of light on water. It has to be Ergal. If I can reach it, I can jump from here, then protect myself from being burned.

I climb within reach, but instinct keeps me from shoving my hand into the fire.

Then Sira climbs to the opposite side of me. She sees it.

This has to be done. I can't hesitate.

My body tenses as I force my hand to reach into the fire, but the second I move, the branch under my feet snaps. I tumble through the tree, my hands clutching to find a grip, tearing away burning twigs and leaves. I hit the large central branch below me, and spin over myself landing in a heap against the stone.

A bone in my leg cracks, and pain shatters every other thought. Vaguely, I sense myself trying to crawl out from under the burning tree, one leg refusing to move. Each breath is fire-filled pain. Smoke squeezes through my eyelids, up my nose. Coughing, I roll over and plant my face in the grass. I claw forward until I hear something snap above me. A flaming branch drops to the right. But, by some miracle, it's the branch with the shimmering leaf. I know it's Ergal. Screaming in pain, I push myself to my knees and stretch out my hand.

Before I can grab it, two thick fingers pluck the leaf. I watch in horror as it transforms into Ergal. The strong sense of safety is snubbed out, the same as when I realized Bazalrak had found his shadow ax. Now one of his goons has my ring.

Through the vapor and smoke, a twisted, cruel smile becomes visible on her face.

"Enough," Sira's voice echoes from behind me. "Help him."

I don't expect a response from the woman, but she steps into the fire. There's a thin flicker of white shielding from Ergal protecting her. She grabs my arm and drags me away from the flames. When we're clear, she heals some of the burns on my body, but the healing power doesn't extend to my leg or the major burns. If she were peerless like me, I would be instantly whole. My body starts to shake. I'm going into shock. I'm never gonna reach my parents.

When Sira steps next to her, I see why the woman followed her orders. Sira clutches Onrix so tightly her knuckles are nearly the same color as the knife itself. Her eyes are wild, saucer huge. "I said, heal him!"

"I-I can't, shieldcraft is my weakness. I was barely able to make a shield."

I see the struggle in Sira's face. She doesn't want me to die.

"Please." It hurts to speak. "Help."

She sighs. "Give him the ring."

The woman pulls it from her finger and jams it onto one of my burnt ones. I would scream in pain, but I'm grinding my teeth into pearls. Ergal takes control, healing all of my burns and my broken leg almost instantly.

I sit up. "I thought you couldn't influence someone if they had Ergal?"

"No, just you, sweet stuff. It's your peerless rating working with the ring. Our ratings were a match, so things canceled out. See? This woman doesn't have your natural ability."

"I guess." I glance at the goldcraft woman. She's standing by Sira, waiting for orders. "Why did you give me back the ring?"

333

Her head shakes slowly. "Nothing really matters anymore. I-I didn't want to see that pretty face all burned. If I took the ring, I'd have to stop using the knife, split the craft between them. That seemed dumb."

"What now?"

She's thoughtful for a second. "We get the mithrium. You and me. Think about it. We make everyone listen. We find a way to create peace. People... they can have their choices back when they've proven they won't hurt each other anymore."

"I don't think it works that way, Sira. We can't bend everyone to our will. That's—"

"Why not? They would do it to us."

"You're not listening to—"

"Then I'll go alone. I'll find your mom myself. She might be able to get the mithrium from the dreamwell."

"Don't send her in there. She'll be lost in nightmares forever. It will kill her."

"If that's what I have to do to get you to listen."

"Don't, Sira."

Rugnus shouts from somewhere outside the room. "Clayson!"

"In here!"

He appears in the doorway at Sira's back. The moment I see him, he budges next to me and, before I say anything, we both budge from the room.

He has Icho.

I'm given no time to talk things over with him. The moment we appear, Ergal flings a wall of energy from one end of the room to the other. Bazalrak and two of his goons are on one side, Andalynn, Hemdi, Rugnus, and I on the other.

Bazalrak jumps down from a ledge, a shadow curled around his body, and smashes his ax into the energy field. The blade bounces off, and he stumbles back.

"Ha!" Rugnus says.

Coolly, Bazalrak says, "Your defense makes little difference. This shield can't protect your mother if I reach her first."

The three of them retreat around a tall statue and disappear through a doorway.

Andalynn hugs me. "You're safe."

"And you have your ring," Rugnus says. "How did you—"

"Sira forced the other ironhead to give it to me."

"Why?" Rugnus says, "I mean great, but why?"

"We can talk about that later," I say. "We have to find the exit keys."

"I already found one," Hemdi says, "but it won't move. Koglim is guarding it. We think it has to be activated at the same time as the other key."

"Winta's searching for the other one," Andalynn adds.

"Okay, let's go find the other key," I say.

Andalynn holds up her hand. "You need to protect Koglim and the first key. Rugnus and I will look for the next one. Hemdi, can I keep Linterna for a bit longer?"

He nods.

"That works for me," I say. "Just find it quickly. Then Rugnus can budge back and tell us when."

"Here we go," Rugnus says.

We budge and appear facing a wall of hexagonal stone blocks, all as big as fists. Some are pushed back, and others are nudged forward. It would be easy to climb. Koglim stands facing me, a glazed-over euphoric smile on his face. Then the wave of crafted emotion hits me from the exit key.

"Okay, wait till I say when," Rugnus says, but he can't keep the grin off his face.

In fact, everyone is grinning ear to ear.

Rugnus shakes his head, and he and Andalynn budge.

A rush of excitement washes over me. I'll reach my parents soon, and the thought makes me almost giddy. I smile at Koglim. He smiles back. It's weird. I'm so excited. It feels like the day Dad said I could climb our cliff without gear. But my newfound eagerness isn't natural. It's coming from some hidden key or object. It's almost euphoric.

335

Hemdi comes behind me, chuckling happily.

I ask Koglim, "Is that...that—"

"I know right," Koglim says. "Get melted! I swear I almost peed myself, and I could barely wait for you. Who am I kidding? I didn't even try to wait for you"—he's in my face now, shaking my shoulders—"I-I tried to climb up there, but I'm as fat as a troll, so I didn't get far, anyway." He slaps my butt. "Get up there, you skinny little outrider."

I take in the small geometric hexagons, which form something like a climbing wall extending to the ceiling. It's an easy climb, to be sure, but it looks awesome.

"This is so cool," I say, immediately realizing how stupid I must sound, but Koglim is bouncing on his toes excitedly. He squeals and claps his hands like a tween waiting for the pop concert of a lifetime.

Koglim's hand shoots to the sky. "Ooh, ooh, ooh."

"Yes, Koglim?" I say.

"Can we come back here like every week...no, every day."

I bounce my chin affirmatively.

"Okay, okay. Come on. Up you go."

Hemdi breaks the moment. "Rugnus wanted us to wait."

Koglim and I roll our heads toward him.

"Who am I kidding," Hemdi says. "Grab that thing."

Usually, I take a moment before a climb to sketch out the best route, but we're so close to getting this key. Before I know it, I'm halfway up the wall, easily pulling myself along the hexagonal handholds, one after another, until they spread out and I'm forced to strategize. But I can sense the key ahead of me. I lock eyes on one of the handholds. It's a different color stone. That must be it. "I see it!"

Koglim's laughing now, rubbing his hands together. "Get it, bro. Get it."

I've never been more alert. It's almost like caffeine has replaced my blood. My chest expands. I'm prepared for anything to happen. I want everyone in the world to share in this euphoria. My mind is prodding me now: hurry up, hurry up, hurry up.

When Hemdi's voice reaches me, I can't process his words. I'm too distracted by the euphoria. His words become louder and louder until he screams. Koglim joins him in yelling. Annoyed at the distraction, I shout back. "What is it?" I glance over my shoulder, and another feeling breaks through the false euphoria —fear.

Below me, the room is filled with black clouds, bursting with countless flashes of multi-colored light. It's Silverlamp's three brothers, the wraiths of this dungeon. Hemdi and Koglim are being forced to the side of the room. I drop from the cliff using Ergal to break my fall. "I'm coming!"

I raise my shield, but the hurricane of wraith clouds passes right through it. I have to get to them. Landred Wolfstaff didn't harm me; maybe these wraiths will be the same. As I build up the courage to run into the black vapor and lights, I can only think one thing: the wraiths will take their craft. Hemdi's voice cries out for me, and I plunge into the cloud.

The wind pushes me to the side. The lights blind me like camera flashes. As it was in Wolfstaff, a cacophony of voices compete with each other. So many words—angry, unstoppable words. The presence of the three brothers becomes clear. They lead the charge to attack, but they are also led by a mass of fear and hatred beyond them. Like Landred, they are part of the whole but have retained enough individuality to exert influence in this dungeon.

"Stop!" I yell, but the noise drowns me out.

I push forward into the cloud. When I reach the other side, I find only Koglim, his fist to the sky, and his pendant glowing brightly. The wraiths don't seem to like it. I come to his side and ignite a shield around us. Still, it doesn't stop the cloud from getting nearer.

If a wraith can take your highest craft, as Rugnus says, wouldn't I have lost my power in shieldcraft by now? Rugnus said it could happen with even a brush of their physical form, but I walked straight through the cloud.

"Where's Hemdi!" I say over the voices.

Koglim grimaces, focused on his pendant. Tapping it rhythmically, superstitiously. He glances to his right, but there are only the swirls of the wraith's cloud.

Frustrated, I try again to appeal to the wraiths, but I use a different tactic. "Stop. You can't hurt me. Landred tried and failed. You can't hurt me."

The swirling cloud freezes exactly in place. After a pause, the lights coalesce into three groups. The muttered screams and cacophony of words become a single word: "Leave."

As the cloud recedes, Hemdi is revealed to our right, curled into a ball on a patch of yellow grass. Koglim pats his own body, checking for holes. "That was crazy."

"Hemdi," I say.

Koglim rushes to his side and pulls him into a bear hug. When real tears spring to Koglim's eyes. "So sorry, Hemdi."

Hemdi hangs his head for a moment but then turns to me. "Did you—did you walk through them? Did they take your shieldcraft?"

"I-I don't think so."

Koglim rubs his face. "But they must have. Sorry, Clayson. You were the best shieldmage I'd ever known. I'm so, so sorry."

I use Ergal to create a shield and shrug.

"What? Trollbrick. How—what did you do? Keep Ide, that's not possible."

Hemdi's eyes fill with hope. "Maybe—maybe I'm okay. I don't have Linterna to check my tincraft."

Rugnus appears back at the wall. "Where are you guys." He sees us. "Get over here! We found it."

Crossing the room as quickly as possible, I bypass Rugnus and climb the wall again.

"Sorry," Koglim tells him. "Fighting wraiths."

"Wraiths?" Rugnus scans all the doors. "Is everyone okay?"

"We're not sure about Hemdi, but Clayson walked right through them, and he can still use shieldcraft."

Rugnus tries to lower his voice, but I still hear him. "I'm not sure you can use Clayson as a guide for what's normal."

The euphoria returns again, and I'm glad. I don't wanna think about how different I am from everyone else. I don't wanna think about the dreams I have, the problems they cause for everyone else. Sira manipulated everything to get me here, and if the cost is my parents, I'm not sure I'll be able to forgive myself.

"I'm ready," I say. "Tell Andalynn."

"She's fending off Bazalrak but give me thirty seconds. Starting now."

He budges, and I start a mental countdown. Another wave of euphoria overtakes me. This situation may be terrible, but I'm ecstatic about it. Joy fills me up from the bottom of my feet to the crown of my head. I laugh. I sigh in contentment.

And then my count reaches thirty, and I grab the different colored hexagon. The key sinks into the wall. The moment it does, the tumultuous waters of my mind are stilled.

No more euphoria.

Below me, Koglim stops talking to himself and looks up. A feeling of unease, almost guilt, fills the base of my stomach. The emotion had controlled me, but I almost want another chance to feel the euphoria again.

Of all the crafts, silvercraft is the single most dangerous one, but it's also connected me to Rugnus and my sister in ways I couldn't have imagine. It could ease people's burdens almost like a drug. I see why Sira wants to flood the world with its power using the mithrium. It's almost convincing. Would it be the worst thing?

Yes. Her father's pain at coming back to himself after so many years, her anguish at losing him—that's all too fresh in my mind to believe an object made from silver and mithrium could be a force for good.

The dome above me disappears. Light bathes a set of stairs at the side of the room, which lead upward. Koglim and Hemdi find the stairs, and I continue climbing until we are balanced on the wall between this room and the next. The wall itself must be ten feet long—a whole bar. The scene looks the same as it did in the first room, more like the model dollhouse.

Not far away, Andalynn emerges from the room she had been in. She and Rugnus and Winta sprint toward us, yelling and pointing behind me.

I whirl around. Within my line of sight, I see a lighted wall darkened only by two small figures past the maze of rooms.

Mom and Dad.

Andalynn nearly plows straight into me. "We beat them. Let's get to the finish."

Hemdi reaches for Linterna, and Andalynn hands it to him.

Bazalrak, now on the same level, charges from a few walls away, striking out with the shadow ax as we run. Winta unleashes a barrage of gears with her new rail gun. And Bazalrak takes cover, but behind him, something massive glows gold. The ironhead woman who came for my father and I grows too large to stay on the wall—twice her height, then doubling, then doubling again. Muscles form and tighten across her arms, legs, and neck. She crashes through the wall next to us like it's made of foam blocks.

Not good. "She'll get there before us!"

Rugnus hands me a small copper bracelet he must have found in the dungeon. "Switch to this. We need offense. You have the highest score."

I slip it on my wrist and immediately sense the creatures patrolling the edges of the maze. This belonged to the ironhead who could control arachnids. I rouse the creatures from the surrounding pit, placing them firmly under my control. I sense their need for purpose, but after having my emotions and thoughts manipulated by the dungeon, after learning how Sira controlled her father, I'm not eager for the work ahead of me.

Coppercraft is like silvercraft for animals.

For a split second, I can't do it. I won't. But my parent's lives are at stake.

I call the creatures from their rest, and they scurry out of the pit onto the stone, made of a thousand furry legs. Their beady eyes lighting the dim cavern. I count five, ten, then dozens skitter their way in a wave toward the golden giant. Their muddy arachnid bodies produce bronze light as they spit webbing around the woman.

"Beautiful, Clayson," Rugnus says. "Onward."

We come to the edge of the maze, the last outside wall. More spiders scurry past us. Koglim grimaces and squeezes his eyes shut. Beyond another chasm, my parents stand on the last few stones, keeping them from falling into a void of nothingness. Another brick at their feet tumbles into the dark.

"Wasn't there a bridge here in the model?" I yell.

"I think we need to make one," Winta says.

"There," Andalynn says, pointing between where we stand and my parents. Out in the middle of the void is a trail of blue-black clouds similar to the threshold, but instead of a doorway, it sits like a finish line.

I yell for them. "Dad! Mom!"

Dad looks up, but the motion sends another rock skittering into the chasm. "Clayson, hurry!"

"How do we get there!" I say.

"Vines." Andalynn turns around, looking to the room below us. The wall at our feet is covered in vines. She tosses Linterna to him. "Hemdi, make a bridge."

We all look at him. Hemdi focuses, then the color drains from his face. He tries to speak, but his face says what he can't. The wraiths stole from him his ability to use tincraft. He shakes his head and passes Linterna to Andalynn. For the first time, Winta lowers the rail gun and finds her husband's eyes. A fresh round of tears attack Koglim, and he makes a desperate effort to angle his face away. Rugnus looks as if he's going to throw up.

Maybe it's the fact that the wraiths didn't affect me, or maybe it's the history this group shares, the dangers they faced together, the friend they already lost to the world, but my body and mind are a hundred yards from everyone else—my existence lies somewhere far, far from here. Everything's make-believe and intangible. I become as foreign to this world as an airplane.

In our frozen state, Bazalrak growls with triumph, seizing the moment to sprint for us. Grimly, Andalynn takes Linterna. Vines crawl over the wall. She knits a bridge leading over the chasm.

"Keep them busy," Rugnus says, running out on the vine bridge.

I command some of the spiders to attack Bazalrak, but they fear the shadows around him. Winta can't keep him pinned down. He's two rooms away. Then one. I switch back to my ring and throw a shield around us, covering every angle to the bridge as well. Bazalrak's ax comes down a moment too late.

He growls. "Don't think this is over."

Behind me, Rugnus shouts, "Got it!" He's crossed the finish.

From the side of the maze, bricks fly toward the wall, reforming the floor around my parents. More bricks assemble where Rugnus stands at the edge of the bridge. Koglim, Winta, and Hemdi rush toward Rugnus.

"Bazalrak won't get on this bridge," I tell Andalynn. "Get to our parents. End this."

Her face beams. "Okay."

Bazalrak raises his ax again and strikes the shield. "It doesn't matter if you get out of this alive. Everyone knows where the mithrium is hidden, and everyone knows you can get it. I have every intention of forcing you to come back here. The council will side with me."

"They won't," I say, but I don't believe it myself. Andalynn's silver oath to the council will make it harder for her to influence their decisions. They used the mithrium in the past. What's to stop them from using it now? Would they attack Tungsten City? Geum Ide?

Bazalrak is right. He's wrong, but he's right.

342

"They will," he says. "And even if they don't. You think I won't find you and your parents again? You'll have to kill me. And then the next person. And then the next. The world will never stop coming for you and your family, Brightstorm."

Sira.

She appears behind him, and Bazalrak drops his ax. She comes to his side, looking at him dismissively. "This one's easy to control," she says. "He's not wrong, though."

But there's nothing left to say to Sira. I know what she wants to do with the mithrium, and I can't let her. As she holds Bazalrak under the power of the knife and I keep my shield up, I feel the balance between the two powers.

Though that's not entirely true. Ergal has a slight edge. I can feel it.

"You were right," I say. "My peerless rating and Ergal versus your peerless rating and Onrix. Sort of equals out."

Her mouth turns. "Sort of?"

"Shieldcraft always has an edge. Doesn't it? Which means I can cancel out your influence on Bazalrak, as if it's not even there. And what would he do? My bet? He'd take the knife from you. That leaves me free to protect everyone else. He won't be able to get through my shield. If you don't give me the knife, I'll free him and let him take it."

Bazalrak is still as stone. It's not clear if he can hear us under Sira's influence.

"You wouldn't."

"Then you understand? I can keep the shield over me and extend it over him. His only choice will be to take the knife from you. He's not peerless in silver. Neither are any of his knights. He's no match for me and Ergal. If it comes down to it, we can get it back from him. That's the hard way."

Almost crying, Sira says, "What's the easy way?"

"I don't want the mithrium hanging over my family. I'll get it from the dreamwell, but not for you. You'll have to trust me with it."

343

She walks past him, through my shield, and holds out Onrix. I shake my head. "Keep Bazalrak under your control and stay next to me. Don't try anything. I have the advantage."

She nods.

We take the vine bridge and step onto the bricks. In the center of the wall, a strange light climbs out from a cylinder of stone. The dreamwell is here at the finish line. Silverlamp seems to want the same thing I want.

Dad sees me and rushes over. "Clayson! You did it!" He tousles my hair like I'm a little kid.

My heart is still pumping. What I have to do sinks like a rock to the bottom of my stomach. My words catch in my throat. "Hey, Dad. Sorry about Geum Ide."

Rugnus stands behind Dad. "Clayson," he says. "Sira is she..."

"She can't use her knife against us. The ring is its equal. Now that I know to defend you."

Rugnus doesn't take his eyes from her. "Oh."

"Sira," I say, "bring the other knights over and have them surrender their relics to us."

She does it.

Rugnus must sense something is happening; his eyes narrow at me. But in a minute, there won't be anything anyone can do to stop me.

Hemdi and Winta stand near Koglim. My mom and Andalynn speak softly at the back of the group. Something inside my heart wants to reach out to her. My ring had the power to affect our curse, but only when I was in physical contact with her. She's too far away. That's how it has been, maybe how it will always be, but at least I can do for her and Dad what they tried to do for me so long ago—protect them.

Bazalrak and all three of his knights step over and drop their relics at Rugnus' feet. Dad stares, his mouth wide open. "What's happening?"

Koglim didn't recover Elbaz from the dungeon. He smiles. Unlike Rugnus he can't sense something is not right. "That's the knife at work. Sira can control people with it. She's Silverkeeper's daughter."

"Rensira. Of course. You were so small. I-I remember you. Where's your father?"

She shakes her head. There's a hitch in her breath, but she holds back tears, her jaw set tight against the emotions she must feel.

"Sira," I say, "the knife."

Rugnus shakes his head. "What are you doing, Clayson." He reaches out his hand, takes a step forward, but Sira is already right next to me. The moment Onrix touches my hand, he and everyone else are under my control. I don't take their minds, or their voices, only the moment of their bodies

"I'm sorry, Rugnus. And Dad, I know this is not what you— what Mom wanted—but there's a way out of this. I think Yinzar has been trying to show me his mistake with the mithrium. That's what the dreams have been about. If I don't do this, there will always be someone chasing us. I want a life together."

Rugnus can only stare at me. "You don't understand what's at risk. The council could use it against Tungsten City."

"Clayson," Dad says as I approach the well. "Don't do this. The mithrium can't be controlled."

I have to avert my eyes from the stark light coming from the well. "You're right," I say. "But I'm not trying to control it."

Sira hasn't left my side. "Do it, Clayson. Make the world what we want it to be."

My hands are shaking, the knife with it. "Not with this."

"Clayson," Andalynn calls out to me. "I trust you. Do what you have to do. I'll help them understand."

I step onto the edge of the dreamwell, trying to close my ears to Rugnus' frustrated mumbling, and jump into the darkness.

FORGE A WAY OUT

FLASHES of light reach for me, draw me out of this cold unknown.

My eyelids flutter. I'm aware of every blink, each tightening of each muscle. My body is shaking but burning with fever. I'm covered in fur. No, dressed like Rugnus. No, naked. I'm strong, but I still can't move. Indistinct whispers fill the space around me.

What's happening? Where am I?

I've forgotten something. I left something in the cabin, on the stove.

With a sharp breath inward, the world appears.

I'm facing the mud lake in Magmadew court. The luscious grass under my feet is bright with dew. Everyone I know—my parents, Andalynn, Rugnus—everyone I've met in Tungsten City, they stand immovable in the churning mud, an arm's length away.

I open my mouth to speak to them. No, I can't breathe.

I scream for help, but it comes out in a hiss. My deflated lungs yearn to expand with oxygen, but there's none in the air. How is this possible?

That's when I die. I fall to the earth, my hands around my own throat, clutching.

Later, much later, I live again. I'm on the same shore, facing the same people, but not in the same body.

When I'm finally able to form words, they leave me in a howl. I'm a wolf. Powerful and strong. I draw power from the glare of the brightstorm far above me. The rays of its warmth and light caress my pelt, heats all my sinews and the marrow in my bones.

That's when all the people start screaming for Clayson Brightstorm. Screaming as they all sink into the bubbling brown liquid past their calves. Rugnus tries to move. He reaches for Andalynn but pulls her down with him. They're consumed by the mud.

Sira next, but she bats her eyes and accepts her fate with a soft smile.

Then my mom screams. "Clayson, where are you?"

My father stands looking at his filthy hands until he sinks into the mud.

I have the power to stop this. I'm strong. But when I try to maneuver my legs, I realize I'm still a wolf. I forget how to move. My legs come up, but I stay in place.

There's nothing more I can do.

Far above me, the brightstorm shrivels, its color a deep blue neon. Granite rises to take the place of the mud. I can move again. Pockets of steam rise up through cracks in the stone at my feet.

Real feet? No, dream feet.

But I can walk again. As I wander over the stone, whispers rise with the steam. The words remain unformed, but I know what they are. Accusations. I run, but the further I go, the thicker the steam, the more powerful the whispers.

I fall to my knees, screaming, "What do you want from me?"

Yinzar, my grandfather, emerges from the steam.

But he should be dead.

Anger enshrouds his features. He draws a large broadsword

from behind his back, heavy enough he has to hold it in two hands. "Are you gonna fail me?"

This is like a nightmare.

My head comes up. This is not *like* a nightmare. This *is* a nightmare.

How could I forget? The dreamwell.

I ignore Yinzar. "Silverlamp! That's enough! I know where I am. I remember."

Confusion fills my grandfather's face. His sword wavers. "Impossible. You can't remember."

I stand and step closer to him. With one quick movement, I yank the sword from his hands. His confusion changes to a look of relief, then a broken smile. "Good. Now get what you came for and never return." The image of Yinzar vanishes.

Somehow, I know what to do. I jam the sword down into the closest fissure. Water erupts in a fountain. The cracks all around me burst and flood over the stone until I'm swimming. Darkness covers the water, black as oil, but a dim light appears deep below me. I dive under. But as deep as I swim, I can't find the floor of this new ocean.

I cast my head back, looking up. In the distance, a dark shape is visible, massive and back-lit with ghoulish light.

It's a monstrous eel. Big enough to wrap around the bluelink building in Tungsten City. That's what the feral wolves are afraid of, what Frrwelhst warned Yinzar about. A vague sense of pride and hopelessness rolls toward me as the beast displaces more water. This is like everything else: an emotion that's given to me. It's trapped in Onthratia, the lake Frrwelhst guided me to. That is what this water represents.

An old voice calls out from far, far below me. For a second, I think it's the eel, but it's something from out of the dungeon.

What do you seek?

"The mithrium." I find I can speak and breathe freely in the water.

What can you tell me about it?

"Who are you?"

I am the dungeon. The lost. The trapped.

"You mean you're Silverlamp?"

Yes, but more. Wolfstaff, Mithriumbane, Brightstorm.

"I don't understand."

Nor do you need to. Why do you seek the heart, the mithrium?

"It's dangerous. My grandfather wants me to make something. Or maybe destroy it. I'm not sure."

The voice is amused. *You believe he's been speaking to you.*

"I see him in my dreams. He showed me a way to make something. Under Lake Onthratia. But in the real world."

Perhaps the reverse is true. You have been trying to tell him something.

"Me? No. He showed me his conversations and his coding for the mithrium. Like a recipe, how to forge it into something useful."

Something else speaks through your connection with him.

"Something else? Like what?"

Ide. The mithrium itself, perhaps. Does it truly matter?

"Of course, it matters. Is it good or bad? Should I try to destroy the mithrium or create something with it?"

It's enough that you question these things. You have everything you need.

Yinzar's voice echoes in the deep. "An opposite energy."

Ergal sends a bright, piercing light through the oily water, highlighting a metal cube floating near the bottom.

Mithrium.

Ergal's light reflects off the cube, and the mithrium becomes as blinding as the sun. Somehow, I know this is real, outside of the illusion. I expect something to try and stop me from grabbing it, but as I circle the light, I feel a vague sense of acceptance.

Maybe the mithrium itself is talking to me, leading me. It greets my touch with a flood of purpose, revealing the connections between the dungeons. They're one place, but many minds, many orientations toward distinct wants and needs. Yet about the mithrium, we share the same goal—protect it and protect others from it.

Go.

The water drains at my feet, and I'm standing at the top of a short staircase, walls closing in on me. I'm holding a metal cube so bright I can't look directly at it.

This is real. This is no longer a nightmare.

The dreamwell is behind me.

A doorway bordered with vines waits for me at the bottom. It's the same as the threshold, the print of a silver vine around it. I cross through the blue-black cloud filling the doorway.

I'm out of the dungeon.

I'm out of the dungeon, but where is everyone else?

The exit lobby is identical to the entrance, another maze. But unlike where Bazalrak forced me through the doors shrouded with fear, the doors to find the exit fill me with gratitude.

I shed all of my parents' judgements and my worries along the way, door after door, leading me downward. I'm filled with an appreciation I didn't know I could feel. The way my father cared for me. The trials my mom endures through our shared curse. The uncompromising love of my sister. They all strengthen my mind and body. We're more alike than different.

Then there's Rugnus' faithfulness to the promise he made to Dad, as well as his friendship, and his honesty which form some fiery core of truth inside him.

I have friends and family who watch out for me, who've tried to protect me.

But where are they?

I hope I haven't broken everything to get the mithrium.

Life on the surface carved me into a new creature. I haven't needed fear, like the people of Whurrimduum, or anger, like the citizens of Tungsten City. And though Dad made every effort to shelter me from the terrible world he had grown up in—like those who have chosen to live in Geum Ide—he also gave me the freedom to grow and express myself in a way that is so distinctly me.

When I take the last step off the staircase, the gratitude only amplifies. It's not something forced upon me by Silverlamp. It's apart from craft. I owe so much to those who've raised me. I want them to be both safe and free.

That's why I have to go through with my plan with the mithrium.

The silver hexagonal tube ahead is identical to the entrance. To my surprise, I find Rugnus waiting for me inside, Icho resting across his lap.

His eyes widen when he sees me—when he sees the mithrium in my hands. "You made it." He stands and hugs me.

"Where are my parents? Where's Bazalrak? Where's Sira?"

"Hold up." Rugnus considers his reflection in a small mirror and fiddles with a blue ring on his hand. "He's here."

Andalynn appears next to him almost immediately.

"What's happening?" I say. "Where's everyone else?"

My sister smiles. "I knew you'd make it. Relax. Here." She moves closer to me and places her forehead against mine, pouring a chain of events into my brain.

I've been in the dreamwell for three days. How has it been that long?

Bazalrak and Sira are being held in Keelcrawl. Silverkeeper's body appeared in the exit and is being prepared for his funeral. My parents are in Geum Ide. The Tungsten City citizens have voted to let me, Rugnus, and the others back into the city on a provisional basis. They've seen what happened in Silverlamp. The game was recorded, all but the dreamwell. There's a coronation planned for early next week. Andalynn will be crowned queen by the Keeper's Council.

"Crazy, huh?" Rugnus says. He nods at the cube of mithrium in my hand. "What are you going to do with that?"

"I think Yinzar wants me to make something."

Rugnus nods. "Down in his forge. Under Lake Onthratia?"

"How did you—"

Rugnus smiles. "Trying to make something out of mithrium in your grandpa's forge? Come on. A feral wolf took you to the lake. And you told us about the cavern forge from your dreams. You're easy to read. But... I'm kinda busy this afternoon," he says.

Andalynn smacks him.

"What? Koglim and I were going to try a new Tacu Tacu place for lunch."

"We're with you," Andalynn says.

The image of them drowning in the mud flashes in my mind. "This is something I should do alone."

Rugnus shrugs and pulls out his club, "Too bad. We're in this mess together."

"No, Rugnus. I'm—"

He pulls Andalynn closer to us. "No time like the present."

We budge into what would be darkness if not for the glow of the mithrium. Gurgling water pulses through a thousand grottoes.

Rugnus groans. "Why does this have to involve water?"

"Would you rather it was lava?" Andalynn asks, extending her own yellow light around us.

Rugnus squints at her. "Absolutely."

"Rugnus. Andalynn. I can do this myself. You should—"

"Give it up, Clayson," Rugnus says. "There's no way you're doing this without our help."

I take a deep breath. "Andalynn, your coronation. You can't—"

"I can too. Look, this—it feels right. I trust you. I trust our grandfather to lead you. He most likely destroyed one piece of the mithrium but didn't tell anyone anything about what he was doing. It was foolish and rash. But he was always kind, and usually, when people didn't listen to him, they were wrong."

"Okay," I say. "Okay, come with me, but if—"

"No buts," Andalynn says.

My head wants them to go back to their lives, to let me deal with this, but all I can think about is how good it is to have these two people by my side. I have to accept their help, but a knot of fear forms in my stomach. I turn toward the sound of water.

"Rugnus, can you budge us down to my grandfather's forge?"

"Down there? Hmm. It'd be guesswork. Probably just as easy to, uh, yeah, wraithspit... just as easy to swim." He produces a set of iron knuckles. "Thought we might need to get in there. I came prepared. Though, fair warning. There's a reason this is not a vacation hotspot."

"I'm aware."

The surface of the lake is more tumultuous than it had been when we passed it on the way to Geum Ide. The tide must be ebbing. The shore has retreated a whole foot in the few moments we've stood here. Is that possible?

Rugnus takes a deep breath. "Good thing you're AMP's not sixty-three or over."

"Why's that?"

"If your plan ends up killing you—and, by extension us—at least you won't generate a dungeon. Koglim might want to live eternal life as a wraith, but I don't."

"It won't kill us," I say, though I'm not sure where the confidence comes from.

"We'll see."

Andalynn pats my shoulder. "We can figure this out when we see what's down there."

I sigh. "It really would be better if—"

"Stop." Andalynn shakes her head.

Rugnus says, "Ide keep us. We're seeing this through together."

The shore is another five feet, but Rugnus wades into the water. "Hold on to me."

Red crystals form along his upper arms and shoulders, like football pads. An icy-hot sensation crawls along my arms, and I find they're covered with the same crystal. Rugnus wades further out and orders us to go under on the count of three.

Beneath the surface, we can breathe freely thanks to the crystal, but a tangle of craggy rock obstructs our view. We navigate the water slowly. A sound like someone screaming into a pillow reverberates around my head.

Andalynn and Rugnus pass each other a knowing look, but we head deeper into the lake. The world is another maze, this one more natural and with nothing to guide us through. After ten minutes of searching, Rugnus moves to the back of us, frustrated, pointing ahead for me to lead the group. The problem is, I have only a general sense of where we can find the forge, somewhere at the bottom of this side of the lake. Another muffled scream finds us in the dim water.

We move as quickly as we can, Andalynn and Rugnus shining their lights like two disconnected submarine headlamps. We hit a dead end and are forced into a grotto where we find a pocket of air.

"Not the best sense of direction, huh?" Rugnus' words echo along the smoothed-out rock above our heads as we tread water.

"I'm trying," I say.

Andalynn opens her mouth, I assume to defend me, but before she speaks, the muffled scream bounces into the tiny space, this time a hundred times more chilling in its effect. In the lowest part of my stomach, I know what we have to do.

"I have something, but you're not going to like it."

"I can already guess," Rugnus says, "We're going toward the screaming monster?"

I nod.

"You saw it in your dream?" Andalynn says.

"Only in the dreamwell. Though it's possible I heard the Great Smoke during one dream."

"Well," Rugnus starts, "not the most pleasant beacon to follow, but should be fantastic as long as we avoid getting eaten."

We dip under, heading toward the screams the best we can. The next time the muffled sound finds us, we're closer—much closer. All three of us slow down without any communication. We weave through one last tunnel and emerge into a large opening. I point out the massive collection of boulders where a dim red fire glows through the cracks, and Rugnus leads us like a bullet downward.

As we reach the rock, I see it. The beast Onthratia, the Great Smoke, is coming straight for us. Its black body is corded with muscle, the gleam of harsh teeth visible in its lower jaw. We're lucky Rugnus didn't have us waste any time. I take the lead at the last moment, and we find the entrance, the large eel still a distance away.

The tunnel leads us down and then back, where we bubble up and crawl out of the water. The red ice fades from our shoulders. Our clothes and bodies are still dry.

"Are we in the right place?" Andalynn asks.

"Definitely." It's the same cavern from my dream, except for the colors cast by two unfamiliar lights emanating from Rugnus and Andalynn. Ahead of us, the faint glow of lava awaits. I lead us through the passageway. The beast's muffled cry penetrates the cavern, and the ground beneath us shakes, droplets of water raining over our heads.

"I should have gone to lunch with Koglim," Rugnus says.

Andalynn passes by him smiling. "There's still time if you're feeling afraid."

"Not a chance, my Queen."

He smiles at her, and she pushes him playfully. I crane my neck around. He looks into her eyes and smiles. Their hands touch, and that brings me to a dead stop. "I've missed something being stuck in the dreamwell for three days. It was only three days, right?" I raise my eyebrows at Rugnus, and maybe it's the light, but I could swear he's blushing.

"Come on," Andalynn says.

The forge greets us with enough light the other two can be extinguished. The only thing missing from my dream is Yinzar himself, but I can almost feel his presence. I step to the forge, turning my face from the heat of the lava flowing around the rock. All his tools and ingredients are still here.

Rugnus points to a long tunnel to my right. "Where's that go?"

I follow the dim red lavalight down the tunnel, but it must stretch out for a long distance. "I think it leads back to Geum Ide. Yinzar must've made this place when Ara and my dad first began healing the brightstorm, when Glaris was establishing her colony for the conjurers."

My hand glows white as I use the power of Ergal to shield us all from the heat.

"What now?" Rugnus asks.

"That barrel of oakwood. I need a bushel and a half."

He blinks.

"Gotta be the dreams," I say. "I know the ingredients exactly."

Rugnus finds an empty bucket and starts pulling the slimy chunks of wood from the barrel. Andalynn and I search for the lambskin bellows. Once I have the bellows, we find the rest of the ingredients and the triangular-shaped mold Yinzar had used for the mithrium the last time he was here, when he chose not to finish the coding. When all the other pieces are gathered, I stand back for a moment and survey the collection of odd ingredients and tools.

"I hope you're baking a taffy cake," Rugnus says.

"Now would be the time to leave if—"

Another scream reaches us, and the cavern shakes this time more violently, raining water droplets from the stalagmites.

"We're not leaving you," Andalynn says.

"Right. Happy to be here," Rugnus adds, taking Andalynn's hand again.

"Here goes nothing," I say.

When I place the oak in the forge, it sizzles and pops like I'm frying steak. I fuel the fire with the lambskin bellows until it's white-hot, sprinkling the oaken coals with peat, which hardens the wood into glowing crystals.

In a few minutes, the mithrium turns to a blazing liquid. Leaving the gypsum in large chunks, I sprinkle it into the mithrium. After that, I add the onyx stone to the oaken coals, which melt and change the color of the liquid metal to a deep silver. Next, amethyst dust. Then, I take the silver bucket, brimming with an unending supply of ice water, and pour enough into the coals to cool them slightly.

Now I'm to the part where I improvise.

I slip Ergal from my finger.

"Clayson," Andalynn says. "What are you doing?"

"This was in the dream?" Rugnus asks.

"Not exactly."

Andalynn steps forward. "You can't combine mithrium with other metals."

Rugnus backs away. "Won't be able to stop the reaction."

I take a deep breath, the ring hovers over the liquid mithrium. "That's what I'm counting on. But the lake provides the opposite energy."

Ergal rolls from my hand and drops toward the liquid. Both Andalynn and Rugnus stumble away terrified, but I've done what has to be done. The ring merges with the mithrium, and it's like a percussion grenade reverberates through the cavern. I drop to my knees. The alloy in the crucible burns white-hot again, growing in intensity until I can't look at it.

I snatch the crucible with the large tongs and pour the liquid into the triangular mold, sealing it shut. The mold rattles and cracks along one side.

I can barely hear Andalynn over the muffled screams above us and the loud buzzing of the mold. "It's going to explode!"

Rugnus crawls over to me. "Time to cool it down?"

"Yeah." I still have the copper bracelet from one of the ironheads. I raise my arm toward the ceiling and pit my will against the will of the creature of Onthratia—the Great Smoke, the eel. It is more complicated than controlling other animals. It has to be reasoned with.

Help me. It says. *I will grant you what your grandfather sought.*

It knows. I send my thoughts out to the eel. *How?*

I have been trapped here. My kind live on the surface, deep in the ocean.
I have a sudden idea.

"Rugnus? Can Icho move animals, like really big ones?"

The mold seems to vibrate the whole room. "I-I... is this important right now?"

"Can you?"

"The eel? I think so!"

I reach out with my mind. *Done. But you will have to trust us to come back for you.*

There's a shudder above us, a sense of peace washes over me. "Get ready to swim!"

As we huddle together, a layer of red ice forms on our shoulders.

The cavern shakes so hard we are forced to the ground. I crawl toward the tunnel to the right. If I'm correct, it will lead back to Geum Ide. I think this was Yinzar's exit plan as well. I hope it was. Andalynn and Rugnus follow me. With the second shriek, the giant eel bashes the ceiling with all its significant might. Stalagmites fall, and the dark, oily water sprays down.

A final, pummeling attack rips a fissure in the ceiling, and the cavern floods with inky, acrid-smelling water. I glimpse the mold engulfed, then the high-pitched buzz becomes softer and muted, along with the light from the mithrium alloy. But that's all I know before a wall of water shoves us down the tunnel.

Rugnus somehow keeps his grip on both of us, and we tumble through the water for nearly a minute. A light finds us. A single piece of metal as bright as the sun, triangular in shape, zips past. The mold formed the mithrium into a flat, triangular shape, as thin as glass—a shield. Ergal is now part of the object. We follow its mesmerizing light like moths to a flame.

The tunnel becomes crowded with vines, and we slow down. The water settles, and the shaft ends in a single tunnel. Now under our own power, we swim until the light from the mithrium shield merges with light at the end of the long tunnel. Something curious begins to happen. The vines on the wall shrink and wither, the water becomes more radiant and transparent.

We pass the edge of the tunnel and swim upward, the water glimmering and silver. I can't tell if the light floating on the surface is the sun or the shield. My lungs catch fresh air as my head breaks a plane of water. We're at the heart of the jungle. Geum Ide. I climb from the water and step through thick ferns.

I turn around to help Rugnus out but catch sight of the shield looping over our heads and resting in the air only a bar away.

As he helps my sister from the pool, he says, "Andalynn, look."

She stares, entranced by the shield made from a single ounce of mithrium and my ring, Ergal. "What is it?"

Ferns fall under my feet as I cut across the ground and reach for the shield. Both Andalynn and Rugnus yell at the same time, but it doesn't stop me. The metal is cool against my fingers even though it shines more brilliantly than a brightstorm.

Andalynn releases a breath. "You must have a real death wish, Clayson,"

"Don't do stupid things like that," Rugnus says, clutching his heart.

"It's fine. It's not even warm. And I can't move it."

I try again, but it won't move from its place.

Under our feet, the plants fade into nothing. Thick vines slink away into the pool. The massive jungle trees surrounding us warp into shadowed shapes and vanish, revealing tall, angled buildings of stone and glass, shattered and empty. The foliage that had darkened the brightstorm far above us shrivels, rays of light cutting to the jungle floor. Lightfalls. With each burst of light, more and more of the jungle retreats into nothing.

"It can't be," Andalynn says, her mouth open in shock.

Rugnus squints at the mithrium shield. "Reversing everything. You did it, Clayson. You did it." In the light, his eyes shine. I don't know how many times he's ventured into a fallout zone, but it's more than I have. This is something he never thought possible. He smiles at me and says, "Let's get a better view."

One of the skyscrapers, now uncovered from jungle life, shines in the glare of the brightstorm. Rugnus squints to the top of it, and we budge there. From our new vantage point, we watch the jungle fade away, block by block, leaving a ruinous city. Buildings large and small are shaped with five sides, hundreds butted up against each other. A pattern emerges, and then, far away, the walls of the citybarrel are revealed. The whole place rests inside a pentagon. A city no longer poisoned by mithrium but protected by it. A warm, white light lines the inside of the citybarrel, like a new coat of paint.

Toward one side, a distinct patch of natural fields and squat buildings becomes visible in the distance, cut in half by a wide ravine.

"Geum Ide," Rugnus says.

"Our parents are there?" I ask Andalynn.

She rests her head on my shoulder. "Yeah."

"You think we'll be able to move the shield to other cities? Heal them too?" Rugnus asks.

"I don't know," I say, "It doesn't seem to wanna be moved."

Rugnus points Icho down to the little settlement.

We're there instantly. We appear on the gravel road, and I recall how much Winta and Hemdi loved it here. My mind flashes back to the wraiths around Hemdi. I wanna ask how he's doing, but I also don't wanna spoil this moment. A pang of guilt shoots through me, and Andalynn must sense it because she squeezes my hand harder as we walk toward the settlement.

A crowd appears staring at us in utter shock. My grandmother is there with Nasur Lavalock. My father too, but when my mom pushes her way through the people, my heart sinks. In destroying Ergal, I'll never be able to counteract the curse keeping her from seeing me, from knowing who I am.

I run for her anyway and throw my arms around her neck. "Mom."

Dad's hands fall on my shoulders as she tightens her grip on me. I dare look into her eyes. "Can you see me?"

Confused, she nods. "And I'm your mother?"

Dad squints at her. His chin lowers. "You can see him?"

"Of course," she says. "Why would I not be able to see him?"

She can see me. I look right into her eyes. "The curse? Maybe the effect of Ergal is in the power of the shield. Do you remember who I am? You were going to tell me something in Keelcrawl. What was it?"

"Sorry," she says, "It's strange. I know you're my son, but I don't remember you."

Andalynn steps to my side. "Mom, it's Clayson."

"Clayson." She mulls the syllables of my name, lingering on the last one.

"She can see you," Dad says. "It's a start."

It's not the same as the full effect of Ergal, but Dad's right. The mithrium shield I created has a part of the ring. Its effect is diffused through the air, breaking the smallest part of this terrible curse we share.

I lift my face to the brightstorm, eyes closed. Will she know me if she moves out from under the protection of Geum Ide, where Ergal is now an inseparable part of the shield? I don't have an answer to that question, but my mom doesn't care about any of this. She trusts the words of her husband, and her daughter, and me. She pulls me toward her. I relax in her arms. I need no craft to heal the years that have passed between us.

EPILOGUE

ANDALYNN'S CORONATION is the most beautiful thing I've ever seen. In the neon-lighted flower garden of Everbloom, surrounded by the keepers and their families, Chainkeeper, now the head of the Council of Ten Keepers, sets a glimmering, jeweled crown upon her head—tin to match her bracelets. She dazzles in a smokey yellow gown. Tiers of the royal guard in their leadcraft vests form symmetrical lines behind her. Citizens of both Whurrimduum and Tungsten City watch the ceremony over bluelink. At her insistence, I stand beside her.

The afterparty lasts through the night, and we're the stars. I've gained the name Mithriumhealer. Not a true name, like a champion, but close enough, Rugnus says.

Not only can the mithrium shield we made not be moved, but no one can enter the city of Geum Ide or the surrounding city-barrel unless someone comes to the very edge of the shield and it draws them in. The whole city is protected. I'm not sure how everything will play out in the end for the settlement, but for now, part of this world is repaired.

Right after the coronation, Rugnus helps me keep my promise to the Great Smoke, the beast under Lake Onthratia. We bring it to the surface, transporting it deep into the Marianas Trench in the Pacific.

With the keepers' reluctant support, Andalynn orders the ironheads to throw open the border, break down the foilgrips that have held her city at bay. Her clarion call, rich with optimism and grace, asks all the keepers and their families to relocate back to Whurrimduum and rebuild the capital. She invites the people of Tungsten City to join their voices as one with her to build a more beautiful and peaceful world. Though her critics on bluelink still decry the monarchy, even they view my sister's coronation as a sign of hopeful things to come, an era of peace.

When the morning comes, I ask to be taken to Keelcrawl prison to see Sira.

The guard hesitates when I tell him I wanna speak with her, but she can't do us any harm behind the transparent aluminum foilgrip.

When she's free to move around, she says, "You made something out of the ring, didn't you?"

"I did." I'm not sure why I owe her an explanation, but even without her knife, I feel compelled to help her. "It's beautiful. A shield over Geum Ide that can't be moved."

"Why are you here? Why are you telling me this?"

"I don't know. I think you've had a hard enough life. Maybe there's a way to help you forward. Let you leave Keelcrawl prison."

She shakes her head, a soft smile forming on her lips. "You're so silly, sweetie. They don't let people out of here. You still don't understand what you're facing. The whole world will turn against you again. You'll see."

"Have some hope."

Sira jingles her gold handcuff at me. "There's more mithrium out there, Clayson."

I shake my head. "It can stay hidden. I have what I want."

"Your precious family? How nice for you. Silverlamp took mine."

"I'm sorry. I don't know exactly how you must feel but—"

She purses her lips. "I bet everyone is so happy right now, aren't they? Living under the illusion the world is safer. No one would dare upset the peace. How long until it all breaks down again? People want to be told what to do, Clayson. They prefer it."

My mind wanders to the Keeper's Council. They have more power over the monarchy now. That's the thing they prefer: power. In Tungsten City, it's not much different. Opinions swell to a majority as people surrender their freedom to the mob, unfeeling about the truth, willing to take every accusation at face value. But they're free to become anything they wanna be, to live a life full of purpose.

Sira clears her throat softly. "How are you sleeping?"

I turn to the guards. "I'm done here."

They freeze her again, but her eyes follow me out of Keelcrawl prison, and I can't shake her last question. I still don't sleep. Though I haven't had another dream. I leave the prison behind and budge to the Royal castlestack.

I find Andalynn in her palatial room. There's still one more task for today. One I've been dreading. "You ready?" I ask her.

"Sure. Will this work?" she asks.

"Worth a try?"

We budge directly to the heart of Tungsten City, inside the high rise where Winta and Hemdi had been trying to raise plants from their homelands. The greenhouse hasn't changed. Emerald light shines on the tin boxes filled with dirt.

A mess of brown hair pokes up between a few boxes, and I lead Andalynn over to where Winta kneels, tightening gears.

"I'll be ready in a second," she says.

She angles away from the table, and our eyes meet. Her usual angry simmer is gone. I'm not sure what has replaced it, but my insides crawl with guilt for involving them in what happened. Hemdi hasn't returned to the nursery to do this work since being back in the city. He doesn't want the reminder of what he's lost—his tincraft.

As Winta stands, Andalynn presents her with Linterna.

"I'm no good with plants," Winta says, "As you can clearly see. I can't get this greenhouse to work. The seeds are there. Automation is set. It has water and light, but I can't seem to initiate a growth cycle." She pushes Linterna to my sister. "I'd ask Hemdi about this, but... he'd want you to keep it. He loved that garden you brought us to—Everbloom. He could've stayed there forever."

"Clayson had an idea," Andalynn tells her.

Winta squints at me. "Is that right?"

Andalynn presses the lantern into the dirt of one of the boxes.

Winta's eyes grow bigger, tearful. Hemdi had never wanted to use Linterna as the catalyst for his nursery, but I figured he would appreciate this. Winta reaches under the table and adjusts a gear bringing the whole room to life.

Atop a dozen rows of tables, thick green leaves pierce through the dirt, soon carpeted with pink and white blooms. Leaves twine themselves onto the metal lattice above us, dropping finger-length, fruit-like flowers in asymmetrical beauty, a perfect lava red.

Winta holds her emotions in check. "They'll love them."

Andalynn smiles. "The people of Tungsten City—"

Winta shakes her head. "That's not what I meant by *they*... Hemdi will love them the most, and..."

"What is it?" I ask.

"Well, Hemdi *did* say we could tell people, might as well be you two. Hemdi and I...I'm going to have a son." Winta smiles softly, and there is something in the green light, a hint of pink in her eyes.

"A baby?" I suddenly know I'll do everything I can to protect her child.

"Thank you for this. It was thoughtful, Clayson—remembering our greenhouse."

"It's the least I could do."

We walk through the rows of plants, Winta smiling. This could be a sad moment, knowing Hemdi can never use tincraft again. The thought weighs on Andalynn's features, but the flowers bring everything to life. These will be waiting for Hemdi's easy laughter and optimism when he's ready to return.

To Ide with his lost craft. He's so much more than his strengths and weakness.

When we've soaked in the beauty of the greenhouse for a long while, we budge out of Tungsten City to the stark, contrasting world of Edium Fiarie and the House of Ide. Below us, Rugnus waits alongside Hemdi with an overflowing crowd of people who've come to pay their last respects to the great Theridal Silverkeeper as we return him to Ide. My parents are here, Koglim standing next to them. Elbaz no longer around his neck. Silver-lamp Dungeon claimed the relic for its own.

Dad acknowledges me. My mom doesn't. Every time she leaves the safety of the mithrium shield, her curse returns. But we spend all our days together.

Rugnus smiles at Andalynn when we approach. He tests strengths with me. There's silence as the keeper's body, wrapped in canvas, is brought out of the building on a stiff board. They've wrapped Silverkeeper in many layers, hiding relics and important objects in the wraps to send with him as his spirit reaches out to become one with Ide.

Behind me, my father tries, but fails, to stop emotion from erupting to the surface. This was his closest friend, a man he thought betrayed him, but in the end, their friendship had never really broken. It only took a temporary detour. I take one side of his body. Rugnus takes the other. We come to the edge of the cliff, where we attach the board and Silverkeeper to large silver chains.

In the crowd, flowers and plants burst in dozens of colors. A song passes over the group, something ancient and unknown to me. Rugnus and I grasp the silver chains and slowly lower the body headfirst down into the lava. My arms strain against his weight, and both sets of our feet dig into the rock for a better grip. Sweat beads up on my forehead, and we inch forward until the silver chains slacken against the obsidian.

Silverkeeper has returned to Ide.

A woman rushes forward to capture the glowing ends of the chains. Bringing them to an anvil, she pounds them into flat pieces. Her job is to make objects to memorialize the keeper, given to his descendants. Though his direct line—all but his only daughter Rensira Silverlamp—has ended. The objects are passed to the council for safekeeping.

The crowd doesn't clear out for a long time, and my father, to the best of his ability, accepts condolences from many, many hands. The pile of flowering plant life left along the edge of the stone grows and grows.

A familiar man moves toward Dad and me. It's Vor. He bows to Dad, and hands him a small square. It's a leaf.

"Vor." Dad seems surprised to see him. "How are you?"

"Greetings, former king." Vor's eyes hold the same eerie noth-ingness as always. "Many of Silverkeeper's objects have returned to Ide, but it was his most humble wish you have this."

He passes the leaf to Dad, but Dad passes it to me. I try to read it, but I can't.

My father bows back to Vor. "I no longer use craft directly. Can it be opened by anyone else?"

Vor averts his eyes, shakes his head slightly, and returns to the crowd. Dad's eyes follow him until he disappears.

"You don't wanna know what's on it?' I say.

"You made it possible for me to keep my oath. I don't want to break it."

"I think Silverkeeper wanted you to know about the knife he found. Onrix. I heard him tell Sira to bring it to you when he—before he died."

"Andalynn has the knife safely guarded at the castlestack. Let her have this too. Maybe she can get someone to read it. But it may be best to leave this undisturbed. Who knows what it says?"

I nod. "Dad?"

"Yes."

"About the other pieces of mithrium... Handler has the same recipe items I found in Yinzar's forge. If we can—"

He leans away from me, straightens his back. "That's not a secret that needs to burden you."

A few minutes later, I walk with Rugnus and Andalynn up the wall where I can view both the sea of lava and the sheet of rainbow-blue ice. When I ask about the ice—or the Foundation, as it's called—Rugnus tells me it was placed there thousands of years ago to protect all of Rimduum from the heat and pressure of living under millions of tons of rock and dirt. And this is not the only one. The other destroyed Loamin kingdoms of the world were all built directly over a span of the Foundation. The scale of the world again increases.

I placed the mithrium shield in Geum Ide. Such a small act of protection compared to this ancient one. I rub the empty place on my finger where Ergal once sat. "This world is still so strange. And I'll have to sleep on the surface. It's gonna take me forever to feel at home down here."

Rugnus shifts in red and blue light, Andalynn next to him. "Well, you've made Rimduum a safer place for the rest of us."

Andalynn grabs Rugnus' hand and rests her forehead on mine, lending me a sense of belonging and happiness. "We'll create something new together. You're good at that, Clayson, and we'll need your help now more than ever."

What had Sira said to me? The world can change so quickly. But for the moment, I accept my place standing on this wall between creation and destruction.

THE WORLD OF RIMDUUM

If you enjoyed the world of RIMDUUM, please consider leaving a review of *Forged in the Fallout*. Another way to spread the word is to share this series with your fantasy-loving friends. Word of mouth is such a positive thing for self-published authors. It takes very little time. Any effort would be supremely helpful, even if you can only leave a quick rating on Amazon or Goodreads.

There are many, many more stories yet to tell. Head to my website below for details about the next two books. And for all the latest information—sales, giveaways, events, short stories, and advanced review copies—sign up for BLUELINK, the official newsletter of RIMDUUM. You'll get a free short story!

www.loamseedpress.com

ACKNOWLEDGMENTS

To my friends and family:

Thank you for letting me hijack past conversations. Everyone seems to have a book inside them, but few people get the help necessary to surgically remove it. I have vomited plot ideas, strange dreams, potential character deaths, and grammar confusion and you have been there with buckets to catch and clean up. As Winta might say, obsession is nine-tenths of the law. That is certainly true for storytellers. Feel free to find me on social media or in-person and reciprocate with hours of information about your passions.

To my wife Karrie:

You've had a front-row seat to my anguish about the writing process. You've heard me say, many times, something to this effect: I should just quit and enjoy my life. I could exercise, spend more time with my kids, and focus on being an amazing teacher and a better husband, father, and friend. You gave me both the space to choose and the support to balance all the other parts of life.

You waited until this book was on draft eight before you read it because you don't like when I change the story. That's fair. I love you. I wish I had your tireless work ethic. Here's to many more decades of supporting each other. I refuse to go through life without you.

To a few critical teachers:

Tony Banto, your influence on my creative writing can't be

overstated. Here's to you for introducing me to Robert Frost, for playing the poetry of Rage Against the Machine in your class, for conversations about chess, jazz, and everything in between. Much respect. I have ramblings of my own because of you.

To my seventh grade teacher with an Italian last name who I can't find anywhere on the internet. Thank you for discovering my interest in writing and for donating an old word processor to my cause. Middle school was a difficult time for me. I had just been kicked out of mainstream school and thrown into a smaller place with a dress code and all new thirteen-year-olds to deal with. Your generosity and thoughtfulness gave me wings.

To my glorious beta readers:

Many of you are writers yourselves. Your feedback hurts in the best way possible. I grew a thick skin and adopted the 'attitude of seven drafts' because of you. In no particular order: Brian Smith, Eric Connett, Heidi Collotzi, Laura Mokrzycki, Anthony Eichenlaub, Amy Thuesen, Rachel Perez, Ryan Langr, and Mike Kalmbach. There's a host of others who read chapters here and there that deserve my thanks as well. Some I've met online, others in local writing groups. Either way, your support and friendship mean the world to me. I truly believe writing is only lonely if you make it that way.

To my editors:

I think Salt and Sage must be an amazing place to work. I will never regret the three rounds of editing we did together to make this book great and to improve my writing overall. Thanks to Carrie Jacks whose countless comments about character, setting, and plot helped shape draft four back when the book was titled RIMDUUM: FALLOUT. Thanks to Erin Olds who broadened my perspectives, challenged my character's beliefs and motivation, and taught me to see the small patterns, the emotional weight of every moment of my book. Thanks to April Jones who contended against all 115,000 words of a debut novel. I don't envy the job of editing RIMDUUM, but I'm certainly jealous of your skills.

To my cover artist:

Stephanie Saw, your cover is like a call to action. It makes RIMDUUM look as awesome as I imagined it. I would put you on retainer and pay you all the money if I had that power. The first moment I saw the cover you made—well, after my eyes popped out of my skull—I thanked all the champions under granite that I found you.

To my writing buddy:

Loury Trader. Here's to many more years of geeking out over speculative fiction and writing together. We've beta read a few things for each other, but really our work has all been in the area of support and encouragement. You've helped me imagine I'm actually a writer. I look forward to many more conversations about the genre and the craft.

To my biggest fan and older brother:

Scott, I'm not sure what I can say here, bro. We're just two kids straight outta the trailer park. When you told me RIMDUUM was awesome and you'd never seen anything like it, I was pumped. Those words continue to inspire me to get through tough rewrites and plot problems. To reciprocate, I promise to make every effort not to kill your player character in D&D, though sometimes things are unavoidable.

To my readers:

There are so many beautiful and imaginative stories floating out in the great void and you choose the world of RIMDUUM. Thank you so much. I'd love to hear from you. Never hesitate to reach out to me over social media. May all of your dreams and wishes come true. May you find something that stokes the fires of your imagination and leads you to be more and more human, and to treat other people the same. Go out there and build a beautiful world.

Ben Green

ABOUT THE AUTHOR

 BEN GREEN has always been a storyteller. When he was a kid, he would tear apart his coloring books and assemble them into crossover stories with lots of drama and lots of glue. Then he discovered action figures and took to burning Cobra agents at the stake and writing/acting out whole episodes of Star Trek the Next Generation. As a teen, he wrote Star Wars fanfiction and began creating his own worlds on a Brother word processor with a tiny screen and floppy disks. Meaning he's also very old.

Though he grew up in Arizona and Nevada, Ben now lives in southern Minnesota where he puts his degrees in teaching, history, and technology to use as a social studies teacher for non-traditional students. He is passionate about teen issues and at-risk youth. This may be why he spends so much time with his four children, telling stories, working in the garden, and encouraging them to find something to be passionate about.

facebook.com/bengreenwrites
instagram.com/bdigitalgreen
goodreads.com/bengreenwrites
pinterest.com/bengreenwrites